# A Girl Called Foote

A Whitehall Romance ~ Book One

by A.E. Walnofer

Visit the author's web page:

www.aewalnofer.com

Cover design & formatting by Jenny Q of Historical Editorial

Cover female model photo by Michelle Partain

Cover female model – Sophia Partain

Photographic artistic consultant – Jennifer Vincent



ISBN: 1511759402

ISBN-13: 978-1511759403

This story is dedicated to

**A MAN CALLED JEFF**

Whom I adore

And for whose presence in my life

I am daily grateful

# Contents

# A Girl Called
# Foote

# Frightening a Maid

~ JONATHAN, AGE 8
WHITEHALL

It was not an unusual occurrence for Jonathan Clyde to urinate into one of his home's many fireplaces. Nor was it unusual for one of the servants to walk into a room, sniff the air unhappily and decide that the baronet's son *had* urinated into the fireplace. What *was* unusual was for Jonathan to be caught in the distasteful act, and that is precisely what nearly happened one morning in late June at Whitehall.

On this particular day, he had been sitting on the library floor, drawing a picture inside of a difficultly-obtained copy of Sir Walter Scott's *Castle Dangerous.* The title had caught his eye as he had pulled various books from their places on the shelf and he thought he would do well to improve the volume through his own efforts.

*Everyone knows that all the best books have pictures,* he told himself*, and besides, I'm the best artist in the family.*

As his drawing of a soldier firing a cannon developed, so did his need to empty his bladder. At times, if an appropriate vessel was available, Jonathan would relieve himself into it and leave it for Ploughman, the aging parlour maid, to empty when she made her rounds. Not seeing a suitable receptacle on hand on this day, Jonathan made his way to the fireplace and proceeded to urinate, drenching the dark, sooty cavity.

*I'm wary not to hit the rug,* he rationalized*, and the rest burns off when the fire's lit.*

At this moment, Ploughman entered the room. Had she not been bungling with an awkward and overloaded bucket of cleaning supplies, she likely would have seen Jonathan standing before the fireplace hurriedly fumbling with the front of his breeches. However, she was busy bumping into the doorjamb and keeping the tin of black from falling onto the floor. After settling her burden upon a table and straightening her cap, the slightly podgy woman selected a cloth and shuffled over to the bookshelves.

*Is she going to climb the ladder?* Jonathan wondered, peeking out from behind an upholstered chair. *She'll snap any rung she steps on!*

To his delight, he watched as the maid positioned the ill-fortuned ladder and ascended it, grunting as she climbed. Her left hand clutched the ladder's side as she started wiping down the top bookshelf with her right hand.

Jonathan felt a familiar rumbling in his lower gut and was struck with what most boys would consider an ingenious idea. Hoping Ploughman was thoroughly engrossed in her task, he quietly climbed onto the settee and positioned himself as if he was napping there. To increase the delicious absurdity of the situation, he stuck his thumb in his mouth as if he was sucking it. He watched Ploughman through barely opened eyes and waited until he felt assured of maximum output. Then, as loudly as he could, he expelled a prodigious amount of gas.

The result was fantastic.

Ploughman let out a cry and gripped the ladder as if her life depended on it. She whipped her head around, frantically looking over both shoulders. Her wild eyes settled on Jonathan who bit his thumb furiously, stifling his laughter.

Just as the fit passed, Jonathan sat up, yawning loudly as if newly awakened, looking as bright eyed and refreshed as he could.

"Why hullo, Ploughman," he said, stretching dramatically and rising from the settee.

"Master Jonathan." She nodded, dislodging her mob-cap from atop her head.

Ploughman resumed her dusting with as much dignity as a frightened woman atop a rickety ladder could as Jonathan casually sauntered out of the library, reining in the peals of laughter which threatened to escape.

*Her face! Too bad Will didn't see it,* he thought, *though he would have likely laughed and ruined it.*

# Impressing Grown Men

~ LYDIA, AGE 7
HAWTHORNE HOUSE

*Ugh. He's telling that horrible story again.*

Lydia tried not to glare at her father as she nibbled the sweet biscuit Mr. Farington had given her.

"She kicked me again, and me down there with my face near her backside. I reached out and swiped at her legs. She fell--BOOM!" John Smythe clapped his meaty hands together. "Just like that!"

"Fell a cow with one swipe, did you, Smythe?" Mr. Farington laughed wheezily. He was a very thin man who, Lydia had noticed, had difficulty opening heavy doors.

"How big was the cow, Father?" asked Lydia.

The broad man looked down at his daughter, the remnants of a prideful smile still on his face.

"What's that, Liddy?"

"Was it a full grown cow?" she asked.

Her father's face shifted uncertainly. "Uh, perhaps not..."

Lydia scrunched up her little nose affectedly and asked, "Wasn't that the calf that the knacker took away because you broke two of its legs?"

Both men looked at the girl who sat at the table, calmly examining the crumbling biscuit in her hand.

The face of the large, rough man broke into an embarrassed grin. He pulled on the scratchy collar of his shirt. "Lydia, you're blowing all the glory out of farming."

*You oughtn't be telling stories of poor little broken-legged calves,* Lydia countered silently.

"Ah, she's an intelligent young girl, Smythe. You can't inflate your stories with her around." Mr. Farington laughed and pushed the plate of biscuits closer to the farmer and his daughter.

"Sharp indeed, she is. You ought to hear her read," Farmer Smythe said, clapping his hand on Lydia's shoulder.

"Ah, you know your letters now, do you?" Mr. Farington asked, peering at Lydia through his spectacles, a kind smile on his face.

"Oh no, Farington! She's known letters since she was three. This one's reading words as long as your arm." He stuck out his own long, bulky appendage.

"Really?" The older man asked and stood up from the table. "I have some things from my teaching days. Let me go and get one of them."

Farmer Smythe winked at his daughter who set down the biscuit.

She suppressed a smile, thinking, *I shall surprise him as I do everyone.*

A moment later Farington returned with a paddle shaped piece of wood and handed it to Lydia.

A thin layer of horn was tacked onto the paddle and words had been carefully scratched into its surface. Hiding her disappointment at the simplicity of the poem before her, Lydia determined to read with fluency and animation. She began:

"For want of a nail the shoe was lost.
For want of a shoe the horse was…"

"No, Farington, none of those silly hornbooks!" interrupted Farmer Smythe. "That book there. Hand *that* to her." He pointed at a thick brown volume resting on the far-end of the table.

"Wordsworth? Really, Smythe?" Mr. Farington smiled and lifted his eyebrows at Lydia. "Would you like to try to read some Wordsworth, child?"

Lydia nodded, delicately brushing crumbs from her fingertips, thankful for once for her father's brashness.

"Very well." Farington cracked open the book. "Let's try the first stanza of *The Daffodils*. That's from here to here."

He held the book open before her, pointing out the first six lines with his crooked, aged index finger.

The book thunked to the table and Lydia pinned the pages down with her small hands, breathing in their distinctive wooden smell.

*Even this looks rather easy*, she thought.

Clearing her throat, she read:

"I wander'd lonely as a cloud
That floats on high o'er vales and hills,
When all at once I saw a crowd,
A host of golden daffodils;
Beside the lake, beneath the trees,
Fluttering and dancing in the breeze…"

Stanza after stanza she read, pausing only once at the word 'jocund' in the third stanza. She pronounced it with an 's' sound for the 'c'. Mr. Farington corrected her quietly as she internally vowed to never mispronounce it again.

"Excellent!" Mr. Farington cried, clapping his hands at the poem's conclusion.

"Thank you, sir," Lydia murmured as she began to flip through the pages. Settling on *The Thorn* she began to read silently.

"How old did you say she was, Smythe?"

"Only seven!"

"Truly, Smythe, for decades I was a schoolmaster, and very rarely did I hear a child of seven read with such ease and fluidity. Child?"

Lydia looked up from the book to see a pair of eyes glowing appreciatively at her.

"To such a reader as yourself, I open my library of books. Any book you want to borrow, you may. Just promise you will keep it safe as I love nothing as I love my books."

"Thank you, sir." Lydia smiled genuinely. She turned her eyes back to the open book before her as the conversation between the two men began anew.

# Counting Windows

~ JONATHAN, AGE 9
WHITEHALL

"12 and 13 for the blue parlor
14 and 15 for Papa's study
Just 16 for the drawing room as it only has one window..."

There was a slight chill in the air as the dazzling sunlight pained Jonathan's eyes. He sat in the crook of his favorite cherry tree, counting the windows of the building he called home. Having visited a few other stately homes, he knew Whitehall was impressive, not as large perhaps, but very grand.

Papa would often give tours to visitors though Mama insisted this should be done by the housekeeper as was done at other great homes.

"But no one knows the place as I do," Sir William would respond, a pleased glint in his eyes. "I know every inch of it and now that I've restored every rotunda and hidey-hole, I want to be the one to show it! Do you honestly think Old Smithy-Pot would be able to answer anyone's questions?"

At this, Lady Clyde would shake her head, though a little smile played on her lips.

Jonathan watched this slightly playful exchange between his parents quietly. It was a rare occurrence and made him feel pleasantly warm.

*Old Smithy-Pot*, he chuckled to himself, thinking of the dour housekeeper who frowned at him whenever she saw him sliding down the bannister.

He accompanied his father many times on these tours of the estate, silently anticipating when people would ask about *this* paneling or marvel at *that* chandelier. Always, the tour's climax was when Papa gathered the group at a specific spot in one of the upstairs hallways and surprised them all by moving a small writing desk. Doing so unblocked a small door in the wall. Once the group had ducked their heads and filed through it, they ascended a narrow staircase to emerge on Whitehall's roof within a belvedere. From there, one could see for miles to the northern rolling hills. The "Lake", which was really a large pond on the Clyde's property, glinted in the sun. On the southern edge, past the forests and fields, the tallest buildings of Wexhall sprouted up toward the skies. Little villages dotted the landscape.

The guests would exclaim at the beauty of the expanse, squinting in the breeze which sometimes grew into an unpleasant gale, causing their eyes to tear.

Once as Jonathan stood alone in the hallway eyeing the desk, Sir William had come along. Kneeling down, Papa had firmly gripped Jonathan's arm and stared into his eyes. Speaking in a voice Jonathan had never heard before, Papa asked, "Remember how high the roof is, Jonathan? You would die if you fell from there. That's why I block the door with the desk. If you ever move it, I'll have Glaser beat you with a riding crop until the blood runs down your back."

As his father's fingers bit into Jonathan's arm, the little boy knew that he would never disobey the order. His stomach lurched at the idea that he had the power to open the small door and ascend the steep staircase up to the roof. He *could* do it, but he never would, especially since the notion of it transformed his father into a threatening stranger. After that, he always felt a sense of relief once the tour group was inside the house again, and his father was moving the small desk back in front of the narrow door.

"22 and 23 as I believe that is my room
24 and 25 for Sophia's room..."

The uppermost story was more difficult to determine. It contained a row of smaller windows, just under the roofline. He thought that was where the servants slept.

*One of those tiny windows must belong to Old Smithy-Pot herself and one to Cook and one to Ploughman. But which ones? And who looks out of those biggest ones at night?*

Built symmetrically, the two final windows at either end of the row were larger than the rest. Jutting past where the others were situated, they were quite prominent.

*I'm going to find out. Why should the servants know when I don't? Maybe Will will go with me.* He bit his lip thoughtfully. *No, I'll tell him when I'm done.*

Dropping from the tree, he headed toward the house. Careful to shut the front door quietly behind him, he stepped across the entryway. Displeased at the loudness of his steps, he slipped off his shoes and proceeded down the hall to the dining room.

"Jonathan?" came a voice from behind him.

Whipping around, he saw his little sister, a puzzled look on her face.

"Why are you..." Sophia began.

"Shhh!" he urged, glancing around.

She ran on slippered feet to his side.

"What are you doing?" she whispered, her blue eyes wide.

"I'll tell you afterward," he murmured back, starting again toward a door at the end of the dining room. It was a swinging door with no handle. At every meal, the servants would emerge from it, their hands full of serving platters and bowls. Then it would swing back into place behind them.

"But you can't go in there!" Sophia insisted, reaching for his sleeve, her voice trembling in its rough whisper. "Who knows what they'll do to you?"

His heart beat quickened at her words, but the boy pushed his sister's hand away and brought his finger forcefully back up to his lips. "Shhh..."

Pushing the door open just enough to see what lay beyond, Jonathan was relieved that none of the servants was there. Letting himself through, he crept down the hallway, past a room with a large table and paused in the doorway of the kitchen itself.

The broad backside of a woman faced him from the stove.

*Cook*, he thought, *that beastly, contrary woman.*

She was stirring something in a large steaming pot.

Jonathan looked around, taking in the row of gleaming copper pots dangling from a rafter and the many shelves crammed with boxes and bottles.

*Is this the right way? How do they get up there at night?*

There were three doors on the far walls. One, Jonathan saw, led outside. Another was shut, remaining mysterious. The third was slightly open. Jonathan positioned himself to see beyond it.

*Stairs. That must be it.*

Hoping it wouldn't creak, Jonathan crept toward the door and prepared to ease himself through, making himself as narrow as possible. He had to push it open another few inches, but the oblivious woman simply reached for a bottle on the shelf overhead.

Up the confining staircase he went, carefully, slowly, his heart beating in his throat.

*Will won't believe I did this. In fact, how can I prove to him that I did?* He paused, thinking.

*I know!*

He felt around in his breeches pocket and pulled out a top that Will had given him earlier that week. He ran his fingers over the marred wooden surface, noting how the paint was chipping off.

*It's broken anyway. I'll leave it in the window and then he'll see it and know I'm telling the truth.*

Up, up he stepped, expecting at any second to be hit over the head by a dripping ladle from behind. At the stairs' end was a hallway. Creeping down it, he quietly pushed open the few doors and peeked inside the rooms, his pulse wild until he saw that even the last door concealed nothing more than a bed and a few pieces of shoddy furniture.

He climbed atop the bed in the last room to peer out the window.

*This must be one of the little ones,* he thought, gazing down at the cherry trees. *But where are the large windows? One must be just on the other side of this wall.*

Stepping back into the hallway, he saw that it had ended. There was nowhere to go but back from where he had come.

*But where are the largest windows? Where will I place the top? Ugh...now Will won't believe me.*

He ran his hand over the wall, wondering if there was a hidden door. His search was fruitless.

Disappointment and frustration turned his wary stepping to a careless tread as he headed back down the hall and staircase. Taking two steps at a time, Jonathan descended the stairs and burst into the kitchen to see Cook, her eyes wide with surprise, her ugly mouth a little 'o'.

"Well, there's certainly no hidden treasure up there," he announced peevishly and ran out of the kitchen. Rushing through the swinging door, he left it swinging in his wake, back and forth, and ran past where Sophia waited, her little hands clasped over her chest.

"You're alive!" she cried.

*Where's Will?* he wondered, careening past her. *He probably won't believe me.*

Will did believe him, but he was no more impressed than usual.

"That's just where the servants sleep, you idiot," he said, sorting through his new set of toy soldiers on the front lawn. He shoved a heavily decorated figurine into Jonathan's hand.

"Here, you be Spain, and I get *all* the horses this time."

***

Days later, as they were in the drive climbing into the carriage, Jonathan looked up and remembered the windows.

"Papa? Whose windows are those?" he asked, pointing at the top story.

Holding back the curtain to peer out of the carriage, Sir William answered proudly, "Those are *my* windows."

"Well, of course, just as Speed's stable is yours and Cook's oven is yours, but who looks out of those large windows on the end there? Who sleeps in those rooms?"

"What, the two largest of the top row?" Papa asked, rumpling Jonathan's hair. "Those are blind dormers."

"What do you mean?"

"There is no usable space behind them. They were put there simply because it makes the house look nicer."

"You mean no one can look through them?" Jonathan asked, baffled, as the carriage jolted into motion.

"The last person to stick his nose up against that glass was the glazer who installed it, nearly 150 years ago, tapping it into place where it would serve no purpose other than glorious pretense."

"What?" Jonathan asked with such incredulity that his father laughed aloud.

*Windows with no purpose but to make the house look more grand?*

"Are you going to score a few runs with that new cricket bat today?" Sir William asked.

Jonathan nodded his head absent-mindedly, still contemplating.

*Windows that are only for show? How perfectly stupid!*

# The Picking Up of Pebbles

~ Lydia, Age 11
Hillcrest Farm

Upon entering the kitchen, Lydia saw her mother peering through the window out at the graveled yard.

"What is it?" Lydia asked, setting the egg basket down on the table.

"Your father's having Jack pick up pebbles again," her mother replied, her mouth arching into a little smile. "Most farmers sweeten their deals with a sip of brandy, but your father prefers to use Jack's spittle."

Walking to where her mother stood, Lydia looked out to see Jack, bending over, a long strand of saliva dangling from his lips. The men on either side of him watched as he suspended it lower and lower until it touched the ground. Its end rested there for a second before he slurped the whole thing back up again.

*Here's his favorite part*, thought Lydia, knowing there was a gleam in her brother's eyes.

Jack smiled smugly at the men, then opened his mouth and stuck out his tongue. Though she couldn't see it from the distance, Lydia knew that on its tip a tiny pebble was perched.

"There's a boy!" Smythe's voice carried across the yard as he roughly pounded his son's bony back.

"Ha ha!" laughed Farmer Midwinter. "He's got the trickiest spit in the county! Do it again!"

"Sally!" Smythe turned to holler toward the house as Jack spat out the pebble. Pert, the dog, bounded about them excitedly. "Bring out a bottle of me best!"

Sally shot Lydia a look. “It sounds as if they reached an agreement on the cow. It’s to be spittle *and* brandy.”

As her mother hurried off, Lydia turned her attention back to the scene outside where Jack, his hands on his knees, was again the men’s focus. She smiled lightly and reached for the egg basket.

# Vomiting Cherries

~ JONATHAN, AGE 12
WHITEHALL

Once again, Jonathan sat in the crook of a cherry tree though his lanky body made this less comfortable than in years past. Every July, he would heft himself up into the burgeoning branches and feast upon their bountiful fruit.

He belched as his stomach reminded him of its limitations.

*Just one more,* he thought, reaching for a dangling ruby fruit. A bee buzzed around his sun-warmed head.

He spat out the stone and the bee flew off to different territories.

*Maybe just one more*, he thought and reached over his head again.

Just as his eye settled on what would possibly be his final mouthful, he heard a shout in the distance, and another. He looked around, seeing no one in the yard or orchard. Then the horizon erupted with screams and anguished cries.

In spite of his painfully full belly, Jonathan dropped from the tree and began to run in the direction of all the noise.

*It's down by the lake*, he thought, tearing westerly through the trees. He flew over the gravel drive and splashed through the lakeside muck.

There he saw Glaser and Hardy out in the small rowboat. Glaser was standing and had a long pole that he kept pushing down into the water and then pulling up again. The other man used the oars to try to direct and steady the boat. A large lump like a soggy blanket was between them. Various servants stood on the far bank. Ploughman was stumbling from the direction of the house, slowed by her age and lack of coordination.

"No! More toward this side!" someone shouted from the lakeshore north of where Jonathan stood.

Hardy rowed this way and that as Glaser used his pole. Ploughman, now at the shore, began to talk with the others and then wailed aloud, her hands at her face.

*What are they doing?* Jonathan wondered, walking towards the people on the shore.

"There! My God! There!" Glaser pointed down into the water and Hardy rowed the boat nearer to the spot. Glaser cried out for Hardy to help him so he stood and the boat began to rock violently. They bent their legs to settle it and pulled up on the pole.

The people on the shore screamed and gasped as something like a humongous fish broke the water's surface. It was caught on a hook at the end of Glaser's pole.

"Too late, dammit!" Glaser shouted. "Too late!"

*Muddle-headed servants. What did they drop in the lake?* mused Jonathan approaching the group on the shore, peering intently at the mysterious lump. *They're always losing their heads over someth...*

The lump had a purplish sleeve and at its end was a hand. A large, pale hand. Realization hit him.

*Father!*

At the same instant, the sight of a dark-haired head lolling atop the soggy thing in the boat became clear.

*Will!*

A scream unlike any sound Jonathan had ever made ripped out of him and all the eyes that had been staring at the boat turned to him. Ploughman began to run at him at a speed that no woman with her physique could possibly reach.

"Don't look!" she screamed. "Don't look, Master Jonathan!" And then she was there, tackling him with her doughy form, blocking out the terrifying sight.

Standing, she dragged him to his feet, and began pulling him toward the house. He wailed the whole way there, weak-kneed and stumbling, but did not resist her determined grip. Up the steps they climbed, both of them shaking.

Once through the door and in the entryway, Jonathan stiffened and pushed Ploughman's hands away. Leaning over, he clutched his stomach and heaved an enormous amount of dark red vomit onto the black and white checkered floor.

He stood, staring down into the foul muck of too many half-chewed cherries, remembering the stillness of the sodden lump in the boat and the soggy mass at the pole's end.

*Will and Father...*

His stomach emptied itself again.

***

One week later, Jonathan sat on a bench beside Sophia at the grotto. His swollen eyelids felt heavy and his nose was rubbed raw.

*Gone*, he thought, the emptiness of the word pinging around in his hollow core.

*Gone.*

Before this week, he had never cried in front of Sophia, but now he did so shamelessly and sometimes noisily. Her own tears fell silently, slipping down her cheeks unchecked, falling onto the front of her black velvet bodice.

They had returned from the churchyard hours ago and the sun was setting over the horrible lake. The sinking sun reminded him of the coffins being lowered into the freshly dug pit.

He raked the arm of his jacket over his nose, the sleeve rough with dried mucus.

"Sir Jonathan," said a voice behind him.

Jonathan turned to see Pryor, clad in his black servant's wear, standing a few feet away.

"Sir Jonathan, Lady Clyde wants to see you in the blue drawing room."

Instinctively Jonathan grabbed Sophia's hand and the two children silently rose from the bench, turning toward Whitehall.

"I wonder why me and not both of us," mumbled Jonathan.

Sophia shrugged one shoulder, tightening her grip on his hand.

Their steps echoed loudly across the entry hall and down the passageway to their mother's favorite room. When they entered, Sophia stayed by the door.

"Come here, my boy," Lady Clyde said from her settee, extending her arms to Jonathan. Her eyes were swollen and red and her head seemed dwarfed by the largeness of her pregnant belly.

Jonathan felt new tears well in his eyes as he crossed the room to her.

"This has been a terrible time for us. And for you to see...what you saw. I'll never forgive the servants for allowing that." She pulled him down next to her and put her arm around him.

He felt stiff and awkward.

"Did you like the monument?" she asked. It took a moment for Jonathan to realize she meant the granite angel that had been erected at the graves. He shrugged, thinking her question odd.

"We can go there and see their gravestone and think..." she paused, her voice gruff, "...of the goodness we had in them." She patted his knee with one hand and stroked his head with the other. He relaxed a little, leaning his shoulder into her.

"Will you go..." he hiccupped as he tried to stop the tears. "Will you go with us tomorrow morning?"

"Yes, darling," she crooned. "We'll go together tomorrow morning. We'll go whenever you'd like."

Jonathan couldn't remember ever crying in his mother's arms before. Once when he was very small, he had fallen on the gravel getting out of the carriage and skinned his knee. She had been right there so he had reached for her.

"Nurse?" she had said. "Oh, blood. Mind my satin, Jonathan. Nurse!"

His nurse had swooped in and lifted him, clucking like a hen.

Now, here he was, her warm arm tight around him, and she was promising to visit the graveyard with him in the morning.

"Can we walk there?" he asked, a little calmer.

"Why ever would we do that?" She laughed lightly. "We'll take the carriage, of course." Then she sighed heavily.

"Darling," she said slowly and sighed again. "You are growing older and I believe I need to familiarize you a bit more with the ways of this world.

"It is good for your sister to hear this as well, I suppose," she continued, though she didn't invite Sophia to join them on the settee. Suddenly, the child within her lurched, pushing against Jonathan's arm.

"Did you feel that?" she asked, laughing and clutching her belly.

Jonathan nodded, his lashes still wet.

"As I was saying," she put her arm back around him and continued, "darling, have you ever wondered how it is that you came to live in such a great house and that you are so well known in and beyond the county?"

Jonathan shook his head slightly, wanting to talk more of Will and Papa.

"Please understand, this is not something we talk about with others, but your father and I made what most would call an 'advantageous marriage'. We both benefited vastly from our union. You see, your father was born with a prestigious lineage but over the last century, the wealth that formerly accompanied his estate dwindled. I, however, was born into the Fanshawes, a rather unknown family that, over the past century, acquired a large fortune through commerce and trade. When my father died, I inherited it all.

"Now that your father and elder brother...have passed from this world...you have inherited the baronetcy." She paused. "Therefore, when you come of age, *you* shall have wealth *and* a title."

Jonathan sighed, picking at the cuff on his jacket.

"Did you know, darling, that your brother was William Walter Clyde the Fifth and your father was William Walter Clyde the Fourth?"

*Was...*he thought and nodded his head. His little sibling bumped against his arm again.

"Yes, of course you did. And you know that your grandfather was William Walter Clyde the Third and so on all the way back to the year 1640 when William Walter Clyde the First was born." She paused. "It is a very old name, dearest."

"Yes, it is," he mumbled, absent-mindedly.

"...and it would be a great shame if it ended now as there has been a Sir William Walter Clyde living at Whitehall since 1697." She paused again and took a deep breath. "Therefore, I have decided that *you*, darling, will carry it on."

She smiled into his face as if she had just promised him a new horse.

"What do you mean?" he asked, suddenly listening.

"From now on, we shall...*everyone* shall refer to you as William Walter Clyde the Fifth."

He stiffened and leaned back from her. "But that is...was Will's name."

"It is a family name and a very important one," she explained.

"But...I'm Jonathan and he was William," he said, with equal patience.

"Don't think of it so much as a name as a title. He carried it for a while and now you shall carry it." The smile had completely faded from her face. Little lines around her mouth grew deeper as her lips settled into a tense pursing. There was a note of annoyance in her voice as she added, "This is all *very* important."

"Important to whom?" Jonathan asked, suddenly wanting her arm completely off of him. Springing up from the settee, he firmly planted his feet in a wide stance and nearly shouted in her face, "He was William and I am Jonathan!"

"I just lost a son and a husband. This is a very difficult time for me!" his mother said. "Don't make it more so by being obstinate. You shall be known as William henceforth and that is final. I trust that as you mature, you will understand the importance of all of this."

Jonathan stared at his mother, her face set as hard as the stone angel's. It was a familiar look, very different to how she appeared just a moment ago.

Jonathan felt something inside him flip.

*No,* he thought. *No.*

He took a deep breath and declared, "I will *never* answer to that name. It is my dead brother's name, which you seem to have forgotten."

She suddenly looked tired, her face loosened into slack blotchiness. "I only want what's best," she said quietly. With a slight wave of her hand she turned her face to gaze out of the window.

Drawing himself up to his full height, he turned his back to her and marched to the door, grabbing Sophia's hand as he passed, pulling her out of the room with him.

Once the door had [illegible] shut behind them with [illegible], Sophia murmured, "Well done, Jonathan."

# Saying the Definitely Wrong Thing

~ Ploughman

*Ohhh,* Ploughman groaned inwardly. She paused in her mopping of the marble entryway to rub her aching calves.

*I musta mopped this floor eighteen times in the past month. Don't the Lady know people are comin' to see the new li'l baby, not the entryway...and with the draining of the lake there's a lotta new muck to be tracked in when people go traipsing about.*

She pushed a knuckle deep into the meatiest part of her left calf, kneading the ache unsatisfactorily.

*Better not let anyone see me doing this. I might be hauled off by the knacker.*

Just then, the front door swung open. The young heir entered, his breeches and shoes splattered with mud.

A lifetime of servitude had taught Ploughman to mask the emotions she felt daily, hiding frustration, anger, even happiness from the people she served, but the sight of those dirty shoes about to needlessly defile the floor she had just mopped weakened her will to do so. The fact that it was *this* boy didn't help, either. Yes, she had done what she could to keep him from the indelible horror of seeing his father and brother dead, but she would have done that for anyone. Any decent person would have. The boy before her was mischievous, perhaps not maliciously so, but carelessly.

She leaned on her mop and woefully cast a fleeting look at the boy's feet, the pain in her calves intensifying.

The boy glanced at the mop in Ploughman's hand as he shut the door and then looked down at his feet where her eyes rested. He stood for an instant, contemplatively. Then quietly, he knelt to undo his laces and removed the shoes. Placing them against the wall, he started across the floor, his stockinged feet silent on the hard surface.

Startled by the unexpected display of thoughtfulness by the boy, Ploughman's face brightened and she burst into grateful exclamations. "Oh, thank you Sir Jona..."

*Oh, when will I learn?* She shook her graying head. *She said we all must call him 'William'.*

"Uh, that is...thank you, Sir *William*. Thank you."

Again the boy halted, but this time the gaze he turned toward her was stony and cold. It bore into the woman, frightening her with its intensity.

Stalking back to the door, he plunged his feet into the muddy shoes. Stomping, he began to circle the woman, the noise of it filling the room.

He spiraled inward, covering more and more flooring with dirty footprint after dirty footprint.

Around and around he marched, drawing closer to her with each heavy step. The thudding cadence was the only sound in Ploughman's ears. She clung to her mop, paralyzed by fear and wonder, her aching calves forgotten.

The eerie ritual ceased when the shoes no longer left a mark. As the boy leaned in to within inches of the maid, she could feel the heat from his breath on her forehead.

In a steady, low voice, he proclaimed, "I am *Jonathan*."

Riveted, the woman studied his face, recalling the sinewy sensation of his elongated body against hers when she had seized him by the lakeside. With wide eyes, she noted the newly darkened hairs upon his upper lip, the cheeks now leaner due to the incessant upward growth of his young body.

Then, he was sprinting up the stairs, gone with only the abundantly gritty floor to remind the woman of the strange and frightening spectacle she had just witnessed.

Ploughman let out a shaky breath and stood for a moment, uneasy in the solitude. She walked toward the bucket to dip the mop, filth crunching under her feet with every step.

The dirt was everywhere, each footprint a testimony of her grievous error. She lifted the dripping mop from the bucket and sloshed it onto the floor, swirling away what she could of the incident.

*Well, I won't be calling him that again, no matter what the Lady says.*

# Forsaking a Room, Gaining a Sibling

~ JONATHAN

With careful hands, Jonathan put the figurines back into the red box. One by one, he placed each soldier and horse standing in its designated spot, and, just as he had seen Will do, wove the woolen strips through the ranks to keep them upright. After a final lingering look, he fitted the lid on top and took the box to his closet where he pushed it to the back of the top shelf. Pulling a number of items in front of it, he surveyed his work.

*Safe,* he decided, then sighed while turning away.

*Hmmm... What to do?*

He made his way to the window and leaned on the sill. It was a beautiful early-winter's day with brilliant sunlight shining down through fluffy white clouds from the crystalline-blue sky. He surveyed the sight joylessly. A bird soaring through the sky caught his eye. He squinted at it.

*Is that a falcon? I wonder if Hodges got that new spyglass he wanted for Christmas. What did he call it? A pair of...binoculars? Well, I suppose he'll bring them back to Heath if he did. One more week...*

*Ha! Am I* longing *to return to school?* He laughed at himself, but it felt hollow in his chest.

Suddenly the bird, barely visible in the distance, alighted on a crooked tree top. Jonathan recognized the tree at once.

*I can see* that *from here?*

He grabbed the chair from his desk and dragged it across the floor, the chair legs drawing dark stripes in the thick carpet. Positioning it by the window, Jonathan climbed atop the chair and stood, gazing out.

*It* is *the crooked one on the lakeside, and...*

Jonathan rocked back and forth on the chair seat, craning his neck and feeling nauseated. Most of what he was looking for was obscured by smaller trees and part of a hillock, but there was a green sliver of the lush pit. Though the lake had been drained, it was still a naturally wet area which plants had overtaken, burgeoning, filling in the space once occupied by several feet of water.

He steadied himself.

*I can't...I won't stay here.*

*Another room. Yes...I'll...*

Jumping down from his perch, Jonathan nearly went to his closet to retrieve the box he had just placed there.

*Don't be stupid.* He shook his head. *Pick the room first and then move everything.*

Going out into the hallway, he headed toward where the guest rooms were.

Jonathan wandered past Sophia's open door which revealed her absence.

*Where is everyone?*

Since his return home for the holiday, the house had felt half-full to Jonathan. Of course there was no loud clattering of Will running up and down the stairs, and the door to the study was closed every day now instead of just when Father was within, wanting solitude. But even Pryor was gone. No longer did the somber looking butler constantly tread the hallways, headed who-knew-where at any moment, his lanky frame silently padding along the thick carpet.

*Six months, it's been...*

He stopped himself.

*Think of other things.*

*Here. This room.*

He stopped and opened the door before him. Gloomy from the heavy drapes drawn closed over the window, the room held a large bed and a few pieces of furniture, ornately carved and marble topped.

Going to the window, he pulled back the drapes, unleashing a huge cloud of dust that hung in the sunbeam like a swirling swarm of gnats. Looking out, he saw the stable and its yard. Beyond that was the kitchen garden. There was no sight of anything having to do with the lake.

*Yes, this will do.*

He returned to the hallway, thinking to begin the moving process immediately.

A noise from one room away arrested him. It sounded like a whimpering puppy on the other side of the nursery door.

*Is the baby back?* he wondered.

Months earlier, he and Sophia had watched from her bedroom window as a big fluffy bundle of blankets was carried out to the driveway. An unfamiliar woman had been holding it, glancing down at a barely visible pink slip of a face in its folds, then up at the front of Whitehall. She had craned her neck, her mouth agape in apparent awe as she surveyed the building. Her eyes had flitted past the window through which Jonathan and Sophia watched the scene. A tiny pink fist popped out of the blanket and waved around in the air, bringing the woman's eyes back to what she held.

"What's she doing with the baby?" Startled, Jonathan had readied himself to rush down and wrestle the infant out of the woman's arms.

"Don't bother yourself," Sophia had said, calmly. "He'll be back. Glory said that he'd be going to live with a family in the village, a family whose mother had plenty to share with a late baronet's baby."

"Plenty of what?" Jonathan had asked, turning to his sister, befuddled.

"I asked that, too. Glory wouldn't answer, but she said he'd come back when he was older."

Jonathan recalled how his heart had sped up as the carriage took off down the drive, steadying himself only because Sophia seemed alright with the idea.

*And now he is here.*

Unhesitatingly, Jonathan opened the door and stepped into the room.

At a table, Sophia and Miss Gloriana sat, both staring at an open book before them. Sophia's face looked hopeful as she turned and saw her brother. Miss Gloriana's looked wary.

"Is there something you...?" the woman began in her unpleasantly high-pitched voice.

Jonathan looked around the large room, memories flooding his mind. Beneath his feet lay the green carpet that padded his earliest memories. The tan swirls on it stretched for what had seemed like miles when he followed them around the room, endeavoring to stay on, not touching his bare feet to any of the encroaching green. The furniture was all in exactly the same spots, but the swirls looked much smaller now.

Looking toward the table at which the two females sat, Jonathan remembered how he used to curl up underneath it, hiding from Will, though that was always the first place Will looked for him.

"Did you need...?" Miss Gloriana started again, her face taking on a hint of annoyance.

The baby gurgled in his crib, then squawked.

Miss Gloriana sighed and began to rise from her chair, mumbling, "And now I must play nurse maid *as well.*"

But Jonathan was quicker and went to peek over the edge of the crib.

A small, dark-haired infant lay on his back, all four limbs up in the air, quivering. The little head tossed back and forth, its mouth working itself open and closed in a growing frustration, sloppily expressed. Locking eyes on Jonathan, the baby awkwardly flipped himself over. Tiny, dimpled hands grabbed the folds of the bedclothes and pulled, dragging the rounded body over to where Jonathan stood. The head, so large proportionally to all else, wobbled atop the straining neck as the baby lifted it to look into Jonathan's face. The pudgy arms, pushing at the mattress, trembled with effort.

Jonathan felt himself smiling, delighted at the determination of his clumsy little sibling.

"Sophia, come look!" he called as he reached out to pat the little downy head. "His name is Elliott, isn't it? He's trying to...aw, look..."

The weight of the head proved too much and the baby tipped over onto his back, looking startled, his arms flailing out on impact.

"Are you alright?" Jonathan chuckled, reaching his hand out to steady those of his brother.

The wet, pink mouth opened in a wide grin as the baby's hands gripped one of Jonathan's fingers tightly.

Suddenly, Sophia was there, her head pressed up against Jonathan's as they hovered above their new sibling.

"Aw, dear little Elly," she said, warmth in her voice.

"Miss Sophia," Miss Gloriana squeaked, tapping the book before her. "You mustn't neglect your German."

"I told you he'd be back, Jonathan," Sophia said over her shoulder as she headed back to the table.

The baby was now pulling Jonathan's hand toward his gaping mouth, panting slightly.

*Oh no you don't,* thought Jonathan. He smiled again, feeling more pleased than he had in a very long time.

*A new brother. And I shall be right next door.*

# The Breaking of a Leg

~ LYDIA, AGE 12
DEVLIN HOUSE

Most of the fourteen or so children at the table were staring at the trifle and nougat almond cake on the side bar, fidgeting excitedly. Though Lydia had determined that she would have as many currant dotted queen cakes as were offered to her, her own eyes were fixed on the bookshelf beyond the dessert display. She had specifically chosen a spot at the table that faced the shelf, hoping it was close enough to allow her to make out the titles on the bindings. So far she had had no luck and was beginning to wonder if it would be rude of her to wander over, after the meal, and examine them up close.

Mrs. Devlin's fluty voice cut through Lydia's wonderings. "Attention please, boys and girls!

"Thank you all for coming." Her eyes were bright, and her hands were clasped together over her bodice as she continued, "I was hoping the Gummit children would be here as well, but I don't want to serve you cold soup, so we will begin. I'm so glad you've all come to celebrate Daffodil Day in my home once again. Let us pray."

The children all assumed a very serious manner, sitting straight up in their chairs, folding their hands before tightly shutting their eyes.

"Dear Heavenly Father," Mrs. Devlin began. "We are so grateful to have all endured the winter, and that we are able to be here today to celebrate the coming of spring together. Thank You for this food and the lives of these dear children. In the name of our Lord Jesus Christ..."

Every voice in the room joined her in loudly stating a solemn, "Amen."

Mrs. Devlin's eyes shone as she looked around the room again and announced, "You may begin with the bread as I come around to fill your bowls."

The gentle murmurs of the children died down as they lifted thick slices of bread from the platters.

Outside, Pert, who had followed Lydia and Jack to Devlin House, barked. Other than that, Lydia heard only the rhythmic sound of her own chewing and the occasional scrape of a spoon in a bowl nearby until there was a timid knock on the door.

"Oh! Perhaps that is the Gummits, come at last," said Mrs. Devlin to no one in particular, moving hastily toward the door. "Do come in!"

Two raggedly dressed children stepped through the doorway to stand on the maroon carpet, nervously looking around. The eldest, a boy, cleared his throat and nudged the youngest, a girl.

Stepping forward, the girl announced in a tremulous voice, "Miz Devlin, we truly thank you for 'viting us to your home for Daffadilly Day. Mumma says thank you also for the two chickens you give us last Christmas when the new baby come." She stopped, her mouth a tight little line as her wide eyes took in the sights on the table.

"Oh, of course, of course." Mrs. Devlin smiled and nodded. "Please, children, do sit and eat your fill."

Two of the only empty seats left were next to Lydia. The littlest Gummit sat in one, whispering to her elder brother, "Did I say it a'right, Bill?"

He jerked his head in a solemn nod as a thick slab of bread was placed on the plate before him.

Lydia couldn't help but smile at the intense concern on the little girl's face and the obvious relief once her brother confirmed her success. It disappeared quickly, though, once the girl's bowl was filled with soup.

Clenching the spoon in her fist, the girl pulled the bowl toward herself. So focused was she on her soup and bread that it seemed everything else around her had vanished. The little girl no longer looked apprehensive as large orange chunks of carrot and tender cubes of beef disappeared into her mouth, followed by big bites of crusty new bread. Faint sounds of contentment escaped her as she chewed.

The girl's inability to disguise or temper her obvious enjoyment threatened to make Lydia laugh, but she bit her lip before spooning some broth into her own mouth. The food *was* very good, fresh and well prepared.

Still smiling, Lydia glanced again at the little girl, but her eye was caught instead by the elder Gummit two seats away. Glowering at Lydia, he hissed at his sister, "Slow down, Bess. Yer makin' a sight o' yerself."

Bill then straightened in his chair and dabbed the corners of his sullen mouth with a napkin before continuing his meal, his eyes resting heavily on the table.

Her eating never ceased, though Bess' eyes widened and she peered around, clearly embarrassed.

Lydia shifted uneasily in her seat, her cheeks burning.

*I didn't mean to gawk at her and shame them. She just looks so pleased with her meal. It's quite endearing.*

*Should I apologize? No, that would probably make them more uncomfortable.*

Lydia stole a glance at Bill, and presumed he was about her own age. *He needn't be ashamed of his sister enjoying a bowl of soup! Ah, well, pride I suppose...*

Returning her gaze to the bookshelf across the room, Lydia took another bite of bread. *Do I dare ask if I could borrow some of those? I could tell Mrs. Devlin that I've been borrowing books from Mr. Farington for years and have always returned them in perfect condition.*

Suddenly, the woman herself was beside Lydia, smiling.

*Should I ask her now?* Lydia's heart sped up.

With her hand on little Bess' shoulder, Mrs. Devlin leaned in and asked softly, "Are you enjoying yourself, dear?"

The little girl turned her face shyly to the woman, but kept her eyes averted. Lydia could see that there was a crumb of bread stuck to her lip. "Yes, Ma'am," she said quietly. "Thank you so much for 'viting us."

"Of course, darling. You shall be invited every year."

The woman placed a hand on Lydia's shoulder, and in the same gentle tone asked, "And you, dear child, are you enjoying yourself? Would you like some more soup before dessert is served?"

"Uhh...no thank you, Mrs. Devlin."

"Are you certain?" she asked, her eyes widening. "There's plenty."

*Why would she suppose I want a second bowl of soup?*

"N-no...though it is very good, I've had quite enough."

The woman gazed kindly at her for a moment longer before squeezing Lydia's shoulder and walking away.

*That was odd.*

Now Mrs. Devlin was hovering above Bill, offering him more food in the same manner, though now it appeared to Lydia to be more charitable than simply courteous. The word 'condescending' slipped into Lydia's mind, though she felt guilty at its appearance.

*She's a very kind woman who likes children,* Lydia reminded herself crossly as she pushed away her bowl, deciding not to ask about the books.

***

"Jack, what do you suppose Mrs. Devlin thinks of us?" Lydia asked on their walk home. The spring sun was warm through the newly-leafy overhang of the tree-lined road.

"Well enough to feed us treacle tart and trifle. That's all that concerns me," Jack responded, throwing a stick for Pert to fetch.

*It's always about your stomach!* Lydia thought irritably. "Yes, but why do you suppose she invites us every year to her house for Daffodil Day? I've never read of anyone else ever celebrating it. I think she may have invented it just to feed the poor children of Shinford."

"So what if she did?" Jack shrugged, then stopped and pointed up into the dark leafy heights of a tree above them. "What's that?"

Lydia halted and looked, though she wasn't thinking about his question.

*But why does she invite* us*? Does she think* we're *poor? I suppose we are compared to her, but we're not* truly *poor. We're not the Gummits!*

*And I highly doubt Mrs. Devlin even reads those books in her parlor. She probably inherited them and didn't have anything else to put up on those shelves so there they stayed.*

Jack kicked off his shoes. "Well, there's one way to find out."

"What?" Lydia asked.

"To find out what that is up there."

"What's up there?" Lydia asked, looking again. "I can't see anything."

Gripping the tree with his hands and feet, Jack scrambled up the trunk, stretching his lanky body to reach the overhead branches. Higher and higher he climbed as Pert pawed at the tree from below, barking in agitation.

"Oh Jack!" called Lydia. "It's too high."

He did not pause until he reached a limb twenty feet above and began to edge himself out on it, away from the trunk's solidity.

"Careful!" cried Lydia.

Many variations of this scenario had played themselves out over the years between the two siblings: Jack attempting some physical feat while Lydia called out, "Careful!" from below, behind or even above, but each time the situation had ended well with Jack smiling proudly and Lydia wishing that the rapid beating of her heart would ease.

This time was different.

Lydia watched in horror as her agile brother misjudged a step and slipped. Grasping wildly at twigs and leaves, he fell. His arms flailed furiously as his thin body plummeted through the air and branches toward the unforgiving ground.

As Lydia screamed, she watched Jack hit, nearly upright as if he hoped to walk out of the fall. There was a nauseating crack and Jack's limbs crumpled into his body as he lay still upon the ground.

There instantly, Lydia knelt in the dirt, begging him to talk, to breathe. Pert circled around, barking and whining. Jack's open eyes fluttered as he dazedly stared up into the branches.

"I...I couldn't see what it was," he said in a voice very unlike his own as he attempted to sit up. "I...I...ahhh!"

He arched his back and fell backward.

"Jack...Jack," Lydia breathed, running her hands over her writhing brother's shoulders.

He emitted a low moan, his face ashen.

"I'll get Father!" Lydia promised as she tore off in the direction of Hillcrest, Pert at her heels.

# Getting Lost

~ JONATHAN, AGE 16
HEATH SCHOOL

"Clyde, you've got a letter and it looks like it's from your mumsy." Widcombe waved an envelope in front of Jonathan's face.

*What? A letter from the Lady? In all my years at Heath, that has never happened.* Jonathan grabbed it from his friend. Sure enough, across the front of the envelope, his mother's hand had addressed it to him. Tearing through the thin paper, he pulled out a flimsy sheet and read:

Dearest--Neither Hardy nor Glaser can be spared to accompany you home at the term's end. You are 16 now. I look forward to seeing you--Mama

The concise note sent a thrill down his spine.

*I'm to ride home all that way unattended?*

Jonathan was uncertain if he felt flattered at his mother's trust in his ability to transport himself home or if he felt abandoned by her to whatever tragic fate awaited him out on the open road.

*Other students ride home alone all the time, but none of them live so far away as Whitehall. It's not even the same county!*

He had traveled the way many times in the preceding years, but it was always either in a coach or with a grown man. He'd never thought to study the way in case he needed to cover the miles alone.

*Perhaps I could hire a man to escort me,* he thought. *No, I'd feel like a perfect idiot asking someone that and besides, it's the end of term, so I've hardly any money left. I can do it alone...can't I?*

Distracted, Jonathan did worse than usual on his final exams that week. He slept and ate little in the days before his journey home. He visited the library and studied whatever maps he could find. This didn't help much because only county names and large towns were denoted, not the many small villages he was accustomed to traveling through with Hardy or Glaser clopping along by his side.

Finally, the night before he was to leave, he privately approached Schoolmaster Townsend who taught geography and explained his situation, hoping his intense anxiety was not apparent.

"What is the closest town to your home?" asked Townsend, his brow furrowed. Of all the schoolmasters, he was mocked the most by Heath's students due to his beanpole like figure and his bad vision. He squinted severely and up close at whatever he was peering, even the faces of students.

"Plimbridge, sir," Jonathan responded, smelling the onions Townsend had had for dinner.

"Hmm, never heard of Plimbridge. Name a larger town near it, Clyde."

"Wexhall, I suppose."

"Wexhall, ay? Hmmm..." He turned to a large map of England on the classroom wall, his nose two inches from its colourful surface and murmured again, hovering there for a moment. "Well, come with me." The gangly man led Jonathan across the cricket green to the stables.

"St. Clare? St. Clare?" Townsend called into the gloomy, earthy smelling building.

"'Ere I am." A short, hairy man in muddy breeches ran to them.

"Sirs." He nodded at Townsend and Jonathan who both towered over him, but his barrel chest hinted that he would win a tussle with either of them.

"St. Clare, you drove a mail coach through the midland counties for nearly ten years, did you not?"

*Mail coach? That's an option as they take passengers! Oh, but no – I cannot leave Skip here for all of the summer.*

"Yessir. Leeds to London." The man thumped his chest proudly, smiling a gap-toothed grin.

"Did your route pass nearby Wexhall?"

"Yessir. Wexhall rings a bell, it does."

"Clyde here needs to get to Plimbridge which is near Wexhall. What would be the best route from here?"

St. Clare's face lit up. Reaching up, he clapped his hand familiarly onto Jonathan's shoulder. "Wexhall, ay? I'll get ya there. Lemme think..."

*What the devil! Am I to be indebted to this stinking troll?* Jonathan thought. Only his desperation to get home to Whitehall kept him from peeling St. Clare's dirty fingers off of his shoulder and flinging the man's hand away.

"Le'see 'ere." St. Clare pursed his lips and squeezed his eyes shut as if a map was drawn on his inner lids. "You'll be wanting to go north from here to Fillmore. Then you'll want to take the Crossley Road. Once you're in Crossley, head toward...Gilston..."

He drew imaginary lines in the air with his free hand, his stubbly face screwed up in concentration. "No, no. It's best to go the Peaslough way, not Gilston. Yes, Crossley to Peaslough. Once you get through Peaslough, it'd be best to turn yourself toward Huppingdon. Straight on through Huppingdon and you'll be at Wexhall soon enough, then from Wexhall to Plimford."

"Plim*bridge*," Jonathan corrected the man.

"Yes, yes, Plimbridge." St. Clare patted Jonathan's shoulder. "You'll get there jus' fine, young man."

*From 'sir' to 'young man' that quickly? And the directions are a bit questionable.* Jonathan scrambled to remember the names that had been mentioned.

He mumbled his thanks to the two older men who had started to discuss turnpike tolls and jogged out of the stables to his room.

He slept fitfully that night and, before the sun rose, he was in the stable mounting Skip, the steed he had brought from Whitehall.

St. Clare was the groom on duty. His face, made even more ghoulish by lantern light, looked self-gratified as he reminded Jonathan, "Remember, take Peaslough, not Gilston. You'll be fine, young man, though it's good you're starting early."

*He'll be calling me 'son' next,* thought Jonathan, eager, though nervous, to canter off into the dark.

The first half hour passed without problem. The road was close enough to Heath and nearby Heathton where the boys went regularly to be familiar even in the predawn. However, once through Heathton, Jonathan came to a crossroad.

*I believe we approached Heathton from this side last autumn, didn't we?*

Jonathan swung Skip around to see which perspective looked right.

*The troll said to go north to Fillmore.*

Jonathan positioned the now rising sun behind him.

*So that would be this way, wouldn't it?* He looked to the right and half-heartedly began to plod in that direction.

Hours later, as the hot noon sun beat down on him, Jonathan lamented that he had not brought anything with him to drink. On the Crossley Road now, he was approaching a small village and decided to stop at the public house and spend his last few pence on his midday meal and a much needed pint. He was feeling a bit more confident about his journey now since he had successfully gained the Crossley Road going toward Peaslough.

After his repast, he remounted Skip and continued on. Soon he came to a crossroad with a large wooden signpost.

It was blistered from standing decades in the sun and rain. Several small arrow shaped boards were nailed to it. At one time, the boards must have declared names of nearby and distant places, pointing travelers in the appropriate direction, but the weather had faded them all to near oblivion. Jonathan studied them fretfully.

"Shinford," he read aloud. Of the six signs, it was the only legible one.

*Someone from Shinford must have taken the time to paint that recently. Where are all the idiots from Peaslough? Have they no civic pride? Where is blasted Peaslough?*

He searched in vain for the hint of a faded capital P.

*Perhaps I should wait for a passerby*, he thought. But the passage of a lonely five minutes proved to be too much, so Jonathan chose a direction, the way toward Shinford, and started out.

It was nearly half an hour later that he overtook a cart full of chickens. Jonathan pulled up alongside it and asked the driver, "This way to Peaslough?"

"Beeslough?" the man asked, wrinkling up his face.

"*P*easlough."

"Never 'eard of it."

*Damn!*

Wheeling Skip around, Jonathan trotted off in the direction he had just come from, swearing under his breath.

Upon arriving back at the useless signpost, he saw that the shadow it cast was lengthening and the sun hung lower in the sky.

The fear he started the day with set in again as he looked around helplessly, passing the reins back and forth between his damp, gloved palms. His mouth had gone dry. He couldn't remember the last time he'd felt so alone.

*Where am I?*

# Kissing a Farmer, Aiding a Gentleman

~ LYDIA, AGE 15
MIDWINTER FARM

Paul and Lydia entered the barn at Midwinter Farm.

"There he is," the boy said.

"Where?" asked Lydia, her eyes adjusting in the dim light. The air was thick with the scents of manure and hay as a swarm of flies hovered overhead.

Paul laughed, "It's a bit hard to see him. His dam and sire are both bay, so that's what we were expecting, but the wee beast came out black."

"Oh, he's just lovely," breathed Lydia as the small form came into focus. The little foal was reclining in the hay, his spindly legs tucked up around him.

*Oh, to stroke his fuzzy little head,* thought Lydia, reaching fruitlessly over the pen wall. The mare beside the colt was alert, her head erect.

"S'alright, Zelda," Paul murmured. "We mean no harm."

"When did she foal?"

"Night before last. I came out to feed her and she was down in the hay, moaning with a hoof hanging out her back end. I called me dad out and it was all over in half an hour."

The two young people stood silently leaning on the pen wall, regarding the new little colt.

*We're touching,* thought Lydia, wondering if Paul had intentionally moved closer to her. She stood very still, focusing on the sensation of his broad shoulder against her own and wondered if he could hear the hammering of her heart. The rough cloth of his sleeve brushed her arm as he leaned a bit forward.

*Keep talking.*

*But I don't know what to say.*

*Think of something.*

"Will you keep him or sell him?"

"I don't know what Da's plans are. They're always changing. I think he'll watch to see how he grows. Maybe we'll keep him and breed him. I hope so for his sake. Midwinter's a nice place to be."

"Yes, it is."

"Do you really think so?" Paul turned to face Lydia.

"Yes, of course."

*He's looking at me.* Lydia stared hard at the foal.

"You like it here?" he asked, quietly.

"Mm hmm," Lydia murmured.

*He's still looking at me. Turn to him.*

Waiting another moment, she forced herself to breath evenly.

*Face him!*

She mentally counted to three and then turned slowly to face him. Their eyes met.

Lydia's eyes searched his face. It couldn't be described as handsome, but it was winsome with its youthful masculinity. She'd admired his manly gait across a farmyard for years. The beginnings of a beard pushed its way out of the boy's chin, short and coarse. It was a bit darker than the hair upon his head.

She felt that her eyes could tell him what she really felt, how he was her first thought each morning, how she sometimes had to shut the book in her hands because memories of him pushed the fictional characters aside on their own stage.

But she wouldn't allow them to, fearful that the fierceness that might manifest itself would seem silly.

*Don't make a fool of yourself. Think on lighter things.*

*His hair is in need of a cutting. It's always falling into his eyes.*

She smiled slightly.

The corners of Paul's mouth turned up faintly in response and he leaned toward her.

*Stay still,* Lydia commanded herself.

Her breath caught in her throat as Paul's lips brushed against her own. He pulled back, his eyes delving into hers, and started to lean in again.

In that instant, a fly circled Lydia's head and landed on her nose.

Paul drew back and snickered.

*Stupid fly,* thought Lydia, though she herself tittered and turned back to look at the colt. The dampness of the kiss tingled on her lips.

"He's right in 'ere," boomed a voice from the yard.

The bulky forms of Farmers Midwinter and Smythe filled the barn's entrance.

"There 'e be." Midwinter motioned toward the pen. "Hey, Zelda. 'Ow are you this morning?"

"Aww, he's a right little fella," said Lydia's father, squinting into the darkness.

"'Ow d'you like our newest bit o' livestock, Miss Liddy?" Midwinter asked, his face beaming.

"I think he is positively resplendent, sir." Lydia's voice was soft as she gazed again at the colt.

"Oh? Ha ha! I *think* that's good!" chortled the farmer as he patted Lydia roughly on the back.

Paul shook his head, smiling. "That's Lydia, always saying things no one can understand."

*Oh? Do I?* Lydia faltered and said aloud, "He's...beautiful."

"Yes he is," offered Farmer Smythe. "Ready, Liddy? I've got to get back to Hillcrest before dark and I know you wanted to stop at Farington's on the way."

***

An hour later, Lydia sat beside her father in the cart, silently moving toward Hillcrest, a book clutched in her hand. She could still feel the light brush of Paul's lips on hers.

*Why was he so intent on knowing if I like it at Midwinter Farm? He can't possibly be thinking about marriage, can he?* Her heart began to hammer again.

*I'm only fifteen and he's seventeen! It would be years before that could happen. And who says he'd even want to marry me, anyway?*

"Why aren't you reading?" Farmer Smythe asked, nodding at the book in her lap.

"Oh, um...It's such a beautiful day. It's nice to just sit here and look around."

"Ha! I've never known you to choose anything over a book. And a book that's new to you at that! What is that one?" He tilted his head to see the cover.

"Uhhh... *The Vicar of Wakefield*," she said lifting it for him to see.

"About a vicar is it? Hmm...doesn't sound too exciting. So you liked Midwinter's colt, did you?"

Lydia nodded, smiling at the memory of it.

"Whatever he decides to do with it, I hope for his sake that he makes back the money on the stud fee. The sire's pretty well sought after and the price proved it. Ho, what's this?"

Several yards down the road, near a dilapidated street sign, was a man mounted on a horse. His fine clothes and the quality of his steed declared him to be a fine gentleman even from a distance. He stood stock still, staring at the approaching farmer and his daughter.

Lydia sensed a hesitation in her father's driving of the cart horse. He glanced around at the tree lines on either side of the road as the cart slowly drew nearer to the rider.

*Why, it's just a boy*, realized Lydia as she took in the smooth, unlined face under the top hat. *But what's the matter?*

The young gentleman's mouth hung slightly open as his worry-filled eyes focused on Farmer Smythe.

"Excuse me," he spoke in the clear, genteel manner of the upper class, his words crisp. "I hope to get to Plimbridge near Wexhall before dark. Have you any advice?"

Lydia suppressed a smile. *He speaks like I imagine Mr. Darcy to.*

"Ha ha!" Farmer Smythe's easy laughter spilled out. "Take a room for the night in Glover. That's me advice. You won't be getting to Plimbridge by dark. That's for certain."

Lydia watched as the boy's face grew more anxious.

"But how should he proceed, Father? Do you know the way?"

"Aye, I take livestock past Plimbridge on my way to Wexhall for the auction, but he's not making it there whilst there's light." Smythe looked up to the lowering sun and shook his head.

The boy's mouth tightened into an ugly knot, a strange appearance for one so finely dressed.

*I believe he may cry,* marveled Lydia.

"Is the way complicated, Father?"

"Not at all, just far. Take this road to Glover, then North through Ramfeld and before you get to Wexhall you'll see the Sharington Crossroad marker. That's a nice big stone marker with the town names carved into it. It'll point you in the way of Plimbridge."

The young man's brow smoothed slightly. He pointed. "So this way to Glover, North through Ramfeld to the Sharington Crossroad?"

"That'd be it, young sir."

"Thank you very much," he said to the farmer. His eyes flitted in Lydia's direction as he lightly touched the brim of his hat. Then he was gone, cantering down the road toward Glover.

Smythe clicked to the horse and the cart started on again, steady and slow.

"I thought that young dandy was part of an ambush when I first caught sight of him. I nearly whipped Dromio into a gallop. I wonder what's at Plimbridge for him."

"I wonder how he lost his way. What's he doing out by himself so far from where he wants to be? He couldn't have been any older than Jack."

"That was a beauty of a horse he was riding."

"Hmm, I prefer Old Dromio," Lydia said.

Her father laughed. "That's good, Liddy because Dromio's about as nice a horse as we're likely to ever have."

Lydia smiled easily. "Quite likely."

*Unless, perhaps someday I'm mistress of Midwinter Farm.*

# Walking the House

~ Wells, Age 9
Whitehall

"So this we call 'walking the house'," said the woman called Ploughman as they exited the kitchen. Her voice, which had been directing Beatrice all day on the upkeep of Whitehall, had lost its cheerful tone. Beatrice knew the sound of exhaustion in a person's voice when she heard it. Her mother always sounded like that at the day's end.

Slowly, they padded down the hall past many darkened windows to the largest staircase. At its base, Ploughman sighed and gripped the handrail to begin the ascent.

"We've already tended to the family's bedrooms, so now we walk the house to check each room. Make sure the fires are dampened and the lamps and candles are all snuffed. Though the house is stone, there's plenty inside it that could burn." She turned to look back at Beatrice, who was two steps behind, a small gentle smile on her face, her eyes looking worn.

Though her meal with the other servants had been hours earlier, Beatrice was still thinking about the yeasty bread they'd eaten, the smell of it, the chewy resistance of it between her teeth. It had been the best thing she had tasted in her nine years of life. No one had looked at her reproachfully even when she had reached for a third thick slice.

Arriving at a door, Ploughman opened it to see nothing but darkness within, so they moved on to the next one. Beside it on the wall was a mirror. While Ploughman opened the door, Beatrice caught sight of her own face, illuminated by the lit candle she carried.

*Is that really me?* she couldn't help but wonder. Outlined by an elaborate and gilt frame, her reflection looked like one of the paintings hanging from the walls, but instead of a smug, well-dressed man looking out from a canvas there was only her, small, pale and dressed in a strange uniform. The clothes were clean, the fabric crisp and devoid of holes and tears. Beatrice nearly smiled as she traced the stiff collar with her finger. Reaching up higher she tugged at a lock of her ginger hair as if to lengthen it.

"It's long enough now that no one's likely to guess you had the sickness," her mother had said, peering down at Beatrice while gently smoothing the hair into place. "Yes, you're ready to go into service now."

Beatrice had cried when her locks had been shorn off, doubting it would make any difference anyway. Benny had died from the sickness and his hair had been short to begin with. Still, off the hair had come, chunks of it falling down around her feet and littering the floor like leaves at the foot of a tree at Michaelmas.

Now the tresses had grown long enough to brush the top of her collar, a suitable length for a girl in service. Over her head was a limp white cap, much like the one atop Ploughman's head.

"Wells?" Ploughman said from within the room, arresting Beatrice in her quiet examination of her altered self.

*Wells? Ah, yes, the Lady says I'm to be called 'Wells'.*

"Yes?"

"Come here and I'll show you how to check these windows to make sure they're shut tight. They got different clasps from the rest."

Into the room Beatrice went to stand next to Ploughman, who was bent over rubbing her calves. Once all the windows and the fire had been checked, they continued down the hall to other rooms. Beatrice curbed her own pace to stay behind the slow-moving Ploughman as they descended the stairs.

"Truth be told, this is my favorite chore of the day," Ploughman said absentmindedly. "When I'm walking the house I know the day's almost done. Now it's back to the kitchen to fetch a couple of stones from the oven to warm our...what's that?"

A loud knocking on the front door had startled them both.

"Who would be wanting in at this time of night?" Ploughman wondered aloud, moving toward the tall, white door.

Her heart thumping, Beatrice stepped back against the wall.

"Hullo?" A masculine voice called from the other side as the pounding continued. "Hullo? It's me! Unbolt the door!"

"Why, I believe it's Sir Jonathan!" Ploughman murmured, throwing the door open wide.

Beatrice's breath caught in her throat as an unfamiliar young man in a riding coat and top hat spilled into the foyer.

"Ploughman! You dear old girl!" he exulted, lifting his hat from his head and tossing it onto a nearby bench. He held his hands out to her as if beholding a magnificent sight. "Ah, I could kiss you!"

The jarring loudness of his voice boomed through the formerly silent entryway.

"Sir!" Ploughman covered her mouth, shyly chuckling, and then bobbed a clumsy curtsey as if it was an after-thought. "The Lady said we could expect you today, but when you weren't here by supper I..." she broke off, still looking embarrassed and pleased.

"Ah, yes. Well, sometimes the same journey takes longer than others. It is *good* to be home!"

Grinning largely, Sir Jonathan stood in the center of the foyer, staring for a moment down each darkened hallway that branched off of it, his eyes glowing in the dim candlelight.

His eyes fell on Beatrice, whose heart jumped to her throat.

She'd seen people like this before. Sometimes they raced sleek horses past her home on the village street, laughing and calling coarse things to one another, the tails of their riding coats whipping out behind them.

"Who are they, Mumma?" she had asked her mother as she watched them through the rag-hung window.

"They're fine gentlemen, Bea. You must stay out of their way," her mother had replied, her eyes large and serious.

And now, here was one before her, examining her.

"I see Whitehall has a new inhabitant." The fellow winked at her as he pulled off his gloves. "Hullo, what's this?"

Looking intently down at his hands and the gloves he held in them, he furrowed his brow. "Slashed right through the leather. You'd think I'd have noticed when that occurred!"

A drop of blood fell heavily from one of his fingertips to the black and white floor below.

Grabbing the candle from Beatrice, Ploughman drew close to him and homed in on the sight, clucking like women do when minor injuries are involved.

"Ah sir, you'd better follow me to the kitchen," she said, her shyness replaced by something approaching authority.

"Ha! You're going to patch me up just as you've always done, are you?" The voice boomed on as the fellow fell into step behind the aging servant.

"I tended to a skinned knee of Master Elliott's just this afternoon," Ploughman said, then called over her shoulder, "Wells, see to the blood on the floor there."

Looking around, Beatrice saw nothing to clean it with. The light was disappearing down the hallway with Ploughman so the girl hurriedly knelt just above the spot and used the inside hem of her skirt to wipe the floor.

Then she rushed after the others to the warmth of the kitchen and its lingering odor of fresh, warm bread.

# Recognizing a Ridiculous Notion

~ Sally
Hillcrest Farm

"Thank you, Widow Smythe and Miss Lydia, for a delicious dinner," the whiskered man called as he walked out the door, winking knowingly at Sally.

She nodded demurely, hoping to appear polite in spite of her raging thoughts.

*Well, that was the worst idea I've ever had*!

She shut the door behind Farmer Stone and his daughter, Barbara, and turned back to the dinner table which was littered with dirty plates and platters. Barbara's plate held nearly a full serving of roast beef.

*Doesn't that girl know how much that piece of meat cost us? What waste!*

"I must warn you, Mama," Lydia's voice cut through Sally's remorse, "that if the banns are called on Sunday, I shall disappear by Monday."

Startled, Sally looked into her daughter's smiling eyes.

"Wha...?" The query caught in Sally's throat.

"You were hoping the sight of him spooning peas into his mouth would inspire me to marry him, weren't you?"

*Such a smart girl! Of course, she saw everything!*

"Only if...you want..." Sally began, haltingly.

*She doesn't* want *to! How could she possibly* want *to?*

Peals of easy laughter spilled from Lydia's mouth.

The knot in Sally's gut loosened a little.

*She hasn't laughed like that since John died.*

Though Sally knew Lydia to be capable and wise beyond her years, the girl suddenly looked so young with her plaits hanging down either side of her face, her smooth complexion softly lit in the candlelight as laughter died on her lips. The reality of what marriage to Farmer Stone would actually mean to the girl rushed into Sally's head. Though she knew him to be a good man, Sally bristled at the thought of his work roughened hands touching her daughter's lithe, unaccustomed body. It turned her stomach and she was filled with shame over the lengths she had gone for such a stupid, unacceptable notion. She crossed the small room to her daughter and sat down on the bench beside her, her cheeks burning.

"My dear, forgive me." Her arm extended protectively around the girl. "I know you can't marry that old man. I just worry for you and what your future holds. Since your father died, and the direction Jack is going, I...I just want you to be taken care of." Tears stung at the corners of her eyes.

"Mama, don't cry!"

Sally bit her lip and tightened her hold around her daughter's shoulders.

"It's quite amusing, really." Lydia laughed again. "When you first said the Stones were coming to dinner, I thought he was to be courting you, but he kept staring at me over his plate and then the thought struck me, 'He's here for me!'"

"I thought you grew suddenly quiet halfway through dinner. He...he expressed interest in you when I last saw him in town and it occurred to me that you would be safe and fed in his house, but..."

"Imagine me as Barbara's step-mother!" Lydia's voice grew shrill as she continued, "'Eat your beef, Barbie, or there'll be no pudding for you!'"

Sally let out a shaky laugh and shook her head. "Sorry, dearest. Let's wash up and forget this ever happened."

*We need to be done and asleep in bed before Jack stumbles in or he may brag to Liddy about the coins I gave him to assure his absence.*

*Yet more waste!*

# Weeping Before Being Choked in the Dark

~ LYDIA, AGE 18
HILLCREST FARM

*Did he kiss her in the barn?*

Tears welled out of the corners of Lydia's eyes, slipping warmly down the sides of her face and into her ears. She laid in bed, staring into the darkness, her chest aching with emotion.

*She* is *prettier than me.*

*Stop it. If Paul is stupid enough to prefer Anne Triver then he's not worth moaning over. He never did read that book I loaned him, though he promised he would. Ugh, this ridiculous emotion. How could I even care about someone who had The Hunchback of Notre Dame in their possession and didn't bother to read it? Oh! How can I get that back to Mr. Farington?*

Her stomach protested at its emptiness. Lydia thought of the eggs on the kitchen table.

*I could go down and cook one...no, that would be one less to sell tomorrow and I'd have to light a candle to see by. More waste!*

She sniffed and dried her eyes with the edge of her pillowcase as she heard the scrape of the front door opening.

*Ugh. Jack's home.*

"Lydia?" Jack's voice drifted up as he ascended the stairs. There was the familiar sound of his clumsy gait as he lumbered down the hall. Thump. Scrape. Thump. Scrape. It was always worse when he was intoxicated.

"Liddy?"

Closing her eyes and letting her mouth fall open, she feigned sleep, breathing as deeply and evenly as possible.

*Leave me alone. I cannot possibly cope with you now.*

Peering through the tiniest of slits, Lydia saw his frame in her bedroom's doorway.

*No! Don't come in! Go away!*

"I know you're awake, Lydia. You'd wake up if a mouse farted in the kitchen." He laughed drunkenly.

Lydia remained still.

He stumbled toward the bed and knelt beside it, breathing his wreaking gin breath into her face.

"Lydia." An edge of anger crept into his voice. He clumsily tapped on her forehead with his finger. "Ly-di-a."

"Stop it!" Lydia pushed his hand away and sat up.

Jack crossed his arms, an empty bottle in his hand, assuming the air of someone wronged by a child. "Where is it, Lydia?"

"What? Can't you just leave me alone?" She dragged the sleeve of her nightgown over her swollen eyes.

" *Where is it*?"

"Where's *what*, Jack? What's so important that you have to wake me up in the middle of the night?"

"I finished *this* bottle." He tipped the empty bottle above her bed, the faint moonlight spilling through the window glinted off its rim. A single drop of liquid fell from its down-turned mouth. "And now...I *want the other one.* "

He belched.

"What makes you think I know where it is?" Lydia asked, waving the foul air away from her face.

"I know you move my bottles around."

Lydia's mind flew back several hours to when she had come across a bottle poorly hidden in some hay in the barn. It was true that she often re-hid them, but that was not what she had done with the one she found that day.

"Hmmm? Where is it?"

"I'm not telling you anything," she said fiercely.

"I am the man on this farm!" Jack's rising voice filled the room. "I bought that gin! You've no right to keep it from me!"

Lydia gaped into the darkness, astounded.

"You *bought* it? You bought it with *what*? The money *I earned* by selling eggs and butter?"

Jack crumpled into a pathetic, inebriated mess. His hands clutched at her bed covers.

"Please, Lydia. Please! Have you no heart? You've no idea what it's like."

Lydia choked on bitter laughter as she sprang from the bed.

"I've no idea what it's like? What? To have a shortened leg? Yes, you're right!" Crouching before him, she stuck her face into his, angry beyond wisdom. "But I *do know* what it's like to watch my dead father's farm fall to ruin because my brother does nothing but drink himself stupid!"

His hands gripped her shoulders painfully and his face leered into her own.

"Give me what is mine." He breathed the words through gritted teeth. "Where is it, you thieving kitchen slut?"

The insult stung like a slap to the face, spurring Lydia on to fearlessness.

"Ha! Would you like to hear what this *slut* did with your beloved gin?" She pushed at the steely grip of his hands. "She poured it out in the yard so...*go lick the cobblestones.*"

Jack gasped with fury and his fingers bit deeper into his sister's shoulders.

"It's *gone*? Altogether?" he roared. His hands flew to her throat, gripping at the soft flesh.

"Jack," Lydia wheezed as his grip tightened. Colored spots appeared before her eyes. "Jack..."

As quickly as it began, his grasp loosened and he fled from the room, shoving past Sally who was rushing in through the doorway.

Falling onto her bed, Lydia began to cry, clutching at her throat as if the fingers were still there.

Her mother was beside her, groping to hold her, weeping.

"He's getting...worse," Lydia coughed. "He nearly...strangled me...over some gin."

"You can't stay here, Liddy. I've thought it before, and now I know."

Lydia raggedly gulped in the night air, leaning against her mother's bony frame.

"Jack's drinking himself to death and...there's so little food...and now...Jack might..." Sally broke off, sobbing as she clutched at her daughter. "You've got to get out of here."

*Leave home?*

"Where would I go?"

"You could...you could...go into service."

"Service?"

"Yes. You're a hard working girl. You could help some nice family. It would only be for a time. You would do well and there would be plenty to eat. You've grown so thin."

*Maybe. Maybe that would be best. But for how long a time?*

Suddenly a new horrific thought struck Lydia.

"But..." she turned to face her mother, "what if he hurts *you*?"

"He won't."

"How can you be sure?"

The moon shone in and fell across the older woman's face. She looked defeated in her tattered nightclothes, perched on the edge of the bed. Sighing heavily, she tightened her grip around Lydia's shoulders and replied, "Because I don't ditch his gin."

# Looking for Placement

~ Mr. Farington
Hawthorne House

Lucas Farington opened his front door.

"Ah, Miss Lydia! Please come in. You haven't finished Bunyan already, have you?"

*She looks a bit tired today.*

"Oh no, sir, though I am close. I was wondering if you had any recent newspapers."

"Come to the table." He beckoned her in through the door and motioned toward the kitchen. "So you've a new interest in current events, have you?"

"If you must know," Lydia said, settling herself into a chair, "I was hoping to peruse the employment section."

The words hung in the air, ripe with multiple meanings, some dire.

*How to preserve her dignity?* The elderly man thought quickly. *Ah, it's beyond that. Might as well acknowledge it for what it is.*

"Ah, so it's come to that, has it?" he asked, sadly. "Well, let me get the papers and a bit of tea for us."

*I wondered how they had survived the previous four or so years since Smythe's death,* he pondered as he filled the tray with tea things. *Of course, I'd heard in town that some of the land had been sold. Once a farm's land starts getting parceled off, it's only a matter of time.*

*Of course, the lamed brother is of no help, too busy staggering around Shinford with a bottle in his hand.*

In the past, Farington had considered asking Lydia to do some housekeeping at Hawthorne House, but Old Betty did just fine and there wasn't enough work for two. He lifted the tray with a somber air and returned to the table.

After pouring Lydia a cup of hot tea, Farington handed her a newspaper saying, "I got this in London, two weeks ago, so I question the currency of its advertisements, but please yourself to look at it."

"Hmmm..." Lydia's eyes scanned the large unfolded pages. "There is only one that looks as if it might be appropriate."

She cleared her throat and read aloud:

"WANTED: IN A BARONET'S FAMILY, A PARLOUR MAID WHO IS TIDY IN HER PERSON AND HABITS. SHE MUST BE A RESPECTABLE, TRUSTWORTHY SORT OF WOMAN WHO IS READY TO SERVE IN THE HOUSEHOLD OF A GREAT FAMILY WITH DEVOTION AND EFFICIENCY. AN AGE OF THIRTY-FIVE YEARS OR OLDER IS PREFERRED. TO APPLY, SEND NAME, LOCATION, SITUATION AND REFERENCES TO DOROTHEA SMITH AT WHITEHALL, PLIMBRIDGE, BEVELSHIRE

"Oh, dear me, I am not close to 35 *and* the '*Great Family*' says I need references. Will one from my impartial mother be acceptable, do you suppose?" She laughed and took a sip of tea.

Farington looked at the young woman before him.

*What a shame that a lovely, intelligent girl such as this is forced into dusting bookshelves just to stay alive. This baronet's family ought to be giving her* their *references to prove they're worthy of her presence in their home.*

"I'll write something up for you, dear." He rose from the table and soon returned with paper and a plume.

He thought for a moment and wrote:

Please consider Miss Lydia Smythe for employment at Whitehall. She is a very good and capable sort of woman who learns more quickly than the average person and achieves whatever she sets her mind to. Sincerely--Mr. Lucas Farington, Former Schoolmaster at Birkhead Boys' School, now residing at Hawthorne House at Cross Street, Shinford.

He blotted and folded the page, then slid it across the table to her.

"Thank you, sir."

Lydia slipped the letter into her handbag along with the advertisement which she had carefully torn from the newspaper. Rising, she thanked Mr. Farington for the tea and headed toward the front door.

"Wait one moment, please," he said and disappeared into his study.

*Which were her favorites?* He asked himself, studying the bookshelves.

He returned to the front door, carrying five books which he pushed into the arms of the astonished girl.

"I'm not likely to read these again," he lied.

"Oh, Mr. Farington," Lydia breathed. "I can't take all of these beautiful books! They belong here. And I never did return *The Hunchback of Notre Dame.*"

"Nonsense! The best home for a book is in the hands of an enamored reader."

*What else can I do for her?*

"Oh! Another thing I've just recalled, and the remembrance is fortunate for you because it will likely cover your travel expenses should you be hired at far-off Whitehall." Farington reached into his pocket and pulled out a few coins. "I owed this to your father for a delivery he made just before he passed. Please forgive me for taking years to make good on the debt."

He held out the money to her.

She stared at the coins in his palm, biting her lower lip. Slowly, her eyes lifted to his face.

He assumed as honest an appearance as possible and shook the handful before her. *Yes dear, of course you know I'm lying, but please, please take it anyway. Please.*

"Thank you...Mr. Farington." She said slowly, picking up the coinage delicately. "Thank you for your...honesty. And, of course, thank you for my one reference...and for a decade of fine reading and..."

She glanced away from him, a tear in each eye.

"It's all been my pleasure," he assured her, his voice husky. "I only wish I could do more."

Clearing her throat, the girl shook the handful of coins and smiled beautifully, gratefully. Then she was out the door and walking down the path.

Farington watched her go. In his mind, a line of Shakespeare pushed itself forward from his vast memorized collection.

*Golden lads and girls all must, as chimney-sweepers come to dust.*

He turned from the door, shaking his head, angry that *that* was the quotation his brain happened to recall just then.

# Arriving

~ Lydia
Whitehall

"Whitehall!" called out the coach's driver.

Lydia reached past the sleeping woman to her left and lifted the canvas flap to look out, eager to see her new home. All that she saw was trees and a narrow drive.

"Whitehall?" she questioned the man who had opened the door and was retrieving her trunk from the top of the coach.

"Down that way, I believe." He pointed down the drive which eventually curved right and disappeared into the woods.

Lydia hesitated, astonished.

*He* believes*? He doesn't know for certain?*

Suddenly, she realized that the eyes of all her fellow passengers and the coachmen were on her. Even the woman who had appeared to be asleep just seconds before was looking at her expectantly, impatiently.

Reluctantly, Lydia climbed out of the vehicle.

The moment her feet hit the ground, the door swung shut and the coach started off again without a word from anyone. She stood in a cloud of dust, watching the coach rush off without her.

*What would Father say if he saw how unceremoniously I've been dumped at the side of the...*

*No! I will not cry. I will not cry. I will sit for just a moment and collect myself.*

Lydia moved the trunk to the side of the road and sat on its lid.

*Why did I leave home?*

*No! I am here now. For the next few months I am to be a parlour maid. No one will choke me in my bedroom at night. I am strong and capable. Many, many girls from worse situations are forced into servitude. They survive and so will I. I will not cry. I will go to my new home and present myself ready for service to make my way in this world. It is an adventure, like in a book. When it is over, I will return home.*

*I will not cry.*

Lydia stood, her knees shaking and lifted the small trunk. Down the drive she lumbered, the trunk's handles biting into her fingers.

Rounding the bend, she stopped, her mouth agape at the sight she saw through a break in the trees.

Before her and beyond an expanse of lawn was a building too dignified and beautiful to be called a house.

*It's like a governmental building or a bank in London*, she thought, recalling drawings she had seen in newspapers.

The entire multi-storied edifice was built from blocks of a cream colored stone. It was symmetrical in design so that every window on the right of the house was matched with one on the left. Six chimneys stretched to the sky from the slate colored roof. Little windows sprouted from there as well. A wide staircase stretched from the gravel drive to the front entryway, which was flanked by two solid columns.

*See? It is beautiful. I will be living with a baronet's family in this grand place...and cleaning every one of those windows.*

She smiled at her little joke and trudged forward with her trunk over the gravel drive. Many breathless moments later, she had ascended the stone staircase to the front door. With relief, she set her trunk down and smoothed out her skirt and bodice.

*Now I will present myself as the capable and intelligent woman that Mr. Farington described me as to Dorothea Smith.*

She patted her hair, hoping her plaits were in decent order and knocked on the door.

A moment of silence passed and she reached for the bell-pull when the door opened a couple of inches.

A plain, austere face filled the narrow space.

"Hello," she began, haltingly. "I am...Lydia Smythe. Is Dorothea available?"

"Go around to the left. That's your entrance," a crisp voice said and the door promptly shut.

A flush of embarrassment and anger warmed Lydia's face, distracting her from the near despair that had threatened to overtake her during the previous fifteen minutes. She stood a moment longer to fortify herself for lifting the trunk yet again and then went in pursuit of *her entrance,* which was apparently somewhere to the left.

Just then, a spry elderly man with muddy knees came into view.

"Oi. I'll give you a hand with that!" he said, reaching for the trunk with a smile.

"Oh, thank you," said Lydia as her burden was lifted.

*A bit of kindness on this adventure,* she thought, gratefully as she fell into step alongside the stranger. They turned the corner and approached a small wooden door over which grew a rambling rose in full bloom.

"You're going in here, I suppose," he said, nodding toward the door. "And I must be getting back to the garden, so here I leave it." He placed the trunk on the ground as the door opened from within.

A thin, tired looking woman exited as the man jogged off to the garden.

"I am Dorothea Smith, housekeeper here at Whitehall," said the same brittle voice which had spoken to her through the ajar front door. "You will call me Smith. Oh, I see you have a trunk. Hmm. Most servants arrive with a small bag. You must have more than just clothes in there, hmm?"

She paused long enough that Lydia began to wonder if servants were not allowed to have trunks, and if they did have trunks were they only supposed to hold clothes, but Smith waved her inside.

"Well, do come in. This is the servants' door and you will always use it when entering the house. You may answer the front door if necessary, but even then you may not exit it. As far as your body is concerned, this is the only entrance and exit, unless you are on the far side of the house where there is another servants' entry." She paused here with her eyebrows raised, looking hard at Lydia.

*I don't like you,* thought Lydia as she nodded and passed through the permissible doorway behind Smith into a kitchen.

At the cooking range, a solid female figure stood, stirring a large pot. Nearby, at a tabletop, stood a tall ginger-haired girl kneading dough. In the corner, sat an older woman mashing something green with a mortar and pestle.

None of them looked up from their work as Lydia and Smith went through the kitchen to a smaller door at the far side. Lydia followed Smith as they passed through and found herself on a dark narrow staircase.

*Ugh...*

It seemed that all the smells that had emanated from the kitchen for years were trapped there in a noxious collection of fumes. Lydia detected the scent of boiled cabbage, onions, eggs and beef, roasted long ago.

The steps were so shallow that Lydia needed to step almost sideways in ascent. This was made even more difficult by carrying the awkward trunk.

Lydia followed the tidy, upright figure in front of her.

"Be careful to never bump this wall."

In the gloom, Lydia could see Smith was pointing at the wall to their right.

"Just on the other side is the family's dining room and we don't want to disturb them when they are dining."

*Yes, we wouldn't want them to hear a single thump, now would we?* thought Lydia. *Mayhem might ensue.*

Once liberated from the stairwell, they continued down an equally narrow hallway.

"Here..." Smith opened another small door, "is your room."

She motioned Lydia into the tiny room behind it. The ceiling was sloped and low, just inches above their heads. Lydia was surprised to see that two beds had been wedged onto the floor space.

"You may put your things there." Smith pointed to a corner past the slightly wider bed as she again eyed the trunk suspiciously.

"You and Wells will share this bed and Ploughman sleeps in that one."

"Excuse me?" Lydia was startled. "Ploughman?"

"Oh, don't worry yourself," the housekeeper said, smiling at Lydia's concern. "The groomsman and gardener sleep above the carriage house. Ploughman is a woman. All the servants go by their family names here, which brings to mind a problem. Because your surname is 'Smythe' much like mine, you ought to think of something we can all call you instead. Perhaps your mother's maiden name?"

'*Stewart*', thought Lydia. *People will assume I am a man when they hear 'Stewart' called out. But I suppose it's better than 'Ploughman'.*

"Another thing I ought to tell you: You may or may not be familiar with servitude in a great house. It differs here from other places where I have had placement. Lady Clyde prefers that all of her servants do many jobs around the house. This means, instead of just doing the work of a parlour maid, you will at times be required to help in the kitchen or even act as a lady's maid to the Lady or her daughter. Lady Clyde believes this arrangement makes for a more capable staff.

"Also," Smith's eyes and voice dropped as she continued. "In most great houses, the head servants such as the butler, housekeeper and head cook eat separately from the other servants, but here we eat all together, once the family's needs are tended to.

"Well, I'll leave you for just a moment to tidy yourself before you go before her." Smith's pale blue eyes rested heavily on Lydia's face before she turned to go. "You will find water in the ewer there on the table."

Now alone, Lydia looked at what little there was to see in the small room. A cloudy looking-glass hung above the table that held the ewer. There were two boards jutting out from the wall as shelves which held a short stack of folded articles of clothing. A few roughly hewn pegs jutting out from the wall were hung with aprons and shawls. The room had one small, highly-placed window.

*It must be one of the little ones sprouting out of the roof.*

Climbing up on the larger bed, Lydia looked out the window and saw the long gravel drive and the lawn. East of there was a kitchen garden. To the west, an orchard stretched far out of sight behind the stables and stable house. There were also rows of hedges in a maze-shape, and in the far distance were the trees of a nearby wood all around.

*See? It is absolutely beautiful and I get to live here now.* She sighed and clambered down from the bed, turning to the ewer on the small table.

She avoided looking at herself in the mirror as she washed her face.

# Presenting the New Maid

~ Smith

In her own room, Smith paced the floor.

*That Mr. Farington called her a* woman *in his reference! I doubt she is older than Miss Sophia! Oh, the Lady is not going to like this.*

She turned to her looking glass and quietly practiced, "I'm sorry, Lady Clyde. I thought she was older."

*No*, she turned from the mirror, disgusted. *That will never do. Then she'll chastise me for not inquiring about her actual age before sending for her.*

*But she was the only applicant! Nearly a month I waited and no one else even inquired about the position.*

*What was I to do?*

*It was a well written advertisement. I'm certain of that.*

*Perhaps people have been warned about serving at Whitehall? No, that is ridiculous. Although, the issue of payment...ugh...*

She thought back to Pryor's dismissal for which Smith had been present, surprisingly. The Lady had told him, "With the passing of the baronet, this household will no longer need your services. Rest assured that I have written out a highly favorable recommendation to aid you in your search for placement elsewhere."

*Did she honestly think that Pryor* only *had valet and butler duties? And who was expected to work her fingers to the bone, making up the difference?*

*We need this girl.* I *need her.*

Smith took a deep breath and looked again in the mirror, trying to relax her features into an unperturbed look.

*Well, let's get this over with...*

Moments later, Smith was leading the new arrival back through the kitchen and servants' hall to the front entryway. They stopped in front of the wall that displayed the Baronets' portraits.

"These," Smith waved her hand with a flourish and began the speech she had many times recited, "are the William Walter Clydes, the First through the Fourth.

"Sir William Walter the First," she pointed to the smallest and most crudely painted of the four, "obtained the baronetcy in the year 1697 at the age of 57 and it has been inherited along with the name over the following four generations.

"He started his life as a humble..." Smith broke off.

The girl was leaning in and studying the portrait of William Walter Clyde the Second, a faint smirk on her face.

*How dare she? What is she looking at?*

Smith turned and saw that directly over the face in the portrait, a small oval of paper had been affixed. On it was drawn a large nose, a crooked mouth and crossed eyes as if the painting's subject was wearing a buffoon's mask.

*Why that spoiled overgrown boy!*

"Oh," Smith said as smoothly as she could. "A bit of Sir Jonathan's tomfoolery, I think. The eldest son enjoys playing jokes on anyone he can, though I fear his mother may not be pleased at this. No, not at all..."

She shook her head, forgetting the historical account she had begun to retell.

"Come this way."

They ascended a wide flight of stairs. Once on the upper level, they started down another hallway and finally arrived at the particularly ornate door of the Lady's favorite room.

Smith stood silently for a moment with her hand on the knob, breathed in deeply and knocked upon the door.

"You may enter," a voice said from within.

The housekeeper opened the door and waved the new girl inside. She was pleased to see that without even being told, the girl followed her example of curtseying to the Lady.

*Good, one less thing to displease the Lady.*

The finely dressed woman who sat on the silken settee uprightly was gazing out of the window. She wore a day dress and her hair was hidden under a heavily embroidered cap. Her eyes were half closed and her mouth was an unamused line. She looked as bored as a person could.

The Lady sighed, still looking outside and asked, "What is her name?"

"Lydia Smythe," Smith answered.

The answer roused Lady Clyde, who turned her head.

"What? Is she a relation of yours?"

"No, Ma'am."

"Well, two servants with the same name in one household will never do." The woman shook her head slightly.

Smith looked at Lydia, a little smile played at the corners of her mouth.

*Yes, I knew that.*

The Lady continued. "She will go by...'Foote'. The other Foote is gone now and we are all accustomed to saying that. Yes, 'Foote' will do nicely."

"Very good, Ma'am," Smith said.

"Have her turn around for me that I might have a look at her."

Smith turned and relayed the message as though the girl had not heard it herself.

The great woman's gaze assessed the young, lithe figure before her.

"Hmm. She's not as tall as a parlour maid ought to be. She doesn't look terribly strong...but she is not so pretty as to incite a wayward temptation for any of the men. Hmm...what qualities does she possess that deem her a better choice over the other applicants?"

Smith had a carefully chosen answer for this question. "She's spent a lot of time in a kitchen, Ma'am, so I thought she could be of help to Cook before the large parties."

"She knows cooking *and* cleaning? That is good. Where was she employed before, did you say?"

"Near Shinford, Ma'am." Smith said, hoping the questions would stop there.

"In what household, Smith?"

"In a farmhouse, Ma'am." Smith said, wanting it to sound like the most natural thing in the world.

"A *farmhouse*?" The great woman stiffened. "What on earth was she doing in a *farmhouse*?"

"She was a...farmer's daughter, my Lady," Smith said, her face growing warm.

Lady Clyde sneered slightly. "A farmer's daughter? What is it that you have brought to me, Smith?"

"Please excuse me, Ma'am. She *was* a farmer's daughter. He has died and left the family in a sorry state and so she has sought employment here."

The Lady stared at the girl, who was looking at the ground. She sighed and turned back to the window.

"Very well," she said. "I suppose that means she has every motivation to please her employer, but make it very clear to her that as long as she is employed by this house, she is not to think of herself as being above hard work, nor above the other servants. She must adjust to her new station in life and she shall behave as a servant in every respect of the word, regardless of the benefits she enjoyed in the past."

"Certainly, Ma'am." Smith bowed her head.

"You may go, Smith. Train her well."

"Yes, Ma'am."

Smith turned to go, silently motioning for the girl to follow.

# Meeting the Other Servants

~ LYDIA

"Oi! Shove down, Wells," said the dark haired man. "This new li'l girl's got nowhere to eat her dinner."

There was some sliding around and a bare spot on the bench appeared.

"Thank you," said Lydia as she took her place amongst the group of strangers, all of Whitehall's servants.

Smith sat at the far end of the table in a chair.

At the other end sat the woman who had been standing at the stove earlier. Now her ruddy face was curled up in a look of mild disgust. Her florid complexion and bristly, colorless hair reminded Lydia of a breed of pig they'd raised at the farm one year.

On the benches sat the dark haired man, the older woman who had small blue eyes and a bulbous nose, the tall ginger-haired girl, and the older man who had carried Lydia's trunk. He sat directly across from Lydia.

"What 'ave you got for us tonight, Cook?" the dark haired man asked, passing his bowl down with the others.

"What do you think, Hardy? Roast venison with oysters," Cook answered dryly as she ladled out a chunky soup.

Hardy laughed.

*Where's the delicious thing I smelled earlier?* Lydia wondered, looking at the disappointing bowlful before her. *Oh, of course, that must have been for the 'Great Family'. Ah well, at least the rolls look good.*

The sound of scraping spoons filled the small room.

The older man across the table nodded his head at Lydia.

"I'm Samuel Glaser, groundsman to Whitehall," he said, sticking his hand out. His tanned face was a mass of wrinkles as he smiled.

"Lydia," she responded, gripping his knobby hand. His forearm was also wrinkled, but the muscles underneath the flesh looked hard and knotted, capable.

"She is to go by 'Foote'," interrupted Smith, giving Lydia a slightly reproachful look.

"Foote? So are you kin to Sarah Foote who was in service here years ago?" Glaser asked.

"No."

"You're not?" queried Hardy. "I never knew there were so many Feet about!" He laughed heartily at his own joke.

Although she didn't find it particularly amusing, Lydia smiled and went on to explain why Lady Clyde had changed her name to Foote and then said, "But I would prefer to be called Lydia."

"Sounds a bit proud," Cook interjected. "I've never balked at being called 'Cook'."

*Yes, well you weren't unjustly named after one of the smelliest parts of the human body, were you?* Lydia thought, focusing on her soup.

"The Lady has decided that she shall be known as Foote," Smith repeated, looking around the table as if to make certain they all heard.

"Where were you in service before Whitehall?" asked Glaser, tearing a roll in half.

"I've never been in service before," Lydia answered, lifting her spoon to her mouth.

Surprise clearly registered on Glaser's face as his hand paused in dipping his roll.

"Truly? I've been in service since I was eight. I was the littlest footman ever employed at Grafton House. What was your situation?"

"My father was a farmer. After he died, we couldn't keep much of the farm. My mother sold most of the land on the condition that we could continue to live in the house and keep a garden and a bit of livestock."

There was interest in Glaser's eyes, though not the pity Lydia had seen in so many others' eyes when she told her story.

*But why would he pity me?* She thought. *I'm temporarily at the level he's lived at all his life.*

"A farmer, was he?" asked Glaser. "It's a shame he didn't have a son to work the land."

"Oh, I have a brother, but he..." Lydia broke off.

"He *what*?" Cook asked, her sullen face suddenly suspicious.

"He broke his leg when he was fourteen, and afterward the left one continued to grow, but the right one never caught up. It makes farm work difficult."

Cook guffawed at this explanation, though Lydia couldn't imagine what was funny about it.

Hardy spoke up. "I came into service when I was seven. On my first day, the housekeeper had me follow her and handed me a china bowl. 'Empty that,' she says to me. It were the finest dish I ever had me li'l hands on, all white with blue flowers painted on it and I were scared to death I'd drop it. 'Go on,' she says. 'Out to the hall with you and empty that in the bucket.' Well, I went careful-like, wondering what fine food was inside. Half way down the hall, I lifted the lid and stopped right where I was. 'Oi!' I hollered back to her. 'Oi! There's piss in this pot!'"

A few others laughed at this, though Hardy laughed the loudest. Lydia tried to mask her own embarrassment by smiling slightly and focusing again on the rolls and soup before her.

*So it's to be pot-humor at the dinner table with this set, is it? Never mind, I can tolerate that for a few months, I suppose.*

Lifting her roll, she cut it in half with a knife and looked around the table. She stopped as she noticed Cook was eyeing her.

"You look as if you're searching for the butter with your knife in hand and your roll split open," Cook laughed then picked up her own knife to imitate Lydia, glancing up and down the table, an expectant look on her plain face. She laughed again as Hardy joined in.

Giving Lydia another reproachful look, Smith said, "When there is a shortage of butter at Whitehall, we servants go without."

Lydia felt herself flush as she put down her knife and took a small bite of the dry roll.

*I will not cry.*

***

The mattress under her was thin and lumpy. Although her own down mattress at home had the occasional feather-point sticking through, it was at least soft and full. Worst of all was her new pillow, if it could be called such. It, too, was thin and so heavy that Lydia wondered what it could possibly be stuffed with.

*Dried peas, perhaps,* she thought. It was at this moment that she began to cry.

*Quietly, quietly,* she told herself.

She dragged the edge of the strange blanket over her eyes. It was rough and smeared the tears around instead of absorbing them. Realizing that even this most basic comfort of being able to dry her own tears was beyond her reach filled her eyes again.

"Do you miss your home?" A voice rose out of the darkness from the prone body lying next to her.

Lydia's breath caught in her throat. She felt embarrassed, but was comforted by the sound. She considered the question for a moment, not wanting to confess what was actually upsetting her and replied, "I can't believe I'm to be called...'Foote'."

Wells didn't seem to recognize Lydia's attempt at a joke and said, "The Lady changed my name as well when I came here. She said 'Wellington' was too fine a name for a servant, so everyone was to call me 'Wells'."

"How long have you been here?" Lydia asked, wanting to distract herself.

"Since I was nine, so four years ago."

Lydia marveled, *She's been away from her family since she was a young child.*

"Being at Whitehall isn't so bad. There's plenty of food and at least *you* won't be shut up in the hot kitchen all day with Cook." Wells sighed into the darkness. "I'd be glad to be called 'Thumb' if it meant I could get away from her."

Lydia chuckled. "Is she really so bad?"

"She's horrible."

"She did seem quite rude during dinner," said Lydia.

"Oh, that was nice for Cook. Just wait, you'll see. Nobody likes her. I'm glad she has her own sleeping quarters. I'd be miserable if I had to be with her all day *and* night."

"Is the soup always that bad?"

Wells laughed quietly. "She gets tired of being careful while making meals for the family, so by the time she puts together meals for the servants she is a bit sloppy. Of course, if *I* made soup that way she'd have my head on a platter."

From across the room came the continued even breathing of the room's third occupant. The sound of it gave Lydia the confidence to whisper, "What about Ploughman? Is she as horrible as Cook?"

"No, she's alright, though she's not happy about you coming here."

"What? Why?"

"She thinks you're here to take her place."

"Why would she think that?"

"Because it's true. She was the parlour maid, but her legs have gone bad. She can't do much more now than sit in the kitchen and shell peas and stir pots. Anyway, she's a nice enough old thing."

There was an awkward silence as Lydia thought through Wells' words, wishing she hadn't been caught weeping.

"Thank you, Wells," she said sincerely, somewhat comforted by the disembodied voice in the dark.

"'S'alright," came the reply as the girl rolled over.

*Well, Ploughman's not happy about me being here, but at least she hasn't tried to strangle me in my bed...yet.*

# Dictating a Missive

~ JONATHAN, AGE 19

Jonathan entered the parlor, holding a letter.

"Oh, good. Here you are," he said seeing Sophia at the writing desk, plume in hand. "Only you could enjoy this as much as me."

"What is it?"

"Listen," said Jonathan clearing his throat. "*Dear Sir Jonathan--Many happy greetings for you out of Hamburg.*"

"Ahhh, the strange German?"

Jonathan held up a finger in response and continued to read, "*I hope this missive find you good. You remember me, yes? My name is called Herman Heldmann and I met at Museum the Louvre in September. We talked of history of art. Now I am by my home in Hamburg. I did ask you to read my missives of English therefore I can learn it and you said yes. Please to read this and write a missive for me. It is important for me learn good English. I want to speak of art to you again. Much regards--Herman.*"

"He was the fellow who kept circling you as you looked at the paintings, wasn't he?" Sophia asked.

"The very one! He asked how he could contact me, but I didn't expect him to do it." Jonathan laughed. "If you think this is poorly done, you should have heard him in person. '*You...mmm...likes the...mmm...the arts, sir?*'"

Sophia giggled. "Herr Herman Heldmann of Hamburg. How harmonious!"

"You will help me, of course, to respond to this, won't you?" Jonathan asked.

"What?"

"You *are* the Germanic expert of the family."

"Oh, yes. Who else in this house can count to zwanzig and translate important sentences such as 'I have a red hat.'?" Sophia waved her hand dismissively.

"Precisely. I expect you will soon be appointed ambassador to Germany by the crown, but in the meantime, won't you help me pen a *missive* in response to our dear Herr Heldmann?"

"Wouldn't you prefer to write back in English? If you respond in German, he may giggle with *his* sister in *their* library over *your* pathetic attempts at communication. Besides, he wants to improve his English, not worsen his German."

"Hmm," Jonathan rubbed his chin. "You may be right. Alright, English it is. Still, will you at least write out my reply? If he's struggling with English, my poor penmanship will only make it more difficult for him."

"Your penmanship is only poor because you don't take the care with it that you do with your drawings."

Jonathan put his hands together, pleadingly. "Please?"

"Oh, fine then." Sophia lifted a creamy new sheet of paper from the stack on the desk and held the plume ready.

Jonathan cleared his throat and began to dictate. "*Hello Mr. Heldmann-I thank you for your letter. Yes, I remember when we met in the Louvre and I have been waiting to hear from you. Your conversation was fascinating and your letter is even better...*"

Sophia paused, looking up from the paper, her eyebrows raised. "Really, Jonathan?"

Her brother cleared his throat and continued in a theatrical voice, "*Please come and visit me the next time you are in England. In fact, my mother will be hosting a ball on the first Saturday in August. I ask that you would be my honored guest for dinner and dancing. With friendly regards—Sir Jonathan Clyde.*"

Sophia shook her head as she finished writing. "You'll never be rid of him now."

"Excellent! Actually, I'm hoping he will come to visit and become determined to make you his wife so that I will forever have a source of amusement near at hand."

Sophia sighed. "That's not likely."

"One can hope." Jonathan rubbed his hands together dramatically.

"Well, I imagine that anyone *I* manage to charm will be a great source of amusement to you." The brightness was gone from Sophia's voice.

"You know I'm joking," Jonathan laughed uneasily, sensing there was more to her statement than the simple wording.

*Oh, no,* he thought as he saw tears in her eyes.

"Sophia, what is the matter?"

She shook her head.

*Dear God, who can understand sisters and who can keep from offending them with every other word?*

"Certainly you don't think I actually want you to marry a stupid German...or a stupid Englishman for that matter!"

"That's probably what I'll end up with."

"What? A stupid husband?"

"Maybe not *stupid*, but whatever sort of person I do attract, he won't please Mama."

"Don't bother yourself with what *she* wants. We all know we'll never satisfy *her*."

"That's easy for you to say. You've already succeeded." The bitterness in Sophia's voice surprised him.

"Succeeded? What can you mean?" he asked, genuinely perplexed. "I balk at anything the woman suggests."

"You're the succeeding baronet! You've nothing to prove! You could do nothing more than hunt pheasants for the rest of your life and that would be enough for her as long as others called you 'Sir Jonathan'."

*She'd prefer they call me Sir William,* Jonathan would have stated aloud had Sophia not burst into a fresh round of tears. Instead, he waited for an uncertain moment and began to pat his sister's shoulder ineptly.

"Never mind, Sophe. She'll never be truly happy with anything, nor anyone. Don't upset yourself like this."

The girl pressed her lips together and, dabbing her eyes, looked up at her brother. She said quietly, "Of course, you are right."

Jonathan gazed down at her.

"And, besides, I'd never let you marry an idiot. Now come, Sophia." Jonathan reached for his sister's hand. "I saw from my window this morning that the peach trees are just beginning to blossom. Let's find Elliott and all have a walk through the grove together."

# Starting Lessons

~ Lydia

"Where did you get that?" Wells asked.

"Get what?" asked Lydia who was sitting up in bed, a book propped open on her lap.

"That book."

"A man called Mr. Farington gave it to me."

"What about those?" Wells pointed at the neat row of five books on the floor, which were leaning against the wall.

"Those, as well."

"Are they the only books you've read?"

*I'd like to get back to my reading*, Lydia thought, but answered, "Oh no. I've read many, many books."

"How did you learn?" Wells asked.

The question surprised Lydia. "My mother taught me when I was little. So you don't...know how?"

Wells' eyes narrowed. "Of course not. When and how would I have learned?"

"Does anyone in your family read?"

"My brother, Joseph, learned a little at a dame's school, but then he became a groom over at Beverly Park. He's probably forgotten it all by now. Did she use that book to teach you?"

Lydia glanced down at the page. Seeing the words *apprehensive* and *congenial*, she chuckled.

"Certainly not. That would have been a bit overwhelming. She started with just the letters, teaching me their sounds. She'd trace them in flour on the table when we were baking or write them in the dust on the windowsills just before she'd clean them. Then she'd show me pages of the Bible and tell me to point out certain letters. Eventually, she showed me how words are just letters linked together and how I could sound them out."

By the look on Wells' face, Lydia could see that she did not understand.

"Look," she said.

Wells sat up and looked where Lydia was pointing at a capital T in the book. "That is a T and it says, 'tuh, tuh'. Do you see any other Ts?"

Wells scanned the page, her brow furrowed. Smiling, she pointed at the only other capital T. "There. So this one says, 'tuh, tuh', too?"

The word Wells was pointing out was 'The'.

"No, actually since it's followed by an 'h', it says 'thh'."

"What?" Wells sounded disappointed.

"Some letters make more than one sound. Find another 'T'."

Wells studied the page for a moment. "But there aren't any others."

The fact that there were many lower case 'T's made Lydia realize she had to explain the differences of the cases.

*This is proving to be rather difficult,* Lydia thought ruefully.

"Nevermind." Lydia shook her head. "It's easy once you know how, but it's a bit difficult to explain."

"You said you learned when you were *little*!" Wells retorted with surprising fierceness. "I'm thirteen and I'm not stupid. I could learn!"

"I wasn't implying you were stupid!"

Over the next twenty minutes, Lydia introduced Wells to 'A' and 'B', their cases and their various sounds. She instructed her on how to trace them on the blanket laying over her lap and identify them in the book.

It was Lydia who suggested they stop and go to sleep.

Once the rush dip had been snuffed out and the girls were settled under the covers, Wells spoke a final time.

"Foote?"

"Hm?"

"Thank you very much."

"You're welcome," responded Lydia. As she said it, she knew that there would be many more reading lessons for Wells in the days to come.

*I guess I won't be using that rush light to read my own books*, she thought, but the idea was not as disappointing as she would have thought. *Perhaps before I'm done at Whitehall she'll be reading avidly and then there will be someone with whom I can have intelligent conversations.*

# Purloining Butter

~ Lydia

Her reflection in the silver serving tray wasn't clear, but Lydia could make out that her hair was coming loose from under her mob-cap.

*These must be the stupidest hats ever tailored.*

She set the tray down on the table and stuffed her straying locks back under the flimsy fabric.

She began to stack the dirty plates onto the tray when she noticed the lid was off of the butter dish.

Inside was a huge soft golden mound. Lydia's eyes flitted around the table and rested on an untouched roll on the bread platter.

Glancing at both closed doors, Lydia reached for the roll and a knife. The butter was the perfect consistency, soft enough to spread on thick, but not so molten that it would drip down the sides and all over her hands.

Her teeth sank into the roll and she began to chew, savoring the slick sensation of its generous layer of butter.

*Mmmmm...*

Taking another bite, she resumed her task of clearing the table with her free hand when she came across a book. Bound in brown leather and with no title embossed on the front cover, it had been pushed under the overflowing floral centerpiece. It didn't appear to be a novel. It was far too large for that.

*What secrets do you contain and which beauties do you offer, dear one?*

Here was a temptation even greater than soft butter and bread. Pausing only to wipe her fingertips with a napkin left crumpled on the tabletop, Lydia flipped the volume open. The heavy cover hit the table and rested open at the first page, which read:

The Nonsensical Notions of an Inattentive Pupil

*Hmmm...what have we here? A book of poetry written during Geography class, perhaps?*

She turned the first page and gasped slightly. Before her was a sketch of what appeared to be Saint George slaying a dragon. However, both the man and the dragon were wrinkled and hunched over with age. Saint George was whacking at the dragon with a cane instead of a sword and the dragon was trying to blow flames out of a puckered, toothless mouth.

Lydia giggled as she turned the page and then another. The entire book was full of drawings. There were a few lovely sketches of normal things like birds and trees, but Lydia leafed quickly past these, pausing instead at the many amusing representations of people that the book held. Lydia recognized the littlest boy of the Great Family whom she had seen that morning throwing a ball on the front lawn. He had been drawn scowling as if he didn't like having to sit so long for the artist.

Smiling, Lydia turned the page and laughed aloud at the sight of an image of Cook. The surly looking woman drawn on the paper could be no one else.

It was at that instant that the door opened. The eldest son of the Great Family entered quickly, heading straight for where Lydia stood.

The half-eaten roll fell from Lydia's fingers as she frantically clattered more plates onto the silver tray.

The young man glanced from the open book to Lydia, a bemused smirk on his lips. Shutting it, he lifted the book and hastily departed, leaving the door ajar behind him.

Alone again, Lydia felt her heart racing inside her chest.

*How must I have looked, flipping through that while I stuffed my face with a pilfered roll and butter?*

*Well, he didn't look angry.*

*Good thing the roll didn't fall on the book!*

In spite of the fright, Lydia chuckled to herself as she lifted the tray and returned to the kitchen.

"What took you so long?" asked Wells as she stoked the fire. Ploughman sat in her corner and Cook was nowhere to be seen.

Lydia smiled as she placed the heavy tray on the chopping board. "Oh, I was caught with my hand in the apple bin."

"What?" Wells asked, smiling questioningly.

Ploughman looked up from her pea-shelling.

"There was a big brown book full of wonderful drawings on the table and I was peeking inside it when the eldest son—Sir Jonathan, is it?--burst in the door and grabbed it from underneath my prying eyes."

"What?" Wells asked, no longer smiling.

"Oh, he didn't say anything. He just tucked it under his arm and rushed back out."

"You oughtn't do that, Foote." Wells shook her head slowly, her eyes full of fear.

"No harm was done."

"You'll be known as 'nosy'. No one wants a meddlesome servant. Ploughman, tell her!"

The two girls turned to the older woman, whose hands paused over a bowl.

"Aye." She shrugged. "I once looked inside one of Sir Jonathan's books meself and have been tempted to since, but Wells is right. It's best not to look like you're rifling through any of the Great Family's things, even if you mean no harm."

The backdoor opened and Cook barged in, her apron full of turnips.

"What, Wells? You haven't got the dishes done yet? They're not going to wash themselves, and you won't wash 'em either if'n you get sacked."

Lydia stood, regarding Cook, recalling the few details she had had time to appreciate in the drawing of her.

"Foote, haven't you got a parlour to dust?" Cook asked, dumping the turnips on the table next to Ploughman. "Save your prattling for mealtimes."

Lydia turned to go, a little smile playing at her lips.

Wells shot her a parting glance with a faint shake of her head.

*Ugh...well, I'm glad I didn't mention the roll and butter. Wells may have felt compelled to report me to the magistrate.*

*Was that a witch's hat he drew on Cook's head?*

# Meeting Pony

~ ELLIOTT, AGE 7

*Stay still! You're too fast!*

The little boy's arm was plunged deeply into the fishbowl and the front of his shirt was soaking wet as he grabbed again and again at the small form of a goldfish.

The large, paneled door opened and in walked a young woman carrying a caddy of cleaning supplies.

"I can't..." he said to the entrant who rushed over to him with a rag. "I can't...*get* him."

"What are you trying to *get* him for?" she asked, wiping away the puddle on the table.

"I want to put him in here," he said, holding up a glass bottle. With a proud smile, he continued, "Then I can take him to the maze. He likes swimming in and out of his little castle, so I know he'd like going through the maze with me."

"Oh." The maid looked from the fishbowl to the bottle and shook her head. "Oh, you can't do that."

*Even the maid is telling me what I can and can't do!*

"And why not?" He crossed his arms, bottle and all, scowling.

"I simply mean that your fish wouldn't last long in that bottle. They need more air to water contact or they die. Trust me, my own fish died when I put him in a lidded bowl."

"You had a fish? Whoever heard of a maid with a goldfish?"

"I haven't been a servant all my life," she said, lifting her eyebrows. "In fact, I even had my own pony at one time."

"Truly?" he asked, his eyes widening. He envisioned the maid cantering across the lawn on Prince's back, her long legs dangling on either side. He giggled. "You'd look funny on a pony."

The maid smiled. "I was much smaller then."

"What's your name?" asked the boy.

"Uh...I go by 'Foote' here," she replied. "And you, master, what is your name?"

*She doesn't know!*

"My name is...Stallion."

"Really?" Foote bit her lip. "I thought I had heard you referred to as 'Elliott'. That must have been someone else."

"I *hate* 'Elliott'!" the boy declared passionately. "Sometimes people shorten it to 'Elly' and that's the *worst* of all. That's a *girl's* name."

*Oh, no! Why did I tell her that? I told Widcombe and now he always calls me 'Elly'!*

"Hmmm, I do understand." Foote said. "Here, I promise to never call you 'Elly'."

Elliott looked at the maid's face. He liked her eyes. "And I shall call you...'Pony'!"

"Hmmm..." Foote paused. "Alright then. Now, I think it very important for your fish's good health that he stays here and you go off to the maze without him."

*It's always so boring alone.*

Elliott stomped his foot, but then an idea struck him.

"Say...why don't you come with me?"

"Oh, thank you very much, but I have work that I need to do."

*Why must grown-ups always be so busy?*

"Work? What work?"

"I've got to sweep this floor and polish the lamps and dust the..." She turned her head as she swept her arm in the direction of the wall of bookshelves and stood frozen for a moment.

"Have you ever been through the maze?" asked the little boy.

The maid didn't immediately respond.

*What's she looking at?*

He moved between her and the bookshelves, but her eyes looked over his head, flitting around. A small smile was on her lips.

*She's not listening. Why do grown-ups never listen?*

"Hmmm?" she asked.

"I said, have you ever been through the maze? It's wonderful fun, but only if you're with someone. Jonathan once cut my leading ribbon and I couldn't find my way out for ages. Now I only go with someone else...not that I'm afraid," he added.

"Of course not, but still, I must do my work." She looked at him now, but glanced toward the bookshelves again.

"But why?"

Elliott knew he was whining, and that Jonathan would rebuke him if he had been there.

Foote sighed. "That's what servants do...Stallion."

*Stallion...*

Elliott smiled, forgetting his disappointment.

"I know, I'll go ask Sophia if she'll go with me."

He headed out the door shaking his head. Glancing back once more, he saw that she had walked nearer the bookshelves and was tilting her head as if to read the books' spines.

*Why would anyone want to be a servant?*

# Returning Teeth

~ JONATHAN

*And you, sir, what use could the Lady possibly have for you?* Jonathan stared at the old man, feeling his mouth twist into a wry smile.

*Will Sophe later claim that the Lady wants this fellow as a son-in-law?*

He lifted his eyebrows quizzically while turning to his sister, who rolled her eyes heavenward in response. They did nothing to hide this exchange as it was clear the man was incapable of seeing it. Since entering the room on the arm of his manservant moments earlier, he had been led to a chair where he sat, staring out at nothing, his cloudy eyes blank.

When spoken to, the man would turn in the direction of the speaker's voice and make a vague response with a slightly imbecilic smile.

*When the Lady said a 'Mr. Spalding' would be coming to Whitehall, I didn't expect a fellow as reedy and wizened as this! And a 'Mr.', hmm? Not a 'Sir'? This one must be rich indeed if he has no title and still received an invitation to dine.*

*I suppose I could ask him about his rheumatism.*

Suddenly, the newest servant, the one whom Jonathan suspected had been flipping through his drawing book, entered the dining room. She placed a tureen of soup on the table and left.

The scent of the ham-laced pea soup seemed to reach Mr. Spalding's nostrils as he roused and looked about, as if curious of its source.

Lifting the ladle, Jonathan began to fill bowls and pass them around.

Spalding was no help in this endeavor, unaware of the bowls passing in front of him once his own bowl was set before him. Again and again he dipped his spoon, lifted it mechanically to his lips and proceeded to slurp soup from its hollow.

Lady Clyde cleared her throat.

*Ah, yes,* Jonathan thought*. Let the sparkling dinner conversation commence!*

"Mr. Spalding," said the Lady loudly. "I believe you live in Milsham, is that so?"

"Hmm? Milsham. Yes, Milsham."

"I hear it's lovely there in the springtime."

"Oh yes, lovely, lovely." Spalding nodded his head, beaming.

*Aren't most places lovely in the springtime?* wondered Jonathan, ruefully.

Spalding's spoon-lifts had slowed and he felt around for his napkin which he used to dab his chin.

The silence was broken by the sound of the maid's footsteps as she brought in a platter of blanched vegetables and sauce.

Settling on an appropriate question, Jonathan asked, "What sort of business are you in, Mr. Spalding?"

"Hmm? What's that? Oh, business you ask?" He smiled and nodded, holding a julienned carrot to his mouth. "Business is good. Yes, good."

Jonathan smiled winningly at the man.

*I give up.*

He glanced at Sophia who appeared to be concentrating especially diligently on her plate.

A moment later, Spalding coughed loudly just as the maid returned with a platter of roast duck.

*At least he has the good manners to cover his mouth,* allowed Jonathan who immediately noticed a strange look on Spalding's face.

The old man's hands began to pat everything within reach, first his lap, then his plate and finally the table around his place setting.

"Do you need something, Mr. Spalding?" Jonathan asked.

Spalding turned towards him, his mouth a strange puckered shape. "Ye*th.*"

The maid stepped between Mr. Spalding and Jonathan to put the duck on the table. Then she knelt to the ground, retrieved something and pressed it into Spalding's right hand.

Jonathan saw a flash of gold and white as Spalding's fingers closed over the item. A look of relief registered on his wrinkled face as he mumbled something indistinguishable.

*I say! I believe he coughed his teeth right out of his head!*

Jonathan pressed his own napkin to his lips, knowing the elderly man would hear the loud laughter that threatened to escape his mouth.

The supposition was confirmed when Spalding shamelessly leaned forward and pushed the object into his mouth.

"They just pop right in," he said, like any man who is pleased with a contraption. "Ah, is that duck I smell?"

Jonathan looked around the table to see the others' reactions, but no one had seemed to notice. It was as if they had dismissed the fellow's presence two courses earlier.

*Well, that maid has proven herself less than squeamish,* he thought, imagining her furiously wiping her slimy hand on her apron on her trip back to the kitchen.

Chuckling quietly, Jonathan wanted nothing more than to get ahold of his sketch book and a newly sharpened pencil. Still, he lifted the carving knife and expertly sliced into the roasted golden duck before him.

"Leg or breast, Mr. Spalding?"

# Arguing Over Books

~ LYDIA

A rush light burned on the table top. It cast an unsatisfactory amount of light onto the open book in Lydia's hands and emitted enough smoke to make everyone present slightly uncomfortable.

Wells lay beside her, tracing the letter 'r' on the sheet again and again.

Ploughman lay in her own bed, eyes drifting closed to open again a second later.

"Mend the light, please," requested Lydia, knowing that if she did it herself the greasy residue of the rush would be passed from her fingers to the book's pages.

Wells moved the rush higher up in the nipper.

"Listen to this," said Lydia and began to read:

"When maidens such as Hester die
Their place ye may not well supply,
Though ye among a thousand try
With vain endeavor.

A month or more hath she been dead,
Yet cannot I by force be led
To think upon the wormy bed
And her together."

"What is that?" interrupted Wells, wrinkling her lightly freckled nose.

"One of Charles Lamb's poems. It's called 'Hester'."

"I knew a Hester once," interjected Ploughman, her eyes opening briefly.

"I don't understand it."

"He's lamenting, that is...he's *mourning* the death of a woman he knew," Lydia responded, disappointed that Wells didn't seem to like it.

"Well, I do understand that a woman called Hester died, but what was all that about a 'wormy bed'?" Wells curled her lip in revulsion. "If you cared for a person at all, why would you talk about them and a 'wormy bed'?"

"That's what he's struggling with. He cared deeply for her and it's difficult for him to acknowl...to think about how she is now in the ground, feeding the worms."

"Eeww. I don't like it. I never noticed that book before," said Wells, tilting her head to see the cover. "It's so small. Where were you keeping it?"

"Hmm?" murmured Lydia, who was engrossed in the poem's next stanza.

"Where's that book been all this time?"

"On the shelf."

"What shelf?" Wells asked, glancing around the sparsely furnished room.

"In the library."

"What? Do you mean that's not one of *your* books?" Wells asked, a familiar hint of fear in her voice.

"No. I only brought six books with me and I've read them all so many times."

"You took one of the family's books from the parlor?" Wells' eyes were large.

"Don't trouble yourself! I was dusting the shelves today and I dropped it into my apron's pocket. It's not the first time. *Rob Roy* came from there as well. No one was there. No one saw me."

"Would you have taken it if someone *was* there?"

Annoyed, Lydia thought for a moment. "No, I suppose not, but still...I didn't do anything *wrong*. All of those books just stay there propped up on the shelves, collecting dust for me to clean off. As far as

I know, I'm the only person in the *entire house* who wants to read them. I'm being careful with it and I'll return it once I'm done."

*I've got to read them before I return home! Farington's collection is paltry in comparison*, she added silently, tired of the conversation which seemed to be turning into an argument.

"Foote," began Wells, "*I* know you won't harm the books, but the family, especially the Lady, *wouldn't like it.* You might even be...*dismissed.*" There was an edge of horror in her voice. "Please put it back tomorrow and don't ever take another. Please?"

"Wells...I'm not worried about it and you oughtn't be, either. And no, I won't promise to not take more. It's one of the few things I actually enjoy and *I'm not doing anything wrong.*"

Wells sniffed lightly and said, "Well...I won't be having any reading lessons out of the books you sneak out of the library." She rolled over as if signaling the end of the discussion.

*As if you could read even* a quarter *of the words on this page*, Lydia thought, rolling her eyes.

Ploughman began to chuckle.

Lydia looked to her questioningly. The older woman was propped up in bed with her aged hands folded over on the bed spread.

Even Wells bothered to ask, "What are you laughing at?"

"Foote's not the only one who's been up to mischief," she said, slyly.

"What?" Lydia smiled.

The older woman clumsily climbed out of bed and knelt on the floor beside it, groaning awkwardly.

*Is she going to pray?* wondered Lydia.

Instead, Ploughman reached under her bed and pulled out a cloth wrapped bundle. Wells was now watching, too, as Ploughman placed the bundle on her bed and drew back the sides of the cloth. Inside were tens of rush lights.

*Each of those would burn for nearly half an hour*, marveled Lydia. *There are* hours *of light there.*

"Where did you get all of those?" she asked, incredulously.

"I made 'em," came the answer. "I knew you needed more light for teaching Wells reading. When I was a wee one, I made dips like these and sold 'em by the dozen on the roadside. Last week I asked Glaser to bring me a bunch of reeds, I soaked 'em, peeled 'em, dried 'em and when I got the chance, I dipped 'em and dried 'em again."

"I wondered what all those reeds on the kitchen table were. Where'd you get the fat for dipping?" asked Wells.

"I won't tell you, Wellsy. You'd have a fainting fit." Ploughman winked. "So you'd better stop up your ears as I tell Foote. When Cook roasted up a joint of meat, I used the drippings before I washed the pan. Cook didn't mind as she's always taking nibbles of what she ought not. I don't tell on her, and she don't tell on me. You're stealing stories from the same Lady I'm stealing fat from." Ploughman winked again, chuckling, setting her second chin aquiver.

"Why, this room is a veritable den of thieves!" Lydia laughed.

Wells huffed and rolled over, her back to the other two women.

Lydia and Ploughman smiled at each other and Lydia mouthed, "Thank you."

"Well, now you know where they are when you need to nick one." Ploughman pushed the bundle of contraband back into its hiding place and found her way back into her bed.

Snuffing out the light, Lydia lay facing Wells' back, which was still heaving with indignation.

*Silly, silly girl. Imagine regarding a dish of fat that's about to be tossed as* illicit*!*

# Frightening Another Maid

~ JONATHAN

Due to a scuttling rat in the floorboards of his bedroom, Jonathan had not slept well the night before. Following breakfast, he wandered into the library for his sketchbook but soon found himself curled up on the settee.

*Ah yes, the old napping place*, he thought, grabbing a nearby decorative pillow. *Hello. You've cradled my weary head before. In fact, I do believe that's a spot from my drooling mouth from ages ago. Ah, soft as ever.*

What seemed like only moments later, the cramping of his knees and the sound of a door closing awoke him from his light nap.

*Who's that?* he thought dully.

The newest servant girl came into view.

*Ah, the Retriever of Fallen Teeth.*

She went directly to the bookshelf ladder, dust rag in hand, and ascended it.

*Servants*, Jonathan considered, looking at the girl through barely opened eyes. *They appear magically when one tugs the bell pull...or simply to awaken one from a much needed nap.*

Jonathan thought back on the times he had played tricks on various servants, recalling how sometimes they were amused along with him, and other times seemed angry in a silent, constipated way.

Most of the servants employed at Whitehall were either mere children or, what Jonathan considered, old. Once he had heard his mother say that young men ate far too much and young women were a distraction to the men so neither would be chosen to serve in her home.

*Yet, here is a girl about the age of Sophia, newly hired. Perhaps the Lady supposed this particular girl would not tempt the men of the household. Though I'm not sure why,* thought Jonathan. *She's reasonably pretty.*

A number of his fellow Heath students had bragged about conquests they'd made of their families' various maids, both attractive and plain. Most of the stories were, Jonathan thought, based on the unimpressive nature of their tellers, highly exaggerated at best and completely fictitious at worst, but a few were plausible.

This girl had dark hair and a figure that was slender without appearing juvenile. Though Jonathan had not seen much of her face, which was presently turned away from him, he recalled it having a nose that was a little short and a chin that was a little broad.

Groggily, Jonathan watched as she put down the dust rag and proceeded to do something very strange.

His eyes flew wide open, though he remained lying still on the settee.

*Did she just take a book from her apron pocket and return it to the shelf?*

His interest piqued, he watched intently to see what else she might do.

The girl hummed a tune quietly as she resumed dusting shelf after shelf. Suddenly, she stopped, saying, "Oh!"

She lifted another book which Jonathan recognized, flipped through several pages and began to read, perched on the ladder. A few years earlier, he had looked through the same book. Upon opening it, he had had little motivation to comprehend the poems. The inscrutable Scottish dialect had muddled his brain.

Jonathan held his breath, aware even of the sound his eyelashes made against the pillow as he blinked, watching for several moments, delighted and astonished.

*A servant girl who reads Robert Burns?*

The girl turned a page and quietly giggled.

*Is it possible she understands and likes that jumble of words?*

Taking something small from her pocket, she put it between the pages and returned the book to its place. Two shelves later, she lifted another book and began to flip through it.

Amused, Jonathan could stay silent no longer.

"Getting the dust from between the pages?"

Her reaction was similar to what Ploughman's had been to the flatus he passed many years earlier in the very same room --a frantic clutching of the ladder and wild turnings of the head.

When she had regained composure, she replied, stiffly, "Sorry, sir. I didn't see you there."

"That's quite clear." He sat up and stretched enormously.

She pushed the book, which miraculously had not dropped from her hand, back into place and resumed dusting, vigorously. Silence prevailed as she finished cleaning the final bookcase.

As she returned the book ladder to its place, Jonathan asked, "Do you really understand the poems of Robert Burns?"

The girl assumed the uncomfortable air that servants often did when Jonathan asked them questions. They would answer him politely, but with a steeliness under the words and facial expression that made him think they just wanted to be done with him.

"I'm able to discern enough to find enjoyment in them," she replied after a brief pause.

Jonathan felt the corners of his mouth twitching.

*Did this parlour maid just use the word 'discern'?*

"You're the 'new Foote', aren't you?" He studied her and saw he had been correct about her face. None of the features were noteworthy, but none were unfavorable. Her eyes were light, though he couldn't tell if they were blue, gray or green from the distance. He also noticed two moles on the left side of her face.

"So says the Lady," she said, then bit her lip and quickly added, "Sir, would you like me to go until you're finished with this room?"

Slightly taken aback, Jonathan said, "Yes. Yes, I would."

Quickly, Foote gathered her cleaning materials and left.

After the door had shut behind her, Jonathan sat for a moment longer, marveling.

*'So says the Lady'? Sounds as if she's been familiarized with the Lady's charms. But what an* odd *servant--stowing books in her apron and marking pages of poetry! What page was that that made her giggle?* he wondered, standing and moving toward the shelf.

Holding the book loosely in his hand, it fell open to where a torn scrap of paper had been placed.

*Why, it's the haggis!*

He nearly laughed.

*That was the only poem in the book that I somewhat enjoyed as it celebrated something so vile.*

There in the margin, next to the title "Address to a Haggis" was a little sketch of a platter overwhelmed by a hulking, steaming sheep-gut. Just beyond was a man's overly large grotesque face, split with a wide grin. In his raised hands, he held a knife and a fork as if he was about to greedily devour the entire sausage-like bag.

*Ahh, yes, I remember drawing this. I'm still quite pleased with the rendition.*

He silently read the first two lines:

Fair fa' your honest, sonsie face
Great chieftain o the puddin'-race!

*Hmmm...*he pondered. *Was it the poem or my drawing that made her laugh?*

He shut the book and returned it to its shelf, a small smile on his lips.

# Sharing a Joke

~ Lydia

Out in the hallway, Lydia bit her lip. *Is he always going to catch me looking through books?*

The thought was interrupted by the sound of quick, punctuated footsteps coming down the hall.

*Ugh...Smith, always treading about...*

Setting the bucket down roughly, Lydia grabbed a rag and began to dust the frames of the William Walter Clyde portraits, or 'those Clyde Fellows' as she had come to think of them. Her heart was still pounding from her exchange with the young baronet.

*Ha! Well I won't be telling Wells about* that*!*

*Did he see me returning Rob Roy to the shelf?*

A shiver of fear ran through her stomach.

*What if he* did *dismiss me?*

*Don't be ridiculous! He didn't seem bothered in the least. In fact, he seemed... entertained. Is that the right word? Maybe, but whatever it was, it wasn't anger or disgust.* This thought settled her a bit as Smith's footsteps grew louder.

*Can't he go nap in his room? Isn't that what a bed is for? I've been looking forward to dusting those books all week!*

Lydia hadn't expected Smith, who was always rushing around in every direction, to halt right next to her.

She stopped dusting and looked up. Smith's attention was normally engaged on anything but the person to whom she spoke, so Lydia found it strange to be staring into her lightly lashed blue eyes.

"Foote?"

"Yes?"

"It's Thursday," Smith said in a low voice.

The words hung in the air meaninglessly. Having no idea what her expected response ought to be, Lydia repeated, "Yes?"

Smith's mouth puckered sourly as she pointed at the door nearest them. "It's library-and-study-day, not hallway-day. I'm sure there's plenty to be done in there." She began to reach for the doorknob.

"The baronet desires to be alone." Lydia regretted saying the words instantly, imagining Smith bursting in on the young man and having her own awkward interaction with him.

*That would have been fun to watch.*

"Oh..." Smith's hand fell to her side and her mouth opened and shut a couple of times.

*Ha! You've nothing to say to that, have you?* Lydia could feel the smugness of her thoughts squaring and lifting her shoulders as she faced the elder woman.

Seeming to sense it, Smith sniffed and looked Lydia over head to toe. "Where is your mob-cap, Foote?"

"My mob-cap?" Lydia felt her confidence wane.

*Where* is *that hideous thing?*

She felt around and pulled the limp, crumpled hat from a small pocket on her bodice.

"Because you've been caught improperly attired, you will lose your free afternoon this Sunday."

"*What?!*" Lydia gasped, her mouth hanging open.

Smith continued quietly, "It is vital that you represent the family well by wearing the designated uniform."

"Yes," Lydia spat, holding her hands out to indicate the empty hallway, "in front of this *vast array* of witnesses."

"Don't make it *two* Sundays, Foote." Smith's voice was low and fierce. "There's plenty of silver to be polished again and again. Now put that on and get to work."

Her quick, clipped footsteps began again, sounding down the hallway and rounding the corner.

Lydia stood aghast.

*How can she...?*

*I didn't know she'd... Ugh!*

She pulled the hat onto her head hard enough to hear a stitch give.

*It's just going to fall off without the pins.*

She found one pin, digging it out of the same pocket and turned to the frame on the wall habitually as if it were a mirror.

Sir William the Second looked back at her, painted as if he smelled a slightly unpleasant odor.

Instinctively, she sneered back and began to rub the rag over his frame, noticing that the caricature face had been removed. A few fibers of paper were stuck to the paint.

*I'll probably be required to clean those off, too,* she thought, peevishly.

Just then, the library door opened and Sir Jonathan emerged. Not even glancing in her direction, he walked past, straightening his coat and went down the hall, out of sight.

Flustered and angry, Lydia returned to the library with her supplies. Once inside, she shut the door and looked behind all the furniture and in every corner.

*Is the little one tormenting a dormouse under the table? Perhaps the Lady is crouching behind the end table, ready to pounce on anyone whose name displeases her.*

Satisfied at the room's emptiness, she walked past the settee where Sir Jonathan had been napping. His sketch book now occupied the place. It was open, but she stayed far enough away as to not see what was on the page.

*Is this an invitation or a trap?*

She envisioned Sir Jonathan lurking for a moment at the other side of the door and then bursting in, bellowing, "Unhand that book, underling!"

*I won't do it,* she decided, turning her back on the book, then gasped.

*The man with the haggis! He must have drawn that as well!*

She giggled at the remembrance of the rapturous look on the man's face.

*Well, even if he is a bit pompous and sly... Sir Jonathan* is *entertaining*. She sighed. *But back to work...*

Lydia tended to her cleaning tasks, though she kept glancing at the settee and the book it held. Once she had finished with the parlour and returned her supplies, except for a single dust rag, to the bucket, she looked toward the door and cautiously approached the book.

*He wouldn't have put it here if he didn't intend for me to have a look.*

She halted, stunned in delighted surprise.

On the page before her was sketched an elderly man with puckered lips, his mouth an empty black hole. A young woman in a maid's garb stood before him, one hand presenting him with a silver platter, the other hand lifting the large silver lid. Upon the platter was a set of teeth as white and gleaming as the cream colored paper would allow.

*That's me!* She chuckled silently, studying the sketched maid. Never before had she seen a drawing of herself, at least not from the hand of a talented artist. She recognized some likenesses, but the focus of the drawing was the elderly man. The look of delight on his saggy face was accentuated by the way his hands were thrown out to the sides. His eyes were lit up with unmistakable joy.

*What a lovely antiquated suitor...and those untethered teeth!*

A feeling Lydia had not experienced for months warmed her, filling her with a quiet sense of excitement. She ached as the long-absent sentiment of understanding another's amusement washed over her.

Words ran through Lydia's mind arranging and rearranging themselves as she continued to stare and giggle. Realizing she would soon be expected back in the kitchen to serve the noon-time meal, she sighed and walked away from the book to leave the room.

It was hours before she realized she had forgotten to slip another book into her apron pocket.

***

That night, Lydia knew Wells was anticipating her reading lesson as they sat in bed side by side. On most nights she hoped to get through the lesson quickly so she could focus on reading whichever book she was making her way through. Tonight she had a different mission altogether. Hurriedly, she scribbled down the easiest poem from *A Pretty Little Pocketbook* that she could recall memorizing as a child.

*This ought to keep her busy for a while,* she thought hopefully. She had sacrificed one of the precious pieces of plain paper she had brought from Hillcrest for the cause. She had plans for a second prized sheet, which she held in her hand.

"Here, read this, then copy it three times."

Wells took the paper from her and stared at it, quietly sounding out the words.

*This paper is so dear,* worried Lydia, gazing at the half-sheet in her hand. *I'll have to think it through carefully before I commit words to it.*

As Wells began to slowly write, Lydia thought and thought, occasionally writing down a short line of words, only to pause to think intently again.

At one point, Wells regarded what Lydia held before her and asked, "Is that my lesson for tomorrow?"

"Mmmm..." Lydia responded indistinctly, resisting the urge to throw her hand over the words she had written.

*Stop talking to me and focus on your work!*

"That looks awful hard." Wells pursed her lips as she peered at Lydia's paper. "Are you sure I can manage it?"

"Only if you master *that* first," Lydia said brightly, pointing at the poem in Wells' hand.

*Oh, do stop distracting me! Now I have to start again with this line. Let's see... 'An antiquated suitor that disregards...' No, the meter is off. 'An antiquated suitor that'...that what?*

Significant time passed before Wells declared herself finished and laid down to sleep.

Still, it was much later after that when Lydia was finally satisfied with her composition.

Her heart beat faster as she thought through what she hoped to do with the now folded half-sheet of paper. She fell asleep silently reciting the same words over and over.

# Attempting to Read in the Maze

~LYDIA

*At last!*

Lydia felt and heard the satisfying crunch of gravel under the thin soles of her shoes.

*No dust rags sullying my fingertips. No oily polish rubbing off on my sleeve. No little brushes to scrub all those cracks...at least for this afternoon...*

*And to think it almost didn't happen...*

The previous morning at the servants' breakfast, she had been delighted to note Smith's absence and to hear Cook say that the housekeeper would be going with the family "to Town" that very afternoon. It seemed that in the rush to ready the family for removal, Smith had forgotten about the loss of Lydia's free-afternoon.

*Enjoy your venture, you tyrannical old crone,* thought Lydia as she headed from the cherry orchard toward the maze.

*I'm probably not supposed to come here*, she thought, approaching one of the maze's entrances. *But the family is all away. Of course, I'll tell none of this to Wells.*

The yew hedges were considerably larger than they appeared from her attic window. They towered over her head and she suddenly realized that getting to the maze's center might be more difficult than she had supposed.

At the entrance was a basket full of spools of ribbon. A pole stuck out of the ground next to it.

*Perhaps I'll need one of these.*

Grabbing a spool, Lydia tied the loose end of the ribbon to the pole and entered the maze, unfurling it behind her. As it unwound, Lydia saw how frayed and dirty it was. It may have been a lovely shade of rose when new, but now it was a faded burgundy. Her fingers felt grimy from touching it.

*Methinks Lady Clyde is unaware that such filth is on her property. What scandal!*

Further in she ventured, down green corridor after green corridor, sometimes finding no outlet. She'd turn around and follow her ribbon back until another option presented itself. Here and there were stone statues and benches between hedges. After several moments, Lydia emerged from the maze into its open center. There on the lawn stood an empty fountain, its basin stained and chipped.

*Lady Clyde must not ever come here.*

The thought was both satisfying and reassuring.

Pleased to find the grass dry, Lydia produced a handkerchief bundle from her pocket and laid down, outstretched on her stomach. Untying the four corners, she laid the cloth next to her and began to eat the cherries it contained, throwing the stones under the nearby hedges.

*And now for the greatest pleasure afforded to me on this fine day...*

She produced a book from her apron's pocket.

Finding this volume on the bookshelves had been especially gratifying because she had so enjoyed *Pride and Prejudice* as well as *Northanger Abbey*. Now in her hand she held *Persuasion.*

*Oh, Miss Austen, I'm certain we could have been very good friends had you consorted with servants...and had you not died.*

She stretched out again on her stomach and began to read.

The heroine, Anne, was just hearing the news that Captain Wentworth might be visiting Kellynch Hall when a melodic whistling alerted Lydia to someone's approach. She sat bolt upright and looked around.

Sir Jonathan and Master Elliott had just emerged from the maze into its center.

*What are they...? Oh, no!*

There was no time to hide herself. As for the text in her hand, she instinctively flung it under the nearest stretch of hedge.

*That was stupid!* she realized immediately. Though the book was well under the bush, she was dismayed to see that a little of the gold foil on the cover was visible from where she sat. A couple of wet cherry stones lay near it.

*Oh, no...hopefully they won't look over there. I could push some leaves around it...no, that would just draw attention to it!*

Her heart pounding furiously, she glanced at the cherries.

*Those are rightfully mine,* she reminded herself. *Glaser told me the servants were allowed to pick as many as they could eat.*

Feeling more awkward than ever, Lydia rearranged her legs and quietly waited for the boys to notice her.

*What ill-fitting part am I required to play in* this *scenario?*

The temptation to simply get up and walk away was there, but she feared looking suspicious.

The elder carried a large book and a small bag. The younger had a red leather ball tucked under his arm.

"Pony!" hollered Elliott as he caught sight of her.

Lydia dipped her head and said nothing, staring at the grass before her.

She began to get up, but Jonathan said, "Don't let us disturb you."

Regardless of his words she rose and assumed a servile stance.

"Do you need anything, sir?"

*Need anything from me during my one afternoon off this entire week? And please don't look under any of the hedges!*

"No. Please sit."

To leave now would be a direct contradiction, so she slowly sank to the ground though she knelt rather than sat. The awkwardness she felt was greatly increased when Elliott plopped down on the grass right beside her. She hoped she was positioned to block their view of the poorly hidden book.

With little hesitation, Jonathan sat himself about five feet away and began to remove a number of things from his bag.

Lydia watched as he took the lid off a small bottle and selected a nib for a pen. Her face flushed as she saw that the book he had was none other than his sketchbook. She looked away, wondering about the fate of the little slip of paper she had left inside it days earlier.

*Has he even seen it yet? I shouldn't have put it there! What if he discovered it when his mother or sister was nearby? What if he finds it right now as I'm sitting here? Oh, why was I so ridiculously bold!*

When everything was arranged, he glanced toward Lydia.

"You look as if you're preparing to flee," he said, his voice low and steady.

"I'm not sure of the propriety of me being here with..." she stopped, realizing that she was explaining what was right and proper to a member of the family. "That is, I would not have presumed to..."

Her voice dropped off again.

"Truly, you speak nothing like a servant," he said, dipping his pen in the ink bottle. "My brother and I don't stand by useless rules of conduct. Those are for idiots and idiots alone."

Elliott, who was looking back and forth between his brother and the maid, nodded sharply, his chin jutting out.

*Well, it was* your *class that wrote those rules...*

Lydia cleared her throat lightly. "I understood that the family had gone to London."

"Elliott was feeling unwell last night. The Lady was determined not to be thrown off her schedule, so I offered to stay behind with him until he was feeling better."

"I hate London," spat the little boy. "The streets are too busy to run in and we hardly ever go to the park. And..."

As Elliott continued to list the deficiencies of the capital, Lydia felt her feet going numb, so she shifted her legs to the side and sat, careful to tuck her skirt about her ankles.

*How can I get out of here? But if I go, will they see the book? It would be obvious that I'm the one who put it there. Oh, why didn't I just put it back into my pocket?*

Lydia felt ill.

*Wells was right! I could be dismissed. Dear God, I don't want to go home to Mama with just a few months' wages and a reputation of thievery.*

*But it's just a book! And I wasn't taking it from the premises. I just wanted to read it. There's no harm there. But would* they *see it that way?*

Jonathan lifted his sketchbook to his lap, opened it and began to draw.

Lydia cringed, wondering if the half-sheet she'd tucked into it would fall out.

*Where is it? Did he find it amusing? Ugh...How different would this occasion be if I were here as myself instead of as a servant?*

She envisioned herself leaning over Jonathan's shoulder, pertly critiquing his sketch and making him laugh.

*Don't be stupid. Even as yourself you wouldn't be so bold with this fellow.*

*But oh, that book!* Unable to resist, she glanced again where the purloined novel lay under the hedge.

*Oh, it's not too visible, actually. In fact, they'd have to be at just the right angle to...*

"You brought cherries," Elliott interrupted her thoughts, glancing at the ruby fruits on the handkerchief.

"Uhh, yes...Would you like some?" Relieved but still flustered, Lydia felt rather foolish offering them. Her rapid heartrate had begun to slow.

Elliott picked one.

"And you, sir, would you care for some?" she asked, raising her voice, though not looking at Jonathan.

*Dear God, please don't let them throw the stones in the same place I was throwing mine!*

She wondered if a cherry stone hitting a leather-bound novel would make a distinctive sound.

Jonathan didn't pause in his sketching. "I take no pleasure in cherries."

"What?" Elliott asked, his mouth full. "You must not have had a very good one then. Here, try this one."

He selected another from Lydia's handkerchief, staining the cloth with his reddened fingertips, and held it out to Jonathan.

Still intent on the paper before him, Jonathan said, "I was sick once after eating a whole tree full. I haven't had one since."

Lydia did not eat any more cherries herself. The thought of digging around to remove a stone from her mouth in front of *these* Clyde fellows was mortifying, so she sat and watched as Elliott ate one after another of her precious little hoard.

*Easy come, easy go.*

She held back the sigh that formed in her chest.

"And another thing," continued Elliott, lifting a finger dripping with juice. "Mama says that I'm old enough to start to enjoy it, says that I'll make friends there, but I don't think so. Do servants have friends?"

Jonathan, at this moment said, "Elliott! Stop eating those. She brought them for herself."

Elliott threw his brother a pout, but neglected to grab another cherry.

"Well, do you?" he asked.

"What?" Lydia asked.

"Do servants have friends?"

"Yes, of course."

"Who are your friends?"

"Oh, Wells is very nice...and Glaser."

"Are you Wells' *best* friend?" asked Elliott.

"Hmm..." She thought for a moment, amused at the childish question. "Actually, I'd guess that Wells' best friend here at Whitehall is a cow."

"A cow?" asked Elliott, incredulously as Jonathan looked up from his paper. "We keep no cows."

"Wells is very fond of a cow...when it's diced in a thick carroty stew and keeping company with a large hunk of fresh bread slathered on both sides with butter."

"What?" Elliott asked.

Lydia felt Jonathan's eyes studying her intently and forced her own to remain focused on Elliott. She hoped she wasn't blushing, seeing that her joke had fallen completely flat.

*Ugh...Jack would have understood. Well, Sober Jack would have.*

But the two people before her were very different from Jack, Wells, and many other people Lydia knew. To these two, *hunger* meant the feeling one experienced three hours after breakfast. That was vastly different from the days' long ache some bellies endured, that sensation that drove all other thoughts from the mind.

"Uh, she...likes beef stew," she explained, doltishly.

The answer seemed to satisfy Elliott who began to talk of his own favorite foods.

Lydia relaxed slightly when she saw Jonathan's pen begin to move again.

As Elliott chattered on and on, Lydia felt a familiar twitching behind her eyes and nose.

*Oh, no. Not now!*

Her hand flew to her face as she sneezed not once, but three times in rapid succession.

Elliott laughed loudly as Lydia felt the wet residue on her hand and face.

Embarrassed, she used her sleeve to dab at the wetness.

Elliott turned to Jonathan. "Aren't you going to give her a handkerchief?"

"What?" Jonathan laughed.

"Mama says that a proper gentleman always has a handkerchief ready to offer a lady," Elliott explained, seriously.

"I haven't got a clean one." Jonathan replied flatly, continuing to draw.

*And I am not a lady worthy of such niceties*, Lydia thought, relieved to see that no sputum had spattered across her bodice.

*Ugh, I just want to get away from here. But...the book!*

Again, she glanced in its direction. *How can I possibly get it back? Perhaps it's far enough under the hedge as to be reached from the other side?*

"If you don't need anything, I ask that you please excuse me," she said, collecting her things and rising from the ground.

Jonathan waved his hand dismissively and Lydia began to leave.

"Don't go!" called Elliott.

"Sorry," she said over her shoulder, retrieving the leading ribbon from the ground where she had left it.

"I *command* you to stay!" he cried out.

"Don't be so despotic, Elly. Really..." She heard Jonathan's voice through the shrubbery of the maze.

"Don't call me that! *Now* who will play catch with me?"

"I might if you stop whining. I'm nearly done with this. Just a moment."

Once safely hidden in one of the maze's alleyways, Lydia barely kept herself from breaking into a run as she wound the grimy ribbon around its spool.

*At least there's no gravel here to proclaim my every step.*

When she reached the spot where she supposed she might be able to retrieve the book, she knelt and looked under the shrubbery. Gnarled roots and low lying branches blocked her view. The novel was nowhere in sight.

*How am I to get that back? My one free afternoon is sunny and perfect and then it's taken over by a prattling, fruit-stealing boy and his peculiar older brother. In my one attempt to say something amusing, I made myself look like a complete fool. And what if it rains before I can get that book back?*

With her stomach churning, Lydia headed back to the house.

# Finding a Furtive Poem

~ JONATHAN

Lifting the pen from the page, Jonathan watched the girl disappear into the maze. Though uninvited, the vision of her, sitting on the lawn at his arrival returned to him. Again, he chided himself for the way his stomach had flipped as he emerged from the maze's alleys to see her there. He was certain the rush of inappropriate and happy surprise he felt had registered on his face.

*Thank God Sophia wasn't here to see it.*

He had tried to offset this by speaking diffidently to her once he had settled himself on the grass.

*Would she have stayed longer had I been friendlier? Bah! She's a* maid*!*

Carelessly, he turned the page before him, no longer pretending to care about the drawing on it.

*Her neck is rather long. Is that how I drew it?* He flipped through his sketchbook to find his drawing of Foote returning Spalding's teeth.

*Hmm...*he thought, looking at the depiction. *It's not one of my better...but what's this?*

A little slip of paper was tucked into the fold of the book.

"You said you'd play catch with me!" Elliott interrupted.

"Umm..." Jonathan grabbed the ball from Elliott's hand and tossed it over the top of the hedges.

"There you are," he said, then lifted the scrap and unfolded it.

"Jonathan!" Elliott cried, exasperated as he ran off. "That's not funny!"

*True, dear brother,* he thought looking down at the paper, *but it ought to buy me some time.* Incredulously, he realized what it was.

*The maid is hiding secretive messages in my things*! The ridiculousness of it nearly made him laugh.

Upon the paper was written in pencil:

The ancient beaux who choose to woo
All must remember as they chew
That teeth untethered within gums
May fall to floors like dinner crumbs

An antiquated suitor that
Ignores this lesson may not get
Another invitation for
A meal spent as a paramour

For slick with thick archaic spit
And crusted o'er with ample grit
A set of gnashers dropping thus
Could dissuade the most amorous

Jonathan sat, stunned.

*Incredible. Did she pen this herself? She couldn't have!*

He read it over again.

*It's so precisely right for the drawing, she must have.*

Elliott reemerged from the maze, the red ball clutched in his hand, a pout on his face. "Now don't do that again!"

"Alright, I won't," Jonathan said, standing. He tucked the poem into his pocket. "Not today anyway. Throw it here."

Elliott's face lit up with a smile as he tossed the ball toward his brother.

*But why would she suppose the old chap was a suitor? Ah well, it's an astonishing bit of poetry regardless.*

Jonathan tossed the ball back and thoughtlessly reached to feel the paper crinkle in his pocket as if to make certain it did exist. He shook his head in appreciation.

*What a clever, clever girl.*

# Choosing an 'E'

~ LYDIA

"Tiny, keep them tiny," Lydia said, watching Wells scratch out letters with the crudely sharpened pencil. "This paper is precious stuff."

Wells beamed, proud of her few little letters.

To Lydia, they looked like the writing of a very young child, but she was pleased that Wells was so happy. Her contentment soured, though, as she recalled for the thousandth time flinging *Persuasion* under the hedge.

*How can I possibly get that back? What if it rains? Or is ruined by dew! Would the shrubbery protect it?* She bit her lip.

*Next Sunday afternoon will probably be my first chance to go and find it. But what if the boys are there again, or what if Wells follows me? She'll never let me hear the end of it if she finds out what I did!*

"And how do I write *your* name?" Wells asked, offering the pencil.

"Hmm...oh, yes." Lydia took it and clearly wrote her name while Wells watched from over her shoulder.

"That says 'Foote'?" Wells asked, looking confused.

"No, 'Lydia'."

"Oh, well I'd rather practice 'Foote'. If I start thinking of you as *that*," she pointed at the paper, "I may accidentally call you that and get into trouble."

"Trouble?" Lydia laughed. "What trouble?"

"Well, if the Lady wants you to be called 'Foote', then I'm not the one to argue with her."

"Very well," said Lydia, mildly annoyed and wrote 'FOOTE' on the paper. It was the first time she had written the name in reference to herself. Even the shape of the letters on the paper irked her.

"F-oo-t," Wells sounded it out slowly, pointing at each letter. "I didn't think it would have an 'e' at the end."

"Well, the word for this thing," Lydia lifted and wiggled her right foot, "doesn't, but I suppose I want to spell it a little differently if it's to signify me." She hadn't thought about this when she wrote it out, but it made sense to her as she spoke.

Wells didn't question it, but took the pencil from Lydia and began to carefully copy each letter.

"Now," Wells said, offering the pencil over with a smile. "Write 'egg' and 'salt'."

"Such *fascinating* words!" Lydia teased as she obliged her.

A shy smile came over Wells' face. "Don't laugh at me! I just thought I ought to learn words to help me read recipes. Do you think that someday I could..."

Wells broke off, looking sly.

"You could what?" Lydia asked, never having seen Wells look this mischievous.

"Do you think I could ever be a head cook?"

"*Of course* you could." Lydia said, wondering why such a thought could make Wells smile.

*Come now, Wellsy, that's not much of a goal to aim for.*

"Don't tell anyone I said that."

"Why not?"

"The Lady wouldn't like it."

"I'll be sure not to mention it next time she invites me to tea."

Wells rolled her eyes as Lydia continued, "Wells, I hardly think *the Lady* would care even if she did hear of it. Besides, servants can have ambitions."

*Even ambitions as base as becoming a head cook.*

"Oh, no." Wells shook her ginger head emphatically. "She wouldn't like it. Smith says the Lady wants her staff to know their place and if she thinks one of them has forgotten it, then *out they go*."

The memory of Smith's face as she whispered threats over a missing mob-cap in the hallway popped into Lydia's mind. Her upper lip involuntarily curled.

"That wouldn't be the end of the world. You could find a place elsewhere."

"No," Wells shook her head again. "If you get dismissed, the Lady won't give you a good reference and then you can't find a place *anywhere*."

*Oh, please*. Lydia narrowed her eyes. "Why are you so fearful?"

"Fearful? Who was it that went down to the kitchen in the dark to relight the dip the other night? It wasn't *you*!" Wells insisted.

Lydia sighed at the recollection. "I didn't accuse you of being afraid of *everything*, but you're constantly thinking about being dismissed or upsetting the Lady."

"I'm just careful." Wells stared at the wall. "I can't go home."

"What would be so bad about that?"

"My family needs the money I earn."

"How many siblings do you have?"

"How many what?"

"Sisters and brothers."

"Well, there were five at home when I left and three in service at Great Homes. There are probably a couple more now."

"You don't even know?"

"How would I? I've not been home since I came."

"You've never visited home?"

Wells shook her head.

"How does your family get your wages?"

"I think Smith arranged for them to be sent to my mother."

"Don't you want to visit home?"

Wells shrugged. "I do miss some of the wee ones, but there was never enough food. I always gave away half my portion to one of my sisters or brothers because I felt sorry for them, but then I felt mad about it later. Here there's always plenty to eat."

A new thought occurred to Lydia. "Maybe when you're done here you can go home and cook them all a big meal like the ones you've learned to cook here."

"*Done* here? What do you mean?"

"When you leave here."

"Why would I leave here?" There was apprehension in Wells' voice.

"I mean when you grow older and can strike out on your own or get married and have a family."

Wells snickered. "Don't be stupid! I won't be having a family!"

"What? Why not?"

"There's no family for me! Once you're in service, that's your life. Surely you know that!"

*What?*

Wells turned her attention back to the paper and began to scratch at its surface with the pencil, seemingly unaware that her declaration had hit Lydia like a kick in the stomach.

*This is my life? No! I'm a farmer's daughter.*

Lydia stopped breathing as the possibility of Wells' words sank in.

*On the contrary, I* was *a farmer's daughter, but now I'm nothing more than a parlour maid. My father is dead and my brother's a drunkard. But...I won't forever dust shelves here at Whitehall, will I?*

Lydia stared at her work-worn hands atop the bed cover, her stomach churning.

*Will I?*

*No. Of course not!*

"Now, write 'peas' if you please," requested Wells, handing Lydia the paper and pencil.

Lydia resumed breathing as she slowly scratched out the word.

"I'm done for the night," she said, handing it back and lying down. "Snuff out the rush dip when you're done."

# Impressing Young Men

~ JONATHAN

"It's my turn to read. Give them here," said Jonathan, clutching his second glass of wine. As the papers were passed around the circle, he asked, "Hodges, when do you go to London?"

"Next week and for a whole month."

Sophia's face fell. "Then you will miss our ball?"

"Certainly not. I'll make a special trip back for it."

"Well, I hope a whole new set shows up while you're there. Our recent trip was quite dull. Upon my soul, Widdy, another misspelling?" exclaimed Jonathan, squinting at the half sheet of paper in his hand. "There's no 'e' in 'truly'! How were you accepted into Heath? Simply jingle a bag of crowns in the headmaster's earshot and he opens the front door for donkeys, I suppose."

Widcombe laughed, reaching for another handful of walnuts. "The nuts are almost gone."

Jonathan reached for the bell-pull. "Alright, I'll read through this muddled mess if I can decipher it. It'll be an act of God with Widdy's spelling."

"And Amelia's terrible scrawl is no help either," joked Widcombe.

"Robert!" Amelia cried, throwing a walnut at her brother's head.

"We all have clearly seen that your handwriting is atrocious," he insisted.

"It *would be* a great misfortune," Jonathan spoke, "if you did not possess in great abundance those *other* qualities which are truly important to an accomplished young lady. Everyone is allowed their faults."

Jonathan grew uneasy as Amelia's face darkened a couple of shades, though he didn't know if it was from Robert's clear insult or from his own ridiculously unfounded compliment.

*I ought to be more careful what I say to her.*

"Let's see here." Jonathan redirected his attention to the paper. "It reads, or *I think* it reads, 'Lawrence Hodges will marry a milkmaid, sire 12 children..."

Here Jonathan paused to raise his eyebrows at Hodges, who was sticking his chest out and gazing smugly around the circle of friends. Jonathan laughed and continued, "...make his living as a reddleman, die a slow and painful death on a sugar plantation in Philadelphia and he will be truly missed by no one.' I say, playing this game with the lot of you is rather boring. Couldn't you have at least married him off to a Portuguese princess? And there is no sugar grown in Philadelphia!"

"I thought my bit about him being a reddleman was clever," piped Sophia. "He'll be a bright shade of red, working in all that ruddle."

The salon's door opened and in came Foote.

"You rang, sir?"

"Uh, yes, Widcombe, has inhaled all the nuts, possibly along with a shoe or two and I'm wondering if there are any left in the house at all," said Jonathan.

"I will see. If there aren't, shall I bring something else?" the maid asked.

"Yes, yes, whatever scraps you might throw to a pig."

He watched the girl as she left, her neat, upright figure briskly walking out the door.

"I suppose it's my turn to have my future determined," said Sophia to the group who immediately focused on the blank slips in their hands. "But include no regimental leaders in my future. That joke has run its course."

Foote's departure still fresh in his mind, Jonathan's attention was arrested by the two young women before him.

Amelia and Sophia sat on chairs that had been pulled in close for the game.

His sister's honey-colored hair hung in thick locks. She hadn't bothered to curl them that morning, a process which Jonathan knew required more than one person and could take hours when done properly.

Amelia, on the other hand, looked as if she had awoken at dawn to groom and preen. Various locks of her hair were curled, twisted and pinned, arranged with such precision and somehow glued into place that Jonathan wondered if she slept at night or simply sat at her toilette table preparing for the next day. Cosmetics, of course, were off limits to a virtuous young woman, but more than once Jonathan had noticed Amelia furtively pinching her cheeks and pressing her lips together, to bring out the colour he supposed.

She'd always been like this. When they were much younger and Jonathan was visiting at the Widcombes' estate, Amelia had sat on the ground under an oak smoothing and resmoothing her skirt and silken sash, watching the boys throw a ball around. Once it was time to go in for the noonday meal, she had risen and walked all the way to the dining room completely unaware that her backside was covered in dirt. Prancing like a show-pony and twirling her parasol, she'd left a trail of clods behind her. Jonathan smiled now at the recollection.

Unfortunately, it was in this instant that Amelia glanced at him. Clearly interpreting his scrutinizing gaze as one of appreciation, she tilted her head at him and smiled back.

*Good God,* thought Jonathan, pushing his mouth into anything other than a smile and focusing on the pencil in his hand. He always knew that some had expected him to take an interest in Amelia by this point in time. The idea had its merits, the foremost being that she was the sister of one of his closest friends. Also, she was neither dull nor churlish in temperament, two characteristics Jonathan disliked in anyone.

*But to draw her close and call her "wife"? Ugh...*

Jonathan nearly shivered at the thought, imagining his hand cut and bleeding from the sharp edges of her carefully arranged hair.

*She might be pretty if she didn't clothe herself in those ridiculous fashions. Perhaps she will catch Hodges and bear his twelve children.*

He looked around at his group of friends who were dully staring at the bits of paper in their hands. Clearing his throat, he offered, "Let's not bore Sophia with our tedious prophecies. Shall we play a different game? One that doesn't require so much wit?"

"You fancy yourself so brilliant, Jonathan," interjected Sophia.

"I have found that people of brilliance are only accused of arrogance by those who lack the intelligence to understand them," he declared, winking at his sister.

Amelia laughed jollily while Sophia rolled her eyes.

Again the door opened and Foote entered, carrying a large bowl of strawberries. She placed it on the table in the midst of the friends.

"Oh, those are lovely!" breathed Amelia as they all reached for the fruit.

"Thank you," said Sophia to Foote who was turning to go.

"Now there's a clever girl," said Jonathan, pointing at Foote's retreating figure.

"Yes, we are all amazed at her ability to carry a bowl of ripened fruit," quipped Hodges, reaching for his second berry.

"No, really. Foote!" Jonathan called.

Foote turned, her hand on the door. "Yes, sir?"

"Say something clever!" he commanded.

"Sir?" the girl asked, her narrow brows lifting in question.

"Don't make a fool of me! Come now. You have on more than one occasion surprised me with your wit."

A look crossed the girl's face, something akin to mischief. "Certainly, sir, even a bear is well-trained and pampered before he is called upon to entertain the masses. You've not even offered me an apple for my performance."

A slight gasp escaped Amelia. Sophia cleared her throat.

Delighted, Jonathan looked around at his circle of astonished friends. "There! You see?"

Reaching into the bowl, he retrieved the largest remaining berry and held it out to the girl. "I'm afraid a strawberry will have to be the reward for cleverness as I have no apples."

But the berry remained in his outstretched hand and the look on Foote's face changed as if she was suddenly a different person.

"Is there anything else that you need?"

"No," Sophia spoke. "Thank you, Foote. You may go."

"She's not really a maid, is she?" asked Amelia as the door shut again. "I've never seen her here before. Is this one of your jokes, Jonathan, dressing up your *cousin* as a maid?"

"She's unlike any of *our* servants," stated Widcombe, grabbing the rejected strawberry from Jonathan's hand.

"You oughtn't tease her like that, Jonathan," warned Sophia. "Or even speak to her so familiarly. You know Mama would not approve."

"At what point did you think I began to care what *she* approves of?"

"I was actually thinking of Foote's sake." Sophia replied. "It would not go well for her here if Mama began to dislike her."

"*The Lady* doesn't seem to know that Foote exists," her brother replied.

"It is only the servants she notices that she dislikes," responded his sister.

*Hmm, there is a bit of truth to that*, thought Jonathan.

"Enough talk about servants," demanded Hodges, throwing a stem at Jonathan. "Get the cards. I'll beat you at Whist."

# Scorning an Apple

~ Lydia

Once again, Lydia stood gazing in awe at the giant bookshelf before her. Anytime she entered the library, even though it was always to clean it, she was struck by the impressive sight. The shelves stretched to the ceiling, laden with countless colourful spines all pushed together to form a collective wall of literature.

*This room even smells differently than the others, like wood...and glue, perhaps.* Lydia sighed contentedly and reached for a rag. *Would anyone notice if I didn't dust those top shelves? I've been here over three months and I've never seen anyone else so much as* open *one of these books.*

It was her love for the volumes themselves that compelled Lydia to climb to the top of the ladder. A bright splash of red caught her attention.

*What's this?*

There, on one of the shelves lay a drawing of an apple. It was on paper that had been cut to fit the apple's shape. Mostly red, it also had tones of yellow in its flesh. A bright green leaf sprouted from the little brown stem. It was lovely and fit perfectly in the palm of Lydia's hand.

Flipping it over, she saw written in a cramped hand,

Is this a proper reward for a dancing bear?

She grunted disgustedly and dropped the paper onto the shelf.

*Arrogant fool.*

*"Say something clever," he commanded. And so I did! Only to see them all shocked into silence as though this maid's uniform relegates me to idiocy.*

She shuddered at the memory of their faces all turned toward her as her words had hung in the air, their mouths open, their eyes wide, all except for Sir Jonathan who grinned at her unabashedly.

The only other time that so many people had gawked at her like that was one wintery morning when she had slipped on an icy step while exiting church. All the parishioners in the churchyard had turned to see her tumbled, wincing and gasping in pain.

*But* those *people hadn't been lounging on silken settees desperately trying to entertain themselves after suffering through a long day of fine food and tedious leisure.*

*No, this is* not *a proper reward, sir, and I am no bear.*

She pushed the apple under some books, and proceeded to dust the next shelf below.

*What is he getting at? Mama warned me of possible "gifts" from male employers.* Lydia scoffed. *But I think she meant ivory combs or bottles of parfum.*

She continued down the ladder to the final shelf. *Apparently I'm not worthy of gifts of* that *caliber.*

A fresh wave of anger crashed over her as she stood, thinking.

*I ought to tear his offering in half.*

Hastily she ascended the rungs and regarded the offensive little scrap.

Imagining Jonathan's grinning face twisting into one of fury at finding it torn in two made her hesitate.

*I'm the one who ought to be angry,* she thought. *Still...*

With a sense of dissatisfaction, Lydia pushed the offensive slip of paper fully under the books, leaving no hint of its existence to the casual observer.

*I don't want to catch sight of that again...*

***

That evening, Lydia and Wells were propped up in bed.

"'P' is such a nice letter," Wells said, looking at an ornate capital P on the page in the book on her lap.

Lydia smiled pertly and wrote a long word on a slip of paper. "What do you think that says?"

Wells began to sound it out, "P-l-ah-uh-g-huh-m-ah-n. That can't be right."

"That was nearly it, but these all stand together to say 'ow'," Lydia pointed. "Try again."

"P-l-ow-m-ah-n. Oh! Ploughman!" Wells turned to Ploughman. "You've got a hard name."

"Let me see it," said the older woman. The beds were so close together in the small room that Lydia was able to hand her the paper simply by stretching her arm out.

"Hmm," Ploughman said, examining it. "It's a long one."

"Here, whisper your Christian name in my ear so I can write it out for Wells," said Lydia, leaning toward the woman.

Ploughman complied and soon Wells was reading, "Juh-oa-n. Joan."

"Let me see," said Ploughman. "I've never seen that one."

Lydia hid her surprise as she handed over the paper.

*She's never seen her first name written out! At times these dear people astound me.*

"So that's what I look like on paper--Joan Ploughman. I certainly look different in person." She chuckled.

An idea occurred to Lydia.

"Would you like to learn to read?" she asked the graying woman. "I could teach you alongside Wells."

"Thank you, Foote, but I've gone this long without it and I think I can go a bit longer. I would like to keep this scrap of paper, though."

"Of course."

Ploughman creakily rose from the bed and carefully put the precious little slip of paper into her sparsely stocked cupboard.

Lydia thought back to the snippet of paper she'd seen earlier that day.

*Did he expect me to pack it away for safe keeping amongst my prized possessions?* She snorted lightly.

"What is it?" Wells asked, looking up from the book.

"Hmm?" Lydia asked and then feigned a cough.

# Not Finding What is Sought After

~ JONATHAN

*It's been a week since I placed it. Surely she's cleaned here since then. Don't they clean each room once a week?*

The narrow rungs felt twig-like under Jonathan's heavy footwear as he ascended the ladder.

*So that would mean...*

The thought was interrupted by the opening of the library door. Jonathan froze and gripped the sides of the ladder, swinging his head around.

Sophia stood in the doorway, looking up at her brother, a sheet of newspaper clutched in her hand.

"Oh, Jonathan, you won't believe this." She pulled the door shut behind her and regarded her brother on the ladder. "What are you doing?"

*I nearly thought it was Foote! Oh, to be caught up here by* her*!*

"Huh? Oh...uh, I'm looking for a book." He continued his climb, cringing internally at the minor falsehood. "What's the matter?"

Reaching the top, he looked from left to right.

*Gone. I did put it right here, anchored by Robinson Crusoe, didn't I?* He examined the length of the shelf again.

"Mama has placed an announcement about our ball in the newspaper."

*Yes, yes, it's gone. She's taken it.*

He imagined Foote ascending the ladder and finding the apple, an amused smile tugging at the corners of her lips as she tucked it into her apron pocket.

"Did you hear me, Jonathan?"

Satisfied, he began to make his way back down.

"Yes. Announcement. Ball. Newspaper. There's nothing unusual about that."

"Well there wouldn't be if she hadn't included *this* bit, 'All members of the Peerage are welcome to attend.'"

"What? Ha ha!" Jonathan laughed loudly. "Well, they'll all be lining up now! The salon will be *bursting* with English nobility." He continued to laugh as his feet hit the floor. "Her absurdities ever increase! Why are you troubled?"

"It's not funny, Jonathan. It's absolutely ludicrous and...and *shameful.* Don't you see why she's done this?"

Jonathan lifted his eyebrows. "Are you able to explain it?" he asked doubtfully.

"Clearly since things with Spalding never progressed she sees this ball as a chance to marry me off and marry me well."

*Here we go with that again!*

"Sophe," he began, "no duke reads the Times to determine which country ball he'll stumble into each week. Even if that was the Lady's hope, it won't be realized. You're worried about nothing."

The lines in Sophia's forehead did not lessen as she bent her head back over the paper.

A thought struck Jonathan and he looked back up at the shelf.

*What if a breeze caught it and it floated down...?*

He envisioned the apple's drifting descent and began to look at the floor and under a nearby table.

*No. Nothing. She definitely took it.*

"What is it?" Sophia asked.

Trying not to let jubilance show on his face, Jonathan responded, "Oh nothing. I thought I dropped something."

He noted the downward turn of Sophia's mouth.

*The poor thing's truly worried.*

Taking the newspaper from her, he crumpled it and tossed it into the fireplace.

"Solved," he said, holding his empty hands out before him.

"Yes, *thoroughly*," Sophia said dubiously, but smiled at Jonathan regardless. She grabbed one of his hands and tilted her head, asking, "What would I do without you?"

He shrugged and forced a broad smile, the lies he had just told her echoing in his mind.

# Wary of a Bottle

~ LYDIA

"Smith didn't tell you what this is all about?" Lydia whispered as she and Wells approached Sophia's bedroom door, their footsteps muffled by the thick carpeting.

Wells whispered back. "All she said was, 'Come to Miss Sophia's room and bring Foote with you.'"

*Of course there is* more *for us to do,* thought Lydia. *If Mama hadn't written that a fox got half the chickens I'd leave tomorrow.*

Settling her face into what she had come to think of as her 'face-of-servitude', Lydia knocked lightly on the paneled door.

"Yes, yes! Come in!" called Smith from within.

They entered to see Miss Sophia who was wearing just a chemise and pantaloons, sitting at a mirrored vanity. Her eyes were wide and her mouth was a thin, hard line.

Smith stood behind her, holding combs in both hands, looking severely agitated.

"Wells, Foote," Smith beckoned them over. "The hairdresser who usually prepares Miss Sophia's hair before special occasions was not able to be here this afternoon, but I told Miss Sophia not to worry as I recall one of you saying that you were quite good at arranging hair."

Lydia was astonished, certain that she had never made such a proud claim, and doubting Wells would ever do so either.

"Which of you was it?" Smith asked, exasperatedly, but did not wait for an answer. "Wells, you come from a large family. Certainly you've done up a lot of hair at home."

"Plaits and such, yes," Wells began. "But..."

"Good, here," said Smith, shoving the combs into Wells' hands. "Go on!"

Hesitantly, Wells began to comb through the thick, straw colored hair. It hung to Sophia's waist in dense waves.

*It is Miss Sophia's greatest beauty*, thought Lydia, *though even it is not a remarkable feature.*

She studied Sophia in the mirror as Wells combed with slightly shaking hands.

The blue eyes were small and lightly lashed. There was an unfortunate fine downiness that covered her broad cheeks, now illuminated in the afternoon light spilling through the window. Her lips were neither fine nor shapely. Neither was her nose. Her forehead was wrinkled with concern, her eyebrows pushing together.

*What miracle can be done with the hair to transform all the rest?* wondered Lydia. *And who are* we *to do it?*

"Let's part it here," Wells said, dragging the edge of the comb down the center of Sophia's crown. The hair would not lie sleekly on either side of the part.

Though she was hesitant to be responsible for any part of the task, Lydia murmured, "Perhaps we can smooth it down with some water." She lifted a comb from the vanity table and dipped it into a cup.

"Don't get it too wet or the curls won't hold." Smith advised, her arms crossed in front of her.

"Curls?" Wells asked.

"Yes, of course. The iron's heating in the fire." Smith motioned toward the hearth.

Wells and Lydia looked at the metal tongs sticking out of the fire and then at one another, questioningly.

*Oh, no*, thought Lydia. *She's never used them before, either.*

"Foote, can you herring bone?" Wells asked softly.

"Pardon me?" Lydia asked.

"Have you ever plaited a herring bone? Come here. I'll show you on this side and then you can do the same on that side."

Although Lydia was relieved that Wells was formulating a plan, she was not pleased to be involved in it. Still, she watched Wells' hands as they manipulated several thin locks of hair at once into a tidy plait. It took her only a moment and soon, with hands that felt too large, she was similarly plaiting on the left side of Sophia's head. Wells then directed her as they looped the plaits and secured them with a sort of hairpin. That took them some time to figure out since neither of them had ever used one like it before.

*Hmm, she won't win any prizes, but it is an improvement,* Lydia thought examining Sophia in the mirror again. *Very good. Now I can go sweep the front entryway and set out the flatware.*

Lydia curtsied, ready to walk out the door with Wells.

"You are not yet excused," Smith murmured, her face severe.

Biting back the words she found forming in her mouth, Lydia turned back to face the vanity, determined to keep her irritation from exhibiting itself on her face. Glancing in the mirror, she noticed that Sophia seemed unaware of anything going on around her.

Steadily, Sophia gazed at her own reflection, the worried look replaced with one of calm resignation. This improved her appearance vastly, Lydia noted.

*Though she'd still not be described as pretty.*

Suddenly, the door burst open and Lady Clyde strode in, startling everyone there. Lydia had never seen her move so quickly before.

The servants silently curtsied and Lydia moved aside as the woman reached the vanity where she began to scrutinize her daughter's appearance.

The look of worry had returned to Sophia's face.

"Smith," she said, meeting the housekeeper's eye in the mirror. "I have a slight headache." She began to rub her temples.

"Of course, Miss Sophia," said Smith who quickly disappeared out the door.

"Hmmm..." Lady Clyde assessed, her arms crossed, her eyes flitting between examining Sophia directly and in the mirror.

"Help me with my dress." Sophia rose from the vanity seat and motioned toward the gown hanging on the wardrobe door.

"The corset comes first," Lady Clyde barked as Wells reached for the gown.

On the bed was a frothy pile of petticoats and a strange looking garment with lots of ties. It was more complicated looking than the simple stays that Lydia wore under her own clothing, but it looked as if it would function similarly. Lydia lifted it and helped Sophia into it.

Sophia grabbed onto a thick column of her poster bed and instructed, "Pull it as tightly as you can."

Wells and Lydia looked at each other.

"Come on then," said Sophia, sharply.

*No need to get waspish,* thought Lydia as she stepped forward to grab the dangling ties. She pulled the laces snugly and began to tie them.

*I thought you were nice, but it seems there's a bit of the Lady within you after all.*

"No. It needs to be much tighter than that," griped Sophia. "Lord, where is Smith?"

*Yes, where* is *Smith*, Lydia thought. I've *never done this before. I've never even* seen *one of these before.*

Lydia tried again, pulling till she feared Sophia would cry out in pain. Clumsily, she tied the corset's laces and stepped back.

"Now the petticoats." Lady Clyde snapped her fingers at Wells who picked up one after another, handing them to Lydia.

Lydia counted four in all as they draped them around Sophia's waist.

Next, they lowered the gown itself over Sophia, who knelt with her arms up in the air.

"Careful! Mind her hair!" the Lady snapped.

*Yes, you wouldn't want to have to stand there uselessly while Wells and I dressed it all over again, now would you?*

Once Sophia was standing with every inch of her dress smoothed and every ruffle fluffed, Lydia surveyed her, looking for any details they might be blamed for missing.

The blue of the dress complemented Sophia's eyes. At the neckline was a broad band of lace. Matching bands hung from the end of each sleeve. The waist and hemline were embellished with a cream-colored braid. Overall, Lydia thought the effect was very pretty, though she found the huge sleeves ridiculous.

*She could hide a side of ham in each of those. May we go now?*

Lady Clyde observed her daughter through narrowed eyes, pursing her lips and sighing several times. Finally, she announced, "It will do. Make certain that you smile often; your teeth are your best feature."

With that, she turned and walked briskly from the room.

*Don't bother expressing any gratitude to those of us who paused in our endless duties to dress your daughter's hair and body, dear Lady!* Lydia thought, then curtsied to Sophia, ready to excuse herself.

Startled, she bumbled the curtsey as she saw that a tear was slipping down Sophia's cheek. Immediately, she averted her eyes, struck by pangs of guilt.

*Clearly this ball isn't the joyous occasion I assumed. Well, how could any occasion be joyous with that gargoyle of a mother staring at you? What did she say? 'It will do? Make sure you smile often'?*

Forgetting how Sophia had snapped at her just moments earlier, Lydia wanted to put her arm around the girl and tell her she looked lovely, wanted to tell her not to pay her own mother any mind. But she knew she could not, so she continued to stare at the floor, regretting her earlier impatience.

At that moment, Smith returned, carrying a small tray. On it were a glass bottle and a tiny cup.

Glancing to see if the tears had stopped, Lydia saw that Sophia's eyes were riveted on the tray Smith carried.

Her mouth slightly open, Sophia watched as Smith carefully poured out a measure of liquid from the bottle and held the little cup out to her.

Lydia observed, engrossed, as Sophia closed her eyes, lifted the cup to her lips and tilted the contents into her mouth. She held it there for a moment as if to drain every drop, then licked her lips and sighed heavily. A look of relief spread across her face.

*What magical fluid is that?* wondered Lydia, taken aback.

Uncomfortably, she looked at Wells, who was arranging things upon the vanity table, and Smith, who was recapping the glass bottle. Neither of them seemed to notice anything unusual.

Sophia gazed into the mirror, now with a dreamy look on her face.

"How is your headache, Miss Sophia?" asked Smith.

The girl simply nodded, a little smile playing on her lips.

*That was an odd answer,* thought Lydia. *And how could it possibly work that quickly?*

"You look very nice, Miss Sophia," Smith declared then turned to the servants. "Go. Ready yourselves to serve the guests."

Once they had passed through the door, Lydia whispered, "What was that she was drinking?"

"What?"

"That glass bottle Smith brought in. What was in it?"

"I don't know," responded Wells. "Her petticoats, though! Her *underclothes* are finer than our *serving* clothes. Ha! We cleaned the *entire* house, prepared *countless* dishes of food and even dressed Miss Sophia's hair! How would they manage without us? Oh, I'm so glad they forgot about the curling tongs. I know I would have burnt her ears!"

"Hmm...yes," said Lydia, thinking, *It seems nearly everything was forgotten once that* bottle *was brought in.*

# Promising to Dance

~ JONATHAN

Jonathan stood in the marble hall, looking out the window at the front drive.

*I thought that at least Hodges would be here by now.*

There was a rustle behind him.

"Jonathan?"

He turned to see his sister descending the staircase.

"Well?" she asked.

"What?"

"How do I look?" she asked, uneasily.

Jonathan turned back to the window. "Fine."

"Jonathan! You hardly looked at me." She held her arms out at her sides as her brother eyed her more carefully.

"You look lovely, Sophia," he said, giving the answer he supposed she wanted to hear, neglecting to add, *Certain to charm all the nobility in attendance.*

"Is my hair alright?" she questioned, then laughed nervously. "The servants did it."

"It's very nice," he said, staring again out the window.

"Jonathan?"

"What?"

"Will you promise to dance with me?"

"Sophia, you know I hate spinning and prancing about like an idiot."

"You don't have to if others are asking me to dance, but I can't bear the thought of sitting in a chair while the pretty girls dance all evening."

"Were pretty girls invited?" Jonathan asked, jokingly. "I wasn't aware of that. Look, if I notice you sitting in a chair for too long, then I will dance with you...but I make no promises that I'll dance well."

"Thank you."

Jonathan continued, "Widcombe likes dancing. Maybe he'll take you for a round or two."

"Jonathan, what was the name of that fellow at Heath who shaved his head because you convinced him he had lice? "

Jonathan laughed out loud. "Edward Morton! That was a while ago. Why?"

"I think he may be coming tonight."

"What? That can't be!"

"Mama said something about a Morton you went to school with being invited."

Jonathan thought for a moment. "No. Even if it was him, he wouldn't come. He once told me that his stable block alone was larger than all of Whitehall, which was an incredibly stupid thing to say since he'd never even been here. And that was *before* I convinced him to shave his head. He considers himself far too superior to step foot on our *piddling* estate."

"Oh," Sophia sounded disappointed.

"What's the matter? Were you hoping he *would* come?" Jonathan asked, a skeptical smile on his face.

"No! Mama said something about him being the most *eligible* young man in attendance, so I know she wants me to impress him and now you're telling me how awful he is."

Jonathan scoffed, "If she finds him so eligible, let *her* marry him!" At that moment, a carriage Jonathan recognized came down the drive. "Ahh, here is Hodges."

Jonathan smiled at Sophia as he bolted to the front door. "Let this blasted ball begin."

Out the front door and down the steps he flew as Hodges emerged from the vehicle.

"Ahoy there!" Jonathan slapped his friend on the back.

"Clyde." Hodges nodded, his oiled hair flopping loose in front.

Just then a lone horse and rider came around the corner of the drive and trotted up to the front staircase. The two young men turned to face the rider as he dismounted.

*One of the Lady's awkward invitees,* thought Jonathan, eyeing the man, but a hint of familiarity was in the face.

"Meestuh Clyde?" the man asked, extending his hand.

The foolish sounding voice jarred Jonathan to realization.

"Heldmann!" Jonathan laughed aloud, grasping the hand which the man held out.

Heldmann breathed in deeply and said, "I am...in England."

Jonathan waited until he realized there was nothing more to come, and nodded, saying, "Yes, yes you are...as we are, as well. Hodges, this is Herman Heldmann. We met in Paris last year."

Hodges and Heldmann nodded at one another.

"Today is the mmmm...dance and eat, yes?" Heldmann asked, uneasily.

"What? Oh yes, the ball! That's right. I mentioned it in the letter, didn't I? Please come in. Hardy! Come take the man's horse. I'm so pleased you've come!"

"I thanks you!" The large blonde man beamed, his broad cheeks rosy in the evening light.

Jonathan motioned up the stairs toward the front door, laughing again as Hardy led the horse away.

*Sophia won't believe it! The strange German is actually here in our own home!*

# Teaching the Dance

~ LYDIA

"Let's help Ploughman get these dishes taken care of," Lydia suggested.

"No! We might spoil our clothes," said Wells. "The Lady would be furious if we looked slovenly in front of the guests."

"But we've been sitting here for half an hour doing absolutely nothing."

"You need to be ready if you're called," Ploughman said, pulling her hands from the sudsy tub and drying them on her apron.

"They've already eaten and the punch is set out. What could they possibly need us for?"

A burst of laughter and cat-calling from beyond the stable could be heard through the open door.

*The grooms and livery servants from the other 'great houses',* assumed Lydia, though no one was in view. She thought for a moment and then began to pile the servants' plain cups onto a platter and fill a pitcher with small beer.

"Come on, Wellsy."

"What are you doing?" asked Wells.

"We're going to go give the lads a drink."

"What?"

"You know, the lads from the other *great houses* out there in the stable yard. They're just waiting for this *great ball* to be over, so we might as well give them some *great small beer* while they endure their *great wait* for their own *great families.*"

"We oughtn't do that," Wells whined.

Annoyed already, Lydia responded, "Well, then *we* won't. *I* will, though you can come along if you'd like. I think I saw your brother, Joseph."

"Don't be stupid. He's at Beverly Park which is counties away."

"Well, I did catch sight of a ginger fellow, and he very well may be thirsty, so if you'll excuse me..." She balanced the platter on her left hand expertly and exited the kitchen.

"And you oughtn't assume all my brothers are gingers!" Wells called out behind her.

The evening air was pleasant as Lydia passed the garden toward the stables. The laughter grew louder and Lydia heard footsteps behind her.

*I knew you'd change your mind, Wellsy.*

Rounding the corner of the stable house, she saw the group was gathered around two tussling men. The taller of the two had succeeded in getting the stockier man in a headlock and they were going round and round. The others laughed and jokingly called out advice to the trapped man.

At her approach, the men fell nearly silent. Even the tusslers let go of each other.

"Oh, don't stop. I'm terribly fond of dancing though I'm not familiar with that particular one you were just doing," she said.

This brought on a fresh round of laughter.

Lydia surveyed the group as she began to pour the small beer for the men. Wells aided her by holding the serving tray.

*They're all a bit rough, though they're dressed in the finest that great families are likely to deck their servants in*, she thought.

Often, the livery staff was dressed in fancier clothing than other servants due to the fact that they were seen out and about. This was unfortunate since most of the livery staff were young men, hardly more than boys, and of all groups, they are known to be the hardest on clothing.

Lydia didn't like the way one of the men was looking at her. He was sitting on a stump, his legs splayed wide as he chewed on a piece of hay.

The look in his eyes was one of assessing, as Lydia recalled her father looking at a heifer he was considering for purchase.

Next to him sat Glaser. The older man lounged comfortably on another stump, smiling appreciatively as he took the cup offered to him.

The strains of a lively tune reached their ears from the ball within Whitehall.

"It's a shame to waste such lovely music. Do any of you lads know the Sellenger's Round?"

"I do," said a boy whose teeth stuck out like a mule.

Usually good looking boys were chosen to be liverers.

*You must really have a way with horses*, thought Lydia, but she said, "Very well then. You shall be my partner. Please come here. And who will dance with Wells?"

A little squeak of horror escaped Wells as many hands shot up into the air.

Careful not to look in the direction of the hay-chewer, Lydia pointed.

"You," she said to the man she had mentioned earlier as a possible sibling to Wells. "Yes, you two belong together."

The young man came forward, looking pleased to have been chosen.

"And you two," said Lydia, turning to the men who had been roughhousing at her approach. "Which of you was the lady of your earlier dance?"

Immediately both men pointed at the other and loudly proclaimed, "Him!"

Everyone laughed.

"Hmm, well it looked as if this fellow was leading," said Lydia, pointing to the taller man. "So you stand here with the men and you come over here beside Wells."

The stocky man refused, looking annoyed. "God ha'n't made me no lady."

"We all praise Him for that!" hollered someone.

The youngest looking boy there was pushed forward into the circle.

"Cadby'll do. His voice ha'n't changed yet and his chin is as bald as the top of Glaser's head."

"That'll do. That'll do," said Glaser, running his hand over his scalp as the others laughed.

Lydia positioned a miserable looking Cadby opposite the tall man, who ducked his head slightly to tell Lydia, "I'll have you know that I'm only willing to dance with this here boy because you kindly brought us the drinks."

"Of course, of course. No one is doubting your natural unwillingness to dance with Cadby. And he, obviously, is lamenting being forced to dance with you. Now let's begin before the song ends."

Standing before the homely boy, Lydia called out, "Bow to your partner and then everyone join hands in a circle. Move to the left for eight."

There was much running into one another as the group struggled to keep up with Lydia's orders.

"Turn to your partner and bow; ladies, curtsey. Now you go this way and you go there."

The observers watched with large grins as the three couples stumbled along, bumping into one another and laughing at their own clumsiness.

"Now all join hands in a circle...ugh, our timing's *completely* off...and two steps in, now two back. You all can count to two, can't you?" Lydia looked to her partner, laughing. "I thought you said you knew Sellenger's Round."

"I'm not sure this *is* Sellenger's Round," retorted the boy, his teeth looking even more obtuse as he smiled.

"I assure you it is! It is!" Lydia laughed aloud.

# Defending a Fraulein's Honor

~ JONATHAN

"God save the king, it's hot in here!" exclaimed Widcombe, throwing himself down on a settee after finishing his third dance of the evening.

"Get off there, sweaty pig!" Jonathan demanded. "You'll leave a watermark. I'll open a couple of windows. You were starting to smell the place up anyway."

Widcombe laughed, prone still on the settee.

It was early enough in the summer evening to still be light outside. Several dancers cheered accordingly as the cooler air rushed in.

Jonathan bowed good naturedly. "As always, I am more than happy to play the hero."

The room held six young men and nine young women in addition to the many parents who had come along to chaperone the event. Some of the guests were Jonathan's school friends and their siblings. Others were fine families from the nearby area.

*Nary a duke nor baron,* Jonathan thought, eyeing his mother who hovered everywhere, rarely sitting down.

Jonathan itched to get Sophia alone to snicker over the ridiculous headpiece Amelia was wearing.

*A turban! And with a little purple jewel dangling from the front, no less!*

One of the young men present was, in fact, the very Edward Morton that Jonathan was certain would *not* attend.

"Excellent," he had said to Hodges, rolling his eyes. "Look who's here with a full head of hair."

Morton had strolled in a little later than the others and sat far from Jonathan at dinner. Even from the distance, Jonathan could see how

Morton had picked at his dinner, wrinkling his nose and waving it away when Foote had offered him vegetables from a platter.

*Hmmm...as charming as ever*, Jonathan thought. Once when Morton looked in his direction, Jonathan vigorously scratched at his scalp.

Noticing Heldmann sitting in a chair watching a dance in progress, Jonathan approached him. "Do you dance the Quadrille in Hamburg?"

"I am...sorry?" Heldmann's eyes focused on Jonathan's mouth.

"Is the Quadrille a dance you've danced before?"

"Mmm...please forgive. I do not...understands." Heldmann repositioned himself in the chair as if preparing for another try at comprehension.

*Ugh, tiresome business.*

"Would you like some punch?" asked Jonathan, sweeping his left arm in the direction of the punchbowl while lifting an imaginary glass with his right.

"No, no thank you," responded Heldmann.

"Very well then. Please excuse me." Jonathan bowed his head and began to move across the room, but not before noting the German's crestfallen face.

*Sorry, old chap, but I've got other things to do than repeat the same question a thousand different ways.*

The musicians struck up another song and a number of couples positioned themselves in the designated dance area to begin a reel. Sophia was not among them. Glancing around, Jonathan saw that she was seated by the door.

*I suppose I ought to fulfill the loathsome obligation. Best to do it now and be done with it.*

He made his way over to her.

"I haven't forgotten my unhappy promise," Jonathan said, extending his hand.

"Thank you," she murmured as she rose.

Halfway through the dance, Jonathan noticed that his mother was standing by the door and that she was looking directly at him, obviously displeased.

*What egregious sin have I committed now?*

Her hand fluttered distractedly.

*If you want to say something to me, you must do so, and not think I can interpret your silly hand gestures.*

He bumbled his way through the dance, only stepping on Sophia's slippered foot once and then moved off to his friends in the corner. Widcombe had sat out the last dance, recovering from three in a row.

"Widdy, be a friend and dance with Sophia, will you?" Jonathan asked.

"You don't hear me asking you or Hodges to dance with Amelia, do you?" Widcombe responded with a grin.

"Quiet, they'll hear you. Please, Sophia's worried sick that no one will dance with her. Just once, won't you?"

"Alright, but don't get any ideas about becoming brothers-in-law." Widcombe walked across the room to where Sophia sat next to her mother.

"Dance with me?" he said to Sophia charmlessly.

Still, Jonathan was thankful to hear it at all.

Sophia began to open her mouth to speak, but it was Lady Clyde whose voice rose above the chatter of the crowd.

"Widcombe, really! You need to leave Miss Sophia available for other suitors to dance with. How will she enjoy herself if she dances all evening with her brother and his friends?"

Unperturbed, Widcombe shrugged and walked off to the punchbowl.

Sophia, however, turned a bright shade of pink and sank as deeply into her chair as she could.

*Well done, Lady,* thought Jonathan. *Not only have you completely mortified your daughter, but you've announced to the entire room that anyone wanting to dance with her will be regarded as a* suitor. *Now she's not likely to have a single dance for the rest of the night.*

Jonathan's prediction appeared to be proving true as three more dances went by and Sophia was not a part of any of them. As he was on the verge of asking Sophia to dance with him a second time, the musicians played the first few notes of the next song.

"Ah!" Heldmann said, his finger in the air as he rose from his seat. "This...*this*, I know!" He smiled broadly around the room though few people paid any attention to his declaration. Crossing the room in a few long strides, he stood before Sophia and asked her to dance.

Smiling shyly, she consented, rising from her seat. Heldmann led her by the hand to where the other dancers stood, tripping on a corner of the rug on the way.

*Off to an excellent start, I see,* thought Jonathan, stifling his laughter.

*Sophe looks quite pleased, though.*

The thought warmed him. However, the sentiment quickly transformed to one of embarrassed amusement for although Heldmann had declared he knew the dance, it became clear that he did not know it well. Twice when the couples changed partners, he reached for the hand of the *fellow* next to him, and once he started to move around the circle in a counter-clockwise direction colliding into several of the other dancers.

Jonathan was pleased to see that Sophia simply laughed and redirected Heldmann each time.

Just beyond her, though, Morton sat, snickering at the display, once even rolling his eyes. When the final notes of the song were played, he rose and stood, mock-applauding an unaware Heldmann who was bowing to Sophia as she curtsied.

Smiling, Heldmann still held on to her hand as they walked over to where Jonathan sat near the door.

"Danke schöen, Herr Heldmann," said Sophia.

"Ich mag Ihre Ärmel." The German continued to smile as he ducked his head. "Sie sind groß."

While the other couples were moving off the floor, Morton made his way past Lady Clyde, who was standing by the punch bowl. In what Jonathan knew as her 'teasing' voice, she said to him, "Mr. Morton. Don't you know that as a guest, it's only proper to dance with the daughter of your hostess?"

"Dear Lady," Morton responded in an equally ingratiating tone, lifting a glass of punch as if he were giving a toast. "Don't you know that as a hostess, it's only proper to offer your guests the very best?"

Someone from across the room gasped. Another snickered.

Jonathan felt his throat tighten with rage when he heard a little sound escape from Sophia who was standing beside him. Turning, he saw her face frozen in angst.

*Oh, no. Here it comes.*

Wrapping his arm around her, he motioned to the musicians to play another song and hurriedly propelled her out of the room. He got her out just before she burst into sobs.

"Why...must Mama...embarrass me...as she does?" She choked out the words between heaving breaths.

Jonathan dragged her up the stairs and down the hall to her door where he fumbled with the knob.

"Why can't she...just leave me...alone?" Sophia stumbled into the room and fell on her bed in a great, blue satin heap.

Jonathan shut the door and began to pace. *How can I punish that insufferable little swine? Think, think!*

*I ought to break his legs!*

Sophia continued to whimper on the bed. The music from downstairs filtered up through the floor and stairway.

*Think*!

Agitatedly, he strode to the window and leaned on the sill, looking out into the weakening light of evening. Below, by the stable block, a strange sight arrested his attention.

Near the carriages stood a group of people. In their midst was a handful of dancers. They were doing a poor job. One girl was obviously in charge, calling out orders and pushing the others this way and that. Everyone was laughing and jostling one another.

Suddenly, a taller girl looked up and saw Jonathan. Fearfully, she halted in her clumsy dance and gripped the shoulder of the girl in charge, leaning in to tell her something. Continuing, the other girl looked around, smiling until her eyes found Jonathan.

*Foote,* Jonathan realized.

With undeniable grace and dignity, she curtsied deeply and then stood, gazing at him for a moment.

The taller girl fled from his view. The men around Foote, at this point, had ceased in their rollicking, their questioning faces turned up to Jonathan.

Foote turned to them and curtsied just as deeply. Then she collected a bunch of cups on a tray and traipsed from the stable yard and out of sight.

*Ah, the delightfulness of a servant's impudence,* Jonathan mulled.

*But wait! What's this?*

A finely dressed man had stumbled into the group. Barking out orders, he was clutching his nose with one hand and gesturing furiously with the other.

Two of the servants flew into action as the rest stared disbelievingly.

"Stop gaping at me, you stupid fools," Jonathan heard through the window, "or I'll have you all dismissed!"

*Why, it's Morton!* marveled Jonathan, his mouth agape.

"Sophia! Sophia, you must come and see this!" Jonathan urged his sister who was still weeping on her bed. "Morton's staggering around in the yard, threatening the servants!"

Within seconds, Morton was clambering into an especially grand-looking carriage which took off down the drive.

"Sophia, come look!"

Without waiting for a response, Jonathan ran from the room and down the sweeping staircase two steps at a time.

The doors of the makeshift ballroom were wide open and though the music was still playing, no one was dancing. Instead, all of the guests were gathered in little groups, some exclaiming excitedly, others looking astonished.

Heldmann stood in the center of the room, cupping his right hand in his left, a look on his face which was something between shock and outrage.

"Ich bin," he began, then started again. "Please forgive...that man have no...mmm... mmm..."

He gave up on trying to convey his meaning and looked around the room. Lifting his hands conciliatorily, he repeated, "Please forgive."

"No need for that, lad. Well done!" Widcombe laughed, lifting a glass of punch high in the air. "Ah, Clyde! You missed it all! When you ran to hide, Heldmann here defended Sophia's honor."

"What?" Jonathan's face broke into a smile.

The German turned to him and said, "I not...know what he...mmm...say. I see Miss Sophia...make sad...mmm...face and I see man...smile...and I..."

Words failed him again as he mimed a swing of his fist.

"So you smashed his bloody face in, you did, Heldy! Well done!" Hodges said, slapping Heldmann's back.

Jonathan laughed loudly. "A true Germanic warrior cannot be tamed!"

"I go now...I go." Heldmann glanced around again at the party guests and started toward the door.

"No, Heldmann. Please don't leave."

"No...no." The German shook his head, his face a wrinkled testimony of remorse. "I go. Thank you for...mmm...dance and food." He walked from the room, cradling his hand again, his head low.

"Auf wiedersehn, Heldy!" called Widcombe, flopping down on the settee.

Throwing Widcombe a sour look, Jonathan followed the German out to the stable.

"Listen, Heldmann." Jonathan strode to keep up. "You only did what my friends and I have wanted to do since Morton first opened his mouth years ago. The fellow's a purebred cur."

Heldmann was staring at Jonathan's mouth. "I do not understands."

Jonathan sighed. "Look...don't go. Stay." He motioned back toward the house, smiling affirmatively.

By now, Hardy was there with Heldmann's gray horse.

"No...tell to Miss Sophia...please forgive. Good bye." Then he was settling into the saddle and trotting down the drive.

Jonathan sighed again, wishing he had made more effort to converse with Heldmann earlier in the evening.

*I suppose I didn't treat him much better than Morton did. Ugh...to be on that idiot's level.*

The thought turned his stomach. Slowly, he walked back to the house, glancing at the retreating figure of the man who was rounding the corner, slouched on his horse.

*The villain and the hero departed within ten minutes of each other. What does this blasted ball have to offer now?*

# Taking a Chance

~ LYDIA

Lydia was smiling happily on her way back to the kitchen. She hadn't danced in ages and although it had been a poor rendition, it had still been enjoyable.

The tray she carried was much lighter now that it held only an empty pitcher and cups.

*Ah!* She was struck by an idea as the path to the maze's entry appeared on her left. *But do I have enough time?*

Glancing toward the house, she saw that Wells had already disappeared into the kitchen. Placing the tray on top of the woodpile, she hurried off to the left.

*If anyone catches me...but who would do so? Everyone's distracted with the ball.*

*What if the book is ruined? Should I take it inside and hope no one notices? No one is likely to pull it off the shelf for the next fifty years. Or should I just shove it further under the hedge? Ugh...*why *did I throw it under there?*

Past the basket of leading ribbons she rushed.

*I haven't much time. Will the bulk of it show in my apron pocket? Well, I need to see the state of the book to decide what I'll do anyway...*

Further into the depth of the green corridors she ventured, quickly correcting the few wrong turns she took.

*It looks so different at this time of day.*

Then, she was thankful to see the fountain at the maze's center, looming before her.

*At last! Just over here...*

She rushed to the spot where she had been sitting when she threw the book. Getting down on her hands and knees, she began to feel under the hedge, the prickly leaves scratching her wrists and fingers.

Suddenly, she heard the clearing of a throat and realized she was not alone.

*Oh, no!* She stopped her searching and waited, wondering, *Young lovers who left the ball?*

A few seconds passed, before she saw, in the waning evening light, a man emerge from the maze. He was moving toward her.

She was on her feet in an instant.

"Hiding, are ya?" he said, drawing closer. "No use in that. We pro'ly ha'nt much time."

He was ten feet away before she realized it was the fellow who had been chewing on the hay, watching the servants dance.

"Pardon me?" she said, feeling very small.

His pace didn't lessen.

Lydia's heart leapt into her throat as she saw the look on his face and how thick his arms were. Though no one had ever before looked at her exactly like that, she knew she needed to flee, immediately.

Without another thought, she bolted, swinging wide around him.

"Bitch of a tease, ay?" he growled as she sped past.

Rounding the corner, Lydia nearly collided with Glaser and a pitchfork he was carrying.

She said nothing but continued on, dashing down the confusion of green alleyways. Turn after turn, she made, until she was out of the maze and back at the woodpile where she had left the serving tray. Breathing heavily, she grabbed onto the stable wall to steady herself.

The little red dog, Sassy, who often accompanied Glaser around the garden, came out of the stable and nudged Lydia's hand with its nose.

With her heart pounding furiously, Lydia eyed the animal and wondered, *Where were you a moment ago?*

Her legs were weak beneath her, but she was comforted by the sound of many young men joking with each other beyond the stable. It was as if nothing ugly and frightening had just occurred.

*Did anyone notice but Glaser? I did nothing to invite the man. What must they think of me?*

Then there was Glaser himself, whistling as he strode over to her.

"I didn't...that is, I wasn't..." she stuttered, so thankful for the presence of the wiry, aging man.

"You needn't explain, Foote," he replied. "I'm familiar with you, and I'm familiar with him. That's why I grabbed this and kept pace with him when I seen him following after you."

He leaned the pitchfork back up against the stable wall. "Best you get back inside now. Thanks again for the draught of beer."

Reassured by his casual response, Lydia lifted the tray and squared her shoulders, though she still felt shaky.

A warm glow of light spilled out of the kitchen door and Lydia headed toward it.

Ploughman looked up from the tub of dirty dishes with wide eyes. "Ah, here you are! The bell just rung! Wells went, but you'd better, too."

Placing the tray within Ploughman's reach, Lydia hurried off, her heart still racing.

When she arrived in the makeshift ballroom, she thought it seemed unsettled. Though the musicians were playing a song, no one was dancing. Instead, they stood about in cliques, discussing something in quietly excited tones.

Wells was kneeling near the punch table with a rag, wiping up a spill where shards of glass littered the floorboards nearby.

At Lydia's entrance, Lady Clyde hurried over to her and asked in an intensely displeased whisper, "*Where* is Smith?"

"I don't know, Ma'am. Would you like me to...?" Lydia motioned toward the mess on the floor.

"You'll do nothing but find Smith," the Lady hissed then turned her back.

Out of habit, Lydia curtsied and left.

*Find Smith?*

Unsure where to begin her search, Lydia went up the stairs toward the family's bedrooms. Striding down the hall, she rounded the corner and saw the housekeeper herself.

"Smith," Lydia began, "Lady Clyde insists you go to her immediately."

The housekeeper did not hide a look of exasperation on her face. She walked over to Lydia, pushed something into her hands and said, "Take this to Miss Sophia in her room at once."

To Lydia's surprise, she saw that she was holding the same tray with the mysterious glass bottle from that afternoon.

Smith rushed off as Lydia wondered again what the bottle held. Resisting the urge to uncap it and sniff its contents, she made her way to Miss Sophia's door and rapped lightly upon it.

"Yes, come in!" said a voice from within.

Lydia entered and stood before Sophia, who was lying on her bed, her face blotchy. At Lydia's approach, Sophia sat up and affixed her eyes to the bottle, her lips parted.

Never having delivered the elixir before, Lydia paused, unsure of what was expected of her.

Sophia ran a hand over her swollen eyes and directed, "Go on then."

Placing the tray on the bed, Lydia fumbled with the bottle's lid and lifted the little cup. When she only filled it half-way, Sophia insisted, "Fill it up. You've no idea what it's like."

*You've no idea what it's like.*

The words echoed in Lydia's mind as she poured a bit more liquid into the cup. Someone had said that to her before.

*You've no idea...*

As soon as the little cup was filled, Sophia took it from Lydia's hand. The swallowing of this dose was not the slow and savory instance that Lydia had witnessed earlier that day. This time Sophia gulped it down and immediately demanded more.

Though she doubted the wisdom in giving it to her, Lydia complied, feeling powerless.

"Ahh, there it is," said Sophia after swallowing the second little cupful. She sighed and a stupid smile spread across her face.

*My God!* Realization crashed into Lydia's mind. *It's Jack and his gin!*

Sophia reclined further on the bed and began to gaze at the wall, announcing dreamily, "You may go."

Lydia capped the bottle quickly and left the room, more than slightly shaken.

*What is this poison?* She no longer wanted to sniff the contents. Instead, she envisioned herself walking through the marble hall and out the entryway to pour the liquid onto the gravel drive as she had once poured out Jack's gin.

*Where should I put this?* she wondered, wanting nothing more than to be rid of the tray and what it held.

Lydia descended the stairs and encountered Smith exiting the ballroom with a dustpan full of glass and a broom.

"Foote, here, you tend to these," she said putting the things down on the floor, "and I'll go lock that up."

She lifted the tray and its contents out of Lydia's hands.

*Lock it up?* thought Lydia.

"Smith?" Lydia relinquished the tray, her eyes meeting Smith's over the top of it. She motioned with her head toward the mysterious bottle. "What *is* that?"

She may have imagined it, but Smith's eyes seemed to linger on her for a moment as she answered. "What, this? Laudanum. Miss Sophia is prone to headaches."

The two regarded each other for a second longer and then Smith was walking down the hall, the tray held out before her.

*Laudanum, is it? Though it's stored in elegant crystal I know* venom *when I see it. Dear God,* she lamented, *not Miss Sophia! It will ruin her.*

She bent to pick up the dustpan.

*But isn't she ruined already? With the Lady for a mother, can there be any hope for a person?*

*No, that's not right. I can't assume she's lost forever just because of her dame. She's generally kind and seems intelligent...except for this.*

*But what's to be done?*

*Sir Jonathan seems fond of her. And he's no fool...even though he does regard me as a "dancing bear" to entertain his vainglorious friends. Such conceit!*

*Still, he could and would likely do something to help her if he knew. But how to tell him?*

She thought for a moment longer, then headed toward the kitchen.

*And what am I to do with this?* She regarded the many sharp shards in the dust pan she held.

*Perhaps Glaser can bury it in the garden. I'll put it in the stable and speak with him about it tomorrow.*

But when she got to the stables, the man himself was there, sweeping a bit of hay off the floor.

"Glaser?" Lydia said, side-stepping a pile of manure on the ground.

"Yes, Foote," he responded, looking up from his work.

She showed him the glass pieces and made her request.

"Ah, yes. I heard there was a bit of a to-do while we were in the maze. Certainly, I'll tend to that for you."

Biting her lip, Lydia paused.

"And, Glaser..." she began, glancing around to see if any of the grooms or stable hands was near.

*How should I say this?* Lydia wondered, the evening air chilling her.

The old man waited expectantly, his eyes resting on her face.

"Um..." she began quietly. "I need to get a message to someone and...I was wondering if you could help me with that as well. You've worked here a long time, so perhaps if you delivered it, it would be...better received."

The usually easy groom bit the inside of his cheek and shifted on his feet. "Who're you sending it to?"

Lydia lowered her voice further. "Sir Jonathan."

A look of confusion registered on the kindly face. "The young sir hasn't done something...*unseemly* toward you, has he? He's always been impish, but I never woulda expected..."

"Pardon?" Lydia's voice rose to its usual level.

"If he's...messing with you, you'd better leave it alone. I know it's hard when he's part of the family and you're supposed to do their bidding, but..." His voice broke off and he looked embarrassed, "...that wouldn't end well for you, Foote."

Lydia smiled in spite of the crassness of the implication. "No, Glaser. It's nothing like that. It has nothing to do with me or him. It's..." she grew serious again. "It's something he would want to know. It's..."

Glaser waited patiently.

"I fear," Lydia began, her voice dropping down to a whisper again, "that Miss Sophia is growing too attached to laudanum."

"Whad'ya mean?"

"I...I see the same look on her face when she is waiting for it that I saw on my brother's when he was yearning for gin. And the effect is the same...a stupification. And that's not all. There's a barely contained...ferociousness before she has it...a desperation."

Glaser's face took on a stern look and said in his lowered voice, "That all very well may be so, Foote, but neither of us can walk up to Sir Jonathan and say, 'We servants think your sister's become a lush', now can we?"

"No, I...I see what you mean."

*Oh, why does this fall to me to tell? How can it be said?*

"Foote," the old man gazed at her steadily, his voice softening. "It's good of you, but..." he shook his head slowly and motioned toward the grandiose presence of Whitehall, "there's *them...*"

Next he pointed to himself and Lydia, "...and there's *us.*"

"And we *all* can be destroyed by drink!" Lydia's frustration sharpened her hushed words. "*I've seen* what it can do to a person. If only we had stopped Jack early on..."

"No, no," the man put his hand up and shook his head. "Now that's something you mustn't do. When you think it's *only money* that makes them different than us, people like the Lady can sense it...*and they don't like it.*"

*He's not going to help me,* Lydia realized, hearing the note of finality in his voice. *But I have to do something!*

She pressed her lips together and dropped her eyes to the ground, thinking.

As Glaser's calloused hand was lightly patting her shoulder, an idea struck her.

*Did Sir Jonathan ever find that poem I hid in his drawing book? I could hide another. But if I did, and he found it whilst Miss Sophia was nearby...what then?*

She fretted as she barely heard the old man say, "You're a good young woman, Foote, but you gotta think of yourself."

"Thank you, Glaser," she murmured, turning and heading back to the kitchen.

*And what if his mother got ahold of it? I'd be dismissed and shamed, for certain.*

*Still, I can't stand by and do nothing.*

*But I must be extremely careful...*

# Finding Another Mysterious Message

~ Jonathan

Jonathan reached for his sketch book on the cherry wood table. Flipping it open as he headed to leave the parlor, a piece of paper fell out and fluttered to the floor.

*Am I losing pages?* He stooped to retrieve the unfamiliar leaf. It was folded in half and its paper was thinner than that of the book's leaves. *Hello, where did you come from?*

He felt his heart flip over.

*Another of Foote's offerings? What have you for me this time, clever girl?*

He smiled and shook his head. Unfolding the paper, he saw written in a clear, neat hand:

I fear the message that is mine
May wrath in you incite
And yet the dangers I foresee
Compel me now to write

The girl you love has grown too fond
Of poisoned cups to drink ~
The grip of this reliance has
Forced me my pen to ink

Regard her closely now yourself ~
Confirm my words or don't ~
The observation of your eyes
Will prove them or it won't

Jonathan stood, bewildered, and read the first stanza again.

*She fears angering me, but decided to write this anyway...*

Though he read the second stanza twice, he couldn't decipher it.

*The girl I love? I love no girl.*

*I am to watch this unknown girl to see if she is reliant on poison?*

Suddenly, he grimaced incredulously, his face warming.

*Could she mean herself? Oh, dear...does she presume that paper apple was a token of adoration?*

*Hmm... such unchecked romanticism...*

*It's like the plot to one of those ridiculous novels that Amelia reads.*

*'A servant girl is convinced of her employer's ardent love for her, but is later tragically made aware of her misunderstanding and opts for a chalice of poison'.*

*Or could she...?*

His mind began to dwell on the notion from a different angle and he shifted uneasily on his feet.

*No. She's never seemed flirtatious in the least...*

His mental image of Foote as a discerning parlour maid transfigured. Suddenly, he envisioned the young woman gazing intently at him from under heavy eyelids, her hair falling down around her face, a little smile playing on her lips.

The confused slurry of excitement and fear evoked by this image sloshed about in the pit of his stomach.

*Well, that won't do,* he thought, his face growing even warmer as the vision lingered.

*Oh, don't be stupid!*

He strode over to the fireplace, crumpling the paper as he went. Just as he was to toss it on the few flames licking up from the logs, he thought better of it. After smoothing the paper, he folded it and pushed it into the pocket of his vest.

*Like a cherished article, tucked away, someone watching me might suppose,* he thought, wanting to assure the imagined observer otherwise.

*Still, this requires more thought.*

*Ah, Foote! What are you aiming at?*

There was a rap on the door, startling Jonathan from his thoughts.

Smith entered, looking around the room.

"Sir Jonathan," she said when her cold eyes found him by the fireplace. Her perfunctory curtsy was slight. "Your mother says dinner is served and that guests will be present this evening."

"Thank you, Smith," Jonathan responded with a nod, hoping his face was not as pink as it felt. Flashing the woman a winning smile, he wondered if she thought her palpable disdain for him went unrecognized.

She barely curtsied again and left.

*Unexpected guests? That means Foote will likely be in and out several times while serving.*

The possible awkwardness resulting from this did not escape him as he felt the crinkle of the poem's paper in his vest pocket.

*Very well, in all my interactions with her, I must resolve to be polite yet disinterested.*

***

Moments later, Jonathan was seated at the dinner table, thankful that his attention might now be effectively diverted. Once the introductions were made, he gladly examined the two strangers who sat at the table with him and his family.

Sir Buffant was short, round and wore the finest of clothes. In his clear, almost feminine voice, he immediately began to praise the situation of Whitehall within its grounds, the density of its surrounding woods, even the stones of the staircase he had ascended to the front door.

Lady Clyde beamed and motioned toward Jonathan.

"Perhaps after we dine, my son will give you a guided tour of the house and grounds, daylight permitting."

*When did I inherit that duty?* Jonathan smiled affably at the man, hoping the sun would drop like a stone.

Sir Buffant's mother, seated next to him, was a quiet wisp of a woman, also finely dressed. With a hint of a smile on her face, she watched her son's every movement, obviously smitten with the fruit of her womb.

Sophia sat, resting her eyes on the table, silently emptying the bowl of soup before her, one scant spoonful at a time.

Elliott was notably absent.

*Gobbling up fried eggs and toast under the disdainful eye of Cook, no doubt,* thought Jonathan, recalling his own childhood meals when his presence in the dining room had not been wanted.

Buffant led the conversation, pausing regularly to admit forkfuls of roast chicken and cream-dripping cauliflower into his mouth.

Many times, Foote came and went, placing dishes on the table and filling glasses. Regretfully, Jonathan recalled how impossible it was to not look at someone when one was determined not to do so. Twice he felt his eyes flit to her face. Both times she was inscrutable, her face stony.

*Perhaps she regrets slipping me that note, already realizing its pointlessness.*

Toward the end of the meal, Foote leaned past him to clear his plate. Jonathan heard a little exhalation of her breath, feeling the warmth of it on his cheek. Then she was on the other side of him, retrieving another plate, her back to him. He noted how slender and pale her neck looked as it disappeared into the dark collar of her serving uniform. Jonathan cleared his throat and tried again to focus on what Buffant was saying about the prior week's weather in Yarmouth.

It was a relief to Jonathan when the meal ended and his mother suggested they move to the parlour to continue conversing. Foote's service was not likely to be needed much for that.

Walking down the hall, Jonathan found himself behind Buffant.

*What does this fellow's tailor think when he has to stretch his measuring tape around that vast midsection? He must hold one end, ball up the rest and toss it across to his assistant on the other side of the room.*

Jonathan tried to catch Sophia's eye, wanting to share his amusement with the simple lift of his eyebrow. His attempt went unnoticed.

Looking uneasy, Sophia clasped her hands before her as she walked, gazing decidedly at the carpet until, and after, the entire party was seated in the parlor.

Buffant's mother perched on the edge of her chair, attentive to each of her son's lively words, smiling appreciatively.

Without Foote hovering nearby, Jonathan was able to realize that just as Buffant's appearance was remarkable, his mannerisms were equally intriguing. His bushy eyebrows seemed to bounce on his forehead as he energetically retold the story of his most recent fox hunt.

*He rides a horse?* marveled Jonathan. *How could he possibly perch on something so narrow?*

Sir Buffant sat very uprightly on the silk brocaded chair across from Lady Clyde, his hands resting on his knees which were pressed tightly together. His poise reminded Jonathan of lessons he had heard Sophia's governess delivering on the importance of sitting tall.

*Perhaps he knew Miss Gloriana as well.*

*And what brings him here this evening?* Jonathan sat wondering when the ginger-haired servant came in carrying a bowl of peaches. She set it on a table near Buffant, curtsied and quietly departed.

Sir Buffant rummaged through the offerings and settled on a particularly rosy one. Lifting it, he suddenly stopped and stared at the fruit in his hand. He smiled and said, "Hmm...it seems Whitehall's birds don't care much for peaches."

With that, he put the peach down on the table and selected another from the bowl. The rejected fruit rolled over, revealing a crusty blob of bird excrement stuck onto the fuzzy peel.

Jonathan watched as his mother's forced smile disappeared and the colour drained from her face. Slowly, her hand reached out to grab the offending fruit. Wrapping it in a serving cloth, she set it aside as her eyes flitted between her guests and the door.

Meanwhile, Sir Buffant sank his teeth into the juicy flesh of his second choice, holding a napkin under his chin to catch the drippings.

"My best dog, Teaser, was injured in the last hunt, bitten by another dog when they were after the fox. It took a few months, but she's healed and spry as ever now!" Sir Buffant, paused here to take the last few bites of his fruit, then dropped the pit into the appropriate bowl. He chose another. "Mmm...it is a good year for peaches."

Dabbing his chin in an almost ladylike fashion, he looked in Sophia's direction and smiled, his eyebrows bobbing about. Sophia squirmed in her seat, looking unequivocally miserable.

*Good lord, what is that about?* wondered Jonathan. The smile had not been leering, but it was too direct to be regarded as mere friendliness.

Suddenly, looking between his mother and Sir Buffant, Jonathan knew.

*He's here to see Sophia...and Sophia knows it!*

He assessed the fellow again, trying to keep his lip from curling in distaste.

*The Lady* can't *be serious! Wed Sophia to this planetary being? He's not as old as Spalding, but he still must be twice her age!*

*Perhaps Sophia has been right all this time about the Lady's marital scheming. No wonder she looks as if she'd like to sink into the ground.*

A silence descended upon the group, broken only by Buffant's occasional slurping of peach juice.

"Whist, anyone?" Lady Clyde asked as the second denuded pit was dropped into the bowl, her mouth turning up at the corners and her eyebrows raised.

*Oh so cheerfully*, thought Jonathan.

Buffant's mother came alive at the suggestion.

"My father always said I enjoyed card games much more than any woman ought!" she said, speaking a full sentence for possibly the first time that evening.

Certain that Sophia, who had remained unmoved at the suggestion of cards, wanted nothing to do with the game, Jonathan went with the three others to the card table.

*Perhaps this will distract the man from paying any attention at all to poor Sophe.*

After the first round, Lady Clyde said in her friendliest voice, "A touch of music would improve this party. Sophia, dear, would you please delight us all at the piano forte?"

*Ah, so that was her plan. Thus now begins the exhibiting of Sophia,* thought Jonathan ruefully.

"Oh, Mama, I...I really don't think..." began Sophia tremulously.

"Not at all, darling. Don't be shy about your talents," Lady Clyde insisted. Her mouth was a hard line as she stared at her daughter over the fan of her cards.

Silently, yet slowly, Sophia rose from her chair and made her way to the awaiting piano bench.

There was a rustling of sheet music and the first few notes were struck. The quiet of the room amplified the timidity of Sophia's playing. Then she hit a sour note.

"Let's carry on then, shall we? Whose turn is it to deal?" asked Jonathan, wanting to fill the room with any noise possible. He cleared his throat and pulled his chair forward, loudly scraping it across the floor. "Who, I wonder, will win the first trick this time!"

His mother smiled at him girlishly and tapped her finger to her closed lips.

*Yes, I know* you *want it quiet,* he thought. *But that is not what Sophia wants.*

Jonathan continued to chatter cheerfully to the card players until the song was over. He then saw her rise from the instrument and reach for the bell-pull.

"Another, dear." Lady Clyde called. "The sonata by Schubert will do nicely."

"Or would you prefer to take my place at cards, Sophia?" Jonathan offered, unsure if she would consider that a preferred occupation over stumbling through a bit of sheet music.

"Sophia is playing the piano forte for us. Of course, she doesn't want to play cards," said Lady Clyde, her thin veneer of pleasantry slipping.

Sophia said nothing in response to either of them and continued to stand next to the bell-pull.

"Ah ha! Mama, you've done it again!" Sir Buffant exclaimed as his mother giggled and picked up the final trick of the round.

At that moment, Foote entered the room and was met at the door by Sophia. Curious, Jonathan watched the two young women speak quietly to one another.

Buffant shuffled the cards and began to deal them around the table.

"Smith has the key. Hurry, Foote," Sophia said as the maid departed.

*Smith has the key? For what?*

"The sonata, dearest!" Lady Clyde called to her daughter as she laid the queen of hearts on top of Buffant's king of diamonds.

Sophia returned to the piano forte and played a few timorous notes. She floundered through the first and second pages as the card game progressed. Reaching to turn the page, her sleeve bumped some of them and several loose leaves drifted to the floor in all directions.

"And now it is my turn to deal," declared the pleased Mama Buffant. Pulling all the cards on the table toward her, she stacked them and began to shuffle them expertly as Jonathan rose and went to his sister's aid. At his approach, he could see that her hands were quivering as she collected the pages from the floor.

It was then that Foote returned, carrying a small tray upon which were a decorative bottle and a little cup. Putting the tray down on a nearby table, she filled the cup and handed it to Sophia who dropped the carefully collected sheet music to receive it.

Foote was a mere two feet from him and Jonathan could feel her eyes on him. He wondered what he would see in them if he turned to her—a look of shy apology or a hint of alluring invitation. What he actually saw when he glanced at her made him flinch.

She was glaring at him furiously. Her eyes bore into him unreservedly and below her flaring nostrils, her mouth was a hard, thin line. She looked as if she might reach out and slap him across the face.

Oblivious to Jonathan's present shock, Sophia handed the now empty cup back to Foote demanding, "More."

Foote whose back was to everyone in the room but the two siblings, took the cup but did not move to fill it.

"Well?" said Sophia, impatiently.

*What is going on?* Jonathan glanced from his sister to the maid and back again.

The pause proved unacceptable for Sophia, who seized the bottle and cup from Foote's hands and poured herself a second dose. Foote continued to glower at Jonathan as Sophia returned the items to her.

Visibly calmed, Sophia lazily pushed Jonathan's hands out of the way, and began to play the song again.

Once Foote had returned everything to the tray, she looked again at him, tilted her head toward the glass bottle and exaggeratedly mouthed the word, "Poison."

She swept out of the room as Sophia played on. This time the song was played no better than it had been previously, but she smiled slightly throughout, as if she knew a secret.

It was with a wrench of his stomach that Jonathan realized he had just been let in on one.

A horrible one.

*The girl I love has grown too fond of poisoned cups to drink.*

*And it was the maid who perceived it all.*

# Dismissing Wells

~ Smith

*Another guest visit evaluation,* thought Smith, making the familiar trek toward the Lady's parlor. *Why she wanted to impress that ridiculous fellow, I'll never know.*

She rapped sharply on the door.

"You may enter," came the barely audible response.

Once she was in the room, Smith could see at once that all was not well.

*Ugh...what went wrong* this *time?*

The Lady's mouth was pulled together more sourly than usual and her eyes danced around as if she wasn't sure where to look. Instead of reclining on her favorite settee, she was seated behind the writing desk.

*She's feeling pious, which means I ought to appear repentant though I have no idea what for.*

Smith stood before her, head slightly bowed, hands folded together. "Lady Clyde?"

*What ax is about to fall and how close to me will it land?*

"Sit," the Lady commanded.

*Ugh, it's that bad, is it?* Smith wondered, lowering herself into the especially short chair placed before the desk.

"Sir Buffant nearly sank his teeth into a mess of bird droppings." Lady Clyde announced, her steely eyes finally settling on Smith.

"Lady?"

Lady Clyde's voice took on the tone that irritated Smith the most, one of forced patience with a sharp undertone. "The *peaches,* Smith. The peaches offered to our guest in a fine silver bowl as he sat upon one of our silk brocade chairs. They were *covered in bird droppings.*"

Her eyes bore into Smith's, and she began to nod her head. "It was the ginger-haired girl, Wells, who brought them in. *This cannot be.*"

"Yes, Lady Clyde," Smith murmured.

"This cannot be," Lady Clyde repeated, turning to the window.

Smith waited, familiar with her mistress' tendency to pause for effect though her insistent declarations sometimes hung in the air to be followed by nothing.

*Oh, good God,* thought Smith when silence had continued for about five seconds. *And how do you expect me to keep the birds from shitting?*

"What would you have me do, Lady?"

"Only what *must* be done, Smith!" Lady Clyde was now well into her wide-eyed indignant stage.

*A loud sigh accompanied by a wave of the hand is surely next,* thought Smith as she waited to hear what it was that 'must be done'.

"Dismiss her; she is not fit to serve in this household," the Lady announced and then sighed loudly and fluttered her hand. "Offering filth to our guests..."

*Dismiss her? But who would replace her?* wondered Smith, incredulously. *And be replaced, she* must *be! There is far too much work in a house this size for our staff to be reduced even by one!*

Smith nearly voiced these thoughts, though of course in a modified manner, but one look at the Lady's face told her that her input was not wanted. Smith sighed internally and said, "Of course. When shall I speak with her?"

"Immediately." Lady Clyde opened a drawer in her desk and pulled out a little velvet bag.

*So it* does *still exist,* thought Smith, eyeing the bag.

Loosening the drawstrings, Lady Clyde dug into it, pulling out a collection of coins which she held out to Smith.

"This, of course, is not her full-year's wage, but she is *not* to expect more."

Smith watched as each coin fell heavily into her palm. "She will be gone in the morning. Is that all, Lady Clyde?"

"Isn't that enough?" the Lady asked before her mouth snapped back into a thin, tight line.

Smith cleared her throat. "Yes, of course."

Turning to go, she wrapped her fingers around the weight of the coins, resisting the urge to shake the handful, and headed for the door.

*This feels about as heavy as what was owed to me on St. John's Day.*

In the hall, with the door shut behind her, Smith peered into her hand, thinking.

*She didn't count it out...I've never seen her keep record...but what if Wells were to complain? Surely even the Lady would know that what she gave me was more than a few crowns.*

Smith envisioned the young girl's freckled face crumpling into despair at the realization of her own dismissal.

*No, Wells wouldn't say a word. That mouse of a girl wouldn't raise a fuss over anything, not even curtailed wages.*

The housekeeper began to walk down the hall.

*In fact, she mightn't expect to be paid* at all *if I stressed to her how damaging the presentation of the peaches was to the family...but no. I ought to give her at least* some *of this.*

Separating a few coins from the rest, Smith dropped them into the front pocket of her apron. The larger portion, she deposited into a snug pocket on the bodice of her dress under her apron. Smoothing the front down, she walked briskly to make certain the coins wouldn't jingle as she headed toward the kitchen where she expected to find Wells.

*Oh, what am I feeling bad about? With all I endure, I deserve far more than a portion of Wells' pittance.*

*Let's get this over with.*

"Smith."

Sir Jonathan's voice startled the housekeeper from her thoughts. Turning, she saw him emerging from the library.

"Sir?" she replied, bobbing a curtsey.

*What now?*

"I would like to speak with you." He motioned toward the library, looking up and down the hallway.

In spite of her definite distaste for the man, she was curious as she stepped into the room. He'd never asked to speak with her like this before.

He swung the door shut and faced her. Three feet away, he peered down at her intently, his eyes riveted steadily on her own.

"Sir?" she asked, looking away from his steadfast gaze.

*Trying to intimidate me now, are you?*

"Where is the laudanum?" he asked, his voice steely.

"Wha...pardon me?" Smith's eyes snapped back to his.

*Laudanum! So that's what this is about?*

"Where is it?"

Through the years, when Smith's gaze had ventured near his face she had beheld amusement, or occasionally disgust, animating his features. Now there was only humorless determination coloring them.

*You want to get sloshed, do you? First the daughter, and now the son!*

Smith dropped her gaze again, suppressing the smile that threatened to reveal her true feelings. Solemnly, she replied, "It is on the top shelf of the tall case in your father's study, on the right...next to the bottle of brandy."

"I'll have the key for the case," he said, extending his large hand toward her.

*What if the Lady...?*

Smith's hesitation was barely perceptible.

*Never mind the Lady! The boy is nearly full grown, and the rightful heir. The Lady can't argue with that.*

"Of course, sir." She nodded, reaching into the pocket which held the money she intended to give to Wells.

*I wondered when he would start laying claim to his place in this household. It's telling that it starts here with a lust for laudanum.*

After a quick search, she identified the requested key and removed it from the key ring. She dropped it onto his palm, watching as the long fingers closed around it.

"Is there anything else, sir?"

"No, thank you. You may go." There was something that sounded like relief in his voice.

*You didn't think that would be so easy, did you, sir? But no, I won't stand between you and drunkenness.*

Curtseying again, Smith swept out of the room in search of Wells, the corners of her mouth twitching.

*Enjoy your new adventure, sir.*

# Nixing Laudanum

~ JONATHAN

As soon as the small silver key was dropped into his hand, Jonathan knew he had been victorious, at least in the first battle.

*Now for the second,* he thought as he approached the parlour door.

His definitive rap upon it echoed loudly down the quiet hallway.

Through the door came a muffled, "Yes?"

Jonathan entered to see the Lady sitting at her desk.

She looked surprised to see him and her hands stretched out over the many papers in front of her. "I thought you were Smith, returned again."

*What are you hiding, Lady?* He wondered as she shuffled the sheets into a tidy stack.

"What is it?" she asked, resting her folded hands on the top page, which bore the large letterhead of Heath School.

Pausing just a moment, Jonathan announced, "Sophia is to have no more laudanum."

"I beg your pardon?"

Just as firmly, Jonathan repeated, "She is to have no more laudanum."

The confusion the Lady must have felt registered clearly on her face. "I was not aware of her having had any, though Smith did say something about headaches."

*She didn't even know?*

Her response jarred him. He assumed she had encouraged Smith to dose Sophia to ensure her compliance.

The Lady tilted her head slightly. "Why would you deny her relief?"

Jonathan forged forward into the crux of his message. "The only true relief she'll get is when you stop hounding her into a wedding chapel."

The Lady inhaled and squared her shoulders, an indignant look on her face. "I am only concerned about my daughter's future."

"Your *concern* is pushing her out of the bounds of propriety."

The cold stare Jonathan expected to see did not manifest itself. Instead, his mother looked at him thoughtfully, worriedly even, and asked, "What can you mean?"

Because the resentment that he had expected did not materialize, the next portion of his prepared speech spilled out somewhat lamely.

"She drugs herself. Others are beginning to notice, which will doubtlessly bring dishonor to the name of 'Clyde' that you cherish so highly."

Jonathan would have relished announcing to her that it was a mere servant girl who had seen what even he had missed in his own sister, but prudence kept him quiet.

Lady Clyde gazed at him a moment longer, then turned to stare out the window, silently.

Seeing that his message had hit a mark, though which one he wasn't sure, Jonathan turned to go. As his hand laid hold of the doorknob, his mother spoke.

"Thank you for telling me."

The words were soft, but clear.

Jonathan paused, aware that something significant had just occurred. Unsure what it was or how to respond, he continued out the door.

# Siding Against London

~ JONATHAN

Once again, a solitary Jonathan was holding a slip of paper, reading over every word. Sometimes it was Foote's first poem, but now it was the more recent one.

*"I fear the message that is mine may wrath in you incite, and yet the dangers I foresee compel me now to write..."*

*Hmm...not only perceptive, but courageous.*

Suddenly, the door opened and Sophia entered, followed by Elliott.

Hurriedly, Jonathan tucked the paper into the fold of his sketchbook and shut it. Simultaneously, he determined to wipe what he was certain was a look of weighty mulling off of his face.

Fortunately, his siblings were arguing as they entered.

"No!" Elliott hollered. "I don't want to go! I won't go!"

"Elly, really..." began Sophia, going to her place at the table.

"Don't call me that! And I won't go to London!"

"But we'll go to the Zoological Society and..."

"I've seen all those stupid animals already. I won't go." At this, he folded his arms and assumed as stolid an appearance as a young boy could.

Sophia looked to Jonathan who simply shrugged and cut himself a bite of ham, the knife squeaking horribly on the porcelain plate.

*What was it? 'The grip of this reliance has'...?*

"Jonathan, please..." Sophia implored. "Elliott, do sit down and eat."

"Please what?" Jonathan asked, chewing vigorously. "I don't blame him."

"Jonathan!" gasped Sophia.

Elliott, whose arms were still folded across his chest, shifted his eyes from one elder sibling to the other.

*It's not often we disagree, is it, Elly*? thought Jonathan.

"Jonathan, please!" Sophia said again.

"What? He'll be stuck inside when the weather's bad which is likely to be *always* at this time of year. I don't understand the Lady's determination to go now anyway. She never wants to go until spring. It all strikes me as rather odd."

"Never mind!" Sophia threw her arms up. "Elliott, if you're not going to sit and eat, I'd like to speak with Jonathan alone."

*Ah, here we go...*

Jonathan belched into his napkin.

Elliott grabbed a raisin bun from the platter on the table and marched out of the room, his face never losing its dour appearance.

Once the door had shut, Sophia whispered, "Jonathan, I agree with you, but there's no use in saying those things. *He has to go.*"

"Why does he *have* to?" Jonathan challenged, forking another bite into his mouth.

"How can you ask such a stupid question? What else is to be done with him?"

"He could stay here."

"Who would take care of him? You'll be at Heath. Even Cook and Smith will be in London."

"That leaves Ploughman and Foote."

"Yes, and Ploughman's hardly of any use at all anymore. We can't entrust a lively young boy to her! And Foote..."

Sophia paused, her plain face dubious.

"Yes?" Jonathan raised his eyebrows. *You have no idea what marvels Foote is capable of.*

"I just doubt Mama would want to leave him in her care, that's all." Sophia shrugged.

Jonathan laughed. "She entrusted you to *Miss Gloriana* all those years, and certainly Foote is better suited for childcare than that fraudulent bit of fluff. Besides, he has refused to go. It's not as if you can tie him to the carriage seat. Remember that time he refused to take a bath?"

Jonathan chuckled, thinking of how he'd found Elliott hiding in a fireplace. The little boy had emerged covered in soot and coughing violently, his clothes ruined.

"You're no help at all," Sophia said, though she giggled.

"That's not what Elliott is thinking." Jonathan smiled and pushed his plate away.

"Yes, very good, side with the sibling who still sucks his thumb at night. Thank you so much."

"Cheer up, dear Sister. You've got an entire season in London *with the Lady* to look forward to."

Sophia threw him a sour look. "Ever the encourager, Jonathan."

"Come to think of it, *you* ought to refuse to go, too."

"But I *want* to go. You'll be off at school and I'm always so bored here when you're gone."

"Please yourself, lunatic." Jonathan stood to go, lifting his book from the table.

"Oh," Sophia said, motioning to it. "Didn't you want to show me your latest drawing?"

Jonathan started and clutched the book to his chest, thinking of the poem regarding Sophia's inebriation tucked inside.

*It may have been her salvation, but the knowledge of it might utterly shame her.*

"Uh...no, not yet. I...I want to finish it completely first."

He winked at 'the girl he loved', and left the room.

# Nearly Breaking a Window

~ Lydia

"Is that *entire* list for me?" Lydia asked Smith who was furiously scribbling on a piece of paper during breakfast.

"Yes, Foote, it is. You're not the only one who will be very busy today."

"Why so much?" Lydia asked, ignoring the jab.

"We always clean the house from top to bottom before the family leaves for an extended period." Smith bit on her pen, thinking.

*Before they* leave*? Shouldn't we clean the house thoroughly just before they* return*?* Lydia wondered. "When do they leave?"

"Thursday," Smith murmured, her hand on her forehead.

*Thursday? That's only three days away!* Lydia despaired. *How can I clean this entire house that quickly?*

"Oh, and Cook," Smith continued, "the Lady wants game hens and new peas for supper tomorrow evening. Sir Jonathan will be leaving for school the next morning."

"How'm I supposed to carry on here with fancy suppers with Wells gone and only Ploughman to help me?" snarled Cook. "Have you spoken to the Lady about hiring on more help?"

"I said something to her. She is considering it."

*Considering it?* thought Lydia. *Maybe when she sees what a horrible job we do, she'll realize it's a necessity.*

"A bit of hard work never killed anyone," said Smith brightly as she wrote two more tasks on Lydia's list.

Cook looked at Lydia over the top of Smith's head and rolled her eyes. Lydia smiled sardonically in response.

"Yes..." Smith said, lifting the list from the table and looking it over for another moment. "That should do...for now."

She extended the paper to Lydia.

Snatching it from her, Lydia walked off to retrieve her cleaning caddy, silently grumbling.

*Wells is gone and Cook and I are becoming friendly! What's next? Will Hardy fall in love with me?*

A heaviness settled over her as she thought again, *Wells is gone.*

Forever she would regret that she hadn't been able to say goodbye. A week earlier she had come to the servants' dinner table to see an empty spot on the bench and one less bowl on the table.

"Wells wishes you all well," Smith had said, looking around at all of them. "She was summoned home this morning by her mother."

"When will she be back?" Cook had asked, gruffly.

"I don't believe she will be back," Smith had replied, sitting down at her spot.

Lydia had felt her heart sink and asked, "What was the matter at home?"

"Perhaps it's best not to discuss the business of others," Smith had responded stiffly as she lifted her spoon.

Lydia continued to wonder about her friend for days.

*Hmmm...where did Wells say she was from?* Lydia pondered, rounding the corner. *Bigley, was it? Oh, why didn't I listen more closely when I had the chance?*

*If I sent a letter to the Wellingtons of Bigley in Bevelshire would it get there? If I wrote in simple words Wells would likely be able to read it.*

*I hope her family is alright.*

*Poor, dear, silly Wells. Always worrying about being dismissed, but she ends up being called home by her mother!*

***

Lydia stood up from crouching under a little table, an oily rag hanging limply in her hand.

*Never before have I had to polish the wood, every unseen inch of it!*

She was in one of the rarely used bedrooms. Her back ached from maintaining prolonged and awkward positions above and under the furniture.

*And I haven't read in days...*

Normally, Lydia would spend some time each evening reading at least a few pages of something before snuffing out the rush dip. However, with the present uproar the house was in, she had no energy to do anything but sleep once released from her increased duties.

*I ought to just go home.*

It wasn't the first time she had thought this since arriving at Whitehall, nor since Wells had departed.

*I work hard there as well, but I'd be with Mama...*She *knows who I am, understands the things I say.*

The image of her mother's face filled Lydia's mind, a lock of brown hair hanging in her eyes, having escaped the linen cap atop her head. Fine lines etched the corners of her eyes and around her mouth.

*She's aged so much since Father died, and grown so thin...*

*Food.*

*There's so little of it at home. I haven't felt hungry once since I got here. Yes, there is sometimes a lack of butter or tea, but bread, potatoes, vegetables...even beef consistently, though the cuts are poor for the servants. Yes, it would be difficult to say goodbye to that.*

*And Jack is there...*

Usually she pushed him from her mind, but in this moment she didn't. She remembered how especially clever she felt when his shoulders would shake with laughter at something she'd said, remembered the sight of little gray pebbles perched on the tip of his tongue as his eyes gleamed with pride. Then she remembered the reek of his gin-thick breath as his rigid fingers dug into the soft flesh of her throat.

*Brothers are supposed to protect their sisters.*

She envisioned Sober Jack rushing in to tackle Drunken Jack, releasing her from strangulation.

*Oh, Jack, why did you give yourself over to that bottle? First we lost Father and then you left us...*

Tears formed in her eyes and she nearly wiped them away with the rag.

*Don't.*

*Stop crying.*

Turning to a window, she began to vigorously polish the wooden sill.

Outside in the drive, the figures of a man and a horse caught her eye. The man's back was to her as he put on a hat and then mounted the animal.

*Is that...?*

She sucked in her breath, incapable of feeling more surprised.

*Paul? Paul Midwinter! But he's...he's* leaving*!*

Though he was only twenty feet away, there was a stone and glass wall between them. Lydia reached to lift the sash, ready to heave, then realized it was a leaded window and couldn't be opened.

"Paul!" she called, pounding on the glass. "No, don't...!"

He was in the saddle now, wheeling around to trot down the drive, his face fully in view.

*It* is *him!*

Lydia pounded harder, calling out more loudly, "No! Wait!"

To Lydia's horror, one of the diamond-shaped panes shifted, loosened from its thick leaden veins. She looked back out of the window as the young farmer cantered away.

"What...?" called a voice as someone burst in through the bedroom door. "Are you...?"

Whirling around, Lydia saw Miss Sophia in the doorway. She was frantically looking around the room until her eyes, large with wonder, found Lydia.

"Foote! Are you alright?" she asked, peering around the room again before advancing on Lydia.

"Oh!" Lydia moved in front of the loosened pane and simultaneously glanced out of the window.

Paul was gone.

"I...I..."

"What's happened? Are you hurt?" The baronet's sister looked Lydia up and down.

"I am so sorry, Miss Sophia. I was startled, I..." Lydia felt her mouth continue to move though nothing came out of it.

"You're as pale as the moon! What's happened?"

*Stupid!*

"Truly, Miss Sophia, I am fine. I saw something...I...I feel quite foolish. Please forgive me."

The features of the young woman before her settled slightly, though her eyes continued to intently delve into Lydia's.

"Foote," she began slowly. "You've been crying. No, no, there's no shame in that...and I won't press you for answers, but we want you to feel safe here."

The well-intended words, though based on ignorant assumptions, relieved Lydia.

*Breathe*, she told herself, dropping her eyes to the ground. She cleared her throat and deliberately stated, "I do appreciate your kindness, Miss Sophia. I am sorry to have disturbed you. I assure you that I am perfectly well."

There was an uneasy silence and Lydia felt Sophia's eyes surveying her again.

"Foote," the words were soft but certain, "if you ever feel anything other than safe here, I hope that you will tell my brother or myself immediately." Her arm reached out as if to pat Lydia on the shoulder, but dropped back to her side as she seemed to think better of it.

"Thank you, Miss Sophia."

Lydia faced her until Sophia had gone through and shut the door.

*Why didn't I tell her I was frightened by a mouse? Although, she may have been insulted by the notion that her house is infested...*

*The window!*

Spinning around, Lydia's eyes fell on the diamonds of glass, all still neatly arranged and leaded together. None had fallen from its place.

Cautiously, she prodded at the few where her hand had beat against them. Two wiggled more easily than the others.

*Oh, dear. It's not visible, but hopefully no one will be pushing on those anytime soon...at least not as long as I'm working here.*

She smiled, embarrassed at the recollection of how frantically she had slapped her open palm on the glass and called out.

*All of that because of a glimpse of Paul Midwinter! How absurd!*

She remembered the last time they had crossed paths on Shinford's High Street. It was the morning that she had left to come to Whitehall. She had been standing outside Wyndell's Tea Room, waiting for the coach to arrive when Paul strode past and jauntily tipped his hat.

In response, she had barely nodded, ignoring the smug look on his face, thinking, *I can't believe I kissed you.*

*Why so different now?* she considered. *I suppose it was the sight of a familiar face in a moment of profound loneliness. Ha! To regard Paul Midwinter as a beacon of light in a time of darkness!*

Lydia began to polish the wooden sill of the next window, glad to be able to laugh at herself.

*But why did he come? I've never noted a farmer on Whitehall's grounds before. It can't be coincidence that the one farmer to come here is all the way from Shinford...*

Jarred to reality, Lydia dropped the rag

*Mama! Something's happened to Mama and he came to tell me!*

She hurried out of the bedroom, fragmentedly thinking, *Who would have answered the door? Did he go to the front or have the sense to go to the side?*

Instinct pointed her in the direction of the kitchen. As she descended the main staircase, Smith was hurrying up it, clearly busy with her own duties.

"You can't possibly be finished with the spare rooms," she chastised over her shoulder. "Time is short."

Lydia made no reply and hurried on.

*I won't be asking* her *if she knows why he was here. Perhaps Glaser saw him in the yard. Yes, he might know. But where is Glaser?*

Heading to the garden, she cut through the kitchen.

"Ah, here she is now," Ploughman said, looking up from peeling potatoes.

"She's not to have it till the day's work is done," Cook said, surly.

Lydia looked at Ploughman, questioningly.

*What? What is it?*

The older woman mouthed something and pointed at the far counter. There, a white rectangle of paper was propped up against a bowl of unshelled peas.

*A letter!* Lydia rushed to it.

"It's for later." Cook growled, glaring out from under her coarse, colorless eyebrows, and then turned her glowering face toward Ploughman who continued to peel potatoes with calm dignity.

*No pig with a wooden spoon is going to keep me from my letter!*

Lydia rushed forward and grabbed it from its place, quickly moving out of Cook's reach, though the woman made no physical motion to stop her.

Staring at the envelope, she recognized her mother's writing. Nothing looked out of the ordinary, which eased Lydia's mind considerably.

*So she's alright? Ah...perhaps she heard he would be passing here so she asked him to deliver this to save a penny.*

It was not unusual for farmers to travel afar occasionally. At times, Lydia's father had gone long distances for business dealings.

With the letter in her hand, she headed back to the bedroom she'd been cleaning, and was startled when she caught sight of herself in the little mirror by the door.

*A bit of polish on my nose! My hair askew and this horrible little mob-cap!* She smiled. *Paul would have galloped away faster had he caught sight of me!*

# Wishing for His Top Hat

~ JONATHAN

"No. Don't pull the bat 'round the back of you," Jonathan called across the lawn. "Come on, then. Stand the way I showed you last time."

Elliott's shoulders sagged, the bat nearly falling out of his hands.

*He hates this*, Jonathan knew. *But I leave for school the day after tomorrow and he really needs the practice. He'll be truly miserable if he gets to Heath and can't hit. Why must so much depend on the crack of a bat on a ball?*

"Alright now, Elliott, here it comes." He drew his arm back, ready to bowl the ball toward his brother.

The little boy dropped the bat altogether and began to run toward Jonathan, pointing and calling, "Who's that?"

Looking behind him, Jonathan saw a horse and rider cantering down the driveway away from the house toward the main road. He wondered the same thing as he examined the man, who had slowed to a trot as he passed.

Dressed in work clothes, the rider was young and broad-shouldered. A wide-brimmed hat was pulled low on the crown of his head. He sat the horse well, the reins slack in his right hand.

"Hullo!" he called, touching his left hand to the brim of his hat and nodding at the Clydes.

Jonathan suddenly longed to be on Achilles' back, wearing his top hat to return the cavalier greeting. Instead, he dipped his bare head, seeing in the same moment that the fellow had kicked his horse into a gallop, and disappeared down the drive in a cloud of dust.

*So you know how to ride a horse. Congratulations to you.*

"Who was that?" Elliott asked breathlessly.

"I've no idea," Jonathan replied, dryly. "A farmer, by the looks of him."

"Why would a farmer come here?" Elliott's eyes lit up. "Are we going to keep cows now?"

*Yes, what business* would *a farmer have here?* Jonathan wondered.

"No."

"Pigs then?" Elliott persisted.

Jonathan laughed.

Suddenly, the little boy was running back toward Whitehall whence the man had just come.

"Elliott!" Jonathan called, but only once as the boy's figure rounded the bend.

*Well, it's not as if I was eager to practice cricket today either…and the Lady hasn't said he's off to school this autumn.*

He walked to where Elliott had left the bat in the long grass.

*What's she waiting for? I was at Heath by this age, wasn't I?*

Assured he had all the equipment, he headed back to the house himself. He felt a pang of irritation as his mind settled back on the mysterious rider.

*But why should I dislike a stranger so?*

*Well, I suppose it's because he seemed so…sure of himself.*

*But what's the crime in that? I've encountered a number of fine men who are low-born. In fact,* he thought hard for a moment, *how many fine men do I know who are high-born?*

He considered the fellows he knew from Heath.

*But none of them are men,* he reasoned. *However, I've met many of their fathers and uncles and such while visiting their homes.*

*Hmm… With whom was I particularly impressed? Anyone?*

Whitehall came into view.

*Hodges' father is a decent fellow. A bit dull, but respectable nevertheless.*

*Widdy's father is amusing, but a lush.*

He recalled the man at meals, always clutching an empty glass and calling out for another bottle.

Visions of his schoolmasters filled his mind as he ascended the steps to the front door.

*Headmaster Grimes might be thought of as admirable, but what class would he be considered a part of?*

*Bah! What does it matter?*

"Oh, here you are!" Sophia turned to face him as he came in.

Elliott was pulling on her sleeve.

"I've no idea what you're talking about, Elly! Jonathan, I must speak with you. Oh, for goodness' sake, Elliott, go check the stables for pigs then!"

His face lit with expectation, Elliott raced out the front door and down the steps.

"Mind where you tread!" Jonathan called after him. Chuckling, he asked his sister, "What's the matter?"

She drew close to him and looked around cautiously. In a low voice, she began, "I'm worried something's happened to Foote."

"What?" Jonathan asked, caught completely off guard.

"I was in my room this morning when I heard someone yelling and pounding from inside one of the spare rooms. I nearly ran for you, but then remembered you and Elliott had gone out. So I rushed in myself."

Sophia paused.

"So...?" Jonathan urged.

"Well, once there, I saw no one but Foote. She looked frightened–I think she'd been crying."

"Was it *her* yelling?"

Sophia nodded vigorously. "Yes! Something like, 'No! Wait! Don't!'"

Feeling sick, Jonathan grabbed Sophia by the shoulders. "You're *certain* she was alone?"

"Yes, yes. I looked all around the room. Jonathan, you're hurting me." She shrugged out of his grasp. "I didn't think you'd react quite like...where are you going?"

Jonathan was up the stairs in a few seconds, calling over his shoulder, "Where is she now?"

"I...uh...don't..." Sophia replied, hurrying to catch up to him.

The siblings rushed down the hallway toward the spare rooms.

"That's where she *was*, though I don't know..." Sophia pointed at the door of the room next to her own bedroom.

Jonathan pushed through the door and strode in, strength and something akin to anger coursing through his limbs.

There was Foote, oddly enough sitting on the floor, looking small, her legs drawn close to her body, her skirt and apron tucked neatly around them. A creased sheet of paper was in her hands. With a look of surprise, she jumped up to a standing position.

"Are you alright?" Jonathan asked, moving hastily toward her.

"Me?" she asked, looking around the room.

"Yes. Are you alright?" Jonathan inquired again, peering at her intently.

"Yes, of course, sir." She looked from Jonathan to Sophia and back to Jonathan. "Oh, are you wondering about...earlier?"

"Well, yes. Sophia said you were yelling, 'No!' and 'Don't!' so naturally I thought..." Jonathan broke off.

Foote looked down and exhaled, seemingly embarrassed. "I...truly, nothing happened. I simply...I saw someone out the window in the drive and it startled me...and he started to leave, so I called out to him."

*The farmer!*

"Did he...Did he *do* anything...?" The words stuck in Jonathan's dry throat.

"No! He never even *saw* me. He climbed on his horse and...and he left...without a word..." Foote looked out of the window as her voice trailed off.

"So you recognized the man?" Jonathan asked. His heart rate was just starting to slow from its reverberating pounding.

"Yes. His family has a farm near Hill...near where I live. He left this letter for me with Cook." She lifted the paper in her hand.

Jonathan regarded her wistful face as she gazed outside.

*She's fond of him...fond of that stupid, galloping fool. He must have come to see her and been turned away by Smith at the door, so he hastily wrote her a letter and left it.*

"Well...all is well, then...but I...that is," Jonathan felt increasingly foolish as each word tumbled out, "if you ever were to feel in danger, I hope that you would...that is..."

Clearing his throat gruffly, Jonathan's jaw ached with tension. "I...I want to ensure that you are safe and all is well with you."

Foote met his gaze, her eyes soft, and said slowly, "I do appreciate that, sir."

She looked away, reaching up to smooth her hair.

"Very well," he murmured.

*I'll let you get back to swooning over your love letter.*

He turned on slightly shaky legs and left.

*Idiot!* he chastised himself while starting down the hallway. He heard Sophia close the door behind them and her footsteps as she caught up to him.

*Agh!*

The urge to hit something surged down his arms, but he put the energy into distancing himself from Foote.

"I suppose it wasn't as bad as I initially thought," said Sophia as she tried to walk alongside him.

"You *suppose*? It was a big upset over *nothing*," he said acidly over his shoulder.

"Well, I thought you ought to know." She sounded hurt, her voice low. "Jonathan, she was genuinely distressed. If you had heard...if you had *seen* her...You just...you don't understand..."

He halted in his steps, nearly causing Sophia to run into him.

"I understand perfectly," he said, tilting his head to glower at her. "Our silly parlour maid is hysterically besotted with some boorish lout of a farmer."

Sophia scoffed angrily and said in the voice she used to correct Elliott, "That is *hardly* fair!"

Jonathan shrugged, his hands outstretched. "I wish them much happiness in their future life together."

Folding her arms across her chest, his sister replied, "How *very* good of you. *Noble,* in fact."

Throwing him a final sour look, she stalked out of the foyer, saying, "Honestly, I can't understand why you're so angry."

Alone, Jonathan stood for a moment, his jaw still aching. Realizing that his hands were clenched into fists, he consciously opened them and took a couple of deep breaths.

*She's a maid,* he told himself.

*She's* just *a maid.*

# Mothering Elliott

~ Lydia

The day of the Lady's departure for London was unusually warm for autumn. Wisps of fine hair stuck to the damp nape of Lydia's neck as she stood by the carriage with Ploughman and Glaser.

Cook crunched along the gravel drive toward the group with her own small bag.

"Where's the wagon?" she asked, the sides of her florid face glistening.

Glaser answered, "The Lady wants to leave it behind."

"Leave it behind? But what of all the luggage--and where will Smith and myself sit?"

"Most of the luggage is already inside the carriage and the Lady says you and Smith are to ride on the perch with me."

He winked at the woman.

"What?" Cook's face was a mixture of anger and confusion.

*The Lady thinks all three can fit on the perch together? Stupid woman!* Lydia tightened her throat, telling herself, *You can laugh about it all you want once the carriage is gone, but* not *now.*

Lydia willed herself not to examine Cook's generous hindquarters though they were directly in front of her. Glaser's twitching face did nothing to help Lydia in her endeavor to maintain composure.

The front door opened and Lady Clyde and Miss Sophia exited, followed by Hardy and Smith, who were carrying even more luggage. Elliott came last of all, hanging onto the doorjamb.

"Good bye, everyone. Thank you," Sophia said. Her eyes fell on Elliott. She grabbed him and picked him up, squeezing him affectionately. "Goodbye, dearest."

"No kisses, Sophie," he responded, squirming out of her grasp.

The servants bowed and curtsied as the young woman climbed up into the carriage.

Turning, the Lady regarded the front of the great house.

Readying herself to climb inside the vehicle, she said to the group before her, "Keep things tidy so that there won't be the usual disorder upon my return."

The servants bobbed and bowed their assent.

"Lady?"

Lady Clyde turned her eyes to Cook. "Yes?"

"I fear that Glaser, Smith and myself will not all be able to sit on the perch together."

"And why not?" The eyes grew cold.

"We won't all fit, Ma'am."

The Lady stepped back from the carriage and surveyed the small driver's seat. Then she looked the three servants up and down.

Lydia bit her lip fiercely.

*Don't even smile.*

"Very well," the Lady said with a sigh. "Smith, you may ride inside the carriage. Cook, you and Glaser may share the perch." She quickly stepped into the vehicle, followed by Smith.

Hardy folded the step up and shut the carriage door.

Lydia dared one quick glance at Cook, who was struggling up into place. The woman was her brightest shade of pink and her eyes were narrowed to slits.

*She could start a fire in the hearth with one glance.*

*Poor Glaser,* thought Lydia, her amusement suddenly gone. *He might fall off the edge! I hope London's not very far.*

"Goodbye, Sophia! Goodbye, Mama!" called Elliott as the horses began to pull the carriage down the driveway.

Sophia held back the window's curtain and waved.

Once the carriage was out of sight, Hardy began to dance a jig, the gravel shifting under his feet. Ploughman clapped along happily.

Surprised, Lydia laughed, joined by Elliott.

"Servants dance?" asked Elliott incredulously.

"We do when we're pleased or pickled," responded Hardy, who was now panting with his efforts.

"Which are you now?" asked Lydia.

"Pleased, of course. Let London take care of 'em. That's what I says."

*Mind what you say,* thought Lydia. *One of the family is still here among us.*

Ploughman chuckled. "That was the strangest sendoff I ever seen. I wonder why she didn't want the wagon."

"I'm just glad I'm not smashed up against Cook all the way to London," said Hardy. "Pity Glaser."

He shrugged and strutted off to the stable house, whistling.

"Aye to that!" said Ploughman, still chuckling and heading with ungainly steps into the house. "Aye to that."

"What'll we do first?" asked Elliott, looking up at Lydia.

*Oh, it really will befall me, won't it?*

She looked into the little boy's shining face.

*I believe he's as happy that his mother is gone as the rest of us are! I don't know why that surprises me. Still, how am I to tend to a child? I'm barely a parlour maid, and now a nanny!*

Yet the shining of Elliott's eyes above his snub nose warmed Lydia.

She smiled, recalling what she had planned and stuck her face into his. "Something you'll like."

"What is it?"

"It's this way," said Lydia, leading him around the side of the house. Stepping into the kitchen, she retrieved a plate of fatty scraps she had set aside.

Elliott eyed the greasy morsels. "Ew. What's that for?"

"You'll see."

Elliott followed Lydia to the stable yard where she called for Sassy. Emerging from the stable, the dog bounded up to them, her tongue lolling out of her mouth, and began to jump up on Elliott.

"Sassy, come," commanded Lydia, leading the others into a stable pen.

The little dog's attention was arrested by Lydia, who held the plate of scraps. Her forelegs danced on the front of Lydia's skirt leaving dusty paw prints.

"Pick up a piece to treat her with," said Lydia. "But don't give it to her until *exactly* when I say. Understand?"

Elliott nodded, his little nose wrinkling as he selected one of the congealed blobs.

"Sassy, sit!" Lydia directed while firmly pushing down on the wriggling dog's hindquarters with her free hand.

"Now!" she said the instant the dog's rear was forced to the ground.

Elliott dropped the fat and Sassy slurped it up, along with a few bits of hay from the pen floor.

The three did this again and again, and in less than fifteen minutes, Sassy began to lower her hindquarters herself each time Lydia said, "Sit."

Elliott was exuberant.

"Sit!" he said forcefully. "Sit!"

"Let's not confuse her," insisted Lydia. "When you train a dog, you don't repeat the command over and over, but only when you have a treat ready. Otherwise they don't learn to obey the command."

"Go get more scraps from the kitchen," demanded Elliott, looking at the empty plate.

"No, she's had enough for the day. We don't want her to grow weary of it."

Sassy, however, looked anything but tired. She jumped around, looking eagerly from one human to the other, giving an occasional yip.

Lydia sat down in the hay and began to rub the dog behind the ears. Elliott followed her example. It wasn't long before Sassy had rolled over, exposing her belly.

One spot Lydia petted resulted in Sassy's hind leg rhythmically kicking out again and again.

Elliott giggled.

"Let me try!" he said, scratching the same spot. His attempts did not elicit as certain of a response from Sassy's leg, but it bobbed around enough to make him giggle again.

The sun shining in through the doorway warmed Lydia's back and head.

"Look, Master Elliott." Lydia took one of the relaxed dog's front paws and gently spread out its toes. The relaxed canine was still.

Elliott carefully pinched the fleshy webs between.

"And feel this here." Lydia placed his little index finger in the various furry hollows of the foot pads. "Aren't dogs marvelous creatures?"

*How many fatty bits fell from my fingers into eager mouths at Hillcrest? How many dog bellies did I scratch there?*

"I like her mouth," said Elliott as he began to stroke Sassy's whiskered muzzle.

The pink tongue flashed out of the mouth to lick the boy's hand.

Lydia closed her eyes and tilted her face up into the sunlight. *Ahh...Cook, Smith and the Lady are getting further away by the moment. How positively lovely...*

*...but it's nearly time for the midday meal.*

"Come on, Elliott. Let's go wash our hands of this stinking pup," she said, rising from the ground and brushing off her skirt.

Suddenly, Sassy was on her feet, barking. Turning, Lydia saw a boy, a few years older than Elliott standing on the footstep by the kitchen door. His face looked wary at the dog's approach.

"Please, Miss," he said, waving a square of paper. "Is this Whitehall? I've a letter."

*A letter!* In an instant, Lydia was across the yard.

"Sassy, hush!" she scolded. "To whom is it addressed? Sassy, go!" She pointed at the stables and ushered the boy inside the kitchen.

"Mr. Cotter says, 'Run this o'er to Whitehall, down toward Kentford way.' I knocked on the front door but there's no answer so I come around the side. Is this Whitehall? I've been looking all morning."

"Yes, yes, but whose name is on the envelope?" Lydia longed to snatch it out of the boy's hand.

*Why am I excited? It's likely for one of the family.*

"I don't rightly know, Miss. Mr. Cotter said Whitehall and that's it." The boy clutched the letter to his chest and stuck out his other hand, palm up. "That'll be two pence."

*Ah, he probably can't read,* Lydia realized, truly examining the boy before her for the first time. He had removed his cap upon entrance of the kitchen. His damp straw-colored hair was flattened and plastered over his ears, and little beads of perspiration dotted his upper lip. Standing ramrod straight, his chin jutted out obstinately and he wouldn't look in Lydia's eyes.

*Who knows how many roads and drives he wandered looking for Whitehall? And on foot!*

"Would you like a cup of well water?" Lydia asked.

"Uhh..." The resolved look in the boy's eyes wavered, but he clutched the paper more tightly. "Mr. Cotter says I mustn't ever hand a letter over until the post is paid."

"I'm not trying to bribe you!" Lydia laughed which resulted in the sullen look returning to the boy's face.

*Ugh, a humorless young fellow. Very well...*

"Please, sit down." Lydia motioned toward the table and filled a glass with water before placing it in his reach. Walking to a shelf, she delved into the petty cash jar and recorded in the log:

Post – 2 d. – Foote

Returning to the table, she placed the money before him, and held out her hand.

Tucking the pence into his pocket, the boy almost smiled as he slid the letter across the table.

It wasn't an envelope, but a single sheet of paper, folded and tucked into itself. Regarding the address, Lydia sucked in her breath, surprised.

*It* is *for me!*

On what appeared to be the front was written in very neat, careful writing:

Foote at Wite Hall
Plym Bridg
Bevilshur

Lydia recognized the printing immediately.

*It's from Wells!*

*Oh dear, I used the laundry money to pay for my own letter. Too late now...*

"I can wait whilst you write back if you'd like, Miss," the boy said, having gulped down the water.

Lydia said nothing, lost in the unfolding of the sheet. The inside had an even stranger appearance than the outside. It was one of Wells' practice sheets, covered in rows of words like 'peas' and 'turnips' over and over. Though it looked as if Wells had initially covered every square inch of writable surface in practice, she had turned the paper sideways and written in whatever empty spots that were left. It took Lydia many minutes to navigate the whole thing and read:

Dere Foote. I did not rede yer leter. I did not hav a penny for the poste but wen the boy wuz at the door and sed ther was a leter I new it was frum yoo. I am ever so shamed that I was dismist. I thot Cook had washt the peeches. I never chekt them beefor wen Cook giv them to me to take into the parler. Mum cride and cride wen I showd up on the doorstepp. But I bin abel to serv in a big farm hous nere by. Thay dint ask for refrinnsis. Also I am teeching my sybleens to rede and rite. Thank yoo for teeching me. Ther ar too new babys sints I left home yeres ugo. A therd wun dyed too wynters back. I do not no if yoo will git to rede this leter sints the poste costs munny, but I hope yoo at leest see it and no it is from me. I am riting it and hopeing thet the poste will take it sints it is goeing to a rich hows thet mite pay the postidg. Yoo are a gud frend Foote. I miss yoo evry day. Beetryss Wellintin.

After reading it over a second time, Lydia put the letter down, her heart pounding rapidly.

*Wells was* dismissed*? Peaches? What peaches?*

"Will you be writing back now, Miss?" the boy asked.

"No," Lydia murmured. "No, thank you. You may go."

Disappointed, the boy pulled his cap back on and walked out the door.

*But Smith said...*Lydia thought, folding and unfolding the letter in her hands. *The Lady must have told her to lie to us!*

*But why?*

*Because the Lady is part of a Great Family and members of Great Families don't have to tell the truth to 'lesser' members of society.*

"Pony?" Elliott spoke from the doorway.

Turning, Lydia saw his silhouette, the bright sunlight behind him making his facial features dark and indiscernible, but the lines of his figure were in sharp contrast. He looked small, his posture slightly uncertain and his hair mussed with bits of hay sticking in it.

"Yes, Master Elliott," Lydia responded, her throat thick with emotion and confusion.

"What are we going to do now?" He walked into the kitchen and sat beside her, grabbing one of her hands with both of his. His guileless eyes looked at her expectantly.

The anger she felt dissipated as she examined his amber-colored eyes.

*It's not his fault he was born to such a woman.*

Lydia let her hand rest in his and replied, "I need to prepare the noonday meal."

"What can I do?" he asked, wrinkling his nose.

"You?" Lydia sighed and looked around the kitchen. "You can...wash your hands and shell the peas."

As he made his way to the basin, she retrieved a bowl of pea pods from the table and placed it on the table. Elliott was delighted as she showed him how to crack one end of the pod, pry it open and run his thumb down the center, releasing all of the little green orbs into a second bowl.

Once the meal was ready, there was the question of where Elliott would eat. Hardy, Ploughman and Lydia would, of course, dine in the servants' hall, but Elliott couldn't be expected to eat all alone in the family's dining room.

*Certainly the Lady would disapprove of her youngest son rubbing elbows with us at our rough wooden table*, Lydia thought. *But what is an acceptable alternative?*

She prayed uneasily that the Lady would never hear of it as she set a folded towel on the bench to boost the small boy higher.

"I like it in here," commented Elliott as he looked around at the three servants, eating a simple meal of bread, cheese and apples. "This is much nicer than that old dining room. The table cloth always gets in the way."

The servants exchanged quiet smiles with one another.

Bedtime presented the most vexing problem of all. Lydia took Elliott to his bedroom where she helped him clean his teeth and wash his face and behind his ears. She then instructed him to change into his nightclothes while she stepped out into the hall. Standing in the dismal silence of the empty hallway, she realized how isolated the little boy would be in this wing of the house.

*Bidding him 'good night' here would seem cruel. If he calls out in the middle of the night, I won't hear him. What if he needs a drink of water? And I certainly can't leave him with a lit candle!*

"Pony! I'm done!" he called.

*Oh, Lady, if you didn't despise me before, you certainly would now!*

Lydia went into the room and said, "Get your pillow and your favorite blanket."

"Why?"

"We're going on an adventure."

"But I'm all ready for bed."

"Yes, I know. Come." Lydia grabbed one of his small hands and led Elliott through the darkened hallways and rooms, downstairs and upstairs to her own small attic room.

"Ploughman, I fear you will have to give up your bed to Master Elliott, and you and I will share the larger one," said Lydia.

Ploughman, who was already situated for the night, looked confused but the wrinkles in her forehead smoothed as she listened to Lydia's explanation.

"I likely wouldn't want to sleep alone over there, either," she said, climbing out of the bed. "There you are, Master Elliott."

"This is great fun!" he said as he took her place.

"Great fun, eh, Foote?" asked the older woman, smiling as they situated themselves in the other bed.

The light had been extinguished for many moments when Ploughman whispered to Lydia, "I've never before slept in a room with a man, great or small. Even when I was a child, the brothers slept in a different room than the sisters."

Lydia chuckled. "I believe we are safe with this 'man'."

"As do I, Foote." The older woman chuckled as she rolled over and was soon breathing evenly.

# Extracting a Tooth

~ Lydia

Over the next few days, Lydia decided not to mention to anyone else that Wells had actually been dismissed. The poor girl was ashamed of it and there was no point in telling Ploughman or Hardy anyway.

Regarding Elliott, she found that the main problem she faced while tending to him was keeping him busy. Eventually she learned ways to distract him long enough to get her work done. He knew some letters, so she began teaching him the others and how to sound out and write words. Soon he was sitting at the kitchen table while she prepared the simple meals, writing out sentences with such ease that Wells would have been jealous.

Another of Lydia's ploys was to tell Elliott that they would play hide-and-seek. He would scamper off to some mysterious location and she would go to find him, but only once she had finished sweeping or dusting a room.

He kept working with the dog, as well. After a while, Sassy, who had mastered sitting on command, was learning to lift her paw when told and to retrieve a stick. Other than his occasional venture out in the garden to play by himself or a visit to the laundress' home to play with her seven-year-old son, Elliott was Lydia's constant companion. He followed her from room to room, asking all sorts of questions and sharing with her the abundance of the workings of his brain. Thus quickly, the strangeness of Elliott's presence at the servants' table and in the attic room wore off.

Early one morning, as Lydia lay in bed drifting toward consciousness, she heard him say, "My tooth hurts."

She was awake in an instant.

"What do you mean, Master Elliott?" she asked, her voice craggy from hours of disuse.

"It hurt yesterday and the day before when I was eating, and now it hurts so much that it woke me up."

Lydia felt her heart sink, and she patted the little boy's back.

*Why now of all times when neither his mother nor even Smith is here?*

Later that morning, she took Elliott out into the sunshine and looked into his widely opened mouth. Peering in, she saw a dark spot deep in the crevice of a back molar.

"What do you see?" asked Elliott.

*No use in frightening him,* she thought and replied, "A whole lot of teeth and a wiggly pink tongue."

Remembering her own experience of having a tooth removed, she worried for the boy. Returning to the house, she sat down and wrote out a letter informing the Lady and asking what should be done.

Two days later there was a knock at the kitchen door. Opening it, Lydia saw the same post boy who had delivered Wells' letter. Supposing whatever the boy held was from the Lady, Lydia did not hesitate this time to dip into the laundry money to pay him. The letter simply stated,

Take him to Plimbridge to see our physician, Chadwick-- Lady Clyde

The next morning, as she set a bowl of porridge in front of him, Lydia saw that tears were running down his face.

"Master Elliott, why are you crying?" she asked, putting her hand on his shoulder.

"I'm not crying!" the boy wailed. "It's just that...I can't eat. My tooth hurts all the time." He pushed the bowl away from him and put his head down on the table.

"Why don't you go rest on the bed for now, Elliott? I'll see if I can get someone to fix that tooth today."

The weepy child shuffled off to the attic room.

Lydia turned to Hardy who was eating his own bowl of porridge.

"Looks like a horrible trip into Plimbridge to see Chadwick today, Hardy. When can you take us?"

"Soon as I gets the horse suited up."

Less than an hour later, the three of them were in the wagon, bundled against a brisk autumnal wind, plodding into the village.

"Who's going to fix it?" asked Elliott as the horse slowly pulled the wagon toward Plimbridge.

"The physician," replied Lydia.

"What's he going to do?"

Hardy coughed slightly and shook the reins.

"I don't know."

*Well, I* don't, Lydia told herself. *I don't know if he's going to pull it or fill it with gold.*

"Will it hurt?"

"I don't think so, Elliott."

*Liar!*

Soon they were pulling up in front of the physician's office. Lydia left Hardy and Elliott behind as she went in.

Inside, Lydia found Mr. Chadwick and explained the situation, adding, "I'd like to keep him unaware of what is happening for as long as possible. He is a very determined little boy and it could take hours to complete if he's not compliant."

"Of course," replied the physician. "I have little tricks I use on children. I see you brought a man with you. I'll need him to hold the boy's legs when it comes down to it. What form of payment will you make?"

*Money? Of course! Ugh, I hadn't even considered that!*

"Oh, I had supposed that Lady Clyde would pay you when she returns from London. She left me with money only for the laundry bills and such. Is that alright?" She suddenly felt foolish, as if she was asking a ridiculous favor.

*Certainly he extends credit!*

Chadwick's lip curled up in a sardonic smile and the formerly intuitive looking eyes narrowed.

"She left you no money? That's hardly surprising." He looked as if he were about to refuse, but then glanced out the window. Elliott was slumped miserably on the wagon seat, his left hand cradling his jaw.

"Well...bring him in. I'll write it on her *tab.*" He said the last word as if it were amusing in a shameful way.

Unsure how to respond, Lydia nodded and went outside to usher Elliott inside.

Soon, Lydia was inviting Elliott to sit in the comfortable reclining chair and look at the lovely lamp hanging from the ceiling. As Elliott got situated, Lydia went back outside to Hardy and informed him of his job in the matter.

"But don't pin his legs until Chadwick signals you or he may panic."

"I want no parta that! I jus' drive the wagon."

"Hardy, get your cowardly carcass in there. Think of the little boy!"

Hardy grumbled as he secured the horse to a post and followed Lydia inside.

Chadwick lit the lamp above the chair and said to Elliott, "Open your mouth, please."

Hardy stood at the foot of the chair, looking miserable. Lydia had positioned herself next to Elliott's side, feeling just as Hardy looked, but trying to appear cheerful.

"A little wider," instructed the physician, aiming the light.

Lydia pretended to see into Elliott's mouth.

"I count 24 teeth. How many do you see, Mr. Chadwick?" she asked.

"Hm, yes," murmured Chadwick as he narrowed his eyes.

"How will you fix it?" Elliott asked, then resumed his wide-mouthed pose.

"Hmm..." repeated Chadwick as he rummaged through his instrument drawer. He pulled out a tooth key and hammer-like tool.

*So it is to come out.* Lydia cringed inwardly.

She would never forget the last time she saw tools similar to these. Her jaw ached at the recollection.

Chadwick unscrewed the key's handle from the shaft.

"Restrain the limbs, please," he said, looking pointedly at Hardy, who was at the foot of the table, and Lydia, who was trembling beside it.

"What are you doing?" asked Elliott as Hardy's large rough hands pinned down his ankles, and Lydia grabbed his arms. "Let go of me! Pony?"

"You must open your mouth so that I may help you," said Chadwick again.

As Elliott did, the physician slipped in a tightly wound wad of treated wool, propping the jaws wide.

The little pink tongue began to bob around frantically and the boy's arms strained against Lydia's weight. A muffled howl of protest rose out of his throat.

Wrapping his arm around the boy's head, Chadwick steadied it and tapped soundly on the tooth as Elliott's protest turned to rage.

Lydia watched as the tooth grew visibly looser in its socket, and blood began to ooze up to the gum line. Feeling light-headed, she squeezed her eyes shut and focused on maintaining control over Elliott's arms which were threatening to fly loose.

When she looked again, Chadwick had expertly fitted the key's band around the tooth and reattached the handle. Giving the key a terrific wrench brought the tooth out as Elliott's lusty muffled screams filled the small room.

Lydia was amazed at the strength such young muscles could exert. Once the tooth was out, she let go of his arms.

Elliott flailed wildly. His right fist flung out and collided squarely with Lydia's eye. It throbbed within her head as she squeezed it tightly shut.

Hardy was still bearing down on the little master's ankles.

Cupping her watering eye, Lydia saw with her functioning eye that Chadwick was calmly examining the tooth's root.

"Excellent," he said over the boy's wails. "The root is completely intact so I needn't root around for shards."

He dropped the tooth on a tray and began to clean his tools.

Still covering her eye, Lydia said, "It's over, Master Elliott. Now that horrible tooth won't hurt you anymore."

Elliott's cries turned to whimpers.

After a moment as Lydia's vision returned, she picked the tooth up from the tray and held it out to the now sniveling boy. "See how long the root is? Would you like to keep it?"

Quiet now, though his dripping lower lip continued to quiver, he nodded.

Lydia dropped the bloody offender, bits of tissue still adhering to it, into the boy's palm. Within moments he was smiling, flipping it over and over in examination, though his free hand was plastered to the side of his face, cradling his cheek.

*And what were the 'tricks' you employ when working with children, sir?* Lydia wondered, looking at the physician. *I didn't seem to notice them. Nevertheless, it is over with...*

"Thank you," Lydia said, pulling Elliott from the chair.

"Hmm, yes," Chadwick replied. "I'll be sending Lady Clyde the *bill.*"

***

That evening, at dinner, Lydia caught Ploughman and Hardy looking at her.

"What is it?" she asked.

Elliott, who had wanted to sit at the table with them while he chewed a piece of gauze, wrinkled his nose and asked, "What's the matter with your eye?"

"Oh, it's better now. I can see perfectly fine again."

"No, I mean, why is it purple?"

"What?"

Hardy and Ploughman began to shake with repressed laughter.

"Aye, Foote. You gotta real blacker there," chortled Hardy.

Lydia rushed to the small looking glass near the door. Staring back at her were her eyes, one normal in every way and the other ringed with an angry bluish smear.

*Ugh...*

"Well, Master Elliott," she said returning to the table with a sigh. "You have succeeded in giving me my very first black eye."

Elliott gasped, "I did that?"

Lydia explained how as Elliott began to chew harder on the gauze. Glancing at Ploughman and Hardy who were chuckling, he smiled and then began to giggle.

"Thank you all so much," said Lydia with mock-irritation.

Suddenly a look of pain crossed Ploughman's face.

"More stomach pains?" asked Lydia.

*She's hardly touched her food.*

"Ugh," Ploughman groaned, rubbing a hand over her abdomen. A strange look flitted across her face as she continued to feel her belly.

Lydia considered questioning her further but decided against it.

"Maybe you need a soft egg like Elliott instead of this chunky stew."

"Nah, I'm not hungry." Ploughman rose from the table and slowly trudged off to the kitchen, still palpating her stomach.

Watching her leave, Lydia was struck by how altered the older woman was. It was rare now that she even saw Ploughman walk across a room. The woman was usually sitting on a stool somewhere, quietly working with her hands. Seeing her backside in retreat, Lydia realized that the woman's figure had shrunk dramatically, looking aged and frail.

***

That night, Lydia instructed Elliott to wait outside the attic room for a moment. Entering, she asked Ploughman, "Why were you groping your stomach like that at dinner?"

With care, the older woman stretched herself out on the bed, motioned to a place on her body and said, "Feel this."

Unaccustomed to exploring another's abdomen, Lydia gingerly reached out to the spot indicated. Her hesitation dissipated as her fingers discerned a large, firm ball under the flesh.

Ploughman's aging body was draped with extra skin and had little muscle. Under these saggy layers, Lydia felt around in the uniform softness, finding the borders of a solid mass, just below where Lydia imagined Ploughman's navel to be.

"What is that?" Ploughman asked, her eyes worried.

"I don't know," Lydia replied, wondering if Chadwick could tell them.

*Yet, if there's no money for Elliott's tooth to be pulled, there certainly is no money to have an elderly servant's abdomen probed.*

"It must be why I have all them stomach pains."

Lydia nodded, unsure of what else to say.

There was a little knock on the door and Elliott said, "Pony? It's dark out here. I'm scared."

# Consulting the Apothecary

~ Lydia

The following day, Ploughman rose from bed as usual, though sluggishly, and descended the stairs to the kitchen where she stayed all day. She parked herself on her little stool in the corner and sorted beans and kneaded dough, all even more slowly than usual.

Lydia again noticed that she ate very little.

A few days passed similarly until one morning, as sunlight spilled in through the attic window, Ploughman declared, "I'm so sorry, Foote, but I can't quite face the stairs yet. I'll be down in a while."

"Alright. Come when you can," said Lydia, though she thought*, Ugh, here I am, the only capable servant caring for an enormous house, tending to an active little boy and making sure we're all fed.*

*I had hoped that she would at least be able to make the porridge while I'm out in the garden. With Glaser gone, the plot is a shamble. Hardy is hardly any help at all! All those cabbages and carrots are going to be wasted on rabbits if I don't get them in soon.*

One glance, however, at the elderly woman, struck Lydia with guilt. She looked as if she had aged 15 years in a week's time. Her ashen face was lined with pain and her mouth hung open as if she didn't have the energy to keep it closed. Her every movement was accompanied by little groans.

*She looks as if she's dying.*

Lydia said, "You stay in bed as long as you need to."

"Thank you, Foote. You've always been so kind to me."

The emotion in these words made Lydia uneasy. "Yes, well, don't get used to it. When I'm in charge here, I'll make Cook seem like an angel of mercy."

Ploughman chuckled as Lydia exited the room.

Arriving in the kitchen, Lydia announced, "Hardy, you must ride into Plimbridge and ask Chadwick to come and have a look at Ploughman."

Hardy looked up from his bowl of porridge. "Chadwick don't look at servants."

"Doesn't look at servants?" Lydia balked. "Is a desperately ill woman to be ignored?"

Hardy continued, "It's Archbold, the apothecary, she needs."

"Well, whoever it is, he needs to come today." Lydia wrung her hands, recalling the plate of untouched eggs she had just brought down from Ploughman's bedside.

***

Before the midday meal, the man called Archbold stood at the foot of Ploughman's bed. He was a sturdy fellow with a red nose and little, deeply set eyes.

"I can't do nothin' if you won't let me have a look." He stared malevolently at Ploughman who was clutching the bedclothes about her.

"You're not touching me."

"Ploughman, please." Lydia was near despair. "I'm right here and he simply wants to feel around that lump to see what can be done."

"Ain't a man who ever touched me there."

Archbold and Ploughman glared steadily at each other.

With an exasperated sigh, the apothecary pulled a little vial out of a leather sack which hung from his shoulder. Holding it out to Lydia, he said, "Give her a draught of this three times a day."

Lydia looked at the bottle. Its content was a greenish brown liquid with mossy looking dregs settled at the bottom.

"No, Foote. I won't drink it!" Ploughman said decidedly from the bed.

*Who knows what's in that witch's brew?* Lydia tried not to wrinkle her nose at Archbold's concoction. *I wouldn't want to drink it either.*

"No, thank you, sir. I fear it would be wasted on her since she insists she won't take it."

With a grunt of disgust, the man dropped the bottle back into his bag and stomped from the room, mumbling about a complete waste of his time. Lydia turned to follow him out, but Ploughman called after her.

"Please, Foote," she pleaded. "If I don't get well from just lying down, then I'll just die here, but no more men like that. Please."

"You won't get well unless you eat. You've eaten nothing for days. You're melting away to skin and bones. Can't I please fix you some porridge?"

The invalid said nothing, but big tears welled up in her eyes, and her lower lip began to quiver.

"What is it?" Lydia asked in the gentle voice she used when speaking with an upset Elliott.

Ploughman shook her head obstinately as an unpleasant odor reached Lydia's nostrils.

*Blast! She's wet the bed!*

"I'm sorry. I'm sorry. I couldn't hold it no longer." The woman wept like a disappointed toddler.

*It couldn't be helped,* Lydia told herself. *She was struggling to use the chamber pot long before she became ill, and she can't even get out of bed now.*

Lydia knew these thoughts were true, but the logic did nothing to eliminate the stench, nor the frustration she felt knowing she was the only person capable of cleaning up the mess.

*And how am I to clean it up?*

"Don't cry, Ploughman. It's alright."

*Alright? What's alright? The woman is obviously dying. Her body is ceasing to function in the most rudimentary of ways and she hasn't eaten for days.*

With tears in her own eyes, Lydia sat down on the other bed and reached for Ploughman's hand.

"Please don't cry, Joan."

The shaking shoulders stilled and the old woman sniffed. "It's been ages since anyone called me that. I'm so sorry, Foote. I didn't mean to."

"Shhh..."

The skin on the wrinkled hand Lydia held was paper thin and dotted with liver spots, so different from how it must have been when others had called the woman 'Joan'. This thought startled Lydia into a realization.

*But how does one ask that question?* she wondered nervously.

"Joan..." she began. "Is there anyone I ought to send for...to come and see you?"

Ploughman met Lydia's eyes. A solemn understanding passed between them. Calmed, the old woman breathed in deeply, her eyelashes still damp with tears.

"I think the only one left is my brother, Joash, unless he's gone, too. I suppose you could write to Rountree House at Sullsby in Cambridgeshire. That's where he was, last I heard. I've a penny in my stocking to pay for the post." Joan motioned toward the socks hanging from a peg near her bed.

Lydia stood and retrieved a coin from its hiding place. A few others jingled in the toe.

"Joash Ploughman at Rountree House in Sullsby, Cambridgeshire?" she asked from the door.

"Tha's right," Joan nodded, her eyes meeting Lydia's once again in an honest and troubled recognition before she departed.

*'...the only one left...unless he's gone, too.'* The words ran through Lydia's mind as her young legs quickly descended the stairs, a lump rising in her throat.

*A few pennies in the toe of a well-darned sock, and one possible relative. That's all there is to show for a dear woman's entire life.*

# Leaving Heath

~ JONATHAN
HEATH SCHOOL

The hands resting on the desktop before Jonathan didn't look like they belonged to an easy living collegiate. The fingers had none of the expected length and tapering, but were heavy and sausage-like. Though the flesh was not rough and thick with manual labor, neither was it smooth and pale like that of a fine gentleman.

These were the hands that most of Heath's students watched with wary expectation at some point or another during their educational years. On more than one occasion, these hands had gripped and swung the 'Cane of Pain', expertly cracking the wooden instrument across Jonathan's posterior.

They belonged to Headmaster Grimes.

The head of Headmaster Grimes loomed above the hands. It was not as familiar to Jonathan since it was the hands that Jonathan had grown accustomed to staring at during his many spells of sitting across from the man in his study, hearing a lecture detailing his sins, and awaiting the corporal punishment dealt by the weighty hands themselves.

Still, it was there, with its ever-receding hairline and its stubbly double chin. What hair it still possessed was thin and gray. In fact, his eyebrows seemed to boast of more substance than did his scalp. Below these ferocious hedges were positioned the blue eyes which had pierced into the souls of innumerable ill-behaving youths.

Upon entering the headmaster's office, Jonathan noted that the pipe, which was usually tightly gripped between the man's teeth, was resting on the desktop. This unsettled Jonathan even more. Even the canings he had suffered through had been dealt whilst the smoking apparatus jutted out of the man's face. In fact, Jonathan was convinced that he would forever feel a burning on his backside at a mere whiff of Harrow's Amber Flake hanging in the air.

*What sort of a visit is this?* he wondered.

"Clyde," Grimes began and cleared his throat. "You are certainly wondering why I summoned you here first thing this morning."

"I thought, perhaps, that you had missed me, sir." Jonathan regretted his attempt at a joke even as it rolled off his tongue.

Yet Grimes smiled. It was not only beatings and lectures that came from the man. On more than one occasion, he had smiled easily at one of Jonathan's quips or even chuckled, which he did now.

Jonathan looked up.

"No, that I did not." The smile faded and he cleared his throat again, looking Jonathan in the eye. His eyes did not possess the fire of anger and frustration that Jonathan had seen many times. Instead, they had a troubled look.

"Clyde, did you bring me anything?"

"Sir?" Jonathan floundered.

"I was told you would play courier for your mother."

*What could you possibly want from her?* Jonathan slowly shook his head, confounded, and said nothing in the pause that followed.

"I see. Hmm..." The man lifted a paper from his desk and glanced at it. "Clyde, I fear you must grow up today and now. You see, for the last three years, we here at Heath have been requesting from your mother the payment of your tuition. Each year, she has made only partial payments. In her last correspondence, she said she would be sending the money from the past years and this year's entire tuition with you at the beginning of this term."

*Why would she do that*? wondered Jonathan.

"Are you certain your mother sent you nothing that she intended for you to pass on to me?" The dreaded eyes peered deeply into Jonathan's own.

*He thinks I'm holding it back for myself!*

"I only have a couple of guineas to pay for my supplemental food and drink, sir."

"So you're telling me that Lady Clyde did not send 25 pounds along with you this term?"

In spite of the discomfort he felt, Jonathan laughed out loud. "I assure you, she did not."

A thought flitted into his mind, *Perhaps Grimes is trying to get money out of me for his own personal use.*

However, this notion did not root itself as Grimes continued.

"The partial payments along with the promises of a formerly reliable patron were enough to keep you here. It is not unusual for us to do so with various families, but with no end in sight for the credit we have extended, I fear all that has changed. I'm sorry to tell you that without payment, you can no longer attend school here at Heath."

*What?*

Though Jonathan heard the words, he sat stupidly in the chair, staring at the headmaster's mouth. The loose, wet lips surrounded by a blackish stubble now formed another sentence.

"You will be required to leave on the morrow."

Jonathan flinched.

"I'm sure there's been some mistake. Are you certain it wasn't lost somehow or...or that she even received your letters requesting payment?"

Nodding his head, Grimes picked up an envelope from the top of a stack and pushed it across the desk.

Pulling the letter out of it, Jonathan saw his mother's fine handwriting carefully scripted across the page. Skimming it quickly, he was bewildered to see that her words confirmed what Grimes had said. The date in the upper right corner proved the letter to be more than a year old.

Jonathan felt as if he had been punched in the gut.

"I'm sorry that circumstances are not otherwise," said Grimes, his hands folding together. "You're welcome to return should the funds accompany you."

Slowly, Jonathan rose from his chair, placing the letter back on the desk.

Grimes also rose and stuck his brawny right hand out to Jonathan.

Reeling, it took the young man a second to realize that Grimes intended for him to shake it.

*From instrument of retribution to instrument of grace,* thought Jonathan, clutching the meaty appendage.

He turned to go, quietly. At the door he paused, glanced back at his former headmaster and said, "Sorry I was such an ass."

The still-standing Grimes smiled and retrieved his pipe from his desktop.

"I wish you well, Clyde," he said, placing the pipe between his teeth.

Jonathan slipped out the door and trod down the still hallway.

*Why would she not pay? It's not that she forgot. She took time to write letters about it.*

Jonathan made his way out of the building and across the campus. Having just eaten their breakfast, most of the boys were down at the field, playing an early morning game of cricket. He went there, but did not join the cheering crowd. Instead, he circled the field, his hands in his pockets.

*Who else knows of this?*

He glanced at the raucous group of boys who were presently hollering at the batter and the bowler. No knowing glances were thrown his way. A couple of teachers were present, just as rapt on the sport as the students.

"Oi! He's out of the crease, he is!" protested a voice.

"Hit his stumps! Hit his stumps!" hollered another.

There was the crack of the bat and the cork and leather ball sailed through the air.

*No one's thinking of me at all. Thank God.*

In the past, Jonathan had known of other students being dismissed for mysterious reasons, but it was something that he himself never expected to suffer.

*They'll all wonder why I'm packing my things. What will I say?*

Suddenly, Jonathan halted in his pacing.

*I won't wait until tomorrow. I'll go now. I'll go straight to London and ask the Lady what this is all about. She won't be able to fob me off in a letter if I'm standing right there before her.*

He nearly jogged to his room.

*But what of Hodges and Widdy? It wouldn't be right to just leave and not say anything.*

Opening the saddlebag in his closet, he saw a packet of gingerbread slices he had brought from Whitehall weeks earlier, nearly forgotten. The rich odor filled the room though the paper was secured tightly with twine.

He pulled the packet out and crossed the room to Widcombe's bed. Lifting the pillow, he shoved the package underneath and smoothed the bedclothes over all.

*I hope it's not green with mold when he opens it,* thought Jonathan, grinning. Sometimes the bread would keep for weeks and other times it wouldn't.

*What can I leave for Hodges?*

He thought for a moment, then grabbed his sketch book and a pencil before sitting on the bed. Beneath his skilled hand, an image of Widcombe clutching hefty slabs of something in both hands formed. The character's cheeks were full to capacity, and crumbs clung to his lips and chin as he appeared to be chewing vigorously. Beside him Jonathan drew Hodges, slight in comparison, his hands waving in the air. Over Hodges' head, he wrote:

Mind the mold, Widdy! You know what it did to your bowels last time!

*That's certain to amuse him,* he thought as he tore it carefully from the book.

He crossed the room and placed the paper under the pillow on Hodges's bed, the corner peeking out enough to declare its presence.

With his goodbyes said, Jonathan stuffed his remaining belongings into his bag, donned his riding coat and stood in the doorway. This was not the dormitory chamber he had always lived in, but he'd spent enough time in it to want to gaze at it for a moment before leaving.

*And now what am I to do with myself?* he thought, hoisting his heavy bag and heading outside.

On several occasions, he had pondered what his life would be like once he finished school, but never bothered to settle on anything because the future seemed so distant. Suddenly, it was here. Upon his father and elder brother's deaths, Jonathan had inherited the baronetcy, but that clarified only his place in society, not what his daily occupation ought to be.

*And what is the value in a mere title*?

In fact, to him, titles seemed pretentious, reminding him vaguely of the dormer windows of Whitehall which had fascinated him all those years ago. Fascinated him, that is, until he learned they served no real purpose.

*Truly, what does it matter that I am 'Sir Jonathan Charles Clyde, Bart.'? Nothing at all! Well, at least I escaped being called 'Sir William Walter Clyde the Fifth, Bart.' as the Lady wished.*

Jonathan shook his head, aggravated anew by his mother's vanity.

He was thankful that he had been born to a baronet and not a duke or an earl. Years earlier, the eldest son of a duke had bragged to his fellow Heath attendants that he would someday have a place in Parliament. Jonathan was unsure what this honor entailed, but he suspected it involved long hours of arguing with other men while wearing an ill-fitting wig.

*If that had been my fate, who knows what the Lady would have tried to wheedle me into? Not that I would have let her...*

Jonathan sighed as he resituated the bag on his shoulder.

*Well, surely the money will make its way here and I'll be back soon. I suppose if the Lady can't be bothered to pay my tuition then I could delve into the estate and do it myself. Or do I need to be twenty-one first? I wonder if she'll answer that question...or if she even knows the answer herself!*

Heavy clouds had blown in since the cricket game, blocking the sun. A cold wind blew. Jonathan secured his coat snuggly across his chest, pulled his hat down low over his ears, and headed to the stables.

*Wait.*

Jonathan paused next to Achilles' pen.

*I've never gone to London straight from school. Would I know the way?*

Vexatious memories of leaving Heath and getting lost on the open roads filled his mind.

*I don't want to go through that again. No. Instead, I'll head home, spend the night there and in the morning I'll head to London. Yes, I know the way from there.*

He climbed into the saddle and dug his heels into Achilles' sides.

*To Whitehall...*

# Hearing, Thinking, Feeling

~ PLOUGHMAN

There was the humming again. It would sound for a few seconds and then cease, only to begin again, unsteadily, then steadily, then stop.

But it was the pain that dragged Ploughman's mind to the surface as if emerging from a pool of thick murky water. The dull ache radiated from her belly up to her chest and simultaneously down to her groin.

*Ah, still here,* she thought, suddenly aware of the lumpy pillow under her very heavy head.

With her eyes closed, Ploughman heard, over the raspy sound of her own breathing, the hum sharpen into words, Foote's words.

"Ah, Joan. Joan..."

There were tears in the young woman's voice.

"I fear you can't hear me...I should have spoken sooner. You're a good woman, Joan. I know you were bullied by Cook and Smith, but you didn't let it sour you. Your sweet nature never faltered."

There was a slight pressure on the ailing woman's hand and then, Ploughman didn't know how, but Foote managed to pick the weighty thing up, and cradle it gently in her own.

"These hands," the voice said. "They've worked hard...so hard at cleaning up the filth of others...and polishing their vain treasures. You made their lives so much easier, so much better, and yet...here you are in a stuffy, smelly attic, slipping away."

*Ah, Foote,* the words formed slowly in Ploughman's haze, *but you have been so kind to me.*

The pain pulsated, insistent of its dominance.

"And where are they?" the voice continued, its edge growing hard. "Where are they? Those thoughtless fools! Off in London in their second house! Or off at a fine school where they're tended by others like you ...others like *us.*"

The voice broke and there was a stifled sob followed by a sniffle.

*Don't cry, Foote. There's pride in working hard, knowing you done a good job o' something.*

"But I know, Joan...although another is dusting their shelves and washing their spoons, *I know* that you are irreplaceable. *I know* that you deserve a comfortable bed in a well-aired room...a hot cup of tea with as much sugar and milk as you like."

Pleased and surprised, the elder woman's chest tightened. Since she was small, any time another seemed appreciative of her, an overwhelming sense of shy gladness would envelop her, constricting her breath. Even now in her prone, immobile state, she felt the warmly familiar sensation wash over her. She felt she was smiling, a gesture done without thought so many thousand times before, but she knew it had not reached her lips. Her tongue, leaden in her mouth, was cumbersome beyond all use to speak any words of thanks. All of this emotion and effort translated into a faint moan from her throat.

In the same instant, the ache in her abdomen grew sharper and the moan thickened into a groan that pushed past her unwieldy lips to escape.

The hand enfolding her own tightened.

"Joan?"

*Oh! Pain...*

Ploughman's eyes fluttered lightly for an instant and the right one remained open, a narrow slit.

*Ah, there you are, Foote.*

"Would you like some water?" the young woman asked, leaning in, her face lined with worry. She reached for something out of sight as Ploughman realized how completely dry her mouth was.

Her eye, unable to do otherwise, drifted shut again as the sensation of a damp rag cooled the corner of her mouth. Laboriously, she barely parted her lips and felt wetness drip in, the small amount pooling at the base of her throat. The liquid seemed to give her strength and she was able to swallow it.

She tried to moan her thanks, but pain seized her around the waist and twisted.

"Ughhh..." a strangled noise gurgled out of her, swelling as the pangs throbbed into a steady burning.

*Pain! Pain!*

Agony contorted her insides, spawning a guttural howl that split her in two as it exited her throat. Above her head, it hung, coiling eerily in the air.

It was followed by another.

# Explaining an Empty Stable

~ Hardy

*A hash of bacon and mash tonight at the Weary Lass*, thought Hardy, jingling the few coins in his breeches pocket as he rounded the corner of the stable block. *A pint of ale and all will be...*

*Sir Jonathan!*

The heir himself stood several yards away, holding the reins of his favorite horse and staring into the stable pens. All but one, which held Stag, were empty.

*Better say something.*

"Oi, Sir Jonathan. I weren't expecting to see you this day."

The young man turned, looking baffled.

"Hardy, where are Hunter and Speed?"

"Uhh, sold, sir...along with Rosefinch and Lynx, as I was told...."

"*Sold*?" The incredulous look on the baronet's face would have made Hardy laugh had he not known better.

*What? 'E don't know? Ahh, why must I be the one to tell 'im? Blast you, Lady!*

"Afore she left for London, Lady Clyde tol' me to sell 'em. Wait for a good buyer, she said, an' I did." The man stuck his chin out instinctively.

*Let 'im argue wi' that! I thought the plan was madness when I heard it, but no one asked me!*

"She told you to *sell* the horses?" Sir Jonathan asked again, his eyes wide.

"Aye, sir, and one of the carriages as well. Tha's what she tol' me to do and I was to send 'er the money but now that you're 'ere, I'll give it to you. The man came for 'em just this morning. I believe I gotta good price for 'em. The money's in my room."

*Don't dismiss me, sir. I just does what the bloody mistress says.* Hardy ran up the flight of stairs in the stable house and returned soon with a small bag, which he handed to the young man.

As if in a daze, the young man handed Achilles's reins over to Hardy and started for the front door, the little bag dangling from his hand.

Suddenly, he turned and called out, "For God's sake, Hardy, don't sell Achilles!"

Hardy wasn't sure if he was supposed to laugh at that or not, so he simply raised his hand in acknowledgement and led the horse away.

# Finding Foote with a File

~ Jonathan

Still confounded by the explanation for the nearly empty stable, Jonathan pushed the front door open where his attention was arrested by the filthiness of the entryway.

*What's all this then?*

Several sets of footprints, small and large, tracked across the floor, some leading to the large staircase and others making paths down the halls.

*Have we been overrun by fetid dwarves?*

"Hello!" he called.

There was no response from any quarter.

*Certainly there will be someone in or near the kitchen,* he thought, heading that way. Upon entering it, he tilted his head at the strange sight that greeted him. On the floor next to the oven was a mattress with two blankets balled up on top of it.

*Someone's sleeping in the kitchen?*

Looking around, he saw newly dirtied bowls on the table, scrapings of porridge still wet in their hollows.

*They were here this morning...*

Returning to the foyer, he ran up the stairs, hollering, "Is anyone here?"

Still nothing.

Throwing open the door to Elliott's room, he saw through dim light that it was tidy, eerily so. The curtains were drawn over the windows. The bed was made, though the pillow was gone. There were no playthings littering the floor. The fireplace looked as if it hadn't been used in weeks.

*Elliott...Did he go to London after I left for Heath? No, Sophia would have mentioned him in her last letter.*

*Elliott!*

Jonathan ran from room to room, throwing open every door. Each room was as cold and empty as the last. Not a single fire burned.

He bolted down the staircase to continue his frantic hunt on the lower story.

*I thought he'd be safe here! Where the bloody hell is...*

*...what? What's this?*

His hand still clutching the doorknob, Jonathan froze, his mouth agape.

Inside his father's old study, every drawer and cupboard was opened. Their contents were strewn about the room, haphazardly. In the midst of the extreme disarray was the most bizarre sight of all.

Before a cabinet, stood a woman who appeared to be prying open its door, or attempting to anyway.

Her back was to him as she agitatedly dug a file into the lock, murmurs of frustration exiting her lips. Meeting with no results, she stuck it into a crevice and pushed on the little lever, groaning with the effort.

*A burglar?*

Jonathan rushed into the room, hollering, "Away from there!"

The woman turned, dropping the file. Her strained face flashed from terror to elation as she beheld the man before her.

"Sir Jonathan!" she cried, her hands flying to her joyous face.

"Foote?"

"Oh, thank God! Thank God! Thank God!" She ran to him and clutched at the front of his coat. "Hurry, you've got to find it!"

Jonathan said nothing, stupefied by the proximity of a young woman grabbing onto him in such an unreserved manner. Though tear tracks stained her cheeks and her eyelids were swollen, there was an earthy authenticity about her that was nothing less than stunning. Her tousled hair, freed from the ubiquitous mob-cap was beautiful in a wild sort of way and her face was animated like he had never seen it before. Gone was the required restraint that she had always maintained in his presence. Here before him was not a curried, proper servant, but a genuine young woman clothed with ivory flesh that coursed with blood.

"Please! Where is it?" she begged, her teeth glinting just beyond her reddish lips.

Jonathan tore his eyes away from her face and asked in a slightly strangled voice, "Where's what?"

"The laudanum! Oh, please. It's Ploughman. She's crying out in pain and I can't bear it!" Her eyes bore intently into his own, her hands regrasping at the folds of cloth on his chest.

"Wha...what's happened to Ploughman?" he stuttered.

*Get ahold of yourself!* he urged himself. *Are you not a man?*

Squaring his shoulders, he grabbed her hands and pulled her down into a chair, then knelt in front of her. "Now...start from the beginning."

Visibly a little calmer, the maid breathed deeply and replied, "Ploughman became ill after the Lady left for London. It wasn't long before she could not leave her bed. Now she can barely communicate, but this afternoon she awoke, screaming in pain. Please, Sir Jonathan, I've been looking for the laudanum ever since. She needs relief. Please..."

The memory of Smith stretching out her narrow hand to give him a key entered Jonathan's mind.

"Yes...yes, I know where it is. Go to Ploughman. I will bring it immediately."

He felt her hands tighten around his fingers and she panted slightly, still winded, but it was the look on her face that took his breath away.

She smiled at him as no one ever had, as he had never known a young woman could. It was a smile full of joy and appreciation, tinged with ecstatic relief.

Relief that, he knew, he alone was responsible for.

"Thank you," she breathed and smiled for a moment longer, then stood, loosening her hands from his grip.

Slightly recovered, Jonathan recalled something else of great importance.

"And where is Elliott?" he asked, watching her move quickly toward the door.

She stopped and turned back to him. The look of shocked realization on her face told him that she had no idea.

"Never mind. I'm sure he's fine," he said, waving her on. "Go to Ploughman."

# Dispensing Laudanum

~ LYDIA

As Lydia returned to the small attic room, the answer to Jonathan's question was there before her. Sitting on the frame of the bed she had shared with Wells for many months, and then with Ploughman, was Elliott. Though it was late afternoon, he still wore his night clothes and his hair was decidedly unkempt.

The room stank of urine and unwashed human flesh, but this seemed to have no effect on the young boy who was peering fixedly at the prone figure in the other bed.

"Why's she thrashing about like that?" he whispered upon seeing Lydia, his eyes wide.

"She's in a lot of pain." Lydia bit her lip, her eyes welling, and silently prayed for the discovery of the laudanum. She sat down on the wooden slat next to the little boy, pulling him onto her lap. They gazed at the old woman in silence.

*At least she's not howling now,* thought Lydia as a low moan escaped Ploughman's lips. Lydia reached for her hand.

"He's looking, Joan. He's looking for the laudanum."

Just then she heard a masculine voice call out from below stairs, "Hello! Where are you?"

"Jonathan?" Elliott asked, sitting up straight. "Jonathan!"

The little boy hurried off, his bare feet padding loudly on the hall floor and down the stairs. In a moment, Jonathan's form filled the doorway as he handed over the sought after bottle with its accompanying cup.

Lydia measured out a dose and held it to the agonized woman's lips, pouring it as slowly as possible into the lax mouth. A thin trickle ran down the cheek to the pillow, and Lydia wiped it with her sleeve.

"There." She watched as Ploughman's head tilted to the side and her wheezing stilled to a slow, steady breath.

She capped the bottle and placed it on the little table next to the ewer.

"What are you doing here?" Elliott asked his brother. "Mama's not here as well, is she?"

Lydia started.

*Yes, what* is *he doing here?* A sick sensation filled her stomach. *Is the Lady here?*

"No, I came from Heath. Come, Elliott."

"Where are we going?"

"Ploughman needs to rest."

The little boy sighed. "Alright. It stinks in here anyway."

The two Clydes exited the room.

*Stinks? Well yes, it would. I suppose I could clean a bit now that Joan is resting peacefully.*

Lydia busied herself, but her cleaning was limited since the worst stench arose from the bedclothes and mattress underneath Joan.

When Lydia rose from a crouching position, she was suddenly lightheaded and gripped the side of the bed to keep herself from falling over.

*Have I eaten today?* she wondered and then was struck by a new thought.

*Sir Jonathan will be expecting dinner! As if it wasn't hard enough to keep Hardy, Elliott and myself fed, and now there's a hungry young man who is used to fine dining for every meal!*

She sighed heavily, and surveyed Joan's sleeping figure one last time before turning to leave.

As she descended the stairs, she was met by a warm and inviting scent. Arriving in the kitchen, she saw Jonathan and Elliott kneeling by the fire.

*Oh, why is he here? This is* my *room. Can't he go inhabit one of his many fine salons or drawing rooms...?*

The thought caught in Lydia's brain as she recalled the filthy state of those areas of the house.

*Well, I've had no time for cleaning!* she thought, indignantly.

"Is it ready?" Elliott was bouncing up and down.

"Nearly. Just wait," replied his brother.

*What's he doing?* Lydia wondered as she washed her hands in the basin.

Jonathan lifted a long handled toasting frame out of the fireplace.

*He knows how to toast bread?* The smell of it filled her nostrils and her mouth began to water.

"Careful!" Jonathan warned and held the frame out of Elliott's reach, carrying it to the wooden table.

Deftly, he popped it open with a knife and dropped its contents onto a plate.

Glancing at it, Lydia saw that it was not ordinary toast. There were two pieces of bread and between them was a blob of pale yellow goo.

*Melted cheese!*

She tore her eyes away from the delectable sight and began to peel a potato.

*So Sir Jonathan can make Welsh Rarebit! I've never seen that done in a toasting frame before. Where did he learn that?* Lydia's stomach rumbled.

"Normally I'd make you wait to eat until the others are made," Jonathan told his brother, "but it's best warm, so you may begin. But don't moan about how good it is or you'll make us all jealous, and I'll have to take it away from you."

*You understand jealousy?* Lydia thought sourly as she lifted the cabbage that would make the bulk of her own dinner onto the cutting board.

Mere steps away, Elliott stood at the wooden table and took his first crunchy bite.

Jonathan placed another slice of bread in the toasting frame, followed by thick slices of cheese and topped them with another piece of bread.

"Mmmm, Pony, this is even better than your rolls. It's so..." he stopped, a bit of yellowish grease dripping from the corner of his mouth, his eyes wide. "Sorry...I forgot."

Jonathan chuckled as he walked toward the fire once again. "Learning how to toast a bit of cheese and bread over the fire in a dormitory is, perhaps, the most vital bit of education that all my years at Heath afforded me."

*Schoolboys, cooking?*

Lydia chopped a few carrots, thinking of how little they would improve the thin soup. Her stomach grumbled again. It was already dinner time and it would be at least an hour before the simple meal was ready.

"Can I have another?" Elliott asked, wiping his hands on his breeches.

"You're the only one who has had even one so far," Jonathan said as he crouched by the fire, slowly turning the handle of the frame. A drop of melted cheese fell from the bread and hissed in the fire.

*They could at least take their torturous rarebit elsewhere,* thought Lydia as she breathed in the thick scent of the burning cheese and headed outside to the well with an empty pot.

*And what's this?*

Against the well was propped her mattress. The two blankets were draped over the nearby wood pile.

Suddenly horrified, Lydia wondered, *What must he think of a mattress in the kitchen? Yet, he saw Ploughman himself. He couldn't expect me to sleep there! Oh! What would he think of Elliott sleeping in the kitchen...and on a corner of the* same *mattress? Oh the decorum of these monied fools!*

*Doesn't he realize how impossible it is to tend to a very ill woman and a little boy and keep a palatial home clean, all single-handedly?*

Ready to speak plainly if spoken to, Lydia returned to the kitchen with the heavy pot, the front of her apron sloshed with cold well water.

Jonathan was no longer hovering near the stove when she entered, so she put the pot on the grate and stoked the fire beneath.

Returning to the cutting board, she saw that there on a plate, next to her neat pile of chopped carrots was the second finished rarebit.

*How thoughtless to put it there.*

Tears stung the corners of her eyes. She grabbed a peeled onion and began to chop it into little pieces, hoping that it could be blamed for her watering eyes if they were noticed.

Jonathan stood nearby preparing a third for the toasting process.

"It's best warm, Pony. You ought to eat it now." Elliott stood near, looking longingly at the coveted cheese and bread.

*Steady your voice,* Lydia told herself. As cheerfully as she could, she said, "I don't believe that's intended for me, Master Elliott."

"Jonathan said I mustn't touch it because it was yours."

*What?* Lydia paused in her onion dicing and glanced at Jonathan's crouching back as he held the laden frame over the flames.

"Oh, I think you are mistaken, Master Elliott. Servants serve their employers, not the other way around."

Her mouth nearly dripped as she spoke.

"Hmmm," Jonathan said, still facing the fire. "Then I guess I shall have to dismiss you and then rehire you once you've swallowed the last bite. Really Foote, for such a clever person, you can be rather thick at times. Please, eat your dinner."

Lydia stood stunned for a moment, then reached for the cheesy bread.

"Thank you, sir," she mumbled lamely before lifting it to her mouth. It was warm to the touch and crunched loudly as her teeth bit into it. Hot, salty goo oozed onto her tongue as she forced herself to chew each bite several times before swallowing.

*Eat it slowly,* she told herself as she felt her mouth taking larger and larger bites. *And don't lick your fingers! Mmm...*

She pushed the last bit of crust into her mouth and wiped her hands on her apron.

By the time Lydia had dumped all of the soup ingredients into the big pot, Jonathan was cutting at the long crusty loaf on the table again.

Elliott bounced up and down at the table. "I'm still hungry, Jonathan!"

His brother cleared his throat affectedly and replied in a high falsetto, "Only polite young gentlemen are rewarded here, sir."

Elliott giggled. "Please, Miss Gloriana, may I have another?"

"Very well, sir. Just give me a moment." Jonathan's voice dropped to its usual register as he glanced in Lydia's direction. "And you, Foote, would you care for another?"

She nearly declined, but as she eyed the large block of cheese that he was now deftly slicing, Lydia instead replied, "Yes, please."

"Oh," he said off-handedly, "and I'll bring the mattress back in later. I kept tripping over it on my way to the fire."

"Thank you, sir."

*That's thoughtful of him,* Lydia thought, recalling the tears that threatened to flow only moments earlier.

*And he found the laudanum for Joan.*

# Observing, Determining

~ LYDIA

The breath laboriously rattled in and out of dying lungs. Each time she came to check on her, Lydia wondered if she had heard Ploughman's final draw at life, only to be startled by another dry, raspy intake.

Attentively, she watched the movements of the declining figure. If they were fitful, she would slowly pour a small amount of laudanum past the chapped lips, praying for relief. It was only once she noticed that Ploughman had lost the ability to swallow that she stopped dosing her.

*Oh God, please let the end be near. Please.*

To pray for another's death was something Lydia had never supposed she would do, but now she did so fervently.

The near-corpse before her had not mouthed a single word for several days and the eyes had not opened in two. She studied Ploughman's loose flesh, mottled and thin, hanging from its framework like worn out cloth. The mouth hung unabashedly open. The arms lay inert at her sides. Only the chest betrayed the presence of frail life as it rose and fell unevenly.

Gently patting the old woman's shoulder, Lydia leaned in and whispered in her ear, "I'll be back to check on you in a little while, Joan."

She straightened up and studied the unresponsive face, finding no evidence of understanding.

*A difficult life lived quietly, without complaint...*

*...and without notice.*

*No one came to see her.*

Lydia thought of the letter she'd sent to Joash Ploughman, never having received any sort of response.

Surveying the small room, Lydia rested her eyes on the little cupboard, thinking of how it held the slip of paper upon which she herself had written 'Joan Ploughman'.

*And so her few treasures will be tossed into the fire, cleared away to make room for the next maid.*

*Oh...*

The thought caught Lydia with its sharpness.

*I'm the next maid.*

Lydia's eyes welled with tears, her stomach churning as she stared at the fading life before her.

*Will that be* me *in forty years? After toiling ceaselessly, will I flicker out in this room, neglected and forgotten?*

Her throat ached with strain.

*No.*

*No, I can't.*

*I won't.*

She thought for a moment longer as she dried her eyes.

*I won't let myself.*

# Thinking in High German

~ HELDMANN
AN INN NEAR PLIMBRIDGE

The man from Hamburg looked down at his plate with disgust. Blood pooled in its base, oozing from the bit of beef, staining the accompanying cabbage and potatoes. His language skills had failed him again.

*Why can I not learn how to say such a simple phrase as 'cooked thoroughly' in English?*

The fellow next to him at the bar cast him a distrusting glance.

Shifting uneasily, Heldmann picked up his fork and began to poke at the meal before him.

*And to think how proud I felt when Father chose me—*me *of all his sons!*

*"Herman," he said, "you are gifted in language. You will go to England and learn all you can about the Herefords. Return with all of this knowledge and our herd will prosper."*

*What a grand adventure for me, the finest linguist of the Heldmann family! Or so I thought!*

He recalled trying not to grin jubilantly in front of Franz and Karl. They, too, had wanted to be chosen, and he had pitied them.

A bark of bitter laughter escaped his lips as he continued to stab at the beef before him.

The look of distrust his bar-mate cast him now hardened into one of disdain with a visible curling of the lip.

Embarrassed, Heldmann cleared his throat and put down his fork.

*Yet another foul meal in a lonely little town, surrounded by strangers who would have no interest in talking with me, even if they could.*

*In the cities it is better—well not much, but any improvement is noticeable. There you can find people who don't look at you as if you're insane when you open your mouth to babble out bits of their confounded tongue. And there was that one man—in Cambridge—who actually spoke German!*

He recalled how beautiful the man's heavily accented voice had sounded, spilling out from underneath his frothy mustache. They had talked of the weather and directions to an hostelry, only for a few moments, yet it had lifted Heldmann's spirits invaluably.

*Yes, near a university, one is likely to encounter people who are familiar with different languages.*

*But the Herefords are not at the universities! They are on farms dotting the countryside, which are inhabited by men who look right through you at best, or glare at you crossly if the wind is blowing the wrong way.*

Heldmann spooned a few diced potatoes off the top of the pile where the blood had not defiled them. He chewed the dry mouthful and stared out the window at the falling snow.

*I may be stuck here for days.*

He took a sip of ale from his mug.

Not even the roaring fire in the inn's fireplace seemed cheerful.

*Although, I believe I'm not far from...*

*No, I couldn't go back there. I disgraced myself the last time.*

*But it's only a few miles from here and he did ask me to stay...It can't be worse than what I'm facing here.*

Heldmann poked uneasily at the chunk of meat, wondering at the amount of gristle it contained. With a weary sigh, he stood, and tossed a couple of coins on the table next to his heaped plate. After draining his mug, he lifted his saddle bag, stepped outside, and went to the stable in search of his horse.

# Entscheidung zu Besuchen

~ Elliott

*If it stops soon, we can play in it before nightfall.*

Elliott stared out at the falling snow, shivering. It was very cold in the foyer away from the fireplace, but he'd never seen it snow like this, settling onto the stretch of lawn and the entryway's windows provided the best view. Large flakes drifted down from leaden skies to rest upon the green blades.

Just then, Elliott was startled by a man rushing up the steps to the front door. His face was wound around with a heavy scarf. A hat was pulled low and his long riding coat was secured tightly around his middle. He reached for the bell pull but Elliott swung the door open before the man could give it a tug.

"Hallo," the visitor said, uncertainly.

"Who are you?" Elliott asked as he examined the collection of snowflakes clinging to the man's clothing.

Surprise registered in the eyes of the newcomer as a hand gripped Elliott from behind.

"Invite him in, Elliott." Jonathan said, towering above him. "There will be time for questions once he's out of the cold."

Elliott held the door firmly. "But what if it's Napoleon? He escaped from Elba, you know."

Jonathan threw his head back and laughed out loud, pushing the door wide to admit the visitor, of whom he asked, "Parlez-vous Francais, Monsieur?"

It wasn't often Elliott succeeded in making his brother laugh like that and he wasn't sure how he did it this time but he felt quite proud nonetheless.

"Herr Clyde. Danke. Danke," the man responded, pulling the scarf from his face revealing a nose, red with the cold.

"Herr Heldmann! Come in to the parlour by the fire! Imagine seeing you here on a day like today! We never have snow like this! But what of your horse? Certainly you didn't walk here? Your horse?" Jonathan looked around.

"Mine horse...mmm...I give to man in...mmm...barn." Heldmann removed his coat and shook it, sending a flurry of snowflakes up around him.

"You've given it to Hardy, have you? Well, I hope he doesn't sell it."

"What you say?" asked Heldmann, his brow furrowed.

"Oh, nothing, nothing at all." Jonathan ushered the man to the parlor's fireplace and hung his outer garments on the coat rack.

"Ja, das ist gut," said the man, stretching his bare fingers toward the flames, a smile lifting his pinkened cheeks.

Elliott studied him carefully. *He doesn't look strange, but what's wrong with his mouth? It moves funny and his words are ever so odd.*

"This is my brother, Elliott," Jonathan said to the man, waving his hand in Elliott's direction.

The man turned his attention to the boy.

"I am nice to...mmm...meet you, Elliott," said the man, bowing his head and offering his hand. "My...mmm...name is Hermann Heldmann."

*This must be one of the 'idiots' that Jonathan talks about,* Elliott reasoned. *I've always wondered what they look like.*

Elliott studied the man's face which was bordered with ample dark blonde sideburns. His thick lips were red, and wavy hair was plastered to his head from much hat wearing.

"Elliott, don't forget your manners. Shake hands," said Jonathan.

*What does an idiot's hand feel like?* Elliott slowly brought his hand up as he continued to study the smiling face.

*Hmm, cold and big.*

"What brings you here? Ah, but first, you'll need a hot drink," Jonathan said, reaching for the bell pull. Then he invited Heldmann to sit on the settee and the two began to talk.

*Why must there always be talking*? thought Elliott, walking over to a window. *Nothing's as boring as talking.*

The snowfall had lessened. The sun hinted at shining through the clouds, illuminating the blanket of snow that lay, blunting all the familiar edges of Whitehall's grounds.

"Jonathan?" Elliott turned from the window. "Jonathan, can we go outside now?"

His older brother paused in his conversation and replied, "Soon, Elliott. But you're not even ready yet. Go don your warmest clothes."

At this, Elliott tore out of the room and up the stairs to his bedroom.

Shivering in the unheated room, he pulled open his armoire, and began to lift out clothing he didn't remember ever wearing. Item after item, he threw to the ground, looking for what he deemed to be the warmest.

Once outfitted, he realized, *Pony will need something as well, but none of my clothes would fit her. I know!*

Now ungainly in his thick layers, Elliott rushed down the hall to his sister's room.

*Where is Sophia's brown mantle?*

He opened the armoire and pushed past the gowns that hung there. A heavy white fold of cloth peeked out at him from among the many garments pressed together. It was embroidered with little blue flowers. The sight of it stirred a memory in his mind.

*We were outside somewhere and we were walking on a gravel path. There were tall trees all around. I could see my breath and tried to catch it with my hand. I told Sophia I was cold. She picked me up and wrapped the edges of this around us both. It was warm and the fur tickled my nose. Then we went inside a large hall. Mama was there with a lot of other people and she told Sophia not to carry me in such a manner.*

Elliott tugged on it. It remained in place, so he gave it a terrific yank. Unconcerned by the short ripping sound he heard, he smiled as it fell into his arms.

*Yes, this can keep Pony warm.*

He fled the room with the surprisingly heavy garment and flew back to the parlor.

*I hope they're not* still *talking.*

The parlour door was open and Pony was inside with the men, collecting sullied teacups.

"Is it time yet?" Elliott asked, panting from his haste.

"Yes, I believe it is," replied Jonathan. "Herr Heldmann, would you care to join us outside for a bit of snow play?"

Heldmann looked confused, staring at Jonathan's mouth. "Mmm...Please forgive?"

"Do you want to come with us," Jonathan pointed at himself and Elliott, "outside," he pointed out the window where the thin sunlight was now wanly shining, "to play in the snow?" He mimed throwing a snowball.

"Ahh, yes. Yes, I like." The man stood.

"Look what I brought for you, Pony." Elliott held up his find proudly.

The maid, whose hands were full with a serving tray, tilted her head questioningly at the boy.

"For when we go outside."

"That is a very lovely cloak, Elliott, but I fear it isn't mine and therefore, I cannot wear it."

"Sophia won't mind. She never wears it anymore."

"Thank you very much, Master Elliott, but I'm afraid it wouldn't be proper."

"Proper? I hate proper!" Elliott dropped the cloak and folded his arms, scowling.

*She doesn't want to play with us. It won't be as fun without her.*

"The girl...mmm...need...a mantle for...mmm...warm?" asked Heldmann, his eyebrows lifted. He walked to where his own riding coat hung on the coat rack and felt it.

"Good. Is no more...water." He held it out to the young woman. "For you. I...mmm...commands."

She stood frozen with the tea tray.

*The idiot is going to get Pony outside with us*! Elliott thought, happily. "I commands, too, Pony."

"Master Elliott and Herr Heldmann seem to insist that you come with us, Foote."

"Sir Jonathan, it isn't proper for a servant to wear the coat of one of Whitehall's guests."

"Of course, you are right, Foote. Therefore, I must relieve you of your position of maid at Whitehall. Henceforth, you shall be a guest who kind-heartedly does everything for everyone and is thanked with a bit of money. Now, please, don the coat."

"But what will he wear if I'm wearing his?"

Jonathan shrugged. "He will wear...*my* coat and I will wear..." Jonathan leaned over and retrieved Sophia's girlish cloak from the floor "...this!"

He dramatically flung the cloak over his shoulders and secured the ties at his neck.

Everyone laughed as he pulled the hood up, his thin, boyish face framed with the soft white fur.

"Wunderbar!" exclaimed Heldmann, grinning broadly.

"You look funny, Jonathan." Elliott continued to giggle.

Jonathan stuck his lower lip out sadly. "I was hoping to look beautiful. Never mind." He dramatically pointed out the window. "There are snowballs to be thrown!"

# Plotting Escape

~ Lydia

Lydia watched from the parlour window as the three males ran around below on a field of white. The white fur cape flew out dramatically behind Sir Jonathan as he careened about, dodging frozen missiles.

Lydia smiled.

She had remained outside with them just long enough to see that Elliott was happily preoccupied, and then excused herself to resume her inside duties.

*Who is this odd fellow?* she wondered, gazing down at the tall blonde visitor. *Good thing he didn't arrive four days ago...*

After Joan's soul had finally departed, her body had been laid to rest in the section of the churchyard where there were no headstones.

*Even in death she's in the servants' quarters*, Lydia had thought, thinking that Joan would have appreciated the thought as a joke, though the fact genuinely bothered Lydia.

She turned her attention back to the newly arrived guest.

*He is German for certain, but why is he here? And how does he know Sir Jonathan? Perhaps he's the son of a Bavarian noble come to visit some of England's finest?*

Just then, the man in question was pelted with an especially large snowball, directly in the face. He roared with feigned rage, his breath a frozen cloud above him, and chased after a fleeing Elliott. Sassy barked excitedly at his heels.

Lydia smiled again.

*He doesn't seem pretentious in the least.*

Looking down, she realized she was still wearing the man's coat. She examined the thick brown cloth of the arm. It was good, durable stuff, meant for warmth and practicality, not thin and shiny like that of more fashionable garments.

*It looks like something a farmer might wear*, thought Lydia. *A well-off farmer.*

A thought stirred in her mind.

*He's young--maybe a few years older than Sir Jonathan--probably not married. Hmmm...*

*Ugh! What am I thinking? I'm no Delilah!*

But then, an image that had recently been seared into Lydia's memory flooded her mind once again. Days earlier, while the gravedigger was carrying Joan's emaciated body down the stairs, he hadn't had the sense to adjust the stiff figure in his arms while coming through the door. The cloth-bound head had clipped the top of the doorframe. Even now, the knocking sound it had made echoed in Lydia's mind.

"Mind her head!" Lydia had snapped, tears springing to her eyes.

"Sorry, Miss," the stocky man had replied, resituating his hold on the rigid form. "I doubt she minds much, though."

"Well, I do!" Lydia had retorted, holding the table to steady herself as she realized, *And I'm the only one who does.*

Recalling this all with a lump in her throat, Lydia hugged the German's coat tightly about her, staring blankly out the window.

In that moment, the visitor looked up toward her and waved, his nose and cheeks pinked by the chill.

She smiled delicately, and lifted her hand in response though she stepped away from the window. A nearby mirror on the wall caught her eye. Moving toward it, she examined herself in the winter afternoon sunlight.

She had thought herself pretty once. Now she wasn't so sure.

*This stupid cap is no help*, she thought, removing the pins that held it in place. Lifting it off of her head, she turned side to side, evaluating herself from various angles. Tugging little locks of hair free from the tight knot above her nape, she smoothed them to frame her face.

*Hmph.* She smirked at her reflection. *A bit better, I suppose.*

*And what impressive meal will you serve to dazzle the fellow and secure his affection? A pot of cabbage soup, perhaps? Maybe Sir Jonathan would be willing to make some rarebit and you can pass it off as your own cookery.*

Giving herself one last appraising look, she sighed and headed for the kitchen.

On the way there, she slipped into the library to retrieve something she had dusted many times, but never opened.

Minutes later she was measuring flour into a bowl on the table with *Fluegel's English-German Dictionary* splayed open beside it.

# Listening to Broken English

~ JONATHAN

The oil in the *magic lantern* was running low. It had burned brightly while Jonathan showed Heldmann the pictures of England's greatest sights--the most common after-dark entertainment for guests of the Clyde Family--but now its light was beginning to dim, dulling the edges of the shadow puppets Heldmann was casting on the salon's wall.

Elliott sat, raptly watching as a raven with outstretched wings transformed into a barking dog before him. The formerly roaring fire on the hearth had died down to a glowing pile of embers, occasionally crackling.

Spent physically from multiple snowball battles, and mentally from trying to converse with Heldmann, Jonathan was sunk deeply into the settee, a pillow under his head. Through barely opened eyes, he watched the dancing shadows.

"Hmm, it's a butterfly," commented Jonathan, watching the shadow wings flap.

"Schmetterling," murmured Heldmann, his forehead wrinkled in concentration as his hands worked in front of him.

"Do the dog again," demanded Elliott.

"Hmm?" asked the tall blonde man, turning to him.

"The dog. Woof woof!"

"Ah. Der Hund." Heldmann was quick to oblige the little boy.

The salon opened and Foote entered to stand before Jonathan, her hands clasped in front of her.

"I've prepared the room overlooking the maze for your guest. Will there be anything else, sir?"

*I suppose I ought to sit up while addressing her...but I'm so comfortable...*

"No, thank you." Jonathan waved his hand toward an empty chair. "Sit and enjoy the nighttime spectacle known as 'Heldmann's Hands'."

"No, thank you, sir. I'd prefer to be excused."

"Pony, he can do the most amazing things! Watch!" said Elliott, then turning to the German, "Der Hund! Der Hund!"

"Elliott, say 'please'." Jonathan murmured.

The young woman remained standing as she turned to watch the much appreciated dog silhouette. Jonathan observed her profile. A small smile curled the edges of her lips though her shoulders sagged.

*She looks weary. She's worked hard today. Her profile is quite pretty...*

Lost in his observation, Jonathan suddenly realized that she had turned back to him.

"Would you like me to put Master Elliott to bed?"

"No, no." Jonathan waved his hand lazily. "Go to your well-earned rest. I will see him to bed. Good night, Foote.

"But I don't want to go to bed! Heldmann, teach me how to do that." Elliott held his hands out to the man, palms up.

"Good night," Foote said, curtseying to Jonathan and then to the others.

"Guten nacht," said Heldmann, rather loudly.

Then she was gone.

Through his heavy eyelids, Jonathan gazed at the door through which she had just disappeared, her footsteps growing fainter as she made her way down the hall.

"Nein, nein. Tun Sie es wie das," Heldmann twisted Elliott's little hands and arms into an awkward shape. The resultant shadow was a malformed dog looming on the wall above them.

"Ja. Das ist gut."

Elliott beamed as he opened and closed his 'dog's' mouth. "Woof. Woof."

"Herr Clyde?" Heldmann asked.

"Hmmm?" murmured Jonathan, his eyelids growing heavier.

"Mmmm...who is her?"

"Pardon me?" asked Jonathan, his eyes now closing.

"Who is...mmm... she?" Heldmann pointed in the direction Foote had left.

Jonathan was suddenly awake. "Foote? She's Foote."

"Yes, but...who? She is your...sister? Your...woman?"

Jonathan laughed aloud, sitting up on the settee. "She isn't my *woman.*"

He laughed again, feeling pleased, though warm in the face.

Heldmann was looking intently at him, leaning forward, his elbows on his knees.

*Good God, he's really waiting for an answer. Who is she? Isn't that clear?*

"Foote," Jonathan began in the slow clear way he had adopted while trying to communicate with the German, "is a *servant.*"

"A servant?" It was clear Heldmann was not familiar with the word.

"Yes, she's a maid. She cooks and... umm...cleans things." Jonathan lifted a polished stone from the table next to him and mimed dusting underneath and around it.

Heldmann looked about dubiously. Even in the dim light, one could see the thick layer of dust on everything within the room. Bits of bark and broken twigs littered the carpet in front of the fireplace. Chair cushions were shifted awkwardly in their places.

Jonathan fumbled for an explanation. "Well, she hasn't been cleaning lately. There's been far too much to do with feeding us and caring for another of our maids who just died. She's had much more than her share to tend to with the..." Jonathan stopped, seeing that Heldmann was understanding nothing. He began again, slowly. "She is a...servant...to my family."

Heldmann nodded, his face serious. "I thinks she is...wise and...kindness and..."

As Heldmann's cumbersome praise spilled out, Jonathan shifted uncomfortably on the settee.

*What do you know of her? You've only just met her.*

"May I...mmm...writes missives...to Foote?"

*You want to exchange letters with her? To what end?* Jonathan wondered if the anger he felt growing inside him was apparent on his face.

*Stuff it. He means no harm. He's asking politely.*

*No.*

"Well, Heldmann," Jonathan paused, taking a deep breath. He leaned forward, his elbows on his knees, his eyes boring into those of the enquiring man. "It might not look good for Foote if she was to receive letters from a guest of my family. People might begin to say things about her that are not true and it might be difficult for her to..."

There was confusion in the eyes of the German.

*Ugh, he has no idea what I'm saying.* Jonathan shook his head firmly and said slowly, "No. Please forgive."

His mouth bent into a smile that he did not feel as he shrugged his shoulders.

Heldmann smiled slightly in return and nodded his head. "I...I understands."

An uncomfortable silence fell in the room.

*Why should I dislike the notion so? He's a decent fellow. His interest in her could actually be to her benefit.*

*But with a mind like hers...to be wasted on this big, stuttering blonde?*

*Yet, isn't her mind presently being wasted as she slaves away in Whitehall's kitchen and parlors? If he has regard for her, it's for her to decide how to respond...*

Jonathan sat with that thought for a moment as Heldmann cast another shadow on the wall.

He nearly opened his mouth to retract his quashing of the plan to exchange letters, but something held him back.

*No. As I told him, it wouldn't be appropriate. In her position, she might feel compelled to respond in a way that is contrary to her true feelings. Hmm...yes, I hardly know the man...and as her employer, I need to protect her from improper advances.*

*Yes. That is right.*

Feigning a jaw splitting yawn, Jonathan announced, "It is late. Shall I show you to your room?"

He stood and motioned toward the door, a strange tightness in his chest. "Come along, Elliott."

"But he hasn't shown me how to make the butterfly!"

"Another time, perhaps." Jonathan put out the light in the Carcel lamp and lifted a lit taper in its silver holder to illuminate their steps to the bedrooms.

"But he's leaving tomorrow!"

"Quiet, Elliott!" Jonathan snapped, a little too sharply. "This way, please, Heldmann."

# Seeking, Finding

~ Lydia

"But you promised!" whined the little boy.

"I said that if I finished with the potatoes then I would, but I haven't yet." Lydia didn't bother trying to hide her irritation.

*I have a job to do, not that that's something you will* ever *understand.*

"Write three more sentences and maybe we'll finish at the same time."

The pencil Elliott had been using remained on the table as he folded his arms across his chest. "I won't do it."

The door opened and in stepped Sir Jonathan. Saying nothing, he walked over to the table and sat down near Elliott, his long legs jutting out into the walkway.

*Oh, good,* thought Lydia, focusing again on peeling the potatoes on the plate before her. *Maybe* he *will entertain Elliott now.*

Glancing his way, Lydia saw that he looked thoughtful, distracted. Her spot at the table allowed her to observe him inconspicuously. She took advantage of the moment by examining him more attentively than usual, feeling that she rarely got to look at him as carefully as she wanted to.

He was tall and lanky, though not in a scarecrow-like way like so many youths. His dark hair hung almost shaggily into his eyes when he leaned forward. His eyes were grayish blue and he had a very nice nose, well-shaped and masculine without being too large. His chin was the least favorable of his features, being a little weak.

*He would do well to grow a beard,* thought Lydia. *On second thought, no he wouldn't.* She smiled at the idea of Jonathan with a face hairier than Herr Heldmann's.

"Hmph!" Elliott rearranged his folded arms demonstratively, tossing his head.

"Well, what ruinous occurrence has marred your day, Sir Surly?" Jonathan asked, turning to his brother.

"Pony says I must write out three more sentences before we play hide-and-seek. I've already written out seven. The paper will hardly hold more." He pushed the sheet across the table to Jonathan, who picked it up and examined it.

"Nicely done, Elliott. When did you learn how to write like this?"

"I've been having lessons ever since Mama and Sophia left."

"This is your doing, I presume?" Jonathan asked, turning to Lydia.

"It was Hardy's," Lydia joked, happy to see amusement in his eyes in response.

*I had to do* something *to keep him occupied,* thought Lydia. *Besides, a boy his age ought to have some schooling. When was the Lady planning on educating him, I wonder?*

"Show me another," Jonathan said to Elliott. "Write about how you smashed a German warrior in the face with a snowball."

The boy smiled smugly, picking up his pencil and asked, "How do you spell 'warrior'?"

His brother answered him and then coached him through two more sentences.

*Nicely done, yourself, sir,* thought Lydia as she finished dicing the last potato and dropping it into the baking dish. She placed the lid over the top and pushed the whole thing into the hot oven.

"And now, I am finished as well," she announced.

"Wunderbar!" Elliott exclaimed, jumping up from the table.

*Herr Heldmann has left his mark.*

Lydia exchanged a quick smile with Jonathan.

"You're the seeker, Pony! Count to one hundred, and don't listen to my footsteps!" he called over his shoulder as he fled the kitchen.

Left alone with Jonathan, Lydia felt uneasy as she always did in those rare moments when Elliott was not nearby. This wasn't helped by the sense of foolishness she felt at playing such a childish game.

"What are the rules?" Jonathan asked.

"Excuse me?"

"Are there places I'm not allowed to hide?"

"Oh, you're going to play, as well?" she asked, laughing. The idea thrilled her, though it increased her uneasiness.

*At least we'll both be foolish.*

She cleared her throat. "Well, I've told him he can't hide in any of the bedrooms except his own, and of course the servants' quarters is off-limits."

"Very well, and where is 'safe'?"

"Right here where I shall count." She motioned to the table.

"Very good." He walked to the door, saying good-naturedly, "Count to one hundred, and don't listen to my footsteps."

Lydia sat on the bench, too distracted to count.

*This all seems quite inappropriate between employee and employer...but no one is here besides us to notice. We haven't seen much of Hardy these past few days, even at mealtimes.*

*And now Herr Heldmann is gone.*

*Herr Heldmann...*Lydia thought. *That was a failed strategy.*

Though she had readied herself the previous evening to be the Coquette of Whitehall to the German guest, when it had come time to serve dinner, she found herself at the little mirror in the kitchen pinning her mob-cap back into place.

*Could there be a clearer bid for attention than suddenly appearing without one's ugly headpiece?* she had chided herself. *Besides, Sir Jonathan would see right through my fraudulent flirtation. It would be better to die in an attic than suffer* that *humiliation.*

So Lydia had determined to simply be herself as she served the meal to her employer and his guest. Jonathan had insisted she join them at the dining table, so she had asked the German a few questions about himself, being patient with his slow answers.

He *was* a farmer, she had learned, pleased with her adroit perception, and he had come to England to learn about Herefords. She had recognized the cattle breed as one her own father had spoken of with appreciation.

And so the conversation had laboriously progressed as the soup, rolls and roast chicken had been consumed. She had realized as it went on that Herr Heldmann was a good man, but the thought of him falling in love with her would have been laughable had she not felt so embarrassed about her earlier intentions to make exactly that occur.

*As of this morning, he is departed, along with my ridiculous ploy,* thought Lydia, feeling her cheeks burn though she was alone with her thoughts.

*And now, no one is here but me and Sir Jonathan...and little Elliott.* The thought echoed through her mind, filling her again with a sense of anxious intrigue.

She had noticed in small ways how lax she had grown in her interactions with Jonathan. Still, she had difficulty looking him in the eye. It felt too bold and improper, but she joked frequently, her eyes turned elsewhere. Words fell out of her mouth that she wouldn't have considered saying in the recent past. His apparent enjoyment of these quips encouraged her to continue doing so. She often wondered how she would behave differently once the Lady and her entourage had returned. A sense of dread always accompanied that thought.

When she felt sufficient time had passed, she rose from the bench. Going through the door to the dining room, she called out, "Ready or not, I'm coming for you!"

She usually knew where to find Elliott. He was partial to a few particular spots, all rather obvious and not difficult for a young boy to squeeze himself into. Thinking she had heard him rush up the stairs, she headed toward the staircase.

*But where is Jonathan?* she thought, anxiously scanning the upstairs hallway. There were many doors to rooms she could search, all concealing so many possibilities. Suddenly, as she padded cautiously down the hall, she noticed something that she had seen a hundred times, but never really thought through.

Just feet away from 'those Clyde fellows', blocked behind a small writing desk, was a narrow door. It could be mistaken for wall paneling since its design closely matched that of the walls on either side of it, but upon close examination, Lydia distinguished hinges and a door knob.

*What is that? A closet? Certainly he's not in there,* Lydia thought.

Suddenly, there was a thump in the parlour to her left. Though still curious about the little narrow door, she moved past it to push the parlour door wide open. It was a room she had dusted and aired many times, though not recently. The hearth was familiar to her knees, where she had knelt to light fires. She had perused the shelves that held a selection of books, which was paltry compared to what the library offered. Still, she saw the room in an entirely new way.

*Is he in here?* she wondered, holding her breath.

*What if he is? It's a stupid game.*

She stepped across the red and gold rug, every creak of the floorboards amplified.

*One of them is in here. I know I heard something. But where?*

Her heart pounded in her chest as she surveyed the possible hiding places.

*Jonathan couldn't possibly fit in there,* she thought, observing a trunk she had swept around many times. She nearly giggled at the thought of his knees up around his ears if he were to contort himself inside it and lower its lid.

*But Elliott would fit.*

Stepping forward, she eased the lid up, determined to steady herself should the young boy jump out.

It was empty.

*Hmmm...where else?* Her heart still beating forcefully, she pivoted on her heel and screamed.

There, a foot before her, was Jonathan, his frame leaning toward and towering over her.

Lydia's hand flew to her mouth, and she felt embarrassed at her visceral reaction.

A slow smile spread across the young man's face, obviously pleased at his clandestine approach.

She felt quite small before him, remembering the stance of his body the day she'd nearly broken a window and he thought she'd been hurt. She recalled how safe she felt when she'd realized his concern for her. The memory warmed her now, and she smiled genuinely up at him.

"Where were you hiding?" Lydia asked, seeing how his hair had fallen into his face.

*Crafty fellow.*

He said nothing, and instead just stared at her, his mischievous smile never wavering.

Feeling emboldened, Lydia realized something. Quickly reaching out, she touched his shoulder and pronounced, "You're out."

A look of pleased surprise crossed the young man's face and he lifted his eyebrows, saying, "Yes, I suppose you got me."

Suddenly, from another room came the sound of a crash and a cry of dismay.

Dashing from the parlor, Jonathan and Lydia hurried to the source which was easy to determine due to the sound of tears being fervidly shed. Following Jonathan as he threw the door open, Lydia saw Elliott blubbering, tears streaming down his face. He stood with his hands thrown out, jagged shards of porcelain littering the ground at his feet.

"I...I didn't mean to..." the little boy wailed.

Lydia recognized the fragments as pieces of the large blue vase that she had always considered ill-placed. Each time she had dusted the end table under it, she had used both hands while moving the vase out of the way.

"I...I was under the table, and...and..."

"Are you hurt?" Jonathan asked, pulling Elliott's hands outward to examine them.

"No, but..." the boy blubbered on.

"Elliott," Jonathan said soothingly. "Get ahold of yourself."

Lydia knelt and began to place the smaller shards into the fractured belly of the vase.

"But...but..." the boy hiccupped, his upper lip slick with mucus.

"But nothing," Jonathan assured him. "It's clear you didn't mean to. Now stop leaking all over the place and let's clean this mess up."

The two boys, one of them sniffing, knelt beside Lydia and began to follow her example.

"Careful," Jonathan said. "The edges are awfully sharp."

Lydia wasn't sure to whom he was speaking.

# Falling Asleep on the Settee

~ ELLIOTT

A cheerful blaze burned in the fireplace and the night sky was dark outside the windows. Elliott's eyelids were getting heavy, but he resisted the urge to let them fall shut.

He was on the settee, between Pony and Jonathan, with the open sketchbook resting on his lap. The fire didn't cast much light on the book, but Elliott was content to sit in the dimness as the two grown-ups leaned towards him, turning the pages, and talking about the various drawings on them.

"That's a new one." Elliott pointed at the image of a young man who was seated on a rock.

Pony leaned in further, angling the book most effectively in the firelight. Peals of laughter, unlike any sound Elliott had ever heard her make, bubbled out of her. He, too, began to laugh, and examined the drawing more carefully.

The fellow had his left shoe off and was staring at his bare foot, which stuck awkwardly up in the air. He looked dismayed as he regarded a prominent bump bulging out from just under his big toe.

"That's Widdy, isn't it?" Elliott asked, glancing at his brother.

"Yes, it is," Jonathan, who was looking at Pony, replied with a broad smile.

The maid's laughter had devolved into barely contained giggles.

"He grew a prodigious wart on his foot this last autumn and I thought I would do well to commemorate it. Though I've drawn him looking mortified, he was actually rather proud of the thing. I've never seen such a large wart."

"But look at the foot's width! And all the hair sprouting out of the biggest toe!" Pony said, still snickering.

"Oh, that's all factual!" Jonathan clarified. "Yes, Widdy's feet are nothing to be trifled with. I always hope to portray people somewhat accurately, though the more I look at this one..."

He turned back several pages to a sketch of an old man. "...the less pleased I am with it."

In the scant light, it looked to Elliott as if the man was being offered a set of teeth on a platter by a maid.

"I fear I failed to capture..." Jonathan paused. "That is, I don't think either subject is properly depicted."

"I've never seen this one before." Elliott said before yawning, though Jonathan, who was still looking at Pony, didn't seem to hear him.

"This was the first time you dazzled me with your verbiage," Jonathan continued. "'The ancient beaux who choose to woo must all remember as they chew...'"

Pony said, "I'm glad it pleased you."

"It astonished me, truly."

Elliott rubbed his eyes as he slowly flipped a few pages to see if there were any other unfamiliar drawings.

"And then there was the other..." Jonathan said, then cleared his throat.

"Pardon me?" Pony asked.

Jonathan glanced at Elliott. "The, uh...other poem. I never thanked you properly...or at all, really..."

*Why are they speaking of poems? Pictures are so much better.* Elliott turned another page, and drowsily slumped further down into the furniture.

"It was...vital," Jonathan proceeded. "I felt quite stupid when I realized what was going on...and ever so thankful that you had discerned it all."

"I've seen the effects of such substances." Pony resettled herself in the corner of the settee. "I didn't want it to...ruin anyone."

"Well, thank you for telling me. It would crush me if she..."

The unfinished sentence hung in the silence of the room.

*Why must there always be boring talking?*

Elliott's eyelids lowered.

"Will you take that off him?" Pony asked, quietly.

Elliott felt that the heavy book was lifted off his legs, and Pony pulled him toward her, guiding his head to rest on her knee. He sighed involuntarily as her hand began to stroke his hair away from his face. His eyes were narrow slits, watching the glow of firelight shift across the walls.

"After my father died, my brother turned to gin. His descent was rapid and distinct."

"So you lost both of them at the same time. I'm so sorry." Jonathan's voice, like Pony's, had grown quiet. "I had the same experience when I was twelve, though the fluid I lost mine to was water. How old were you when your father passed?"

"Nearly sixteen," Pony replied. "We think it was his heart..."

Elliott breathed heavily, feeling the warmth of Pony's hand as it continued to caress the side of his face, and he allowed his eyes to fully shut.

# Witnessing Happiness, Then Plotting to Destroy It

~ Smith

The parlour door swung open before her silently, and Smith was happily startled by what she beheld.

*Better and better*, she thought as she stood in the doorway. *The filth in the entryway was delightful, but this sight is the most welcome of all.*

Before her eyes, Sir Jonathan and Foote were slumped on separate ends of the settee, their legs lax in slumber. Master Elliott was between them, curled up in a ball, his head resting in Foote's lap.

*You all look so comfortable...and happy together.*

It was the little boy's eyes that opened slowly as Smith cleared her throat. He rubbed them and squinted at her, his hair sticking up in all directions.

"What is *she* doing here?" he asked, his voice peevish.

Smith willed herself not to smile as the two others awoke simultaneously and realization dawned on their faces.

Foote looked startled, and frightened.

*Good,* thought Smith.

Jonathan, on the other hand, yawned loudly, then stretched his far-reaching limbs as he smiled up at the woman. "Hullo, Smith. Are you only just arrived? And where is the rest of your party?"

"I am the only one returned from London, sir."

*Much to your benefit! Oh, if your mother were to catch sight of this! I rather wish she* was *here.*

Sir Jonathan finished his stretching. "Well, welcome back. I hope your journey was comfortable and free of any unwanted adventure."

*Ever the smug gentleman. Your words are right, but your manner is as smarmy as always.*

"It was fine, sir. May I request the favor of an audience alone with you?" She stated the words deliberately as she eyed Foote who had stood up from the settee and was smoothing her skirt.

"Of course. Let's just venture into the study down the hall." Sir Jonathan stood, rubbing a hand over his belly. "I'm feeling a bit peckish. Might I have some porridge, Foote?"

The maid barely nodded and disappeared out the door, never looking up from the floor.

At Foote's heels, Elliott asked again, "Why's *she* here?"

He was promptly shushed by the maid.

Smith suppressed a laugh. *That's right, young woman. Your indolence is at an end. It's back to being an* actual *servant. Oh, if the Lady could see this!*

She hoped to look as stern as possible as she followed the young man out of the room.

The study door opened with a creak. Jonathan stepped in and sat at the disorderly desk, motioning for Smith to sit in an upright chair before him.

"Foote has been keeping house, I see," she said, looking around with haughty pleasure.

"Yes. Yes, she has." He nodded, his smile never wavering.

"You all looked like a very happy family just now...comfortably sleeping on the sofa. Are those your intentions, Sir Jonathan, to set up house with a servant?" She trusted that the glint in her eye looked dangerous.

"My intentions are my own, Smith. Now for what did you want the pleasure of my company?" He crossed his legs comfortably and hooked his hands around his knee.

*You think yourself untouchable, don't you? Let's see you smile at what I'm about to say.*

"Yes, I will get to the matter quickly." She cleared her throat with the air of someone who has been rehearsing a carefully planned speech.

"Though I have served this family faithfully for upwards of twenty years, I have been paid only half of my full wage for the last three years. At first, I chose to encourage myself with the fact that I had a secure position in a great and distinguished household, certain that I would be reimbursed fully at some point, but...last week, when my wages were again due to me, your mother informed me that I would have to wait until you, as the handler of estate affairs, would give me my due. Sick to death of not being paid for my tireless and excellent work, I boarded the night coach from London last night and have returned here to collect my things and go. Imagine my delight when I came upon you, not at Heath as all had supposed, but here at Whitehall, keeping house with a servant girl.

"Thus, my plans have changed. I will require of you ten full years of payment and a letter of excellent reference so that I may seek employment from a household that will actually *pay* its servants."

She stared brazenly into the young man's eyes, an action she had never before taken.

There was a flicker of something indistinguishable in his face, though he continued to smile tranquilly. Interpreting this as a precursor to refusal, Smith continued.

"If you do not meet my demands, then I shall go back to your mother and tell her of your truancy from school and your presence here with the young *and vulnerable* Foote...and, I will tell the servants of all the other Great Families. It won't be long before everyone in your social circle is aware of your questionable behavior...and your poor taste."

At this, Jonathan's smile faded. He lifted his eyebrows and swallowed, seeming to think for a moment.

"Is that all?" he finally asked, solemnly.

"I beg your pardon?"

Jonathan leaned back in his chair, rubbing his chin. "Is there anything else you want?"

*He doesn't believe me!*

"I will make good on all I have promised." Smith set her shoulders straight and her chin high.

"I have no doubt of that, Smith. I have always known you to be thorough and diligent. Thank you for making your terms so clear. It makes this whole regrettable situation much more manageable."

He sighed and looked around the desk. "However, I will need a little time to put things in order. Please leave me to it. I imagine you have some packing to do upstairs?"

*That was even easier than I expected.*

"Yes. Very good, Sir," she replied, her apparent victory soothing her back into civility as she rose from her chair.

"Oh, Smith?" Jonathan called just before she exited the room.

"Sir?"

"What is your yearly wage? I want to make sure I get the figures correct."

Smith suppressed the victorious smile that threatened to split her face in two and replied, "Forty-one pounds, two shillings."

"Thank you." Jonathan removed the quill from its stand as Smith walked out the door.

*To be free at last from all the Clydes!*

She inhaled deeply as she felt herself floating down the hall.

***

An hour later, Smith descended the stairs from her servant's room for the final time with her belongings. Both Clydes and Foote were in the servants' hall, eating porridge.

"Ah, here you are, Smith," said Jonathan, rising and wiping his mouth with his hand. From the table, he picked up a drawstring purse and a fat envelope.

"These are for you," he said cheerfully, handing the items over to her.

The bag felt splendidly heavy in her hand.

*No need to count that,* she thought.

"I've included several copies of the reference letter so that you can send it out to multiple prospects at once. Also, I have asked Hardy to drive you into Plimbridge where you can board the coach and begin your search for the new life you desire."

His easy acquiescence to her plan softened her heart toward him, just slightly. "Thank you very much, sir."

*If he wants to save face in front of Foote, I will allow it.*

"Would you like some breakfast before you go?"

"No, thank you." The weight of the bag in her hand drove all thoughts of hunger from her mind. She placed it, along with the envelope, into her trunk and shut the lid securely.

"Very well. I'll summon Hardy for you."

Moments later, Sir Jonathan stood by the wagon as Hardy lifted Smith's trunk into it.

Smith felt nearly regal as she climbed onto the wagon seat, smiling slightly in spite of all recent occurrences.

"Smith, thank you for your many years of service." Jonathan said, bowing his head.

"You're welcome, sir," she said, dipping her head in return.

Hardy clicked to the horse and the cart rolled forward.

***

*At last,* thought Smith, after settling herself down behind the closed door of her room at an inn in Wexhall.

In times past, she would have climbed on the next coach to Spearside immediately to get there before nightfall, or possibly taken a place at the Jug and Platter on the other side of the Plim, but not this morning.

Today, she allowed herself the luxury of a private room at the Silver Swan. She sighed contentedly as she opened her trunk and retrieved the heavy purse. Hoping the jingle of coins would not alert anyone who happened to be near of her good fortune, she loosened the drawstrings and poured the hoard out onto the blue bedspread.

*But...but where are all the* crowns? she thought, surprised at the sight of so many pennies and shillings.

A frantic precursor totaling of the money proved that she'd been given far less than the ten years of salary she had demanded. In fact, it looked to be little more than the amount owed to her for her last three years of service.

*That conniving devil! If he doesn't expect me to do just as I threatened, he will be painfully surprised!*

A thought jarred her.

*And what of the reference letter?*

Snatching the thick envelope from her trunk, she tore at it and hastily unfolded the papers within. With shaking hands, she read:

To Whom it May Concern--

Dorothea Smith has served at my home, Whitehall near Plimbridge, for more than twenty years. She did an excellent job of keeping the house stocked and functioning and overseeing the other servants. She is a tough old hen who managed to endure many difficulties in her unprivileged life. Recently, she has aspired to be an extortionist, though she has failed miserably since no one feels bullied by her ridiculous threats. Consider Old Smithy-Pot for employment if you have no other applicants and you'd like to hear all the stories of what happened at Whitehall though you'll never know if they are true or simply born out of her own embittered and pathetic mind.

Sincerely—Sir Jonathan Charles Clyde, Bart.

# Cleaning Up the Place

~ The Hosteler
The Silver Swan

The screams he heard emanating from inside the Blue Room that morning were the loudest noises the innkeeper had ever heard on the premises of the Silver Swan, including in the yard and stables. Once he had rammed through the door and determined that the woman inside was neither under attack nor bleeding profusely, he quickly slammed shut the lid of her trunk, and carried it downstairs, calling over his shoulder, "You won't be staying here, Ma'am. Try across the river at the Jug and Platter."

# Visiting the Butcher

~ JONATHAN

Jonathan had spent all morning mulling over how to share every detail of his response to Smith with Foote, but the entire business had included so many slights to Foote that he wasn't sure which parts he ought to exclude. He feared any exclusions would dim the light of his obvious ingenuity. Now he sat alone in the parlor, gazing out the window, thinking.

*Is it possible that Foote would be offended by the insults of such a woman?*

*Why would she? Would any servant balk at the idea of their employer falling in love with them as Smith suggested? Isn't that the happiest story of all for any maid...a besotted, rich employer liberating them from a life of servitude?*

*Still, this is no story in a book. She might feel toyed with at the mention of such notions.*

*But...*

He bit his lip.

*What if I* were *to fall in love with her?*

*And she with me?*

"Jonathan, here you are!" Elliott burst in through the door and hurried over to tug on his brother's arm. "You must come and see the most wonderful thing! I can't believe I forgot to show you until now."

*But how would I know her affection was genuine and not merely for the contents of my coffers?*

"What is it?"

"It's a surprise," insisted the exuberant little boy, pulling him down the hall and into the kitchen. "Pony! Let's show Jonathan!"

The servant girl's back was to them as she was washing another load of dishes.

Jonathan silently appreciated the revealed nape of her neck just above her collar, a few strands of hair dangling down around it. Her sleeves were pushed up above her elbows, baring her firm, slender forearms.

"Show him what?" she asked, rinsing a cup.

Elliott ran to her and whispered excitedly in her ear, his little feet dancing underneath him.

Foote assumed the overly animated expression that friendly people often have when interacting with a child. Her eyes were large and her mouth hung delicately lax as if she was enraptured with the secret being shared with her.

"But *I* want to be the one to show him," finished Elliott loudly.

"Fine, fine. Do you remember everything I taught you? You must be firm and don't keep repeat..."

"Shh..." Elliott's eyes swung over to Jonathan suspiciously. "I remember everything. Where are the treats?"

"Foote's making treats, is she?" asked Jonathan, curiously.

"Not for you!" said Elliott, giggling. "You wouldn't like these."

Foote dried her hands on her apron and glanced around the kitchen. Biting her lip she said, "Treats? Treats...Let me see..."

She found a few crusts of bread, dipped them in the cold, congealed drippings of a roasting pan and put them all on a plate.

"You're right. I wouldn't like those," Jonathan told Elliott who was dancing around by the door.

"Come on!" Elliott sprinted outside.

The recent snow had been followed by two surprisingly warm days, melting and drying up most evidence of the previous weather.

"Sassy! Sassy!" Elliott cried.

Immediately, the little reddish dog was jumping around his feet, yipping happily. However, she abandoned this when Lydia approached with the plate.

"I'll take that," said Elliott gravely as he took it from Lydia. He pointed at the porch step. "You two, stay there."

Jonathan sat, smiling to himself about Elliott's sober demeanor.

The step was wide enough for him and Foote to sit side by side, but the girl lingered.

"You as well, Pony."

"Say 'please', Elliott," spoke Jonathan. "You're being a bit saucy."

"Please sit," the boy corrected himself.

Foote complied.

Sassy, hearing the command, had also lowered her hindquarters to the ground, which caused the three people to laugh aloud.

"Excellent!" Jonathan laughed, clapping his hands.

Elliott rewarded her with a bit of bread crust. The dog swallowed it whole and jumped around the boy.

"That's not all! Watch this!" Elliott cleared his throat and clearly stated, "Pleased to meet you, Sassy."

The dog's left paw flew up and Elliott grabbed it in mock greeting.

"Very good!" said Jonathan, applauding again.

"Oh, but there's more." Elliott furrowed his brow, squinting into the sunshine. "Where's that good stick?" He looked around the yard.

Off he ran, plate in hand, the excited dog bounding along beside him.

Grossly aware of the hip just inches from his own, Jonathan stared off into the distance at his brother's figure as it roamed around the grounds.

Wondering where Foote was looking at this moment, Jonathan asked, "You taught him this?"

"We always had a dog or two at Hillcrest," replied the girl.

"Hillcrest?"

"The farm where I grew up."

Jonathan steadied his voice. "Is that nearby?"

"It's near Shinford in Coddingshire."

*Shinford. Shinford? That sounds familiar.*

"I can't find it, Pony!" called Elliott who was down by the rock wall.

"Go get a bit of kindling from the woodpile," offered Foote. "But be wary of spiders."

"Why does he call you 'Pony'?"

"Oh, it's rather silly, really," began Lydia. "I told him that I once had a pony and he was quite struck by the idea of a parlour maid on a pony."

Jonathan chuckled, immediately wanting to draw the girl atop a pony, feather duster in hand.

"So how long have the Footes inhabited Hillcrest?" Jonathan asked.

"Actually, *the Footes* have never inhabited Hillcrest, as that is not our name."

"What can you mean?"

"My surname is Smythe, like the housekeeper's, but with a 'y' and 'e'. Upon my arrival here, your mother deemed it appropriate to rename me."

Jonathan sat silently for a moment.

*Just as she tried to change my name so many years ago. Of course, this poor girl was incapable of defying the action.*

"And she stuck you with 'Foote'? I am terribly sorry. What is your name then?" he asked.

"Hmmm? Smythe."

"No," Jonathan began. "I meant your Christian name." He felt his tongue thicken as he awaited her response.

*Good God, man. It's not as if you've just requested to see her in her shift.*

Foote cleared her throat and responded, "My mother named me Lydia after her sister who died at the age of four."

"Oh, I'm sorry to hear that," Jonathan said, lamely realizing that it sounded as if he was sorry her name was Lydia. He nearly began to explain himself, but didn't, fearing it would only make things more awkward.

"Sir Jonathan?" Foote said.

"Yes?"

"I fear that we are low on meat and other foodstuffs. I've a joint for tomorrow's dinner and a side of bacon, but beyond that we are without meat."

He asked, "What would Cook do to acquire more?"

"Well, she would send word to the butcher...which I did."

"And?"

She paused. "He says he will send no more until he is paid for both the last delivery and the newest order."

"Alright, I will see about it."

He recalled how adoringly she had looked at him when he said he knew where the laudanum was for Ploughman. He envisioned her regarding him similarly in a few short hours when he returned with a large slab of bacon.

Just then, Elliott reemerged with a short stick and jogged up to them, breathlessly.

"Watch this, Jonathan!" He hurled the stick across the yard.

Sassy tore after it, gravel spraying out from under her rapidly flying feet. She soon returned, the stick clenched in her jaws, slime dripping from either end.

"Eww," said Elliott. "You can keep it, but here is your treat."

"Well done, Elliott." Jonathan patted his back. "Truly, very well done."

The little boy beamed.

"And you as well for teaching him, Lydia." Jonathan said the name as casually as he could, but it rang in his ears as if he had said 'darling'. Somehow he managed not to cringe.

At this sentence the two young adults looked at each other straight on, and quickly glanced away.

However, it was not before Jonathan noted a pleased glow in her eyes.

***

Within an hour, Jonathan had saddled Achilles and was riding toward the butcher in Plimbridge. Having paid Smith with money from the sale of the horses, he had grabbed a few of the remaining coins for his jaunt into town.

When he was a child, he had seen the gutted piglets hanging from the porch's rafters. There were other dangling carcasses, some quite large, but none as easily identifiable as the piglets. Therefore, from an early age he had thought of that place as the Dead Pig Shop. It was later that he learned it was the butcher's and that much of the flesh he ate passed through there before landing on a platter at Whitehall.

Plodding down High Street, Jonathan passed the haberdashery, the milliner and the coffee house. These were all places he had visited by himself or with Sophia. Inside the butcher shop, however, he had never been.

After dismounting and securing Achilles to a post out front, Jonathan entered the shop, stepping past a young girl. She was scrubbing a stain on the wooden floor with a brush and wet sand.

There was a thick, sickly smell of blood filling the room. Spots of it were everywhere, on the walls, splattered on the open shelves before him. The fresher smears were bright red and the older were brown.

*Why bother*? wondered Jonathan as he saw the girl was scrubbing at the particularly large stain.

The shelves held crudely hacked large joints and finer cuts which had been more carefully carved.

Jonathan stood for only a moment, when the girl with the brush abandoned her task, and came to stand before him.

"Can I help you, sir?" she asked, her eyelids drooped as she ran her hands down her apron.

"Yes, I'd like to have some beef and pork delivered to Whitehall."

"One moment please, sir," she said and walked behind the shelves. There, perched on a little table, was a large book. The girl flipped through many pages, which were edged with bloody fingerprints.

"Whitehall, did you say?" She stopped at a page and stared at it a long time, biting her lip.

*Come on then,* thought Jonathan, longing for fresh air.

"One moment please, sir." She disappeared through a doorway at the back of the shop.

Jonathan stood awkwardly, sickened by the heavy scent in his nostrils and wondering how many stains his clothing would have once he left.

Soon, the girl returned. Seemingly reluctant to meet Jonathan's eyes before, now she focused completely on her own feet and informed him, "I'm sorry, sir, but my father says Whitehall must pay before you get anymore."

"Of course," responded Jonathan. "How much is owed?"

"Two pounds, six shillings," announced the girl, still staring at the ground.

*What? That's quite a bit. Good thing I brought as much as I did.* He counted out the coins carefully into the girl's palm.

"And how much for three more joints of beef and a rash of bacon?"

He flinched as she told him the amount.

"Uhh...just one joint of beef for now, I suppose," he said, tallying up the remaining coins in his hand before passing them to her.

"The carter will deliver it tomorrow morning."

"Thank you." Jonathan turned and left the shop.

As he rode away, he glanced toward the doorway and saw the man who must be the butcher himself. His heavy leather apron was the bloodiest item of all. In his hand he held a large cleaver. There were smears of gore across his face and a malevolent smirk as he watched Jonathan depart.

The air of it was grossly unsettling to Jonathan.

*He might have at least put down the cleaver,* he thought, perturbed that someone so obviously disliked him. He was used to similar expressions on faces of boys at school whom he had bested with a prank, but a muscular man from the working class holding a sharpened tool had never dared to glare at him so forebodingly.

*And why was the unpaid bill so high? Where's all the cursed money?* He wondered, thinking for the first time in a couple of weeks about his dismissal from Heath. *What the bloody hell is happening?*

*I meant to go see the Lady about it immediately, but first there was everything with Ploughman...then Heldmann's arrival, and now...*

Jonathan realized he had no valid excuse to put off his trip to London any longer, though recollections of the previous evening made him hesitate.

*To sit again tonight in the parlor, talking with Lydia until we drift off to sleep on the settee...*

He smiled. Though he'd had a crick in his neck all day from the previous night's discomfort, he could think of no way to spend an evening in a more pleasant manner.

*Yet, Lydia will still be here when I return. Hopefully the Lady won't return with me...*

As he circled back onto High Street, some words painted on a window caught his eye:

ANTHONY HARRIS, ATTORNEY OF LAW AND SOLICITOR

"*I'll have to take that up with Harris.*"

The words, stated by his father's voice, echoed in his memory. Sir William had said them many times to the Lady over dinner.

*Ah, yes, Harris. I haven't thought of that name in years! I'd no idea he was right here in Plimbridge. Perhaps he will have some answers for me. In fact, he probably knows considerably more than the Lady,* thought Jonathan, stopping in front of the building.

*Paying him a call just might save me a trip to London.*

# Explaining How Things Are

~ HARRIS

The door's bell jangled, announcing a new arrival.

"Hello?" a voice called.

"Yes. I'm back here," Harris called from his back office.

The narrow body of a tall young man filled the doorway. "Mr. Harris? My name is Jonathan Clyde. I believe you might be able to help me."

*Ah, the young Clyde has come at last*, thought Harris, suppressing a groan.

"Yes, yes. Please sit down, Sir Jonathan," said Harris, proffering a chair.

*Still dressed in finery, I see*, thought Harris, eyeing the dark blue vest under Clyde's frock coat. *Apparently the creditors have not run out of patience. Not yet, anyway...*

Once settled, the young man held his hat between his hands and jiggled his knee.

*Hmm, yes, let's get this over with*, thought Harris.

"What can I do for you today, sir?"

"Are you...aware of my family's financial situation?" Jonathan asked, stumblingly.

"Yes," was the unadorned answer with a slight nod.

"Can you...explain it to me?"

*Of course his fool of a mother has left it to me to tell him.*

Harris prepared himself for the regrettable transformation he had witnessed multiple times in that very room.

*So many of the upper class are thinly veiled animals who at the mere mention of reality turn into either enraged bulls or whining dogs. Which sort of beast will you become, Young Clyde?*

*Oh, get on with it.*

He cleared his throat and began.

"Obviously there was great wealth associated with the name of Clyde at one time. I did not begin to handle your family's financial affairs until about twenty-five years ago, so I'm not aware of anything beyond the paper records that exist. Studying these several years ago, I saw that the troubles started when Sir William Clyde the Third began selling the estate's farm land."

"The troubles?" the young man interrupted him.

"Well, yes. At first it was just a few acres on the north side to settle some debts, but eventually he sold the entire portion as well as the eastern section. This eliminated a vast source of your family's yearly income. Thus the expenses remained to maintain the grand home and its customary lifestyle, but there were fewer and fewer ways to fund them."

The young baronet blinked, his mouth hanging slightly open as Harris continued.

"At the transfer of your mother's dowry, your father acquired a great deal of money, your mother being the daughter of Miles Fanshawe. Your father and I met to discuss various options of what to do with it. I recommended investments, but he was set on restoring Whitehall to its former glory. This took more than ten years and cost the vast majority of what Lady Clyde brought into the union."

Young Clyde held up his hand, asking, "Is...is she aware of all this?"

"Your mother? Hmm, yes. I sat with her shortly after your father's death and explained to her the state of affairs. She informed me that you, as the heir, would take care of matters once you were of age, and that I needn't bother her. As you know, that was more than five years ago. Since then, each of my letters requiring an audience with her has been unanswered. Might I ask, sir, are you yet twenty-one years of age?"

Jonathan's eyes focused on the floorboards, his brow knit tightly together. "Uh, no, not for another thirteen months, actually."

*Hmm...well with everything falling apart, perhaps the Lady won't stand in the way if he takes the reins...*Harris thought.

"But, Mr. Harris," Jonathan continued. "I don't understand. How was I able to travel across Europe? How do we still have a house in London?"

"How your tour was funded, I've no idea. Perhaps your mother sold some jewelry? As for the London property, it was never transferred to your father's name and was, thus..." Harris nearly said 'safe', but caught himself, "...retained by your mother."

*At least Old Fanshawe had the forethought to require that contingency at his daughter's marriage.*

"Are you telling me...there's no money left?"

The older man pursed his lips, pleasantly surprised at the calm delivery of such a question.

"No, there is some. The exact figures, I would have to read up on to determine, but there are a few investments that earn interest each year, which is why I'm still involved at all. I collect it every quarter and deliver it to your mother. However, the only thing of considerable value is Whitehall itself. Your father spared no expense in restoring it, ensuring that it would stand solid and sound for decades to come. Truthfully, I am surprised that you've all maintained the baronet-lifestyle as long as you have. I thought your mother would respond to every one of the letters I sent once she realized money was running low. May I ask what has happened that brought you here today?"

Harris listened unblinkingly as Jonathan relayed to him his dismissal from Heath, the empty stables and his recent trip to the butcher.

"Now we come to it, Mr. Harris..." The young man took a deep breath. "What should I do?"

Harris studied the person before him.

*Hardly more than a boy, yet more rational than either of his parents. Perhaps he will be alright...*if *he follows my counsel.*

"I fear you will dislike my recommendation, but honestly, I see no other option."

"Carry on."

Harris stared intently at Jonathan, sighed heavily and explained the exact course of action that he had suggested to the boy's father nearly two decades earlier, recalling that it had been met with haughty ridicule.

At its conclusion, Harris was bemused as his client sat silently, chewing on his lower lip.

"Hmm..." Jonathan murmured, sitting for a moment longer before rising to his feet. "Well then, thank you for your time and advice, Mr. Harris."

*Neither a whimper nor a roar?* Harris reached out to firmly shake the hand extended to him.

*Well done, young sir.*

# Speaking with One's Eyes

~ Lydia

Of the countless tasks she could have performed that afternoon, Lydia chose to clean the windows at the front of the house. They afforded the best view of the front drive.

The dust on the furniture was far thicker than the grime on the windows' glass, she knew. Still, it was with great care that she wiped every inch of the panes, watching always for the sight of Jonathan's black top hat upon his return from Plimbridge.

Much earlier, she had left Elliott happily employed with teaching Sassy to roll over, and now she saw him climbing a small tree on the edge of the lawn.

Alone in the hallway, her heartbeat quickened again at the thoughts she had been previously pushing down.

*Don't think so much of yourself! Such arrogance!*

She felt her face warm.

*But I know it's true. The way he's been speaking to me...and looking at me. I know genuine appreciation when I see it in someone's eyes.*

Turning, she saw the paintings of 'those Clyde fellows' staring out at her from their places on the wall. She abandoned her post at the windows to study them more closely, looking for any resemblance to Jonathan in their features.

*Would you fine gentlemen be horrified at your young descendant's leanings?*

Only William Walter Clyde the Second seemed to gaze at her disapprovingly. The First and Third looked disinterested altogether, while the Fourth nearly appeared jolly at the prospect.

*Dead relatives are of little consequence,* Lydia told herself. *It's the living ones who are scandalized.*

An image of Lady Clyde stepping into the carriage after surveying the servants on the day of her departure filled Lydia's mind. It was a sobering thought.

*But he's not like his mother,* she assured herself. *He didn't flinch at the broken vase. He says nothing that smacks of snobbery.*

*Still, her presence would forever be a dark cloud over our life.*

*"Our life"?* The thought jolted her. *Am I so bold as to think of ourselves as intertwined?*

*Steady, Lydia. Steady. You may be disappointed...and gravely so.*

*But there's no mistaking it! His feelings are clear...*

*As are mine...*

*Stop it! You ridiculous girl! You were setting your cap for the German only days ago.*

*But I didn't know the man, whereas, Sir Jonathan has lived his life clearly before me for months. I've seen his constant and genuine affection for his siblings, which is a testimony to his character...and he's exceedingly clever!*

She thought back over the previous evening, how exhaustion had laid hold of her, but she had refused to excuse herself to bed, unwilling to end their evening in the parlour together. Instead, she had sat with Elliott's little head on her knee, her backside numb from immobility, until the next thing she saw was Smith's scornful face lit by early morning light, looming in the doorway.

*Oh, but the disappointment that may come! Losing that boor, Paul, to Anne Triver would be nothing by comparison...*

*Stop it. Think about something else, you silly fool.*

Her eyes drifted from the paintings and rested on the little door, blocked by the writing desk, ten feet away.

*The mysterious, narrow door. That's a worthy distraction,* she thought, moving toward it. *What secrets do you hide, little one?*

She heaved her weight against the oddly placed desk. It moved with a screech of protest, its thin legs resisting the slide across the floor.

Turning the oval shaped handle, she felt a surprising click and the door swung open, towards her. Behind it was a staircase, even steeper and narrower than the one leading up to her sleeping quarters. Peering into the darkness, she saw sunlight sharply outlining a door about twenty steps up.

*It leads outside! But surely that door will be locked.*

Her foot slipped slightly on the dust of unknown years which had settled on the wooden steps. There was no handrail. She wiped cobwebs from her hands and face as she ascended. Upon reaching the top step, she patted around where she imagined the doorknob would be and found it much higher than expected.

Grasping it, she breathed in sharply, steeling herself for the letdown she was sure would come. To her delight, the knob turned and she pushed the door out, letting in the piercing light of the sun.

She stood in the small doorway, squinting for several moments until her eyes adjusted to the light-filled world before her. A wind blew, flapping her skirt and apron. Slowly, she stepped outside under the belvedere.

*The roof!*

Unsheltered, she was now fair game to the wind which whipped at her clothes and stung her eyes.

This was a far finer view than the one afforded her in the servants' chamber, and she gazed out on it, transfixed, for several moments. The whole of Whitehall's grounds lay below her, verdant with the slight growth of a dawning season. Beyond, she could see the High Street of Plimbridge flanked by its stone buildings of commerce. The Plim flowed past them, straddled by its humpbacked bridge, the sun glinting off of its ebbings. In another direction, she saw acres and acres of newly furrowed fields and laborers, small as ants, preparing them further for crops. The fields were bordered by hedges which ran straight and thick, dividing the world into distinct sections. Multiple small villages dotted the landscape, their church steeples pointing to the sky. Turning, she saw in the distance, the encroaching woods abutting the fields, the many trees blending to form a dark green border on the horizon.

Just then, an especially strong gust of wind bore down on her, snatching the mob-cap from her head, the flimsy pins holding it in place proving ineffective. She laughed as she watched it fly like a crazed pigeon released from its cage high up into the air, over the woods and out of sight.

*Smith will be enraged when she learns that that is gone!*

Still laughing, she turned so the wind would blow her hair out of her eyes, and was startled to see she was not alone.

There, looking tall and stark beside the little doorway, stood Jonathan, his hat in his hands.

Delighted to see him, Lydia smiled broadly.

"Sir Jonathan!" she called above the gale. "Why have you never brought me here before? This is positively glorious!"

His eyes never wavered from her face as her hands motioned generously to the landscape around them.

In that moment, she knew she had a choice to make.

Making it, she allowed her eyes to bore playfully into his.

*I know your thoughts, sir.*

Knowing they could speak for her, she felt buoyed up by the fierce truths her eyes could convey.

*And your feelings are not unrequited.*

*If you'd been born a few degrees lower or I'd been born a few higher, we'd have known long ago and there would have been no hindrance whatsoever.*

*At balls, I could watch you grow jealous as I danced with others, forcing you to dance with me yourself.*

Lydia's mouth relaxed into a little smile that was just as eloquent, her eyes still intently gazing into Jonathan's.

*You could chase me through the maze and kiss me in every corner.*

Lydia tilted her head coquettishly.

Jonathan's lips parted, and Lydia noticed for the first time how somber he looked.

*Why so serious, sir? Last night, looking at your drawings alongside my writings, you said we work well together. I understood what you really meant.*

He said nothing, though his eyes looked apologetic.

*Isn't that what you meant?*

Suddenly, she felt the sickening stirrings of uncertainty in her gut.

Peering at his almost worried looking face, she felt the smile slip from her lips.

*Am I mistaken?*

*Jonathan? Jonathan!* She felt his name bubbling up within her. *Do you, even now, think me beneath you?*

The thought was a blow to her stomach as her eyes continued to speak, peering into his own.

A hollowness gaped within her as she dropped her gaze.

*Of course. Of course!*

Gripping the solid railing before her, Lydia pulled herself around and looked out again at the expansive view, now swirling below her like the deep waters of a rough sea.

*He's a baronet!*

*And I...am a parlour maid.*

*We are who we are who we are...*

She sighed deeply, shakily, defying the tears that threatened to fill her eyes.

*I mustn't shame myself further.*

She slowly counted to five.

Turning back toward him, she said in as casual a voice as she could feign, "This view of the Clyde estate is truly impressive. Now if you will please excuse me, Sir Jonathan, I've spent enough leisure time upon your roof. I have many duties I ought to see to."

She curtsied heavily before moving toward him and the little door. Her face, rigid as stone, burned.

A jolt passed through her as his fingers splayed outwardly, brushing her hand as she moved past.

"Lydia?" he breathed her name softly.

She paused in the doorway, gazing down into the gloom of the narrow stairwell.

*It means nothing, you stupid, stupid girl.*

"Sir?" she asked with forced cheerfulness.

She turned her head toward him, unable to look into his eyes.

His mouth slightly parted and gaped for a moment, though it formed no words.

The silence persisted.

*He saw all of your presumptuous, ludicrous thoughts. You've frightened him.*

"I've dinner to see to," Lydia murmured before stepping through the doorway.

*I've ruined everything.*

*I cannot stay here.*

*I won't.*

# Mulling, Regretting, Aching

~ Jonathan

"Why didn't Pony come with us?" Elliott asked. He had asked the same question at the beginning of their walk, but Jonathan hadn't bothered to answer him then.

"Hmm?" murmured Jonathan as he stood on an embankment.

*Harris' plan is extreme, but seemingly unavoidable...*

Elliott, leaning against a tall, crooked tree near him asked again, "Why didn't Pony come, too?"

"Uh...she has things she needs to do, Elliott. She takes her duties very seriously."

"Nothing's as fun without her," Elliott said, breaking a twig off the tree and pulling it to pieces.

"I whole-heartedly agree, dear brother."

"Is this what you wanted to see?" the little boy asked, staring out at the lush green hollow, clearly unimpressed.

"Yes," Jonathan replied. "It was a lake when I was your age."

"A lake?" Elliott questioned. "How does a lake just disappear?"

"It was drained."

*After it took our father and elder brother.*

Suddenly, he turned to Elliott and smiled. That is, his mouth smiled, but he knew the gesture didn't reach his eyes.

Uncharacteristically, Elliott approached Jonathan and grabbed his hand. Jonathan didn't resist, enveloping the small hand in his own.

Together they turned back toward the house, walking in silence for many minutes.

They were nearly back to the house and Jonathan felt Elliott tugging him toward the kitchen door.

*Lydia's in there,* thought Jonathan, and gently he resisted, maneuvering them toward the front entryway instead.

The memory of her on the roof, laughing and stunningly beautiful as her cap flew off into the distance filled his mind.

*And what have I to offer her?* He sighed, and felt Elliott's hand tighten around his fingers. *A few amusing drawings and some stories of successful pranks?*

Just as they rounded the corner, a wagon rolled into the side yard, slowing by the garden fence.

Jonathan stiffened and dropped Elliott's hand, turning to watch the familiar figure on its driver's seat.

"The idiot farmer," he muttered, his jaw tense.

"Who?" Elliott asked.

Jonathan gave no answer while he watched the stocky man secure the brake and jump from the seat.

Apparently unaware that he was being observed, the farmer approached the kitchen door on his booted feet and knocked, the sound of his thick knuckles on the wood thudding across the yard.

Jonathan heard the distinctive squeak of the kitchen door opening and saw the man hesitate for only a moment before disappearing inside.

He felt frozen in place, his upper lip curled and slightly quivering as he stared at the spot where the man had just been.

"What's *he* doing here?" Elliott queried, then bolted for the kitchen.

Jonathan followed with long strides, his arms rigid.

The sight that greeted him inside was mundane, surprisingly so. The man was seated at the servants' table, his hat beside him on the bench, enthusiastically digging into a bowl of porridge with a spoon.

Standing beside the stove was Lydia, motionless, her eyes riveted on a sheet of paper clutched in her hand.

"Who are you?" Elliott was asking the man.

Instead of answering, the man ducked his head at Jonathan and called out too loudly, "Good morrow, sir. I brung Miss Liddy a letter and she offered me some breakfast."

Jonathan nodded stiffly back at the fellow. "Enjoy it. You are welcome here."

He kept back the bitter bark of laughter that nearly followed the dishonest words as he turned to watch Lydia. She seemed to be reading through the letter a second time.

Finally, she folded it and returned it to its envelope, but stared at the ground for a moment longer. Then, without lifting her eyes, she said quietly, "Are you able to wait a few moments, Paul? There's more porridge on the stove."

The man lifted his bowl cheerfully in agreement.

Turning to Jonathan, she asked. "May I speak with you, sir?"

"Of course," Jonathan replied in an unnatural tone and motioned toward the door. "Shall we go to the study?"

Elliott followed them both out of the kitchen.

*Oh, what to do with him?* Jonathan asked himself, as they walked down the hall.

At the study's door, Jonathan opened it and said, "I'll be back in a moment. Come, Elliott, I've something to show you."

Taking the staircase two steps at a time, Jonathan was up it in a few seconds with Elliott trailing behind.

Once inside his own bedroom, Jonathan reached up to the highest shelf in his closet, pushed many things aside and retrieved a red box which he placed on the ground before his little brother.

"What is it?" Elliott asked.

"Some things that are very important to me. You may play with them, but you must be very careful and you mustn't leave my room with them," Jonathan said, lifting the lid.

Inside were rows of toy soldiers, wound round with strips of wool.

Elliott pulled one out and held it up before digging back into the box.

"There are even horses!" he said, delighted, but Jonathan was already out the door, shutting it behind him as he left.

# Paying the Wage

~ JONATHAN

*What was in that letter?* Jonathan wondered for the hundredth time in five minutes. He was back at the study door in a few seconds and pushed through it.

Lydia was sitting uprightly in a chair before the desk.

Silently, Jonathan moved to the desk chair and sat, wondering how long it would be before either of them spoke.

She stared at her hands in her lap. There was no sign of the letter.

*What's happened?*

Finally, Lydia took a deep breath and announced. "I'm afraid I must leave Whitehall."

"Leave?" Jonathan felt a lead weight in his gut.

"Yes. My mother needs me at home."

"Has some misfortune occurred? Can't..." Jonathan nearly said 'that fool brother of yours' but caught himself. "...can't Jack tend to it?"

"Apparently he disappeared several weeks ago."

"I...I can send Hardy. He'll see to whatever her needs are."

Lydia looked at him and laughed a little. "Hardy? Thank you, but I hardly think that's necessary when I can just go myself."

"But..."

*She's going...I've* nothing *to entice her to stay!*

"When will you go?" Jonathan asked, the words sticking in his throat.

"At once, escorted by Farmer Midwinter."

Jonathan cleared his throat and shifted in his chair, hating the man, hating his muck-caked boots, hating the hat he wore upon his head, and hating, most of all, the man's broad shoulders and swaggering gait.

“I hate to leave without my replacement present,” Lydia continued. “I ought to train her, whoever she may be...”

She stopped, her eyes flitting around the long-neglected room.

Jonathan looked, too, his eyes taking in the dust-covered furniture, the firewood dumped in a careless heap on the rug by the fireplace.

A sound drew his eyes back to her face. It was laughter, bubbling out of her as she continued to glance around the room.

“Clearly,” she said, “she will need *rigorous* training in order to maintain the high standards that I have set.”

Jonathan stared at her smiling face.

*Come, Man. Take it bravely. Don’t let her final memory be of you sniveling and pouting.*

Jonathan forced a laugh, knowing it probably sounded as hollow as it felt.

“Well, no one was ever meant to keep an entire house, play governess *and* cook all at once. You’ve done admirably considering everything. And that brings me to the next issue at hand. How much is your wage?”

“Fifteen pounds, three shillings for the year, but I’ve only been here for eleven months so thirteen pounds, two shillings will do.”

He retrieved the pouch of coins received for the sale of the horses from the desk drawer. There was still a good amount in it after the payments to Smith and the butcher. Attempting to keep a steady hand, he opened it and began to stack coins into little piles on the desktop.

*Let’s see, twenty shillings per pound...here’s a crown. That’s five shillings... What’s a florin again? Two shillings? Is this right? Don’t start over again as she’s watching! What idiot can’t count out fifteen pounds, three shillings?*

All the coins blurred into a mass of jangling metal. He grabbed at what might have been the required amount, but was likely much more and pushed the clinking pile across the desk to her.

She made no move to pick it up.

“What will you do?” he asked. *Besides spend the next several hours riding alongside the farmer?*

Lydia thought for a few seconds. "I will go home and milk cows...churn butter...sell eggs in town...tend the garden. Each Sunday after church I'll walk to Mr. Farington's house and borrow a book or two." She stared at her empty hands and sighed.

*Say something, you idiot. You may never see her again.*

"Well, I must thank you for not only all of your hard work, but also for your..."

*Damn, why couldn't I have practiced this? What am I thanking her for?*

"...for your...companionship. It has been...very enjoyable."

*The most enjoyable of my life.*

"It has been for me, as well," she responded.

Their eyes met.

"And of course, thank you for the employment," she said and smiled, motioning to the room around them. "I hope that if I ever request a recommendation for another placement that you will be willing to lie profusely about my effectiveness as a parlour maid."

"You will always have..." he broke off. He had nearly said that she would always have a place to work at Whitehall, but knew that was not something he could offer, nor was it what he *wanted* to offer.

*But what* can *I offer?*

*Nothing...*

He began again. "You will always have the highest of recommendations from me. The care you have given to Elliott has been invaluable, and...and..."

He trailed off again, uncertain how to continue.

They sat in silence for a moment.

"Sir Jonathan?"

"Yes, Lydia?" he answered, refusing to match the formality of her words with his own.

"I must confess something to you."

Jonathan's breath caught in his throat. "Wha...what is it?"

"I'm afraid I ruined a book from your library."

"I beg your pardon?"

"I left it outside, in the maze, and I've been too afraid to retrieve it for fear of seeing the state it's in. It's been through rain and even snow." She smiled apologetically and pushed a few coins from the pile towards him on the desk. "I think that ought to be enough to cover it and the letter I paid for with the laundry money."

"No, please," said Jonathan. "Take your money. You have more than earned it. The book is nothing."

Seeing that she made no move to retrieve the proffered coins, Jonathan stood, walked around the desk and clumsily picked up all of them himself. Kneeling beside her, he lifted her hand and pressed the money into it. Knowing he was violating innumerable rules of propriety, he held her warm, soft hand closed around the coinage as some of it slipped out onto her lap.

She didn't flinch at the contact, but stared at their joined hands.

He watched, immobile, as a single tear slid down her cheek, feeling a tiny splash as it fell onto his wrist.

Lydia began to pick up the stray coins with her free hand, and stood, disengaging herself from Jonathan's hold.

"Please excuse me," she murmured, dropping the money into an apron pocket, and then she was gone, her footsteps sounding down the hall.

# Fleeing Without the Apple

~ Lydia

Still feeling the touch of Jonathan's hand, Lydia's one goal was to get to her room without bursting into sobs.

*He meant* nothing *by it,* she insisted to herself. *You've seen him with his sister. He is gentle and kind to sensitive females.*

*Breathe,* she told herself.

She was relieved he hadn't pressed her for answers as to why she was needed back at Hillcrest. The few excuses she had quickly formulated would not have seemed sound after much questioning.

Lydia had prayed for a way to leave Whitehall, and two days later, Paul Midwinter rode in on his wagon with a letter, the contents of which she alone knew. She hadn't lied to Jonathan. Her mother had written that weeks ago, Jack had declared his intention to go to Tortmouth to join the Royal Navy, and that he hadn't been heard from since. Still, she doubted her presence back at Hillcrest was the necessary thing that she had implied.

Moving past the parlor, she suddenly stopped, halted by the memory of something within it.

Entering, she shut the door behind her, and ascended the bookshelf's ladder to seek the little paper apple, the initial sight of which had angered her so many months earlier.

Every book, she saw, was covered with dust.

*Oh, my beauties, I have neglected you far too long, and now I'll never tend to you again,* thought Lydia as she climbed. Reaching the top, she pulled some books off the shelf to begin her search.

*Nothing.*

*Surely it's here.*

She lifted more volumes from where she knew the little treasure had been.

*It's gone!*

Panic seized her as she shoved more and more books aside. Tears filled her eyes, blurring her search. She swiped them away with the back of her hand.

*Did it fall to the ground?* From the height, she surveyed the scene below, scanning it for a glimpse of red, fruitlessly.

Her search was over, she knew, but still she stood for a moment as the rung dug into the arches of her thinly-shod feet.

*Stop crying.*

*Stupid.*

*Stupid!*

*It was just a little piece of paper.*

She envisioned herself sitting on her bed back at Hillcrest, pulling the apple out of some hiding place, tears spilling down her cheeks, pointlessly.

*Yes, it's better this way.*

*Now stop crying. You need to pack your things and leave with Paul.*

She breathed in deeply, and resituated the books upon the shelf before slowly climbing down the ladder.

*Stop crying.*

# Watching a Departure

~ JONATHAN

"Master Elliott," Lydia said as they stood in the side yard. "I'm afraid I have some bad news."

Jonathan saw Elliott's little nose crinkle as he gave her his full attention.

"I've just received a letter from my mother and she needs me back at the farm."

"What farm? Is it far away?" His little hand reached out and grabbed hers familiarly.

"Yes, I'm afraid it is."

Looking concerned, he asked, "When will you be back?"

"I...I won't be. I am very sorry to have to say goodbye."

"You're *leaving*?" Elliott asked.

His lower lip began to tremble as Lydia nodded. He motioned toward the man who was several feet away, rearranging things in his wagon bed, making room for Lydia's trunk. "With the Idiot Farmer?"

"Elliott! There's no need to be unkind! Farmer Midwinter is taking me home to my mother." Her voice broke on the last few words.

"But you can't go!" he insisted. "You may go for a...a week, but then you have to come back."

Though he wished he could say the same words, and that there was power behind them, Jonathan interrupted, "Elliott, she's leaving. Don't make it unpleasant for her."

"I don't want her to go, so she can't!"

"Elliott..." sighed Jonathan.

"My mother needs me," Lydia said softly.

"But *I* need you!" the little boy wailed, throwing his arms around the maid. Sobs shook his body as she held him, tears streaming down her own face.

"I'm very glad to have had all the time I've had with you," Lydia said, rubbing her hand across his back. "We've done so many fun things together and you've made me so proud with how smart you are."

Pulling his head back, Elliott looked up at her. "Is it because I gave you a black eye? I didn't mean to!"

"No, it's nothing to do with that. Please, Elliott..."

Looking completely unaware of the doleful scene before him, the farmer approached, nodding and said, "It's a good thing I brought the wagon on this trip, Liddy, or we'd be squeezed into Zelda's saddle together."

Jonathan felt his chest tighten.

"Such crassness is unbecoming!" he barked.

The farmer shrugged, mumbling, "No harm meant."

Lydia continued to shush the little boy who was clinging to her, then looked up at Jonathan and said quietly, "I must go now."

Jonathan nodded and began to pull at Elliott's arms, which quickly clasped themselves around Jonathan's leg.

"Goodbye," he said thickly, reaching to shake the hand she held out to him.

Their eyes met for one last confusing, misery-fraught moment before she walked to the wagon.

*This can't be goodbye,* Jonathan determined as he watched her climb into the seat beside the now disinterested farmer.

*But why wouldn't it be?* he asked himself. *What could possibly bring us back together?*

As he watched the wagon take the turn in the drive, the feeling of dread that had balanced itself on Jonathan's shoulders from the day he sat in Harris' office threatened to swallow him whole.

Elliott continued to clutch at Jonathan's leg, sobbing.

Though Jonathan pressed the little boy's head against his side, his eyes never drifted from the departing wagon.

When it had disappeared around the bend, Jonathan stood for a moment, knowing it was not going to reappear, then picked Elliott up and carried him into the kitchen. Settling himself at the table, he sat for an uncertain amount of time, staring out into nothingness.

Curled up on the bench, Elliott had laid his head on Jonathan's lap, his sobs having devolved into an occasional hiccup or shaky inhalation. Jonathan patted the boy's shoulder every now and then, as he continued to sit and think in the near stillness.

Finally, Jonathan reached for a pencil and his sketchbook, which lay before him on the table.

There, poking out of the leaves, was a crisp white corner of paper.

He felt a stab of hope and curiosity.

*Has the dear girl left me something?*

Opening the book to where the paper had been placed, he saw the drawing of Widdy examining his foot.

His mouth felt dry as he lifted the loose sheet, unfolded it and read:

'Twas not enough 'tis grossly wide
(Can barely in its shoe abide)
Nor that its scent which lingers long
Is putrid and unearthly strong.
Its biggest toe baits all to stare
And festers with unruly hair.
The coarsened skin across its sole
Well imitates the hide of troll.

One more misfortune to report...
Alas, a newly sprouted wart!

*Apt, as always,* Jonathan thought, a wry smile lifting the heavy corners of his mouth.

After reading it over several more times, Jonathan sighed and pulled his sketchbook toward him. Turning to a blank page near the back, he began to draw.

Within moments, the page was filled. In spite of the ache in his gut, he was pleased with the drawing as he tore it out of the book.

He thought for several moments as Elliott hiccupped beside him and then wrote a few lines of poetry of his own invention beneath the drawing. Reading it over, Jonathan smirked.

*That's perfectly awful,* he thought before adding a final sentence.

Grabbing a candle on the table, he said, "Elliott, sit up for a moment. I need to light this."

Unsteadily, Elliott did as he was told, peering out miserably from between puffy lids, his upper lip slick with mucus.

"For heaven's sake, clean your nose," Jonathan said as he stood up from the table. "You could grease an axle with it."

He walked over to the fire, and stuck the candle's wick into flame as Elliott dragged his shirt sleeve over his face.

Taking a few coins from the jar he had seen Lydia pay the laundress with, Jonathan returned to the table and tilted the burning candle over the bottom of the paper. Molten wax dripped onto its surface and Jonathan pressed the coins into it.

"What are you doing?" Elliott asked, his red-rimmed eyes fixed on the page.

"It may be a hardship for her to pay the postage, but if the post boy hears jingling, he might steal the money inside and throw the letter in a ditch."

Tearing a second page out of his book, he fashioned it into an envelope, stuck the folded drawing and poem inside, and sealed the whole thing with more wax. On the front he wrote the address he had memorized a few days earlier:

Miss Lydia Smythe
Hillcrest Farm
Shinford, Coddingshire

Standing again, Jonathan announced, "Come, Elliott. We're riding into town to post this and speak with Harris."

# Confounded by a Limerick

~ Lydia
Hillcrest Farm

When her mother went out to the hen house, Lydia let her face relax into the look of misery that had been attempting to seize her features for days.

Nearly a week earlier, Lydia had arrived home from Whitehall.

Sally had turned, startled from washing a few dishes in the sink. Bursting into tears, she had rushed to enfold Lydia in her arms, crying out, "Oh, dearest! Why are you here? What has happened?"

"All is well, Mama," Lydia had lied, then added truthfully, "I wanted to come home and be with you."

"Oh, my beautiful girl." Sally, her eyes streaming, had smoothed Lydia's hair away from her face and said gravely, "We shall face our trials together."

Lydia nodded, though she wondered to which trials her mother was referring. She studied Sally's features, noting that they had grown less distinct in her absence. It was as if their lines had been blurred, leaving a looser arrangement of nose, eyes and mouth, all sagging at the edges.

*She is troubled, and I shan't burden her further with my own worries*

Squeezing her mother's hand, Lydia had asked, "Have the chickens been fed yet this evening?"

Now, Lydia was taking the bottles and tins off the shelf in the kitchen, wiping the dust off each one and returning it to its place.

Examining a small bottle of ground nutmeg, Lydia recalled the occasional prodigal purchases Farmer Smythe had surprised his wife with years ago, when the farm was prosperous.

Suddenly, Lydia heard a knock on the door.

She answered it, still clutching the nutmeg, and saw a stranger standing before her.

The man's hair was streaked with gray, and his face was tanned and leathery. Still, there was an element of youthfulness about him, as if his outer shell had aged far sooner than had his inside.

"Letter for Lydia Smythe," he said.

"A letter?" Lydia's mouth went dry.

The man nodded and examined the front of the envelope in his hand. "From...Whitehall in Bevelshire."

Lydia's eyes were riveted on the white rectangle.

*Whitehall?*

"I..." Lydia stuttered, her heart beating wildly. "I've only a penny..." She nearly added 'to spare', but caught herself. If the man knew she had more money, he might hold out for it before handing the precious envelope over to her. Even the one penny was an extravagance to spend when the hens weren't laying well.

The man shrugged.

"That'll do," he said, thrusting his hand out, palm up.

"One moment, please." Lydia hurried off to retrieve the money, hoping he wouldn't overhear the jangling of any other coins as she dug the one out of the jar.

As if in a dream, Lydia dropped the penny into the man's hand and he, in turn, handed her the letter. Then he was across the yard, swinging back up into his saddle. By the time he was gone, Lydia was still standing in the doorway, staring at the envelope.

*It's Sir Jonathan's writing.*

On shaking legs, she walked back into the kitchen and eased herself down into a chair at the table. With trembling hands, she loosened the waxen seal and pulled out a single sheet of paper. Two pennies were affixed to it with wax.

*That was thoughtful.*

She popped them off.

Unfolding the paper, she saw on it a fine example of one of Jonathan's drawings. This one was of herself, she recognized immediately, on the roof of Whitehall. Standing, she was smiling happily, her hair blowing wildly around her face. Before her was Jonathan, tall and lanky. Leaning forward, he held out to her a stack of papers. Some of the sheets had broken free from his hands and were being swept away in the wind.

Below the drawing was written:

There once was a girl called Foote
Whose influence firmly took root
On all at Whitehall.
Then she left with Paul
(Who seemed to be a bit of a brute)

Underneath that, in smaller letters was penned:

Perhaps you could critique my rhyme and meter.

Lydia sat immobile, a mélange of emotions swirling within her.

*What can he possibly mean? My 'influence firmly took root on all at Whitehall'? Who is 'all'? Elliott, of course. And perhaps Sophia with my noticing of the laudanum...but is he including himself? How did I influence* him*? And this bid for critique at the end...certainly that can't be what he's truly after...*

She looked again at the picture, noticing that in the top left corner was a mob-cap flying off in the wind. The whole presentation was slightly amusing, yet it lacked the absurdity of so many of his other drawings.

Her mouth was drawn open, as if she was laughing.

Lydia's face warmed as she remembered what thoughts had filled her mind as she stood on the roof that day.

*I was such a fool.*

She shifted her focus to the rendition of Jonathan.

*He's offering me...what? Papers that blow away in the wind?*

*What does that signify?*

She studied the lines of his face. There was no trace of amusement in them, only solemnity, as his lengthy arm held the papers out to her.

*Ugh...This is why I fled! Such confusion and ridiculous notions...I stopped searching for the apple for this very reason...but now I have* this *token to weep and wonder over.*

She recalled the look of apology in his eyes when she realized she'd been wrong, realized that regardless of how he felt, he couldn't allow himself to love her.

*He was sorry for me...and still is now.*

Tears pricked her eyes as she folded the paper and slipped it back into the envelope.

*He's apologizing for being born a baronet when I was born a farmer's daughter.*

*He's only trying to be kind. If I don't send a response he might think I despise him.*

The two pennies lay on the table.

*I could post it tomorrow when I'm in town to sell the eggs...but what ought I to say?*

*I know that money and grandiosity on one side, and* nothing *on the other, makes for a disastrous imbalance, regardless of equal minds and temperaments.*

*But I can't* tell *him that!*

*No, I must veil my meaning and emotion as well as he hid his in this.* She laid her hand atop the letter.

*Levity,* she thought. *Yes, levity has always worked well between us.*

With a sigh, she rose from the table in search of paper, determined to concoct a witty reply, despite the ache deep within her.

# The Selling of the Birthright

~ Elliott
Whitehall

Of all the strangers Mr. Harris had brought to Whitehall over the past several months, Mr. Caspar was the strangest.

He had a long flowing mustache that reminded Elliott of a dog he'd seen once in Plimbridge, and his voice was odd. He didn't speak slow and choppy like Heldmann, but he pronounced words as if his mouth was full of something that he was about to start chewing. Mr. Harris said he was from a place called 'America'.

Mr. Caspar's enthusiasm for Whitehall was evident from the very beginning of the tour. He asked more questions than any of the other people had and wanted to look at certain parts of the house more than once.

Normally Elliott enjoyed accompanying Jonathan as he led the strangers around the house, but this tour was taking much longer than the previous ones had. He nearly wandered off to play with Sassy, but knowing his favorite part was drawing closer, he stayed with Jonathan.

Months earlier, at the end of the very first tour with two unknown women and a man, Jonathan had surprised Elliott by pushing aside a desk in the hallway. Behind it was a door that Elliott had never noticed before. To his delight, it was a passageway leading up to the roof of Whitehall.

All together, they had stood looking out over what Mr. Harris termed "the length, breadth and beauty of the estate". As they gazed out on the villages, near and far, and the woods, blackish green on the horizon, a small herd of deer appeared, running along in wild formation in the distance.

Elliott was entranced.

Once they had tromped back down the little staircase, Elliott had asked Jonathan excitedly, "Why did you never show me this before? We ought to go up there every day!"

Though Jonathan had not seemed to hear a number of other things Elliott had said that afternoon, he paused at this and peered down at his little brother.

"Erm...one moment, please, Ma'am," he said to the visiting woman who had begun to ask him a question. "Elliott, you're never to go up there without me."

Then looking around, he walked over to a bookshelf.

"Elliott, would you help me move this a few inches to the right?" Jonathan asked.

Surprised at the request, Elliott had made his way over. At Jonathan's prompting, Elliott pushed with all of his strength on his side of the shelf, and was somewhat shamed at their apparent inability to shift it.

"Harris, would you be so good as to move that writing desk aside and help me position this there in its stead?" Jonathan asked.

Elliott watched as a few moments of the grown men straining resulted in the heavy shelf blocking the mysterious door.

*I don't think Jonathan was trying very hard when it was* me *helping him*, Elliott thought peevishly.

There the shelf had stayed until each time a tour was concluding with Harris and Jonathan moving it aside to reveal the little door.

Now they were finally making their way down the hallway with Mr. Caspar, though he paused a long time to study a section of the wall.

"A fine example of late $17^{th}$ Century solid oak paneling," he murmured, his mustache nearly brushing the siding. This was one of the few things that came out of the man's mouth that Elliott understood.

*Come on then!* Elliott wanted to push him from behind. *There might be a herd going past at this very moment!*

When the man's curiosity of the immobile piece of wood was at last satisfied, he turned to Jonathan and asked, "What wonder awaits us next?"

"This way please, to see *the hidden passageway*," Jonathan replied with a flourish of his hand and a lift of his eyebrows.

Mr. Caspar's face broke into a grin under his dense hedge of lip hair and he nearly trotted after his host.

"It's just behind here," Jonathan said, and squatted beside the heavy bookshelf. Seeming to anticipate what was about to occur, Caspar beat Harris to the other side.

"Which way?" the American asked, placing his hands under its base.

"Toward me, about two feet," Jonathan responded.

Once the small party had ascended the staircase and emerged on the roof, Mr. Caspar spun around, staring in every direction.

"I must have it!" he declared, exultant laughter bursting out of him as he raised his arms up into the air.

Elliott was mortified by the man's exuberance, but this lessened into minor embarrassment when he heard Jonathan chuckling beside him.

"We can return to the study and sign the papers this instant," Harris, who had been nearly silent until this point, said.

At this, Caspar stuck his hand out to Jonathan, who readily accepted it. Suddenly, Elliott saw that the large hand was being offered to him as well. Reaching out, he gripped Caspar's hand and was rattled by the most vigorous handshake of his entire life.

***

That evening, Jonathan sighed as he popped open the toasting frame above Elliott's plate and dropped a fresh rarebit onto it.

"And with just a few strokes of a pen, our birthright is sold," he said as Elliott burned his fingertips on the toast's perfectly golden surface. "Now, dear brother, we must go and find our *future*."

Elliott didn't understand these statements, but had recently grown weary of asking about everything he didn't comprehend. He found that even when his questions were answered, he still felt confused much of the time.

Lifting the rarebit to his lips, he crunched into it, thankful for the familiar tanginess of the hot, salty cheese.

# Lamenting a Loss of Solitude

~ HARDY

*Ugh!*

Having run through the stable for decades, even in the dark, Hardy was not used to his knee crashing into anything while doing so. Yet, this was the second time in a day that he wondered what bruising would result from his clumsiness. Now the stalls were housing only two horses while the other pens were overloaded with furniture and boxes.

Things had changed so much over the last few months. They could hardly feel more different.

Some changes were likely for the better.

*I'm supposin' the new owner'll pay on time and in full,* Hardy thought, rubbing his knee, then ventured forth in the gloom trying to avoid any other obstacles. *That'll be good!*

When Sir Jonathan told him that Whitehall was to be sold, Hardy had worried for his own future. He had stopped expecting full payment from Lady Clyde a few years earlier. Having heard stories over pints at the Weary Lass from other grooms, he was thankful that he had a place to sleep, food to eat and an easy job to fill his days. He'd never wanted to risk his preferable situation with a complaint over short pay.

*But I wonder how long before I understand a word that Caspar fella says. They say it's English he speaks, but tha's not what I hear.*

His shoulder collided with something else.

*Ugh! Still, the mess down here is nothing to the change upstairs!* he thought, wondering how long before he had his living space all to himself again.

Somehow Mr. Caspar had offered Sir Jonathan and Master Elliott a place in the carriage house until they found a home to purchase and move into.

"Stay as long as you want!" the mustachioed man had declared. Hardy had stood by smiling, but thinking crossly about the noise of a little boy filling his personal quarters.

*At least at night they bunk in Glaser's old room, so's there's no complainin' about me snorin'.*

*Still, I want me chair back,* thought Hardy, recalling how Master Elliott would often hang from the sturdy arms of the seat nearest the fireplace.

Finally past the clutter and at the base of the staircase to his quarters above, Hardy began to hurry up the steps.

Halfway there, the sound of Sir Jonathan's voice reached his ears.

"So Harris may have finally found the place." The words drifted down the passageway. "His inquiries turned up a farm in Coddingshire that sounds suitable. We are poorer than we've ever thought possible, but there is still enough for that."

*Who's he talking to?*

"Oh, and rest assured that your dowry will remain untouched...in case Buffant or Spalding should reappear."

A familiar sound--Miss Sophia's laughter--rang out, halting Hardy's ascension.

*Damn! And now the girl's up there as well? I suppose the Lady's pouring 'em tea outta me kettle at the table.*

Turning on his heel, Hardy headed back down the stairs. *If there's no peace above stairs, I might as well pack up more boxes...get 'em outta here sooner once they* do *find a place...*

In moments, he was in Whitehall's library, climbing the little ladder to reach the top shelves. What looked like a hundred crates were on the floor below, some already filled to capacity. Hardy had been told that though most of the furniture would be left behind for Caspar's use, every single book in the house was to be packed.

Hardy wondered why it was *his* job to put things into boxes since he worked for Caspar now, but the irritation had lessened when Sir Jonathan, and even little Elliott, had joined him in the library earlier that day to fill boxes.

*Sir Jonathan's turned out a'right. He's not a blowing show horse like his father. 'S'a shame he's lost Whitehall.*

Filling his right arm with a load from the top shelf, Hardy descended the flimsy ladder, gripping its side and wondering when a rung would snap under his heavy feet. On the floor, he dropped the books into the nearest box.

*Hmm...wha's that?* he wondered as a sliver of red peeking out from the pages of a book caught his eye.

Had he been literate, Hardy would have noted that the book containing the mystery was *Robinson Crusoe.*

Pinching the little puzzlement between his calloused thumb and index finger, the man pulled and found himself holding an apple-shaped piece of paper. Though severely bent by the way it was stuck in the book's pages, it was a lovely representation, rosy with a narrow green leaf jutting out of the top. Even Hardy, who rarely noticed the aesthetic value of anything beyond the golden brown of a well-roasted potato or the swell of a plump woman's bosom, was vaguely charmed by its appearance.

Flipping it over, he saw that someone had written something on the back, but the inscrutable lines didn't hold his attention, so he regarded the front again for a moment. He nearly slipped it into his pocket, thinking he would ask the Clydes if it meant anything to any of them.

But the memory of the invasion of his living space irked him again.

*Ahh...*

Crumpling the little drawing in his fist, he tossed it into the nearby fireplace, which was cold and dusty from disuse.

*It's pro'ly nothin'.*

# Fretting Over a New Address

~ LYDIA
HILLCREST FARM

Lydia smiled as she watched the graying postman head down the drive to the main road. In his saddlebag was a letter, headed to Whitehall, and in her hand, she held one from there.

*Mama will not mind if I pause in the baking to read this,* she knew, heading for the kitchen.

At first, the letters exchanged had been thin, but within a couple of weeks, they were fat and arriving two or more times per week. Now Lydia was always listening for the sound of the postman's horse trotting into the yard, hoping for a delivery.

Each letter that she received contained two pennies, pressed into blobs of wax, stuck to a page. Lydia would place them on the windowsill in the kitchen where they would lay until the next letter arrived, and postage needed to be paid.

When the stack of fresh paper in the farmhouse's desk had been depleted, Lydia had taken an old newspaper and written her response to Jonathan between the text lines of the articles. Since then, every letter that he had sent included two clean sheets of paper.

Eventually, Elliott began to add a few sentences to the end of each of Jonathan's letters, telling Lydia of Sassy's latest exploit or the snake he found in the woodpile. Lydia was pleased with the progress she saw in his writing, and she always wrote a few lines directed to him in her letters.

It had been nearly a year since the confusing drawing and limerick from Whitehall had arrived. When Lydia responded to that, she had carefully worded a light-hearted reply, wanting to leave a pleasant final impression in Sir Jonathan's mind.

But almost immediately, a second letter from Jonathan, equally entertaining, but devoid of mystifying poetry and unsettling drawings, had arrived. As Lydia read it over again and again, many droll responses formed in her mind, and she felt especially clever as she wrote out her reply. Shortly afterward, a third letter arrived and they hadn't stopped since. For the first two months, she wrote back thinking, *I won't respond so quickly next time. I should wean myself of this.*

Her face still grew warm when she recalled the ridiculous thoughts that had run through her mind during those last few wonderfully horrible days at Whitehall. She had never spoken of them to her mother, hoping that they would cease to exist if she pretended she'd never thought them.

Sometimes while she sat at the table reading a letter, Lydia sensed that Sally's gaze was lingering on her. When this happened, Lydia would laugh lightly about an anecdote in the text and hand the page to her mother, wanting Sally to see that the letters contained no proclamations of undying love, nor promises of futures intertwined.

*Sir Jonathan and I are friends*, thought Lydia, emphasizing the 'sir' in her mind as she settled down into a chair. *Unusual friends who live very different lives...who appreciate each other...but that is all. Besides, his letters give me something to look forward to. Something beyond books from Mr. Farington, or an especially beautiful sunset. And there's no risk of making a fool of myself because I am here in my place, and he is there in his.*

With a gentle tug, Lydia tore through the wax seal and pulled the newly-arrived letter from the envelope.

*This one's much shorter than usual,* she thought, disappointed as she began to read.

Dear Miss Lydia-- I'm writing to ask that you send future correspondence to a new address:

Sir Jonathan Clyde, Bart.

formerly Warren Farm

Peaslough, Coddingshire

Elliott and I are to be living there for now. I apologize for the brevity of this letter, but we are in the midst of much upheaval due to the move. I shall write more very soon—Jonathan

*The Great Family has acquired another property? And it's here in Coddingshire?*

Her heart began to thump. *Where is Peaslough? I've never heard of it, so perhaps it's not too close. But still! What if he were to...?*

Lydia fretted, poring over the lines again, hoping to see evidence that she was safe, safe in merely exchanging letters, safe from feeling unsettled and foolish when he looked at her.

She found no assurance in the letter. Pushing it back into the envelope, she hoped fervently that its writer would remain in Peaslough, wherever that was.

# Finding Peaslough

~ HELDMANN
THE OPEN ROAD

Heldmann thought that by now he would be accustomed to feeling lost in the English countryside, but it still filled him with a sense of dread when he realized he had no idea where he was, nor how to get to where he hoped to be.

Herr Clyde had invited him to visit his new home on a farm near a village called Peaslough. Looking again at the letter he held, Heldmann saw it was located south of a town called Huppingdon. Huppingdon he had found, but Peaslough had thus far evaded him.

Even the energetic trot of Heinz beneath him had slowed to a lethargic clopping as the unmarked road stretched out under their feet.

Right around noon, as Heldmann stood by a large wooden signpost at a crossroad, he took one of the last swigs of water from his bottle. As he was trying, fruitlessly, to make out any words on the sun-blistered sign, a cart appeared down the road. Urging Heinz to a trot, Heldmann soon found himself riding alongside the chicken-filled vehicle, which was driven by a grumpy looking, hunch-shouldered man.

Having prepared his tongue for the dexterity required to ask the question, Heldmann stated, slowly and clearly, "Please forgive...where is *Peaslough*?"

The cart driver's face crumpled as he hunched further into himself, never looking up from the donkey's backside in front of him. In a sudden burst of energy, he whacked the donkey's rump with the long, swishy stick he held, and remained silent.

*Ugh...the chicken-man is above speaking with a foreigner,* thought Heldmann, wheeling Heinz around. In a moment he was back at the crossroad, squinting at the sign.

It was then that a modest, one-horse chaise rounded the corner and slowed next to the sign as well. A young woman driving it passed the reins to her other hand as she shaded her eyes and looked up at the sign.

*Ought I to ask her?* Heldmann wondered, frustrated at the barely civil reception he anticipated from the young woman. *Certainly she finds herself finer than the chicken-cart man.*

"Please forgive," Heldmann began almost sullenly. "Where is *Peaslough*...do you knows?"

Turning her gaze from the sign to the German, the woman gasped and declared, "Herr Heldmann!"

The shock he felt at hearing his name spoken by the stranger left him dumbfounded.

"Pl...please forgive?" he stuttered, studying what little he could see of her face, which was mostly obscured within her riding bonnet.

"It's Sophia Clyde!" she said, pulling the bonnet down to hang by its ties around her neck as she began to chatter in English. Taking in the honey-colored locks now framing her face, Heldmann was too startled to even attempt to follow the words she was saying.

After several sentences, Miss Sophia seemed to sense his complete perplexedness.

"So sorry," she said with a laugh. Clearing her throat, she started to speak again, this time in a halting, oddly-pronounced jangle of German words.

It was one of the most beautiful sounds Heldmann had ever heard.

She was good to see him, but surprising, and she was to visit brother at farm where he purchase. The journey is new, but Jonathan says easy very.

Heldmann swallowed hard as the somewhat understandable information spilled out.

*She is traveling to see Herr Clyde as well?*

"You go...mmm, to see...brother?"

She smiled happily, nodding.

"I go!" His own face broke into a grin. "We goes...together?"

"Ja," she accepted his invitation.

Thus, Heldmann restarted his search for the new Clyde residence with a sense of joyous levity that he had not felt since arriving in England.

***

It was nearing dinnertime when the German and the baronet's sister found the farm which they sought.

Herr Clyde hurried out of the house, a stout farmhouse made of stone and timber, calling out something undecipherable. His joy at seeing them was apparent as he urged them inside with a wave of the hand and a broad smile.

The little brother was there, sitting at the table, shelling peas. He hurried to embrace his sister at their reunion, and then solemnly extended his hand to Heldmann.

During a meal of cheese on toast and peas, the three Clydes conversed happily, occasionally turning to Heldmann in attempts to include him. After the meal was finished and the four of them had tidied the kitchen, Herr Clyde walked the two newcomers around the house and grounds, pointing out various sites. There were several bedrooms, and Herr Clyde indicated to Heldmann which one he would sleep in that night.

Heldmann regarded everything with interest, now and then murmuring, "Ja, ist gut."

Still, in the solitude of his own brain, Heldmann thought things within the house were odd. He wasn't surprised that Herr Clyde had moved to this property from the ostentatious place where he had lived before. That was perfectly understandable.

*Who would want to live in a cavernous, cold, enormous building when a comfortable farmhouse such as this exists? Clearly this is preferable, and much easier to keep clean,* he thought, recalling the layers of dust he had seen on everything during his second visit to Whitehall.

No, the man's removal from there didn't confound Heldmann. It was how things had been arranged in this new house that confused him.

First, there were the paintings. On the wall, in the farmhouse's one parlor, hung four portraits. Their frames were overly-large and crammed together on the wall space.

Miss Sophia laughed merrily at the sight as the group paused before them.

Studying the faces, Heldmann recognized strains of resemblance running through the features of all four.

*Ancestors,* he determined.

Their glaring presence in the cozy room seemed a little overwhelming, but Heldmann dismissed it as the way Englishmen honored their forefathers.

But then there were the bookshelves.

In nearly every room, even the kitchen, there were whole walls laden with shelves, which held rows and rows of books of various colors and sizes. The smell of newly cut wood, though pleasant, hung heavily in the air, making Heldmann wonder if all of the shelves had just been constructed. The vast number of them throughout the rooms certainly looked incongruous with the original plan for the house.

*Why so many?* Heldmann wondered. *Ah well, these English...they are certainly odd in more ways than one.*

Once they were outside on the farmland itself, Heldman felt more at ease. Herr Clyde led them to the barn, a solid structure, built of stone, and similar in shape to the house.

*This,* Heldmann thought, patting a wall almost affectionately, *this will stand for generations. My father would be proud to own such a barn.*

Miss Sophia stepped delicately around, lifting the hem of her skirt a few inches, examining the dirt floor beneath her. Heldmann looked away, determined not to be caught staring at her ankle.

She had little reason to be so careful. No animals except for two horses were stabled there, though Heldmann heard Herr Clyde say 'cows' and 'pigs' as he motioned to different pens, so he supposed there were plans to stock the farm.

Stepping out of the gloom of the barn, they walked a few paces out into the arable land. Kneeling, Heldmann picked up a handful of dirt and sifted it through his fingers. It was good, dark earth.

*Yes,* Heldmann thought, his many years on a farm leading him to a conclusion. *Herr Clyde has a good situation. All is much better here than the grandiose Whitehall.*

He stood and saw that the siblings were now silent and intently watching him, pleased expectation on their faces.

"Is good," he said, sweeping his arm to indicate all of the property around them. "I am farmer...I knows...mmm...Is good."

"Danke, Herr Heldmann." Herr Clyde held a hand over his chest and dipped his head, smiling. "Danke."

The sun was nearly setting now, turning the clouds on the horizon red and purple. Jonathan waved his guests back inside the house and they were soon settled in the parlor.

The two eldest Clydes began to talk again while Elliott played with some toy soldiers on the carpet. At first, Miss Sophia would occasionally turn and involve Heldmann by interpreting a few words, letting him know the topic that was being discussed. However, after a while, her efforts became sparse, and Heldmann sensed that the conversation had taken a serious turn. Miss Sophia's face looked thoughtful as Herr Clyde spoke on and on to her. Heldmann heard the word 'Foote' many times.

*Yes, where is Foote?* Heldmann wondered, but refrained from asking.

"Heldmann." Young Elliott, nudged his shoulder. "Look. Der Hund."

The boy held a contorted hand out into the glow of the firelight, casting a malformed shadow on the far wall.

"Ah, is good..." Heldmann nodded.

"Jonathan." The earnest tone of Miss Sophia's voice arrested Heldmann's attention. She continued slowly, deliberately, and Heldmann had no trouble understanding each word as she said, "You must speak with her."

She was leaning forward, resting her hand on Herr Clyde's knee, a look of intent sincerity on her face. She repeated herself.

"You must speak with her. Go. Soon."

Herr Clyde stared into the fire with the most unsettled look Heldmann had ever seen upon his usually jovial face.

Suddenly feeling that he was intruding on an intimate and vulnerable moment, Heldmann turned his attention back to Elliott, who was nearby, still playing with the shadows.

Taking the boy's little hands in his own, Heldmann gently manipulated them into place, saying, "Ja, ist gut."

Elliott's face broke into a grin as he cast the silhouette of a butterfly flittering across the faces of the four ancestors.

# Vomiting Porridge

~ JONATHAN
THE OPEN ROAD

Though it was a cool day, Jonathan could feel the perspiration collecting under his arms and dripping down his sides. His palms, too, were clammy as he passed the reins back and forth between them.

Two days earlier, he had started out on this same journey, made it to within half a mile of his destination, and then retraced his steps all the way back to his home.

*Well, now I know how to get there*, he had told himself.

Now, the clopping of Achilles' hooves beneath him jarred his innards mercilessly. He'd had no appetite that morning, but knew he had a long ride ahead of him, so he'd forced himself to eat. The few bites of porridge hadn't settled well.

Inhaling shakily, he thought through what he would say on his arrival.

*'How do you do, Farmwife Smythe?' No...no. 'I am pleased to meet you, Widow Smythe.'*

He cringed.

*Ought I to call her 'Widow'? I don't want to remind the woman of her husband's death the moment that I meet her. Must I call her* anything*? Well, I would think so. One doesn't introduce oneself and ignore the fact that the other person has a name. Ugh...*

Still unsure on that point, he thought a little further into the conversation and began to practice it aloud.

"Might I speak with...? I...I...mmm, uh, that is..."

*Good God, I sound like Heldmann!*

Pulling Achilles to an abrupt stop, Jonathan nearly jumped from the horse's back. Just in time, he planted his hands on his knees before his stomach turned inside out, emptying itself into the dirt. Fortunately, the projected mass missed his top hat, which had tumbled from his head to the ground a second earlier.

Achilles stood by, pawing the ground uneasily, as Jonathan removed a bottle from his saddlebag. Taking a swig of water, Jonathan swished his mouth and spat, then ran a shaky, open hand over his face.

"Steady, boy. Steady," he said, perhaps to Achilles, then leaned his forehead against the animal's warm neck.

He rested there a long moment before climbing back into the saddle.

# Abandoning a Letter

~ LYDIA
HILLCREST FARM

The rotten tooth's eviction was
Concluded with a yank,
A wrench so strong it...

*It what...?*

Lydia sat at the kitchen table, biting the end of her pen, and thinking.

*What rhymes with 'yank'? 'Prank', 'clank', stank'? No, none of those will work.*

In his latest contribution, Elliott had requested that Lydia write a poem about his long-ago tooth extraction. She was working diligently, hoping to have the verse done and sealed in an envelope by the time the postman arrived.

Older letters from the Clydes formed a mountainous pile in front of her. Too fat and rounded to stack neatly, they had slipped off of each other, and were scattered across the table's top. Earlier that morning, Sally had joked that soon Lydia would need to store them in their own pen in the barn.

*A wrench so strong...*

Lydia bit the pen harder.

Suddenly, she heard the sound of a jangling stirrup outside the kitchen door.

*Oh, no! He's never here this early!* she thought, disappointed for once at the postman's arrival. *Still, he must have a letter to deliver, or he wouldn't likely have stopped at all.*

With the unfinished letter in hand, she arose from the table, grabbed a penny from the windowsill, and opened the door.

"You're early today!" she called out to the rider in the drive. "I've not fini..."

Her words were cut off by a mixture of rapturous, yet horrified, shock.

There, in the yard of Hillcrest Farm, sitting astride his fine horse, wearing his top hat and riding coat, was Sir Jonathan.

Lydia clutched at the doorjamb as the penny fell from her grasp.

She and Jonathan regarded each other in silence, their mouths slightly open, their eyes wide.

*Why...? What...?*

Lydia's legs began to quiver beneath her.

At the same moment, her mother's steady hand was on her shoulder.

"You may tie your horse to the post by the water trough, sir," Sally said from behind her. "And then please come inside for a cup of tea."

Jonathan dipped his head and turned Achilles toward the trough.

"Go, seat yourself in the parlor," Sally whispered while smoothing Lydia's hair down from the crown of her head.

"But I...I..." Lydia stammered.

"Shhh, dearest," Sally soothed. "Go to the parlor."

Lydia somehow wobbled her way there and sat on the room's one settee. She struggled to arrange her legs in a way to stop them from shaking.

*What is he...? What will I...?*

In a moment, Jonathan was filling the doorway, and then settling himself in the chair beside her.

Looking down, Lydia saw that she still held the paper.

"I was just writing to you...and Elliott," Lydia murmured, loosening her fingers' hold on the now severely crumpled sheet.

Jonathan nodded mutely, staring at the paper in her hand.

As he did so, she studied his face, seeing details she had nearly forgotten in the year of his absence. She gazed at the length of his eyelashes, the straightness of his nose, the way his upper lip protruded slightly further than his lower one. He had removed his hat, which now rested on his knee, and his dark hair was stuck to his head, damp in places.

*He is here,* she thought, her heart thumping wildly, *sitting, just feet away. He is here, with me.*

She eyed the sparse growth of stubble on his chin, the faint flush of colour in his cheeks.

From the doorway, Sally cleared her throat.

"You must be Sir Jonathan," she said, stepping into the room, extending her hand. "I am Lydia's mother, Sally Smythe."

Jonathan shot up out of his chair, his hat tumbling to the ground. "Yes...yes, I am and...you are...That is...might I...might I speak with you?"

"Speak with *me*?" Sally raised her eyebrows in surprise.

"Yes, ummm, privat...that is...alone?"

*What can he mean by this?* Lydia thought incredulously.

"Uhh...yes," Sally looked around the room. "Umm, in the kitchen perhaps?" She motioned toward the doorway, and threw Lydia a wondering glance.

Jonathan shut the door as he left.

Lydia longed to flee, but the smallness of the farmhouse, its kitchen and parlour below stairs and its three bedrooms above, offered no practical place to hide without it being clear to all that hiding was one's objective. So there she sat, her stomach turning over.

*Why would he want to speak with her?*

She gasped, convinced of her own perceptiveness.

*He's going to offer me a place to serve at his new property! His mother can't spare any of her staff, so he needs to find more servants! When I left Whitehall I told him that Mama needed me here, so he's come to persuade her to let me go.*

Her mind flew back to that final conversation in the study at Whitehall when he had filled her hand with money, and then held it gently for a long moment in his own.

*What did I say then? That I hoped he would consider me for future employment? No! I wouldn't have!*

*And I can't! I can't go back to living under the same roof! Seeing him every day...hearing his voice...watching his hand as he lifts a glass to his mouth...*

The corners of her eyes began to sting as she plucked at the settee cushion agitatedly.

*I can't. I won't.*

*The letters, they're torturous enough, reminding me that he exists...that he's walking, breathing, laughing* somewhere *in England...but to see him day by day, alive and real right before me...*

*No. I won't.*

Outside the window, the sun shone brightly. Lydia considered lifting the lower sash and climbing through, into the yard.

But then, he was there again, coming back through the parlour door, alone this time.

"Mama?" Lydia called, peering past him down the hallway, her voice shaking.

Jonathan waited a moment, his hand on the door, but Sally gave no response, and he shut it.

Slowly, he walked a few steps closer to where Lydia sat.

Lydia's mind was reeling. *How can I decline graciously...and believably?*

"Miss Lydia," Jonathan said, then paused.

Lydia turned her face to him, composing her own as serenely as she could.

*He looks unwell,* she thought, surprised.

*Oh, but what am I to say?*

"Miss Lydia," he began again. "I...I hoped to come here and...and ask you...that is, I must first tell you that...mmm, I mean..."

To Lydia's humiliation, she felt tears begin to run down her face, washing away any pretense of her composure.

"Sir Jonathan," she cut in, her lower lip quivering. "I...I..."

Then she was interrupted by an abrupt sob heaving up out of her chest.

*Damn these emotions!*

There was a creak of a floorboard just outside the door in the hallway.

"Why...?" he asked, his eyes filled with a mixture of pity and horror as another sob escaped her lips. "Why are you... crying?"

The parlour door flew open and both young people turned to behold Sally, standing there in the doorway, tears streaming down her own face.

"Tell her!" she said, marching up to Jonathan, looking small and worn next to his tall, hale form.

The look of confused alarm had not faded from Jonathan's face as he looked at the woman.

"Tell her!" Sally repeated, wiping her eyes, then motioning wildly with her hands. "Tell her what you told me!"

Lydia's sobs were arrested at a new mortifying thought.

*Has Mama gone* mad?

"I...I..." Jonathan stuttered. "I...

Apparently losing hope in the fellow's ability to finish his sentence, Sally broke into a fresh round of tears as she turned to Lydia and announced, "He loves you! He wants to *marry* you, but..."

Here, the woman paused and began to chuckle. The malapropos sound grew, swelling into a rolling belly laugh though Sally's cheeks were still streaked with tears.

"But he -- *heh heh* -- he hasn't got a *vast fortune*." She struggled against the laughter as she continued. "All he's got is a -- *ha ha* -- a farm of 200 acres and -- *ha ha!* -- and forty head of Herefords!

"And he's afraid -- *HA HA HA!*" She bent over, holding her sides as she convulsed with mirth, and howled, "*He's afraid you won't want him!*"

Jonathan stared, aghast, at the woman.

Lydia stood as the unbelievable meaning of Sally's words sank into her mind.

Suddenly, her now giggling mother was holding her, kissing her face. "My dear, dear girl..."

Stunned, Lydia was immobile as Sally grabbed ahold of her hands.

Standing four feet away, Jonathan's face was as pale as milk.

Nothing was said or done for a lingering moment until, having somewhat recovered herself, Sally looked back and forth between her daughter and the young man.

"Well," she sighed, letting go of Lydia's hands. "I'll go put the kettle on."

She left, shutting the door behind her with a final chuckle.

*Is it true?*

Unsure where to look, Lydia stared at the floor. She heard Jonathan's shaky inhalation.

"Miss Lydia." He moved two steps closer and reached out toward her. "May I take your hand in mine?"

Though her heart was in her throat, Lydia lifted her hand to meet his and raised her eyes to his face.

"Though this is not the manner in which I hoped to declare myself, what your mother has said is true...all of it."

His gray eyes were solemn as he continued, "Just before you left Whitehall, I learned that the wealth I had always...that *everyone* had always believed existed, had dwindled, not *entirely*...but I was forced to sell Whitehall. It is lost to my family forever, and I wanted you to know that before I asked you if you would consider...I've bought a farm not far from here, where we could live comfortably, and I...that is..."

He sank to the floor on one knee, barely fitting between the settee and the little table in front of it.

Lydia, suddenly light-headed, lowered herself onto the settee, feeling the firm grasp of his hand around hers.

"Miss Lydia," he asked, his eyes steadily gazing into her own. "Would you consent to be my wife?"

# Picking Pony a New Name

~ Elliott, age 9
Ignoble Acres

Elliott's eyelids fluttered open as the rooster's crowing roused him from his slumber. In the past several months, this had been a daily occurrence, but on this particular day he did not immediately drift back to sleep.

*It's my birthday,* he recalled drowsily. *Sophie wrote that she will arrive today and Jonathan said the German Warrior was coming to visit as well. Oh, and Pony said she'd bake me a nougat almond cake.*

*'Pony',* he thought, suddenly realizing how juvenile it sounded. *A nine-year-old shouldn't call anyone 'Pony'.*

*But what ought I to call her? 'Foote?' No, no one calls her that anymore. 'Lydia'? Hmmm...that just seems so strange.*

*And I wonder if she's forgotten that there's still wedding cake left over. She mightn't bake me a birthday cake if she knows there's still some of the other.*

Groggily, he gazed at the ceiling above him, pondering these dilemmas as the first rays of light filtered in through the window.

The wedding had taken place a week earlier at a church near Pony's home. Sophia had been there, though Elliott's mama had decided to remain in London with Cook and Glaser that day. Widcombe and his sister, Amelia, as well as Hodges, were also there.

While sipping punch after the ceremony, Elliott was studying the furry, lavender hat Amelia was wearing when he saw her lean toward Widdy and whisper, "I *knew* she wasn't *really* a maid."

Elliott had gone to stay with Sophia and his mama for that night and the next, but on the third day, Jonathan had brought him and Pony back to the farm.

When she first walked into the farmhouse, Pony had gasped at the many bookshelves, hurrying from room to room to see them all.

Like Sophia, she had giggled at the sight of the paintings of the grandfathers.

"I'm so glad you didn't leave those Clyde Fellows behind at Whitehall," she had said, reaching for Jonathan's hand. "I wonder how they enjoy gazing out over such ignoble acres as these."

"'Ignoble Acres'? Hmmm...I like the sound of that," Jonathan had said. "I think you've just renamed the farm, my dear."

Elliott had felt pleased as he saw Jonathan lift Pony's hand to kiss it.

He fondly recalled this as he resettled deeply into his warm down mattress.

*But I still don't know what I ought to call her now...*

And it was this thought that slipped out of his drowsy head as he drifted back to sleep.

# The End

## A Page of Gratitude and Possible Apologies

Thank you to my daughter who, at the age of fifteen, showed me how a serious writer commits herself to birthing a story, no matter how vexing the process becomes. Your pep talks quelled my frustrations and warmed my maternal heart. I continue to learn so much from you.

Thank you to my wonderful parents for paying my tuition as I earned a degree in Creative Writing *twenty years ago*. (Look! I finally did something with it!)

Thank you to all of the Lonely Scriveners, both past and present. Though my ego sometimes bristled at your feedback, I know that this book was *immeasurably* improved by your honest and helpful words. I am honored to call you talented people my friends and partners in creating stories that would otherwise remain untold. May they fill the earth!

Thank you to Diana who was the very first person to read through this story in one of its earliest forms. Your encouragement and enthusiasm were invaluable, as is your friendship.

Thank you to the extremely helpful Beverly Matthews of Tonbridge School in England who sent me *A Look at the Head and the Fifty* by Barry Orchard, as well as Septimus Rivington's *A History of Tonbridge School,* and D.C. Somervell's work by the same name. I am truly grateful for the resources you took time to send to a stranger in the U.S. and I hope that Heath (my rendition of an aged English boys' school) doesn't cause you to shake your head in chagrin.

Many thanks to Jenny Quinlan. You met my every request in the design of this book's new cover with grace and amazing skill. I love the end result!
Thank you to Jo Beverly, the bestselling author of multiple historical novels, as well as Grant Bavister, the Assistant Head of the Crown Office and the Assistant Registrar of the Peerage & Baronetage. They answered questions for me regarding baronetcies and an heir's coming of age. Hopefully I have not shamed them by getting it wrong in spite of their generosity of time and information.

Thank you to the readers of this book. It is my great hope that you enjoyed reading this story which I ached, labored and even wept over. You get points if you caught the reference to Jared and Jerusha Hess' *Napoleon Dynamite* that I couldn't resist hiding in these pages. Double points go to the readers who also perceived my references to Delaney Walnofer's *Dragon Clutch,* a gripping tale of dragons and humans...

To anyone who is an expert on early-nineteenth century England and who found errors and/or inconsistencies upon these pages, then know that (in the words of my friend, George) that is *my gift* to you: Enjoy your superiority. ☺

Finally, many thanks to Jesus. You tucked into my little human brain a desire to create the people on these pages, and gave me the resources to make it happen. I am truly grateful for the life, grace and purpose which You continue to grant me.

Please visit my web page and sign up for my newsletter to be notified when new titles are released:

www.aewalnofer.com

Other Books by A.E. Walnofer

## Out of the Bower

**London, 1817:** Celia Woodlow is trapped in Titania's Bower, a brothel disguised as a coffee house. She is wretchedly resigned to this fate until high-spirited Honora Goodwin appears. Shared tragedy quickly bonds the two girls in friendship and they determine to flee the Bower together, though they wonder at their survival outside its walls.

Suddenly, Honora vanishes without a word, and Celia is left feeling betrayed and hopeless.

Barclay Durbin, a kind, young street preacher, desires little more than to help London's destitute masses. After he encounters Honora, injured in her flight from the Bower, he comes to believe she is divinely appointed to become his wife. Honora knows that encouraging the good-hearted gentleman's attentions may prove to ensure her future security, but she is intent on liberating Celia. Telling Barclay only parts of her own story, Honora enlists the besotted young man to help her.

When their plan goes awry, Honora realizes that only the truth can deliver them from the emotional and societal maelstrom in which they find themselves. But what will become of Honora and Barclay's budding attachment? And will Celia ever gain her freedom?

*Out of the Bower* tells the tale of a forbidden romance, an ardent friendship, and the ever-essential redemption of self.

## With Face Aflame

**England, 1681:** Born with a red mark emblazoned across her face, seventeen-year-old Madge is lonely as she spends her days serving guests and cleaning rooms in the inn her father keeps.

One day, she meets an unusual minstrel in the marketplace. Moved by the beauty of his song and the odd shape of his body, she realizes she has made her first friend. But he must go on to the next town, leaving her behind. Soon after, while she herself is singing in the woods, she is startled by a chance meeting with a stranger there. Though the encounter leaves her horribly embarrassed, it proves she need not remain unnoticed and alone forever.

However, this new hope is shattered when she overhears a few quiet words that weren't intended for her ears. Heartbroken and confused, she flees her home to join the minstrel and his companion, a crass juggler. As they travel earning their daily bread, Madge secretly seeks to rid herself of the mark upon her cheek, convinced that nothing else can heal her heart.

*With Face Aflame* is the tale of a girl who risks everything in hopes of becoming the person she desperately wants to be.

Made in the USA
Columbia, SC
05 September 2024

41793298R00231